ACTIVE MEMORY

ALSO BY DAN WELLS

ACTIVE MEMORY

A MIRADOR NOVEL

DAN WELLS

BALZER + BRAY
An Imprint of HarperCollins*Publishers*

Active Memory

Copyright © 2018 by Dan Wells

All rights reserved. Printed in the United States of America.

No part of this book may be used or reproduced in any manner whatsoever without written permission except in the case of brief quotations embodied in critical articles and reviews. For information address HarperCollins Children's Books, a division of HarperCollins Publishers, 195 Broadway, New York, NY 10007.

www.epicreads.com

Library of Congress Control Number: 2017954059
ISBN 978-0-06-234793-0

Typography by Torborg Davern
18 19 20 21 22   PC/LSCH   10 9 8 7 6 5 4 3 2 1

First Edition

*This book is dedicated to the OG: Ada Lovelace.
She wrote the world's first computer program, so long
ago that computers were only theoretical and computer
languages didn't even exist. Our entire world is built on
the dreams of a young woman who had a cool idea and
invented the future. Don't let anyone tell you
that you can't be just as great.*

ONE

Mario Fortino Alfonso Moreno Reyes High School was lit with a swarm of beautiful floating lanterns: solar-powered LED lights attached to large Mylar balloons, neutrally buoyant so they hung in the air, and just barely smart enough to maneuver back to their designated spot if an errant gust of wind came by and blew them out of position. Or, Marisa supposed, if an errant high school boy came by and jerked them out of position on purpose. Which was probably more likely. She was seventeen herself, and prided herself on knowing everything she possibly could, but if there was one thing she'd never understand, it was high school boys.

"How much do you think those cost?" asked Marisa's father, looking at the lights through the window of their autocab.

"It's a special night," said Marisa. "It's the science fair."

"It's called STEAM Power," said Pati, Marisa's twelve-year-old sister. You could hear the capitalization in the way she said it. "Science, technology, engineering, art, and math. It's *everything*."

Gabi snorted. "It's just a science fair." She was two years older than Pati, and much harder to impress. "Why are we even here?"

"Your brother has a nuli in this science fair," said their father. "None of you have ever built a nuli."

Marisa rolled her eyes. "It's not a competition, Papi."

"Of course it's a competition," he said. "There's a prize and everything."

"I mean between your children."

"It's not a science fair," Pati insisted. "It's a robotics show and a hack-off and Gama said there was going to be a nuli fight—"

"It's not a hack-off," said Gabi. "The school's not going to let people just hack into stuff on school property."

"Mari does it all the time," said Pati.

"She'd better not," said their father.

"Ay, que niña," said Marisa, "cállate."

"Apologize to your sister," said their father.

"Yeah," said Marisa, "apologize."

He scowled. "I meant you, morena!"

Pati looked at Marisa smugly. "We don't say 'cállate,' remember?"

"Fine," said Marisa, "I'm sorry. In Spanish: lo siento. In Chinese: bi zui."

Marisa's father gave her a suspicious look from the corner of his eye. He didn't speak Chinese, so he didn't *know* she'd told her sister to shut up, but she could tell from his eyes that he suspected.

"There's not going to be nuli fights, either," said Gabi. "It's just going to be, como, fifty boys standing next to some dumb little robots they made."

"And fifty girls," said Marisa.

"Who cares about them?" asked Gabi. "I'm only related to one of the boys, which leaves forty-nine who want to tell me all about their projects."

"High school boys," said Marisa with disgust. "You can have 'em."

"I intend to."

"My ears!" shouted their father. "Can you at least wait until you're out of the car?"

The autocab pulled to a stop by the curb, and slid its doors open with a rickety clatter. Normally they wouldn't have bothered with a cab at all, but their father was still recovering from surgery—a liver replacement—and while he could walk well enough, the doctors didn't want him doing so very often. So, the cheapest possible auto-cab it was. Marisa climbed out, adjusted her T-shirt—the Intruders, her favorite new Nigerian metal band—and looked at the school. *Her* school, though she studied from home more often than not. She braced her metal arm against the doorframe, and reached back in with her flesh one. Her father took it, and she hauled him to his feet with a grunt. The joints and servos in her metal arm—a slim, elegant prosthetic—handled the exertion with perfection but left a row of tiny divots in the cab's flimsy roof. Whatever. She shook her head and helped Gabi pull the medical nuli out as well.

"Triste Chango," said her father. "I hate that thing."

The phrase meant "stupid monkey," more or less, but it had become the family's name for the medical nuli. Marisa smiled and patted its top. "It's keeping you alive, Papi. You don't want to pop a stitch or get infected, do you?"

He shook out a foldable cane and started walking slowly toward the high school doors. "I don't need a babysitter." Triste Chango followed eagerly after him, emergency equipment at the ready.

Pati and Gabi climbed out of the cab, and Marisa blinked on the payment link in her djinni UI, a soft glow the computer implant displayed around the edges of her vision. She didn't have much in her own account, but their mom had given her enough to cover the autocab fare. It asked for a tip, which she gleefully declined, and drove itself away with a high-pitched squeal somewhere in the engine.

"That's why teenagers don't care about anything," said Marisa, taking Pati's hand as they followed their father into the school. Pati, like Marisa, was dressed in black jeans and a black T-shirt. "Like, a hundred people just saw us get out of that thing, and if I cared what they thought I would literally die. Not caring about things is *the best*."

"Ugh, you're so stupid," said Gabi.

Marisa smiled at Pati. "See?"

The LED sign over the big front doors had been modified for the fair, and announced the name "STEAM Power" in bright yellow letters. The hallway inside was lined with trophies and news articles—most of them about sports rather than science—and several people waved at them as they made their way to the cafeteria where the projects were on display. Los Angeles was huge—the largest city in the world, in surface area if not in population—but Mirador was a tight-knit community, and most people were at least passingly acquainted with everyone else. Thanks to their restaurant, the Carnesecas were even better known than most.

"Buenas tardes, Carlo Magno!" An older man waved jovially at Marisa's father, and put his hands on his hips as if appraising a cut of beef in a butcher shop. "You look good. Recovering well."

"Thank you, Beto." Carlo Magno smiled, and Marisa saw the genuine gratitude on his face as he stopped to talk. He liked to pretend he was a picture of health, but tonight was going to put him flat on his back.

"Come on," said Pati, and pulled on Marisa's hand. "Let's find Sandro! Have you seen his nuli? It's amazing!"

"I've seen it," said Marisa, "Our bedrooms are right next to each other." Still, she let herself be pulled forward. Gabi had already disappeared.

"Wait!" said Carlo Magno. "Don't leave me here alone!"

"You're not alone," said Marisa, "you have Triste Chango."

"Excuse me?" asked Beto.

"It's the nuli," said Marisa, "not you!" But Pati was already pulling her through the doors into the cafeteria. The tables had been rearranged from long lines into a network of triangles, though Marisa couldn't immediately see how that made the drab room any nicer to look at or easier to navigate. Each triangular island was covered with STEAM projects, some with posters—the obvious overachievers—but most with simply a nuli or a robot or a monitor showing off some fancy new software. The wall screens had been set to display generic footage of animals and wilderness: the Serengeti, or the Amazon, or the ruins of Old Detroit. The theme of this year's fair was "City in the Wild," and most of the projects focused on some aspect of nature, or of LA's unique symbiosis with it.

Gabi was standing at a nearby table, wearing her best vest and pleated miniskirt, listening raptly while Jordan Brown explained the new garbage collection algorithm he'd developed for a groundskeeper nuli:

"It can identify not just more kinds of waste, but it can sort them more efficiently into recyclable categories: food and organics, paper, and even metallic material such as one-sided foil. . . ."

Marisa left them alone and wandered deeper into the room. Jordan was cute enough, she supposed, but he was also a senior with a handful of incredible scholarship offers. Gabi didn't stand a chance, but why ruin her dreams?

A message popped up in her djinni, a little picture of her friend Bao bouncing cheerfully in her field of vision. She blinked on it, and read the text message:

Three minutes.

"Chamuco," she murmured.

"What?" asked Pati.

"Apparently Bao's here," said Marisa, looking around. Bao was one of her best friends in the world, and one of her most frequent partners in crime. Sometimes literally.

"Omigosh," said Pati, her eyes going wide. She'd had a crush on Bao for years. "Do I look good? I didn't even try to look good— Gabi looks good but I look like I slept under a bridge, what do I do?"

"You look fine."

"I'm wearing a training bra," said Pati. "Can you tell? Do you think he'll notice?"

Marisa laughed. "Bao is way too much of a gentleman to notice a twelve-year-old's boobs."

"But that's what they're for!"

"Ay, Pati, cálmate. Bao loves you—like a sister."

"I won't be twelve forever."

"You'll be five years younger than him forever."

"And when I'm twenty that won't matter anymore."

"Fine," said Marisa, looking back at the crowd. "When you're twenty and he's twenty-five, you have my permission to marry him."

Pati frowned. "Why do you keep looking all around?"

"It's a game Bao and I play," said Marisa. "He gave me three minutes to find him."

"Split up," said Pati, suddenly laser focused. "We can cover more ground. Go!" She turned and raced into the crowd.

Another message popped up: **No fair using your sister to help look.**

Marisa scanned the crowd again—wherever he was, he was watching her.

Did you hear what she said? she sent back.

No.

Thank goodness.

So he was close enough to see but not hear. Where was he? The ceiling was low, with no balconies or other elevated positions to give him a long-range sight line. **Give me a clue.**

I just did, he sent, followed by a picture of a cartoon cat sticking its tongue out.

Bao was unique among Marisa's friends in that he didn't have a djinni—the supercomputer installed directly into your brain, wired seamlessly into your senses and nervous system, and through which you interfaced with almost everything in the world. If he'd had one, she could have simply fed her GPS app his ID and let it lead her straight to him, but without one he was practically a ghost. And that's the way he wanted it, because he supported his family picking tourists' pockets.

She walked as casually as she could past all the nearest tables, but found no smirking Chinese boys hiding under any of them. Where, then?

She checked her clock: one minute left.

He could have already moved deeper into the crowd, staying hidden by staying ahead of her—

Don't just stand there, he sent.

He was still watching. He had to be nearby. . . .

Or maybe not. What better way to stay hidden than to stay out of the room altogether? She looked up again, running her eyes along the edge of the ceiling, and found it: a little black security camera. She made a gun shape with her fingers and pretended to shoot it. **Found you.**

With thirteen seconds to spare.

You broke into the principal's office?

You make it sound so criminal, sent Bao. **I didn't break in, I let myself in. It's different.**

That's not a difference most cops would be willing to consider.

I prefer that cops don't consider me at all.

Then maybe you should stop letting yourself into places.

And leave all this incriminating footage of me just sitting on the server? I don't think you've thought this through.

What footage?

Footage of me breaking in to delete the footage.

Marisa laughed. Your logic is unassailable.

I agree, sent Bao. I'm done, though, so I'll meet you in a minute. Sandro's table?

Sounds great. And one more thing.

Yeah?

Please say something nice about Pati when you see her. She sent the message, started walking, and then almost tripped herself sending a sudden, urgent follow-up: But not about her . . . shirt! Don't mention her shirt.

Is something wrong with it?

Don't say anything either way. I'd die of embarrassment.

You're the boss. A pause, then another message: A weird boss who I don't understand, but a boss nonetheless. See you soon.

Marisa looked at the crowd; it seemed like everyone in Mirador was there, but finding Sandro would be easy—he had a djinni. She blinked on her guidance app, and a blue line appeared in front of her, leading her through the crowd. She followed it with a smile. Other kids on every side were hawking their projects like vendors in a street market: this girl had a nuli that cleaned pollution from solar trees, improving their energy transfer rate; that boy had a small-scale factory robot with a new kind of joint that required less maintenance. Marisa stopped by one of the tables and read through her friend Rosa's new code for a ranger nuli—the kind that followed endangered species around and protected them from poachers. Rosa Sanchez, eighteen years old and living in the barrio, had modified the AI to start actively hunting the poachers instead of just passively shocking them anytime they got too close. It had the potential to change the entire balance of power between poachers and rangers.

Everything in the room was amazing, and Marisa felt a swell of pride for her friends and neighbors. This was the future, right here and now. A hundred kids with big ideas, and a room full of people telling them yes instead of no. It was the greatest thing Marisa had ever seen.

She found her brother Sandro by the back wall, telling the crowd about his forestry nuli. He had a poster, because of course he did.

"Just like animals, plants can get sick," Sandro was saying, "and when they do, it can spread through an ecosystem like wildfire. A single parasite, like the blight you see in this image, can destroy an entire orchard or forest in weeks." He held up a screen with a picture of a tree; massive patches of the leaves were shriveled and black, almost like they'd been burned. "This is called Fire Blight, and it's caused by a bacterium called *Erwinia amylovora*, which targets fruit trees. We can spray for it, but the spray is poisonous and gets on everything—the sick leaves, the healthy leaves, and even the fruit. My nuli can sense this bacteria and dozens of other plagues and parasites, and spray for them precisely—with no collateral damage. It patrols its area 24/7, and the precision also means it uses fewer chemicals than traditional methods, so it's cheaper."

The small crowd applauded, and Marisa whooped more loudly than anyone: "Ándale, Sandro! Lechuga!"

"You know he hates that nickname," said Bao, suddenly standing next to her. Marisa hadn't even seen him approach.

"Why do you think I use it?" she asked, and then started chanting the name loudly: "Le-chu-ga! Le-chu-ga!"

Sandro looked at her as the crowd moved on to another project. She wanted him to sneer or roll his eyes, but instead he simply raised his eyebrow; he was one year her junior, but always treated her like the younger one.

"Thanks for coming," he said.

"Claro que sí, hermanito. Your presentation was perfect."

"You think?"

"It was great," said Bao. "Do you have a video to show it in action?"

"It's on the tablet," he said, gesturing with the screen in his hands. "I'm keeping the presentation short for now, but I'll show it to the judges."

"Pop quiz," said Bao, glancing at Marisa. "What do you call a reptilian ferret with wings?"

"Those are called MyDragons," said Marisa. "There's ads for them all over the city. Why do you ask?"

"Correct," said Bao. "If you've ever wanted to see one in person, La Princesa has one right over there." He pointed, and Marisa's mouth fell open as she looked. There she was:

Francisca Maldonado, La Princesa de Mirador, with a bright purple MyDragon perched on her shoulder.

"They're here?" asked Marisa. It wasn't just La Princesa, it was the whole Maldonado family: Omar, Sergio, and in the middle of the group was Don Maldonado himself. The richest man in Mirador; the head of a massive crime family that ran the neighborhood like a personal kingdom. Don Maldonado and Marisa's father hated each other with an old but ever-burning passion, and that feud had shaped much of Marisa's life. Worst of all, they refused to even tell her how the feud began.

Hey, Mari. It was a new message, bouncing at the edge of Marisa's vision in a window she never closed: a private conversation with her best friend, Sahara. **Don't look now, but your favorite people are here.**

Just saw them, Marisa sent back. **And with a frakking MyDragon. Just to let us know how much richer they are than the rest of us.**

I'm wearing a bouquet of flowers on my shoulder, sent Sahara. **Franca's wearing a gengineered custom pet.**

I drove here in a taxi so old it still had a steering wheel, sent Marisa. **They look like they were carried here on a palanquin while someone waved palm fronds over their heads.**

"Earth to Marisa," said Bao. "Are you volleying insults with Sahara again?"

"I applied my own makeup in under five minutes," said Marisa out loud. "She looks like she has a closet full of 3D-printed faces, and just swaps them out whenever she goes somewhere."

"Don't compare yourself to them," said Sandro. "You'll just make yourself feel bad."

Why are they even here? sent Sahara.

Pati and Carlo Magno walked toward them through the crowd, with Triste Chango following behind like a box-shaped puppy.

"I couldn't find Bao but I found Papi—" yelled Pati, and then stopped instantly when she saw that Bao was already there. "Hi, Bao! Good to see you! Did you see Sandro's nuli? Isn't it awesome?"

Marisa smiled. At least Pati wasn't shy.

"I saw it," said Bao. "It's the best one here by a mile and a half."

"For all the good it's going to do him," said Carlo Magno, angrily shaking his cane toward the knot of people that had formed around the Maldonados. "Do you know why that chundo's here?"

"I was just wondering that," said Marisa, but she felt her stomach sink as she realized there was only one possible answer.

"He's the judge," said Carlo Magno, confirming her fears. "Don Francisco Maldonado is picking the winner of the science fair, and handing out the check with his own filthy hands, and do you think he's ever going to pick a Carneseca?"

"I think he'll let the work decide," said Sandro, but their father cut him off with a loud *bah*.

"You're a fool," said Carlo Magno. "A genius, but a fool as well. He hates us, and he always has, and no science project is ever going to change that. No matter how brilliant."

Marisa realized that she was clutching her metal arm with her human one. She'd lost the arm in a car accident when she was two years old, and the mysteries that surrounded that one event seemed to permeate every aspect of her life. The basic details were well known to everybody in Mirador: Don Francisco's wife, Zenaida, went for a drive—actually driving herself, like people used to do before self-driving cars were the norm—and got into an accident. Nobody knew where she'd been going, or why, and since she'd been thrown from the car and died on impact, no one had ever been able to ask her.

But that's where things got weird. The first people to arrive on the scene had found three children in the car with her: Jacinto Maldonado, their second child, very nearly dead as well; Omar Maldonado, their fourth and youngest child, completely unharmed—and Marisa Carneseca, who had absolutely no reason to be there whatsoever. Her arm had been severed just below the shoulder.

Why had Marisa been in that car? Why had Zenaida been driving it manually? And why did any of that cause Don Maldonado and Marisa's father to hate each other so intensely?

Great. Holy. Handgrenades, sent Sahara. **That's not just the purple MyDragon, it's the iridescent purple MyDragon. They only made three of them!**

Yeah, sent Marisa, and closed the chat window. She didn't feel like gossiping anymore.

"Good evening, Mr. Carneseca," said Bao, trying valiantly to cut the tension that had silenced the group. He reached out to shake his hand, and Carlo Magno absentmindedly shook back. "It's good to see you up and moving around."

"I'm doing my best," said Carlo Magno. "Well enough I don't

14

need this stupid thing." He kicked feebly at Triste Chango, and it beeped cheerfully in response.

"We couldn't afford one of the really good livers," Marisa explained, "or even a midrange one. The cheapest ones come with a ten-week nuli rental to make sure nothing goes wrong. Hospital subsidy to help prevent lawsuits."

"Way to clip the coupons," said Bao.

Carlo Magno sneered at the Maldonados. "My wife couldn't even be here tonight because we can't afford to close the restaurant, and he brings his entire family."

Bao smiled. "I always forget how much like Marisa you are."

Carlo Magno and Marisa looked at each other, neither one certain if they liked that comparison.

"Not the whole family," said Pati. "Not Jacinto."

"Jacinto hasn't left home since the . . ." Carlo Magno looked at Marisa again, then gave another loud *bah*.

"Here comes another group," said Sandro. "Give me some room, I'm going to do my presentation again."

They moved to the side, away from the Maldonados, and Marisa found her father a bench to sit down on. Triste Chango scooted in close. "Your heart rate is approaching the upper limits specified by your doctor. Please take deep breaths as follows: in, out. In, out."

Carlo Magno hit it with his cane.

Another message popped up from Sahara, and Marisa leaned her forehead against the wall. Why wasn't anything ever easy? Sahara sent a second message, and then a third, and the icon started glowing faintly red. Marisa blinked on it, and the messages exploded across her vision.

Omigosh.

Are you seeing this?

MARI, ARE YOU SEEING THIS?

Marisa frowned, confused, and sent a response. **Seeing what?**

Look at Don Francisco!

Marisa snapped her head around, searching through the crowd, but there were too many people. She craned her neck in various directions, trying to get a look at whatever Sahara was freaking out about, and finally just stood on the bench next to her father. A space had cleared around the Maldonados, and a woman was talking to Francisco.

A woman holding a badge.

"What's wrong with you?" asked Carlo Magno. "Get down from there before a teacher sees you."

"It's a cop," said Marisa, still wondering what exactly was going on. "Don Francisco's talking to a cop."

"He talks to cops all the time," said Carlo Magno. "They're practically his own private army. His son's the captain of the local precinct!"

"But that's not a Mirador cop," said Marisa. "I know all the locals. She's not in uniform, either. And she's not happy."

"Off duty?" asked Bao.

"She's showing him her badge," said Marisa.

Found her, sent Sahara. **I ran an image search through the LAPD database—her name's Kiki Hendel, and she's a homicide detective from downtown.**

Why is she here? sent Marisa.

How am I supposed to know?

"Maybe they finally got him," said Carlo Magno. "Maybe they finally caught him on some charge, and he's going to prison—taxes, maybe. That's how they got Al Capone."

"Who?" asked Pati.

"Tā mā de," whispered Bao, standing on the other side of the bench. "She's taking him away."

"What?" asked Carlo Magno. He stood up so fast that the bench unbalanced, and Bao and Marisa had to jump clear to keep from falling. The bench clattered to the ground, and Carlo Magno raised himself to his full height. "Are they arresting him?"

"It didn't look like it," said Bao, trying to stand the bench back up again. "Just . . . leading him outside."

What the what? sent Sahara.

I know! sent Marisa.

I'll see if I can get Cameron outside after him, sent Sahara, and across the room Marisa saw one of Sahara's small camera nulis rise up above the crowd and race toward the door.

"Look online," said Marisa, blinking on her djinni. "All of you—look for everything you can. What's in the news, what's going on here or downtown or at their estate in Mirador, what's going on with any of their investments or their enforcers or anything at all." She started running searches on the internet, going through all the local news blogs.

Hold up, sent Sahara. **What was his wife's name again?**

Zenaida, said Marisa, **but you're not going to turn up anything on her, she's been dead for fifteen years—**

Are you sure about that?

17

Marisa froze.

The LAPD found her . . . hand, sent Sahara. **At a crime scene in South Central. Her left hand, severed at the wrist, lying on the ground.**

Marisa couldn't move. She could barely comprehend the words in Sahara's next message:

I don't know what happened fifteen years ago, said Sahara, **but Zenaida was alive last night.**

TWO

"This changes everything," said Sahara. She'd left her own coding project—a social app for tracking fashion memes in real time—and found Marisa by the back wall. Sandro had righted the bench, and Marisa was sitting on it, still in shock, while Sahara tried to keep her calm. "This changes *everything.*"

"You're not really keeping me calm," said Marisa.

"Sorry, sorry," said Sahara. She was wearing a bright yellow dress with a high neck and long sleeves but no shoulders, the fabric replaced with sprays of deep red flowers. She had both red and yellow flowers in her hair. The warm colors contrasted flawlessly against Sahara's dark brown skin, and the whole effect was perfectly designed to help sell the value of her fashion app. "What should we talk about instead? Alain? Have you heard from him?"

"We need to talk about Don Francisco," said Marisa. "Wait—where's Pati?"

"With Bao," said Sahara, "and she's practically floating with joy, so chill."

"And my dad?"

"Ten feet away from you, calling your mom and abusing a nuli."

Marisa turned and saw Carlo Magno on a nearby bench, arguing in Spanish while fending off the medical nuli with his cane. His heart rate was probably through the roof. He was talking to Guadalupe, Marisa's mother, but it was a djinni call, so it looked like he was a crazy person howling at his robot wife. Marisa laughed at the image, and the laugh broke down her emotional barriers, and seconds later she was bawling into the flowers on Sahara's shoulder.

"Shhh," said Sahara, rubbing her back. "It's okay."

"She was alive this whole time," said Marisa. "I thought she was dead my whole life, but . . ."

"What does this mean?" asked Sahara.

"I . . . I don't know," said Marisa. "But I guess I don't know anything anymore. That crash was my whole life: the feud between my parents and the Maldonados started that night. It's everything. And it was a lie."

"They took Don Francisco downtown," said Sahara. "I saw it on Cameron's video feed."

"In handcuffs?"

Sahara shook her head. "She didn't arrest him, just . . . took him. They're probably questioning him."

"Do they think he knows something?" asked Marisa. "Did he hide his wife for fifteen years and then . . . cut her hand off? Or did he even know she was alive?"

"We don't know," said Sahara. "And we won't know until it breaks on the news, so calm down."

Marisa sat up straight and wiped the tears from her face with the back of her hand. "We could hack the police station's security cameras."

"In the next ten minutes?" asked Sahara. "You're good, but you're not that good."

"Then we can . . . I don't know," said Marisa. "We can call Omar."

"Are you serious?" asked Sahara. "I think Omar Maldonado's got enough to worry about with his mom's hand turning up out of nowhere. Besides, how many times has that bastard betrayed us?"

"We used to be friends. He might . . . understand."

"You used to be little kids," said Sahara. She rubbed Marisa's back again. "Just be patient. We'll know soon enough."

"Soon enough for what?" Marisa rubbed her eyes again, and then looked at her hand in disgust. "Did I smear my mascara? I must look like a raccoon."

"Sexiest raccoon I've ever seen," said Sahara. She stood up, and dragged Marisa up with her.

"Why are we standing?"

"Because it's time for the award ceremony," said Sahara. "We're going to watch me lose the coding category to Rosa Sanchez." She pulled Marisa through the crowd, to where Principal Layton was standing awkwardly in front of a microphone nuli, the two assistant principals behind him. It looked like he was already done with the standard litany of thanking all the teachers and volunteers and school district bigwigs, and Marisa had just enough presence of mind to be ironically grateful that this world-changing news had distracted her from that. He started on the first category—chemistry—and Marisa tuned him out while she looked for more news about Zenaida. She found several news blogs talking about homicides—dead bodies were hardly a rare occurrence in LA. She skimmed through several stories before finding the one she wanted: a severed hand in South Central. Even finding the right story didn't mean she'd found any useful information: blah blah shootout, blah blah dangerous part of the city, blah blah gang activity. She refined her search and found a POV video from a bystander's djinni, but even that didn't include a lot of useful information. At least four shooters that she could see, both male and female, but at such a distance that she couldn't make out anyone's features.

"Clap," whispered Sahara.

Marisa started clapping immediately, and blinked on the video to pause it and refocus her eyes on the school cafeteria. Polite applause filled the room.

"What happened?" asked Marisa.

"Sandro won third in his category," said Sahara.

"Whooooo!" shouted Marisa, much louder than before. "Ándale, moreno! Viva la lechuga!"

Sandro accepted a certificate from the principal, then turned and smiled at Marisa. She whooped again, and leaned toward Sahara.

"You win anything?"

"I promise you would know if I'd won something."

"True," said Marisa. "Have you lost anything?"

"You'd know that, too," said Sahara. "My category's next."

"I'll give them twenty seconds," said Marisa, "and then I'm watching this video again."

It ended up being forty seconds before they announced the winners of the coding category, and Sahara officially lost to Rosa Sanchez. Marisa gave her friend a squeeze, watched the shootout video again, and growled in frustration. It barely showed anything.

"Just calm down," said Sahara, and took Marisa gently by the shoulders, planting herself firmly in her friend's center of vision. Marisa focused on her, and Sahara spoke: "Take some deep breaths, okay? Feel better?"

"That depends. Better than what?"

Sahara squeezed her shoulders with a reassuring grip. "You're going to find out, okay? Maybe tomorrow, maybe next week—sooner or later you're going to learn everything. You're going to know the whole story. You've been chasing that darknet hacker Grendel for months now just to get whatever scrap of information he has about the accident and your past. But now you don't even need to. You don't have to hunt, you don't have to freak out, you just have to breathe and stay calm and wait."

"Grendel's not the only one who knows what happened that night," said Marisa, and looked at her father, still ranting into his phone call. "My dad knows, too." It bothered her, all over again, how angry it made her that he refused to tell her what he knew about the crash. Like the news had peeled a scab off her emotions, revealing a fresh red wound underneath.

"You'll find out soon," said Sahara. "Whether he wants you to or not."

Marisa kept her eyes on her father. "How soon?"

And then her father froze.

"Disculpe, corazón," he said softly. "I have another call." He blinked, closing the call with Guadalupe, and shot a glance at Marisa before blinking again. "Mándame," he said firmly. "This is Carlo Magno Carneseca."

Marisa took a step toward him, as if being closer could help her overhear a conversation being fed straight into his auditory nerves. He watched her for a moment, then turned away.

"Yes," he said. He listened for a moment, then said yes again.

"Papi?" asked Marisa.

"Tonight?" asked Carlo Magno. "No—out of the question. I'm at my son's science fair." Another pause. "Yes, I saw that. No, I already told you, it's completely—" Another pause. "Fine. I'll be there as soon as I can."

He blinked one more time, and sighed.

"Papi?" asked Marisa. "Who was that?"

"You're not coming with me," said Carlo Magno.

Marisa stepped toward him, her suspicions confirmed. "Was that the police station? They want to interview you, too, don't they? Because you know what happened."

"You're not coming with me," he said firmly.

"You can't go alone," said Marisa. "The doctors said one of us has to accompany you at all times."

"I need you to take the girls home."

Marisa folded her arms and looked him straight in the eye. "Sahara, would you mind taking my sisters home?"

"On it," said Sahara.

24

Carlo Magno shook his head. "Absolutely not. I've told you you're not going, and you're not going. My word is final."

A police badge icon popped up in Marisa's vision, and her heart skipped a beat at the shock of it. Why were they calling her? She recovered, stared at the icon, and then blinked on it, patching the audio into a small external speaker built into her metal arm. Her father would have no trouble overhearing the conversation.

"Hello?" she said.

"Marisa Carneseca?" said a voice on the other end. "My name's Kiki Hendel; I'm a detective with the LAPD. Do you have a moment for a few questions?"

It was the same woman who'd come to fetch Don Francisco in person. "Sure," Marisa said, "but I don't know what you want with me. I was only two years old when she was killed . . . or disappeared, or . . ."

The woman's voice took on a hint of weary amusement. "Looks like news travels fast. Are you at that school thing too?"

"The whole neighborhood is."

"Then you and your father can travel together," said the woman. "I should have just told him to ask you along, but I've got a teenage daughter of my own and she wouldn't be caught dead with me in a public setting. Good to know at least some families stay close."

"Enjoy it while it lasts," said Marisa. "My dad's going to disown me by the time we get to the station. But we'll be right there."

"See you soon," said the detective, and closed the call.

"I urge you," said Carlo Magno, "with every scrap of paternal authority that I possess, to stay home tonight."

"She said she wants to talk to me," said Marisa. "What am I supposed to do, tell a cop to stick it?" After a moment she blinked and added: "And I already ordered us a cab."

Carlo Magno sighed and looked down at his medical nuli, as if expecting it to commiserate. "You see what I have to put up with?"

"Your blood pressure is abnormally high," said Triste Chango. "You should consider a dinner low in sodium, and avoid stressful situations."

Carlo Magno smacked it with his cane. "Fine," he said, and started walking toward the door. "Let's get this over with."

The South Central police station was an older building, renovated in the 2020s, so instead of the bright colors and 3D holodisplays Marisa was used to from the movies, it was all polished steel and full-length window walls. Practically ancient design. The officer at the front desk took their names and signed them in, and left Marisa to sit in the waiting area before taking Carlo Magno into one of the back rooms. They were apparently interviewing Don Francisco at the same time in a different room; she didn't hear any belligerent shouting, so they might have been totally oblivious to each other.

It was nearly ten in the evening, but the station was still humming with activity; officers and detectives and nulis moved purposefully through the halls, all too busy to even notice Marisa, let alone answer any questions. She bit her tongue and forced herself to wait, remembering Sahara's advice—she'd know the details soon enough—but then the desk officer returned with another person and told him to wait with her.

It was Omar Maldonado.

"Hey," said Marisa.

"Hey."

She never knew how to talk to Omar anymore. They'd been friends as kids, but only when their fathers weren't looking, because the two men hated each other so much they'd forbidden their children to associate with each other. And then they'd grown older, and Omar had gotten more involved with his father's business, and Marisa had started to see in him an undercurrent of . . . something. Deception was maybe the best word for it. The subtle sense that everything he said was an act, like a smooth, trustworthy interface over a website riddled with malware. He was wickedly good-looking—that she could appreciate no matter what he said or did—but he was impossible to believe in. He'd betrayed Marisa and her friends, sometimes horribly, but he'd helped them as well, sometimes even saving their lives at the risk of his own. And what bothered Marisa most of all was that she could never be sure, good or bad, what he really wanted. How much of his assistance was a calculated effort to win their favor?

It's an abusive relationship, she told herself. *Once a Maldonado, always a Maldonado.*

She looked at him now, sitting in the bright lights of the featureless gray police station, and saw something in his face that she'd never seen before. She'd seen him friendly, angry, two-faced, charming—so, so charming—but until tonight she'd never seen him *afraid.*

She wanted to ask if he was okay, but was that the right thing to say? How could he possibly answer? He'd thought his mother was dead, and then he'd found out she was alive and then maybe dead again, or at least maimed. She hadn't shown up in any hospitals. Had she died—for real this time? How many pieces was she in? It made Marisa sick just to think about it, and she forced herself to talk even if only to quiet the voices in her head.

"They want to talk to you, too, huh?"

Omar looked up, facing her directly for the first time that evening. His eyes had lost their usual spark, but they weren't red; whatever was bothering him, he hadn't been crying. She wasn't sure if he could.

"No," he said, and as he shifted in his chair, a mask seemed to come over his face, hiding all the fear and the damage and replacing it with slick, affable calm. "I'm just here if my father needs anything. I assume you're here for the same?"

Marisa rolled her eyes. "My papi would sooner cut out his own liver than ask me for help right now. He doesn't want me here at all—didn't say a word to me in the cab."

"But you came anyway," he said, and pointed at her. The gesture struck her as incredibly odd for some reason. "That's loyalty."

"Tell that to him. If the cops hadn't demanded that I be here, he'd have left me chained to a lunch table back at the school."

Omar's left eyebrow went up. "They demanded that you be here? The cops, you mean?"

"Yeah, they . . . want to talk to me." She frowned. "Not you? We were both in the car that day."

"But we were too young to remember any of it," said Omar,

leaning forward. Even through his facade, she could see the gears turning in his mind. "They want to talk to my father and to Sergio, but Franca and I are out."

"And Jacinto?"

He dismissed the notion with a shake of his head. "He's always out. Maybe they'll want to talk to him later, but . . . Mari, you were two years old. What could they possibly want to ask you?"

"I . . ." Marisa shook her head. "I don't know. I thought I knew, but if they're not interviewing you, then maybe . . ." She shrugged. "Maybe they knew Papi was sick, and that he needed someone with him?" But even as she said it, she knew that couldn't be it—the detective had said on the phone that she wanted to ask her some questions.

"She came to me last night," said Omar.

Marisa's jaw dropped open. "What? Your mother? She came to see you?"

"No, I don't mean . . ." He was staring at the wall, his eyes never moving. "She didn't come in person, she came in a dream. Or I guess really I came to her in my dream, and she was trying to get away. Running and running, and she kept looking back over her shoulder, and she'd see me, and then she'd turn away again and keep running. Running and running and running. And I thought she was scared, but maybe she was angry. Maybe she was just anxious to get away. But she didn't want to be with me, so she ran away, and now she's . . ."

Marisa watched him, stunned by the pain in his voice. When was the last time she'd heard any real emotion from Omar, let alone pain? "I'm sorry," she said at last. "That sucks."

He laughed once—a short, derisive cough. "Yeah."

"Brains are stupid sometimes."

He looked like he was about to say something, but didn't.

"Why was she running?" asked Marisa. "Usually in dreams you just . . . know things."

"Not in this one," said Omar.

"Sorry," said Marisa again, and then followed up with another weak "That sucks." What else could she say?

Before she could come up with a good answer, the desk officer brought a third person to the waiting area: a woman, maybe thirty years old, and almost impossibly attractive. Her hair was dark but lustrous, and her face was like delicate porcelain. She looked beautiful in a way that real people seldom did, more like a dream than a human being. Sahara would be all over her, and she assumed Omar would be as well. She glanced at him, and saw that he was, yes, watching her, but coolly—more like a wary evaluation than the blatant admiration she had expected. Always wearing a mask. She looked back at the woman, trying to be casual about it, and studied her more closely; it was hard to focus on anything but her face, to the point that her clothes seemed to almost blend into the background. When Marisa looked at them, she saw that the stranger was dressed completely in black: black trousers, a black suit coat, even black gloves. Who wore gloves in LA in the summer? She looked efficient and professional, like maybe she was a lawyer or a business executive.

For her part, the woman didn't bother looking at Marisa or Omar at all, but simply watched the row of office doors where Carlo Magno and Don Francisco were being questioned.

A message from Omar popped up in Marisa's vision, and she blinked on it.

Do you know who that is?

No, she sent back. **You?**

No idea.

Marisa glanced at the woman again, and blinked to take a photo and send it to her friends—but then stopped, staring at the still photo, and decided to go a step further. She wasn't using the bandwidth for anything else, so why not send a live video? She blinked again, setting her djinni to start streaming, and sent a quick message to Sahara and their friend Anja:

Fijense a esta mamita.

The first response came from Sahara: **What the crap does that mean?**

Just blink on the video feed.

Fine, sent Sahara. Her ID appeared in the streaming window, followed almost immediately by another message in the conversation: **Hot damn, Mari, why I don't I hang out in more police stations? She's gorgeous.**

Right?

She can't be real.

Marisa moved her head slightly, so that the video feed could see more of the room. **See? I'm in a real place. This is a real person.**

Whoa, said Sahara, **is that Omar?**

Yeah, he's here with his dad.

Kick him.

Come on, Sahara, his mom just died.

Did her death magically transform him into a decent human being again?

Anja joined the conversation with a string of incomprehensible German: Ich beschlagnahme Eichhörnchen!

What on earth? asked Marisa.

I'm sorry, sent Anja, I thought we were playing "Random phrases in languages our friends don't speak."

Ay, que feas, sent Marisa. You live in LA and you still don't speak Spanish? Or at least have autotranslators set up on your djinnis? How do you even survive?

And you don't have one set up for German, either, sent Anja, or you would know that I confiscate squirrels.

I don't think Anja's making sense in any language right now, sent Sahara.

Blerg, sent Marisa. Blink the link, huera.

Anja's ID appeared in the streaming window. Whoa, she said. Check out the hot chick.

That's exactly what I said, sent Marisa. Any idea who she is?

A model? asked Sahara. An actress?

Maybe she's a lawyer, sent Anja.

She's not Don Francisco's lawyer, sent Marisa. Omar doesn't know her, either.

You asked Omar before us? sent Anja.

Show her, sent Sahara.

Marisa moved her head again, looking at Omar.

Tier, sent Anja. **Kick him.**

Marisa rolled her eyes. **I can't kick him in the police station.**

Too bad, sent Sahara. **The police station is one of his more sensitive areas.**

Hang on, sent Marisa, and shot her glance over at one of the office doors. The lock clicked, and the knob was turning. When the door opened, Carlo Magno stepped out, looking even more furious than when he'd gone in. Detective Hendel stepped out after him, wearing a shirt and tie, a long skirt, and a headscarf. Muslim? Marisa shook her head. Based on the name, she guessed the detective was Orthodox Jewish.

"Thank you again for your time, Mr. Carneseca." She offered Carlo Magno her hand, and he shook it grudgingly. "Would you like to wait here while I talk to your daughter?"

"Absolutely not!" Carlo Magno roared. "I've already told you everything—she doesn't know any more than that, so I'm taking her home!"

"Mr. Carneseca," said the detective, but before their argument could go any further, the woman in black stepped in between them, smoothly cutting off Carlo Magno and clasping the detective's hand in a firm handshake.

"Good evening, Detective Hendel, I'm Ramira Bennett. We spoke earlier on the phone?"

"Yes, Ms. Bennett, if you'll please have a seat I can—"

"I'm afraid my employers are on a very tight schedule," said Bennett. She didn't let go of the detective's hand, and was

33

somehow smoothly maneuvering Hendel back into her office. "My questions will only take a short time, and then you can return to your interviews."

She's here to ask the detective questions? sent Sahara. **Now I really want to know who this is.**

"Yes," said Carlo Magno, "talk to her. I'm taking my daughter and we're leaving."

"No," said Detective Hendel, and in the same instant Marisa said: "Papi! Stop making a scene!"

"I'm not making a scene!"

He's definitely making a scene, sent Anja.

"Sir," said Ramira Bennett, and turned the full strength of her attention on Carlo Magno—though still, Marisa noticed, keeping herself firmly between the detective and the rest of the hallway. "If you and your daughter will wait here for just a moment, I'll see what I can work out to help you."

Carlo Magno stuttered, shocked by either her offer of help or her blinding facial symmetry, and before he could summon a proper response, the woman had maneuvered Hendel into the office and closed the door behind them.

THREE

Omar whistled. "She's good."

"Cállate," said Carlo Magno, pointing at him fiercely and then walking toward Marisa. The medical nuli followed close behind. "Vámonos."

"We're staying," said Marisa.

"We're not."

"This is important."

"*Education* is important," said Carlo Magno. "Family. My mother's recipe for adobada. This is just spectacle—this is nothing."

Your dad is so weird, sent Sahara.

Shut up, sent Marisa, and then pulled on her father's arm as he tried to walk away. "Papi, sit down."

"I don't want you to talk to her."

Marisa held her ground. "Tell me what's going on."

"Nothing is going on. This is over."

Look at Omar, sent Anja. **I want to see his reaction to all of this.**

"Shut up!" said Marisa, and then she realized with a jolt of terror that she'd said it out loud. "Sorry!" Her eyes went wide. "I'm so sorry, that was meant for Anja, not you."

Carlo Magno threw his hands in the air. "You're texting your friends *now*? You can't even take *this* seriously."

"Why does talking to my friends about it mean I'm not taking it seriously?"

"Because I've met your friends," said Carlo Magno.

Burn, sent Anja.

Marisa blinked on the conversation, closing it and turning off notifications. "Don't change the subject. This isn't about my friends, this is about you—I'm talking to them because you won't say two words in a row to me unless one of them is no!"

"That's not true."

"Not is a derivative of no."

"That's not the point!"

"There it is again!"

"No it—" He clenched his fist in frustration. "Mari. You need to—" He stopped again, glancing at Omar, and then lowered his voice and looked back at Marisa. "You need to understand. What I'm about to ask you will be hard for you, but I need you to do it."

Marisa frowned, caught up in his suddenly serious tone, and matched his solemn whisper. "What?"

"I need you to believe me."

Marisa sighed and rolled her eyes. "Santa vaca."

"I'm not joking," he said. "I need you to listen to what I'm saying and recognize for once in your life that maybe a forty-four-year-old father knows more about something than a seventeen-year-old child. That maybe sometimes when I tell you to do something it's because I understand the ramifications and surrounding circumstances better than the girl I have dedicated my life to raising and protecting."

"We're in a police station," said Marisa. "I think I'm protected."

"From violence, yes," said Carlo Magno. "Sometimes that doesn't hurt as much as the truth does."

"The truth will set you free," said Marisa. "They tell us every frakking week in church."

"You're already free," said Carlo Magno. He glanced at Omar again, then back at Marisa, and his voice softened even more—not just quiet but earnest. Pleading. "Dredging up the past is like picking at a scab. It feels good while you do it, because you think you like the pain, but then it bleeds, and it aches, and even if you're lucky it leaves a scar you can never get rid of. And if you're not lucky it just never heals at all, and you bleed and ache forever. I don't want you to have to live with that."

Marisa was touched by the change in tone, but the words just made her furious, and the discrepancy between those two feelings left her feeling unbalanced and upset. "Papi—"

"The past is in the past," he said.

The door to the office flew open, and Ramira Bennett stalked out of it, calm and imperious.

"This is an outrage," said Detective Hendel.

Bennett didn't even look at her, and focused her attention instead on some kind of tablet screen in her hand. "Feel free to take that up with your local government representative," she said. She tapped the screen a few times and then slid it into the breast pocket inside of her suit. "It's the law, and you will comply with it."

"You're a real piece of work," said Hendel.

Bennett turned and looked at her, saying nothing.

Marisa was desperate to know what they were talking about, and had to restrain herself from blurting something out. She gripped her father's arm tightly for support.

Hendel fumed, grinding her teeth, then looked at the desk officer and shouted in a clipped, angry voice, "Lopez! Give Ms. Bennett the evidence we recovered for case number 957."

The desk officer blinked, scrolling through some list of case files on his djinni, and then blinked again in surprise. "The . . . The hand, ma'am?"

"Yes," Hendel hissed. "The hand."

"That's evidence in an ongoing investigation—"

"Federal statute 7o.3482," said Bennett. "By running a blood test on that hand, you have violated my employer's rights, and as such you have opened yourselves to full legal reprisal, even in the instance of an active investigation, as explained in substatute 2.6r4. Surrender the hand immediately and we will not press charges."

The desk officer looked back and forth between Bennett and Hendel. "I'll have to talk to the chief."

"I've already talked to her," said Hendel, barely containing her anger. "Do what she says."

"Please move quickly," said Bennett. "I don't have all night."

The desk officer turned and hurried through an unmarked door. Hendel practically growled her next words to Bennett.

"You can wait here," she said. "He'll be back in a second. Carneseca, you're with me." Carlo Magno started to protest, but Hendel cut him off with a glare. "Don't even start with me, sir. Miss, in here, please."

Marisa looked at her father one more time, seeing the pain in his eyes; she saw the confusion in Omar's, and the passionless triumph in Ramira Bennett's, and the grumpy fatigue in Hendel's. Marisa grabbed her purse from a chair and went into the office.

Detective Hendel closed and locked the door behind them.

"What on earth is going on?" asked Marisa.

"I wish I could say it was just another day in the LAPD," said Hendel, "but this is unusual even for me." The detective sat in a chair behind the desk, and gestured at another chair for Marisa.

Marisa stayed standing. "Why does she want the hand?"

"I'm supposed to be the one asking you the questions."

"It's not evidence," said Marisa, ignoring the comment completely. She planted her fists on the desk. "It's human remains."

"Please don't argue about laws that you've obviously never read."

Marisa's eyes went wide, and then she narrowed them in a tight scowl. "Those laws sound stupid."

"I'm glad you're reacting so maturely," said Hendel. "Now: I need you to calm down, and stop asking questions, and answer just a couple of minor—"

Marisa wasn't done. "How are you supposed to find out what happened to Zenaida de Maldonado without the only piece of evidence that she might still be alive?"

"I assure you that we are doing everything in our power,"

said Hendel. "Which is precious little these days, but even with megacorps running the government, we can still investigate a murder. And we are still very good at it."

"So, Bennett works for a megacorp," Marisa said. The slight change in Hendel's expression told her she was right. "Which one?"

Hendel straightened up, fixing her posture and taking a deep breath. "I'm sorry, Miss Carneseca, but there are certain aspects of this case that I am not at liberty to discuss. Let me tell you the part that I can discuss, and we'll see if maybe you can shed some light on it."

"We can try," said Marisa, and after a moment she sighed and sat in the chair. "But I was only two when it happened, so I don't know what I can tell you."

"You people are all so hung up on that car crash," said Hendel. "That was fifteen years ago; this attack happened last night. And I wanted to talk to you because the attack went down involving a gang called La Sesenta."

The words hit Marisa like a punch in the stomach. "That's my brother's gang."

"It is," said Hendel. "My research tells me that most of your family has no communication with Jesús 'Chuy' Carneseca, and your very angry father confirmed that. But I understand that you stay in touch with him."

"Is he okay?" asked Marisa. She didn't talk to her oldest brother often, but the detective was right—she was probably the only one in the family who talked to him at all.

Was this what her father didn't want her to know? That Chuy was somehow involved with all of this?

"As far as we know, your brother is fine," said Hendel. "The severed left hand was the only bodily remnant recovered at the scene, aside from a few blood spatters that our forensics team is still sorting through. It's possible someone was shot, but we've been watching the hospitals—if any of the gangsters from either side were hurt badly enough to need one, they haven't gone."

"They probably can't afford it," said Marisa. "I know Chuy can't." She hesitated a moment, then quickly sent him a message: **Are you okay? Call me.**

Detective Hendel watched her. Had she noticed when Marisa sent the message?

"Do you know where your brother is now?" asked Hendel.

"No."

"Do you know where he lives?"

Marisa paused, wondering if she should tell the truth or not. She didn't want to be the reason her own brother ended up in jail, but if he'd hurt someone—if he'd killed anyone, let alone Zenaida de Maldonado—then he needed to be stopped.

She thought about Chuy's girlfriend, Adriana, and their little boy, Chito.

She thought about a woman's severed hand.

She felt torn in half.

"Hmm," said Hendel, watching her. "Let me ask you another question while you think. Has your brother ever mentioned anything about a chop shop?"

"Is that another gang?"

"A chop shop is a *type* of gang," said Hendel. "The one that shot up La Sesenta last night is called Discount Arms."

Marisa frowned. "Are they arms dealers?"

"Please don't."

"Please don't what?"

"I've heard every joke you could possibly make," said Hendel, "and they're all bad, and it's very late, and I'd rather we just skip over them and focus on the useful information."

Marisa narrowed her eyes, staring at the detective. "What are you talking about?"

Hendel narrowed her eyes back. "Do you genuinely not know what a chop shop is? I thought you had to, what with your prosthetic and everything."

Marisa looked at her metal hand. "Are they—" And then the pieces all clicked into place. "Holy crap, they really are arms dealers!"

Hendel rolled her eyes. "The black market for replacement body parts—either natural, cybernetic, or gengineered—is booming. How much did you pay for your father's liver?"

"More than we could afford."

"You could have bought it off the street for half the price. But it would have come from someone else, someone in the wrong place at the wrong time, who someone like Discount Arms or Body Style or half a dozen others kidnapped and literally broke down for parts. They're kidnappers, murderers, and dealers of the worst kind."

Marisa's jaw was hanging open. "And you think—I mean, these are real?"

"Unfortunately. They're a much bigger problem in Asia, but we're starting to get offshoots and copycats popping up on the West Coast as well."

"And you think they have something to do with Zenaida's hand?"

Hendel watched her for a moment, probably looking for a new way to say *stop asking about the details of the case*. Then, to Marisa's surprise, she answered the question. "Maybe. Probably. Our forensic people couldn't figure out how or when the hand was severed from the rest of her body, but there is evidence that it was kept on ice for at least a day, which implies a chop shop."

"One day?"

"Maybe more."

"Fifteen years?"

Hendel shook her head. "Three, four days at the absolute most."

"So maybe . . ." Marisa still couldn't believe that something this disgusting—this reprehensible—could be real. With a shock, she realized that that was probably why Hendel had been so open: she'd shared this one detail of the case to help convince Marisa that Chuy was either in real danger or the cause of it. She was trying to make her doubt Chuy enough to give her his address.

"Maybe Chuy and his friends were trying to stop them," said Marisa.

"Maybe," said Hendel. "Or maybe they're fighting for territory. Black-market body parts can be more lucrative than drugs if the gang can hold on to their market."

"Chuy would never do this."

"Chuy's in a gang," said Hendel, her voice rising. "Chuy makes his living by ruining people's lives—no matter what he's told you about the group all hanging together, looking out for each other, blah blah blah, that's the truth at the core of it. He might not be murdering homeless people for eyes and livers, but he's not exactly planting flowers and teaching kids to read, either."

Marisa stared at her, and frowned at a sudden thought. "You don't need the address," she said.

"Yes we do."

"His ID is public," said Marisa. "His address is easily searchable, along with every other aspect of his life. With police access, you can probably tap into his apartment computer and find out what he had for breakfast." She looked at the detective. "What do you really need?"

"We need to know where they are," said Hendel. "Not where they live, but their current location—we've already looked, and they're completely off the grid."

"His family?"

"His whole gang, and all of their families. We can't find any of them anywhere."

"I don't know where they are—"

"But you know how to find out," said Hendel. "You've probably already messaged him about this just in the last couple of minutes. Am I right?"

Marisa said nothing.

"Chuy trusts you," said Hendel, "in a way that no one in La Sesenta will ever trust anyone who works in this building. And after what you just learned about the chop shops, and about what probably happened to Zenaida, now you understand exactly how important it is that we find them."

FOUR

Marisa pulled the trigger and held it, feeling the rifle buck in her hands and watching the stream of bullets eat through the drone like a firehose spray through a sand castle. The magazine emptied and the rifle clicked, and Marisa snarled as the drone fell to the asphalt with a clatter. She slapped a new magazine into the well and fired another burst into the dead drone.

"Easy there, sparky," said Anja.

"Sorry," said Marisa. She gritted her teeth and fired one last, short burst. "I just really needed to destroy something."

"In that case," said Anja, and her eyes glinted wildly behind her glasteel visor, "I'll join you." She fired a burst from her own weapon—not bullets but a hot stream of liquid fire, melting the shattered drone fragments into slag. "This game is the best for that."

Marisa looked around at the blasted landscape: a virtual reality simulation of a postapocalyptic city, inside of a video game called Overworld. The game had dozens of different maps—a fantasy castle, a pirate island, a space station—but Marisa and her friends had grown obsessed with the apocalyptic one lately because it gave them a chance to cosplay as characters from their favorite book series.

And, of course, it was a really great way to work out some stress.

"Come on," said Marisa. "Let's go find some more gun drones to murder."

"You watch your mouth," said Anja, slinging her flamethrower over her shoulder and following Marisa through the ruins. "When a true AI finally emerges and we have to start recognizing drones as people, that kind of talk will be super racist."

Sahara's voice crackled through the comm system, shouting their in-game call signs. "Happy! Heartbeat! Do you two intend to actually play the game at some point? Quicksand and I just got triple-teamed by some enemy agents, and some backup would have been, you know, your gorram jobs."

"Sorry," said Anja. "We were punishing a nuli for its species' future insolence."

"It's okay," said Marisa, "we'll be right there."

"Right where?" asked Sahara. "The fight's over now; we lost a whole wave of minions."

"Lighten up," said Quicksand—their friend Jaya, who lived in Mumbai. Virtual reality made the distance meaningless. "It's not like this is a real match."

"Two points for Jaya," said Anja. "This was specifically established as a blow-off-steam match."

"I don't know about the rest of you," said Fang, the fifth player on their team, "but I blow off steam by winning."

"Exactly," said Sahara. "Losing is only going to ruin your night."

"Day," said Fang. "Some of us live in real cities." Fang hailed from Beijing, a full fourteen hours ahead; while the girls in Los Angeles were pushing midnight, Fang was already well into tomorrow afternoon.

"Heads up," said Anja, and pulled Marisa down into cover. "Enemy agent in the fallen silo."

"Take him out," said Sahara.

"The most dangerous game," Anja whispered dramatically. The drones on the map were neutral, guided by the game itself, but the agents were other players: five on five, on a mission to destroy each other's vaults. Anja grinned. "*This* is how you blow off steam."

Marisa had been near a few real-world firefights, and she'd even been shot at a couple of times, but she'd never been an active participant outside of Overworld. She propped her gun across the top of a ruined wall, and closed one eye while she looked down her scope. The other agent was alone—the enemy Sniper or Spotter, she wasn't sure which—and easy pickings for a team of two. Anja slithered forward, hidden by rubble, trying to get into range with her flamethrower, and Marisa watched the agent approach, oblivious. His in-game avatar was some kind of fantasy ranger, with a black cloak and a spiky longbow, which wasn't a perfect fit for the postapocalyptic city but didn't feel out of place, either. She watched through the scope, waiting for Anja's signal, as he passed in front of a crumbling brick wall.

"Now!" shouted Anja, leaping up and letting loose with her flamethrower. The ranger cast a wind spell that launched him up and backward, and at the apex of his leap he nocked and fired an arrow back at Anja. She dodged, but only barely, and screamed at Marisa to take the shot. "Get him! He's getting away! Shoot him!"

Marisa thought about her brother Chuy, trapped in a real shootout, Zenaida's hand lying on the ground beside him, and her hands shook so much that when she finally squeezed the trigger the bullet went far to the side. The ranger landed behind a crumbling building, disappearing into the ruins, and Marisa dropped her rifle.

"I'm sorry, girls." She blinked, opening the Overworld interface, and left the game. "I can't do this." The city disappeared, and she hung in black emptiness for a moment before appearing in their team lobby. She trembled, remembering the video of the shootout—thinking of the chop shop, and Zenaida's hand, and of the rest of her body, and it was too much, and then her friends appeared in the lobby with her: first Jaya, then Anja and Fang. Jaya wrapped her in a tight hug, no less comforting for being in virtual reality—she could feel it, and she could appreciate the love behind it, and she hugged Jaya back. Last of all came Sahara; she'd probably stayed behind to apologize to the other team for jumping out before the match was over.

"I'm so sorry," said Marisa. "I just couldn't."

"No worries," said Sahara. "We can forfeit a game without the whole world ending."

"Who are you?" asked Fang. "And what have you done with Sahara?"

"It's a blow-off-steam game," said Anja. "That's different."

Fang feigned disgust. "This is why your nation isn't a world superpower anymore."

"My nation is a verdammt Wunder," said Anja. "Don't lump me in with the Americans just because I live with them."

"This is how I blow off steam," said Jaya, smiling and holding Marisa tightly. "Listening to my best friends argue about stupid crap."

Marisa laughed. "It is kind of comforting, isn't it?"

"You heard the girl," said Jaya, scowling fiercely at the other girls. "She finds pleasure in your antics! Dance, monkeys, dance!"

Anja blinked, and her apocalyptic avatar was replaced with a chimpanzee, complete with a tutu and a tiara.

"Yes!" shouted Jaya. "Now say something stupid about things that don't matter!"

"Fang!" shouted the Anja Chimpanzee. "That's it. Just, Fang."

"Tā mā de," growled Fang, and blinked herself into a VR tiger. The two girls chased each other around the room, while Sahara rolled her eyes and Marisa and Jaya laughed themselves silly.

"Okay," said Sahara, walking toward the center of the room. "Okay. Calm down. Everybody ca—" A chimpanzee flew by her head, and she glared at it for a second before speaking again. "Everybody calm down. We have an actual job to do here, you know."

"Blow off steam!" chanted the chimp, dangling from a light

fixture while the tiger leaped after it again and again, missing by millimeters. "Blow off steam!"

"I'm not talking about the game," said Sahara. "I'm talking about this severed hand."

Fang immediately turned back into a human, peering at Sahara suspiciously. "You have my attention."

Sahara blinked, summoning a table in the center of the room. It bore a 3D model of the Overworld map, designed for teams to plan their strategy, but Sahara swept it away, leaving only their team logo: the Cherry Dogs.

"We've brought down a digital drug dealer and a frakking megacorp," said Sahara. "I think we can figure out what's going on with this Maldonado business—and when we do, then it can end. The secrets can be out, and the stupid feud behind the Maldonados and Marisa's family can finally be put to rest." She looked at Marisa. "It'll be a start, at least. Marisa's always there for us, no matter what the problem is. Let's solve this thing and give her her life back."

Marisa felt a renewed surge of affection for the other girls. This was what she'd been searching for, for years: the truth behind the night her life, and her family's lives, had changed forever. And they were going to help her find it.

Sahara drew with her finger as she talked, leaving 3D stick figures hanging in the air above the table. "Zenaida de Maldonado died in a car accident fifteen years ago—or so we thought. What we do know—and what we assume is still true—is that Mari was in the car with her, though we don't know why. Omar and his brother Jacinto were there too. Mari lost her arm, and

Jacinto lost . . . more than that. He was badly injured, but we don't know how."

"And Omar didn't lose anything," said Anja. "Lucky bastard."

"He lost his mother," said Marisa. Anja scowled but grew more somber.

"So last night," Sahara continued, "La Sesenta and a chop shop gang called Discount Arms—I can't believe that stupid name—got into a shootout, and though none of them died, that we know of, a severed left hand was found at the scene." Sahara sketched a hand into her diagram, and Sahara being Sahara, it was a better-looking sketch than it needed to be. "Police forensics determined that the hand had spent at least a day on ice, and DNA tests confirmed it was definitely Zenaida's hand."

"Or someone else in the family," said Fang. "Zenaida's children share enough of her DNA to maybe fool a forensic test."

"Not likely," said Jaya. "Maybe thirty years ago. Maybe even fifteen years ago, honestly, which might be how they identified the wrong body. But not today. Modern DNA tests are crazy accurate."

"But Jacinto is such an obvious lead," said Anja. "Right? Marisa's seen everyone else in their family in the last few hours, and they all still had their hands, but no one's seen Jacinto in years. Assuming he's even still around, maybe he got out and—" Her eyes went wide. "Heilige Scheiss."

"Please don't pose a ridiculous conspiracy theory," said Sahara.

Anja's grin spread from ear to ear. "What if Jacinto is the one who died in the crash, and Zenaida's been hiding in their house ever since, pretending to be him and pretending to be psychologically damaged as an excuse not to leave the house! Boom! I just blew your minds."

"Your nose, maybe," said Fang.

Sahara covered her face with her palm. "Oh my word."

"Jacinto was ten years old at the time of the accident," said Marisa. "There's no way a ten-year-old boy's body gets mistaken for an adult woman's."

"Fine," said Anja. "We'll stick a pin in this idea and come back to it later."

"Meanwhile, back in reality," said Sahara, "we have two potential leads: Chuy, who was involved in the shootout, and Mystery Babe Ramira Bennett, who works for some shadowy megacorp and claimed the severed hand as that megacorp's property."

"Federal statute whatever-the-hell," said Anja, and looked at Marisa. "I like the detective, by the way. Hendel."

"So Bennett's a corporate liaison," asked Marisa. "Or a lawyer, or an . . . I don't know. A corporate enforcer?"

"She's someplace to start," said Sahara. "Anja, Fang, and Jaya: that's your job. I'll forward you the footage Mari recorded at the police station, and you see if you can find any more clues about who she is, or an image search of her face, or whatever."

"If she works for a genhancement company, that could explain her face," said Anja. "No way someone that beautiful isn't running some custom DNA."

"We're on it," said Jaya. "What are you two doing?"

"We're going after the other lead," said Sahara. "We're going to talk to Chuy."

* * *

Mirador wasn't a rich neighborhood, but it wasn't really a poor one, either. Don Maldonado, for all his faults, did manage to keep the place lively enough to get by, and while vast swaths of Los Angeles had essentially become shantytowns, Mirador was still clinging to the edge of viability.

Some blocks were clinging much more desperately than others.

Chuy lived in a quadruplex on the western edge of Mirador, in a fading slum that was not, Marisa realized, all that different from the apocalyptic ruins they'd been playing through in Overworld. Each building and house had a cinder-block wall around it, topped by razor wire and shards of glass bottles set into cement. The roofs were festooned with ad hoc solar collectors, and black, ragged cables spread out from each one like fraying spiderwebs, carrying illicit power to whoever was savvy enough to steal it. Marisa and Sahara and Bao walked down the sidewalk warily, blinking at the morning sunlight and trying not to look like outsiders. Only Bao was succeeding. Suspicious locals watched them from porches and corners, and Sahara's camera nulis hovered overhead like protective guard dogs.

"Both Cameron and Camilla have several taser charges each," Sahara whispered. "And I've been taking tae kwon do since I was four."

"Taking it doesn't mean you can beat people up with it," whispered Bao.

"Trust her," whispered Marisa. "I've seen her take down groups of four at a time."

"Nice," whispered Bao. "Now I kind of hope we get jumped."

Marisa sighed. "Sometimes I think it would be easier to drop this whole thing and start searching for Grendel again." Grendel was a mystery—a hacker lurking in the darkest corners of the internet, sometimes helping her and sometimes masterminding horrific plots to frighten and destroy. The last time they'd talked, he'd said that he knew about the car accident that killed Zenaida and took Marisa's arm, and the girls had spent every day since trying to track him down. He may as well have been a ghost.

"What do you mean, 'again'?" asked Bao. "You don't expect us to believe that you ever stopped."

"Fine," said Marisa. "No, I didn't—I've been combing every darknet forum I can find for him, even with all this stuff going on. This morning I left two messages on old dummy forum accounts I'm pretty sure he used as aliases. So at the very least, he knows I want to talk to him—maybe he'll just talk to me first."

"Fat chance," said Sahara, and then nodded at a dead, yellow lawn. "We're here."

They turned at the lawn and walked up the short driveway to Chuy's building. The iron gate stood open, and despite the security elsewhere on the walls, it didn't look like the gate was even capable of closing. An old man in a shaded folding chair stopped them with a brusque bark:

"Oyen! What are you doing here?"

"I want to see my brother," said Marisa. She looked closer at the shaded man and realized his eyes were clouded over; he was probably blind, but he seemed to be able to see them just fine. "Chuy Carneseca, in 2B."

"He ain't here."

"You mind if we go knock anyway?"

The man seemed to take that as an affront. "You think I'm lying to you?"

"We want to leave an analog," said Bao, and the man grunted.

"Well, that's different," he said, and waved them by.

Marisa leaned in close as they passed the man and tramped up the stairs. "What's an analog?"

"A real-world message," whispered Bao, "like, on a piece of paper. Poor neighborhoods like this one use them all the time to pass notes." He nodded at the building. "Chuy's front door's probably full of them."

"They don't text?" asked Sahara.

"They don't trust each other enough to share their IDs," said Bao.

They reached the door to 2B, and Marisa gave a cursory glance to the five or six fluttering, tacked-on notes. Most were from people wondering where Chuy's girlfriend, Adriana, was, which wasn't a good sign; it didn't look like anyone had been here in days. Marisa knocked loudly, and they waited.

Bao pulled out a small notepad and started writing. "We'd better leave an actual note—I know that blind guy can see me."

"Probably hear you, too," said Sahara. She was scanning the street, one hand shielding her eyes from the bright LA sun. "This whole neighborhood is watching us."

Marisa knocked again, even more loudly. "I've sent messages to him and Adriana both," she said, "and neither one is answering."

"Hey!" said a voice. She looked around, startled, but didn't identify the source of the sound until it spoke again. "Chica, they're not home."

The voice was coming from the window of the next apartment over, in 2A. The lights were off inside, but behind the wire screen and the wrought-iron bars Marisa could just make out the shape of a face.

"Órale," said Marisa, greeting the man. "Chuy's my brother. Do you know where he is?"

"Chuy don't have sisters."

"He has three," said Marisa. Did the man really not know, or was this a test to make sure she was for real? "And he has a girlfriend named Adriana, and a son named Chito—or, uh, Jesusito. He's named after his father, but I always just call him Chito."

"So what's your name, then?"

"I'm Marisa," she said. "I really need to talk to him."

The man in the window was silent for a moment, and then the half-glimpsed face broke into a smile. "Este cuñado! He never told me his sister was so fine. What's up, baby girl?"

Marisa wrinkled her lips into a grimace. "Can you tell me where he is?"

"They're gone, guapa, the whole group."

"But do you know where?"

The man paused, and a moment later something cylindrical and metallic appeared in the window. Marisa and her friends ducked immediately, throwing themselves down and to the sides, but the man only laughed. "Kind of jumpy? It's not a gun, niñitos, it's a Wi-Fi scanner. I gotta make sure you're safe." A series of colors lit up on the end of the cylinder, and the man hummed and muttered over the results until suddenly he dropped the scanner and disappeared, just as jumpy as they had been.

"You got cameras?"

Marisa looked up at the nulis. "Yeah?"

"Everyone has cameras," said Sahara, glaring at the man impatiently. "Even if we didn't have nulis, we have cameras in our eyes—so do you, and so does everyone on this street. Including the lights and the stop signs."

"Chuy—" the man started, still hiding out of sight, but he stopped before he went any further. "Listen, I can take you to him, but not on camera."

"Where do you expect to go that doesn't have cameras?" asked Sahara.

"La Zona Muerta," the man whispered.

"The Dead Zone?" asked Marisa.

"I don't really want to go to a place called the Dead Zone," said Bao. "Just a personal preference."

"You're the only one who can go," said the man. "Scanner says you got no Wi-Fi."

"No djinni," said Bao. "I've got a handheld phone, but it's off."

"Smart," said the man. He was still hiding.

"Listen," said Marisa. "I have to see him, so if you can take us, let's go. I can . . ." She hesitated. "Turn my djinni off." She'd done it before, to protect herself from a virus, but it was intensely unsettling. To go from a real-time connection with the entire internet, including a full heads-up display overlaying and supplementing her vision, to . . . nothing at all. Trapped in her own head with no way out but her own senses. It made her shiver just to think about it.

But if it meant helping Chuy, she'd do anything.

"I'm not going to let you just take them somewhere," said Sahara, stepping closer to the window. "We don't even know you."

"Fine with me," said the man, "I didn't want to go anyway."

"Just turn yours off, too," said Bao.

"These cameras are my livelihood," said Sahara. "People pay to watch this stream, and if I turn them off I don't eat."

"We'll be okay," said Marisa. Sahara was their protector, and probably terrified to leave them alone. "We've got this."

"Are you armed?" asked Sahara.

"We're in La Sesenta territory," said Marisa. "No one's going to mess with Chuy's sister."

"Take this anyway," she said, and handed Marisa a slim black rod about the size and shape of a lipstick tube. "Not as good as the tasers in the nulis, but it'll help you in a pinch."

"Whoa," said the man behind the window. "Those cameras run a live feed? Are you famous?"

"I don't know," said Sahara, "do you recognize me?"

"You're that girl with that show," said the man. "Sahara Cowan."

"Well, what do you know," said Sahara, and Marisa could see how surprised and pleased it made her. "I guess I am."

"I love your show," said the man, "I watch it every night."

"Then why didn't you recognize Marisa?"

"I only watch while you're sleeping. It's kind of a thing with me—the girl's just lying there, totally at peace—"

"Here," said Sahara, and handed Marisa another item: a black plastic gun. "If creepazoid goes for you, skip the taser and kill him."

"We'll be fine," said Marisa. "Now go, before he changes his mind."

Sahara gave them a last look, then walked down the stairs and back to the street. Cameron and Camilla followed her, using their carefully calibrated algorithms to catch her and her surroundings from all the best angles.

"You realize," said Bao, "the more successful she gets, the less of this kind of stuff she'll be able to do with us."

Marisa watched her walk away, and then banged lightly on the window. "Okay, cuate, she's gone."

"Your djinni's not off yet."

Marisa clenched her jaw, bracing herself for the shock of it, but Bao stopped her.

"Can't you just . . . turn off the satellite connection or something? Leave at least the interface? That might make it more comfortable."

"The interface can still take pictures," said the man in the window.

"Djinnis don't work like that, anyway," said Marisa. "That's like saying 'Can't you just leave the car turned on, but remove its engine?' Very few of a djinni's programs are run locally; I have my own data stored in here, but all the processing is done server-side. My djinni just taps in via the internet. It's either on or its off; no half measures."

"Let's get it done," said the man in the window.

She took a deep breath, and blinked through the long series of menus and confirmations required to shut down a djinni. She hit the last one, a timer icon started spinning, and then all of her icons disappeared completely. Her chat windows, gone; her GPS tracker, gone; the overlays and interfaces that augmented her reality, giving meaning and order and a personal touch to everything she saw, all disappeared. Her mind was accustomed to filtering a dozen worldwide internet connections at once, and now it had nothing. The world felt smaller and more isolated, and she shivered involuntarily.

"It's okay," Bao whispered. "I got you."

"Ándale," said the man in the window. "I didn't think you'd do it—kids these days and their HUD apps, man, it's like cutting off their air supply."

"Which is of course a thing you've never done and would never do," said Bao.

"Wait right there," said the man. "I'm coming out."

Bao and Marisa stood on the walkway for a moment, Marisa blinking at the strangeness of the unmodified world, and when the door to 2A opened they saw the man for the first time—tallish, thin, and with a long, wispy beard matched in disarray by his long, unkempt hair. He was older than Marisa expected, and he scanned them one last time with his Wi-Fi wand before grinning, shoving the tool into his belt, and pulling his hair back into a ponytail. He wound it tight and locked it in place with a chopstick.

"I'm Raña," he said. "Let's go." He walked to the stairs, and Marisa hurried to keep up, Bao close behind.

"Where's La Zona Muerta?"

"There's a lot of them," said Raña. "All over the city. This one's close by. It's not a place like a named place, like a coffee shop or a VR parlor, but it's like a *kind* of place, you know? Like a park or an intersection. It's not about branding, like everything else in the megacorps' world, it's just what it is."

"This whole explanation sounds herbally augmented," said Bao.

"That's how you see the world for what it is," said Raña.

"So where are we going?" asked Marisa. They were out on the street now, walking quickly to keep pace with Raña's long legs. "And why's it called a Zona Muerta?"

"Because it's dead," said Raña, and patted the Wi-Fi scanner on his waist. "No signals, no cameras, no radio frequencies playing songs in your teeth."

Bao looked at Marisa, obviously worried about what they'd gotten themselves into. She smiled back and kept walking.

They followed Raña for several blocks, past old, run-down houses and a long parade of improvised storefronts, thrown together with paint and desperation to sell everything from chip phones to groceries; knockoff shirt brands and chapulín tacos and sets of mismatched dishes piled high on rickety shelves. Some of them had scraped together enough cash to add holodisplays to their windows, and Marisa blinked to make sure her ad blockers were all in place, only to remember that her djinni was off. She smirked. At least they couldn't send her ads, even if they wanted to.

"This is what you live like all the time?" she whispered to Bao. He lived in a similar shantytown, built in the husk of a half-finished hotel.

"You get used to it," he answered.

Marisa wasn't sure she wanted to.

Raña led them to an empty lot, blocked off by chain-link fences and filled with huge piles of dirt; they'd obviously been intended for a construction project, but at some point it had been abandoned, and now they were covered with tracks where local kids raced bikes around the hills and valleys. "This was going to be a mall," said Raña, picking his way through the rubble and weeds, "but they never finished it."

"Looks like they barely even started it," said Marisa.

"Well, yeah, not the building," said Raña, and pulled aside a sheet of corrugated tin. A narrow tunnel of packed dirt and cement stairs yawned before them. "The underground parking was finished twenty years ago, though. Most people forget it's even here."

They followed him in, replacing the makeshift door behind them, and Marisa felt her uneasiness building, slowly but relentlessly. A tall man emerged from around the first corner of the tunnel, his arms replaced by bionic limbs so large they might have been taken off of pile drivers.

"Raña," said the guard, "what the hell, man?"

"Chuy's sister," said Raña, and held up his Wi-Fi scanner. "They're clean."

The man grunted, and crossed his giant piston arms in grudging acceptance. "Fine," he growled, and stepped to the side so they could pass. "Next time use the damn secret knock—why do we even have a secret knock if none of you blowholes ever use it?"

Raña led them past the guard, barely squeezing through the space between the wall and his bionic arms. Marisa came through last, and held her own prosthetic up in a fist of solidarity. He tapped it with his own fist, a metal monstrosity the size of a toaster oven, and the force of it reverberated through her entire skeleton.

It occurred to Marisa that they'd made her give up her djinni, but hadn't even asked about her gun. They were more worried about a digital footprint than a bullet. The thought made her shiver.

The tunnel was short, and after just a few meters turned another curve and opened into a wide, sloped parking garage, lit by fluorescent tubes and filled with pipes and makeshift walls and so many more people than Marisa expected. It was an entire community, complete with homes and market stalls, with each room or home or store separated by rugs and blankets hanging from wires. She smelled grease frying, and saw a man with an old metal barrel set up on cinder blocks, with a bright blue flame burning below it; a hose snaked out from the burner to a propane tank, and the man stirred the barrel with a two-by-four.

"Fried rat?" asked Bao.

"Crickets," said Raña.

"Just like home," said Bao. But his home had never spooked Marisa the way this one did. An entire hidden community, closed off and secret.

"So no one here has a djinni?" she asked Raña. He led them down the ramp, and then circled to the left and went down another level.

"No one," said Raña. "Or if they do, they have them turned off."

"I've wondered about this," said Bao. "Or this kind of thing, at least. It's really the only way to keep a criminal organization secret."

A group of children ran by, shouting and chasing a dirty gray ball.

"Criminals?" asked Marisa.

"You know what I mean."

Raña led them to the very bottom of the parking garage, down where the ad hoc city gave way to an ad hoc arsenal: here they saw not the families of La Sesenta but the gangsters themselves, along with motorcycles and racks of guns and large wooden crates that contained things Marisa could only guess at. In the center of the last open space, someone had made a room of translucent plastic sheets, which glowed a pale blue from the powerful lights inside of it. Power cables snaked in under the makeshift walls, and vague silhouettes of people and equipment moved slowly inside.

"What's that?" whispered Marisa.

"Surgery," said Raña. "La Sesenta has their own private djinni extractor."

"Marisa!" The shout echoed through the cement space, and Marisa recognized Chuy's voice. She turned, trying to spot him in the gloom, and saw him waving from the far corner. A group of men sat behind him in mismatched chairs, watching her; none of them looked particularly pleased to see outsiders.

"Hombre Araña," said another voice, and as they drew closer Marisa recognized the speaker as Calaca, one of the highest-ranking gangsters in the group, instantly recognizable as he was completely covered with tattoos—his entire face bore the image of a skull. He was short and powerful, not muscle-bound but twisted tight with brutal energy. He looked like a demon, which only made his calm and measured tone all the more threatening. He approached Raña until he was no more than a few centimeters from his face. "Am I to understand that you, in whatever passes for wisdom in whatever passes for your mind, saw fit to bring not one but two strangers into what I feel I must remind you is a secret hideout?"

"This is Chuy's sister, güey." Raña arrived at the circle and stepped in without hesitation, holding up his hand for Calaca to slap or embrace or otherwise acknowledge and welcome him. Calaca kept his arms at his sides, leaning against a folding metal table.

"You say that," said Calaca, "as if it provided some form of explanation or excuse for your behavior."

"Déjalo," said a deep voice, and Marisa knew that this must be Memo—the leader of La Sesenta, and the brother of their former leader, Goyo. Memo wasn't nearly as frightening as Goyo had been—and not as frightening as Calaca was now—but he had an obvious, easy authority, and the rest of the group was arrayed around him like a satellite dish. He had a stark white bandage on the back of his head, held on with fiber tape. He shook his head at Raña and finished his thought: "It's like arguing with a cat." Calaca frowned but stayed silent. Memo pulled a wad of cash from his pocket and handed it to Raña. "Gracias, carnal. Nos vemos en la próxima, eh?" Raña nodded and left, and Memo looked back at Marisa and Bao—and at Chuy, who stood beside them. "This is your sister?"

"The oldest one, yeah," said Chuy. "She's the one who helped us out with that Bluescreen thing."

Memo fixed Marisa with a stare, and she felt like a cockroach pinned to a board.

"My brother died in that *thing*," said Memo, and Marisa felt her heart leap into her throat. Memo stared at her a moment, letting the tension build, then nodded slowly. "Without you I think I would have died, too. A lot of us, maybe. Thank you."

"Thank *you*," said Marisa. She didn't know what else to say, so she jerked a thumb toward Bao. "This is Bao."

"I'm not important," said Bao quickly. "Feel free to ignore me completely."

"You shouldn't have come here," said Chuy. "It's dangerous, for you and for us."

"That," said Calaca, "is an impressive grasp of the truth, from which your sister would be wise to learn."

"We're here to warn you," said Marisa, realizing in this moment that, in spite of her promise to Detective Hendel, she could not bring herself to betray her own brother. "The cops are looking for you."

Calaca laughed. "They are? Then we should do something about that, like maybe . . . I don't know, hiding ourselves in an underground bunker completely cut off from all digital signals. Dios en vivo, Chuy, I'm so glad your sister's here to save us from our foolishness."

"And I'm here to ask you—" said Marisa, though she immediately regretted it, and didn't have the heart to finish her sentence with the full underworld leadership of La Sesenta staring at her.

"Ask us what?" said Chuy.

"I, um . . ." She paused, and looked back at the glowing plastic enclosure, finally understanding what it was. *A surgery tent.* She thought about the chop shop and her throat dried up completely.

A panel in the wall of the surgery tent moved, and a man emerged in a white apron stained red with blood. He walked toward them, carrying a bowl, and entered the circle of gangsters without any thought to what they had been talking about. He set the bowl on Calaca's folding table; Marisa tried to see what was in it but could discern only the wet glint of bloody wires.

"That makes seven today," said the doctor. "I can do one more with the resources I have here, maybe two, but I wouldn't have enough anesthetic for either of them."

"We'll wait," said Memo, reflexively touching the bandage on his own head. "Calaca, get a list of what he needs for next time, and we'll put it together."

Marisa couldn't help but notice that the fetch order was given to Calaca; the doctor wasn't part of La Sesenta, but he held a lot of power in the group.

"This is Dr. Jones," said Chuy. "He's helping us free ourselves."

"From whom?"

"From everyone," said Dr. Jones, looking at her with unsettling intensity. "From the vast web of software and commerce and propaganda that you have invited inside of your skull. I am disinviting it." He looked at Memo. "New recruits?"

"Chuy's sister," said Memo, "and her boyfriend." Marisa didn't dare to correct him.

"Good," said the doctor. "The fewer golems, the better."

"Excuse me?" said Marisa. Her heart skipped a beat at the sudden fear that gripped her, and her leg started trembling, but her anger was hotter. She raised her metal arm, showing him the back of her hand and splaying her cybernetic fingers. "That's not a very nice word."

"Esa muchacha," muttered one of the gangsters, but Marisa couldn't tell if he was calling her out for bravery or stupidity. Or maybe both.

"And what," said Dr. Jones slowly, "am I supposed to call a

golem, other than a golem? Or is it not true? Is that a real human hand merely disguised as a borg hand? Some sort of sick joke?"

Marisa bristled. "Dímelo otra vez, culo."

"Easy," said Memo. "We pay the doctor for his services, not his principles."

"He has principles?" asked Marisa.

"Transhumanism is a plague," said Dr. Jones calmly. "But as sins go it's one of the easiest to repent of."

"Stop talking," snarled Marisa.

"Better damaged than corrupted," said the doctor.

"Thank you for your services," said Memo, ending the argument with a growl of authority. "We'll have more supplies tomorrow."

"I'll walk you out," said one of the gangsters, and gestured respectfully for the doctor to precede him. Jones shot one last look at Marisa, then at Memo, then walked away. The gangster followed.

Marisa watched him go, then glanced at Chuy. He kept his eyes on the floor, not meeting her gaze.

"He's from the Foundation," said Marisa, guessing out loud. They were the most active anticybernetic group in LA. She turned back to Memo. "You're working with a human supremacist from a terrorist organization."

Memo answered calmly. "Freelance surgeons are hard to find."

"He called me a golem," Marisa snapped.

"And I'm sorry about that," said Memo, and his hand moved again to the bandage on the back of his head. "Look: if we all still had djinnis, the cops would already be here—they're useful, but they've become too much of a liability. Even people who still have them can't ever turn them on, or they'd be zapped and tied by a police nuli before they got to the end of the block. Djinnis threaten our entire community here—all our families, which includes some of your family. We don't agree with everything that zealot doctor spouts, and frankly I think he's a madman, but he's one of the few people I could find who has the skills that we need and the willingness to perform them, and he's my guest here. Don't forget that you're a guest here, too."

"Chuy?" said Marisa, but he didn't answer.

"Chuy's a bigger dog than he used to be," said Calaca, "but he's still a dog. And dogs have collars and leashes to keep them in line." He planted himself in front of Marisa and spread his arms wide. "He works with us, and he lives with us, and out of respect for that loyalty we tolerate your presence here. Disrupt that loyalty and you are infringing on your own safety."

Marisa held Calaca's gaze just long enough to show she wasn't afraid of him—though in truth she was terrified, and had to clench her jaw tightly closed to keep it from shaking—and then turned slowly to look at Chuy. "So I guess now there are two reasons why you aren't answering my calls. You don't have a djinni, and you have a new family anyway."

"It's not a replacement," said Chuy. "La familia está sagrada." He licked his lips nervously, his eyes darting over her shoulders toward Memo or Calaca and then back to her. "And I still have my djinni—for now. I haven't turned it on because I haven't left the complex since yesterday."

"Not since you cut a woman's hand off," said Marisa, her fear turning to fury now that she was talking to someone she knew well. She regretted the words even as she said them, but it was too late to take them back.

"How much do you know?" asked Calaca.

Marisa shot him a quick glance; he was tense but no angrier than usual. "You were in a shootout with a chop shop in South Central. There's camera footage. They found a severed hand at the scene, but there were no positive IDs. The cops can't find you anywhere, which is why they questioned me."

Calaca's face clouded. "You're talking to the cops?"

"That was literally the first thing she said when she came in here," said Bao. "We're here to warn you, not turn you in." Marisa put a hand on his arm and squeezed it gratefully.

"What's this about a hand?" asked Chuy. "We shot up some cabrones there, but we didn't cut anyone, let alone cut something off."

"It was a woman's left hand," said Marisa, calming herself with a deep breath. "And I know you didn't do it, because they said it had been on ice." She looked at Chuy, locking their gazes together. "The hand belonged to Zenaida de Maldonado."

Chuy's jaw fell open. "Eitale."

"Relative of Don Francisco?" asked Memo.

"His wife," said Chuy.

"His wife's dead," said Calaca.

"Maybe," said Marisa. "But she was alive two days ago at the earliest."

"Where's she been for fifteen years?" asked Memo.

Bao shook his head. "We don't know."

"How she'd die?"

"We don't know," said Marisa. "We were hoping you could tell us."

"We didn't kill her," said Chuy.

"One of the chop shop guys had a case," said Calaca. "Like a cooler. Maybe he was carrying merchandise."

"Just say body parts," said Chuy. "It makes you sound less like a sociopath."

Marisa kept her face solemn but marveled at the sudden jab. Chuy might have been subservient to Memo, but apparently he could stand up to Calaca when he felt like it.

Marisa summoned her courage and looked at Memo. "What happened between you and the chop shop?"

"It's a turf war," said Memo.

"It's none of your business," said Calaca, and glared at Memo. "Sister or not, she's still an outsider."

"Just tell me you're not starting a chop shop of your own," said Marisa. She looked at the medical tent, standing like a ghostly blue cube in the center of the dark cavern.

"Of course we're not," said Chuy, but he didn't say any more, and Memo and Calaca didn't appear to be offering any new info either.

"Look," said Bao, breaking the silence. "Your affairs are your own. We don't want to get in the way, and we're definitely not going to talk to the police. But if you know anything about Zenaida de Maldonado and how her hand showed up at that scene—"

"She was killed and harvested by the chop shop," said Calaca. "Surely that's the only reasonable explanation."

"We don't know anything about her," said Memo. "But it looks like our goals are aligned, at least for a little while. We need to find the leaders of that chop shop, and if you want to find out what happened to Zenaida, it looks like you do, too."

"No," said Marisa, "we definitely don't want to find the chop shop."

"I snagged a bunch of IDs at the shootout," said Memo, ignoring her protest. "What I don't have are the hacking skills to track them down."

Chuy looked at Marisa. "You do."

"Maybe," said Marisa warily. "But I don't know how comfortable I am with tracking down gente for you to murder."

"They kidnap and dismember innocent people for money," said Memo.

"Good point," said Marisa. She nodded. "Okay." She jerked her chin toward the bandage on Memo's head. "If you don't have a djinni, how do you have the IDs?"

Memo smiled. "Oh, I have a djinni. It's just not in my head at the moment. Chuy."

Her brother walked to the edge of the circle, took something from a box just beyond the shadows, and handed it to Marisa. It was a sealed plastic container, like the kind you'd use for leftovers in the fridge, and a strip of tape on the lid read simply "Memo." Inside was a pile of ceramic and circuits and wires, dripping with semi-congealed blood.

"Be careful with that," said Memo. "It's my brain."

FIVE

Marisa grimaced. "I am not comfortable holding a gangster's brain."

"You're not technically holding it," said Fang. "You're in virtual reality."

Marisa stared at her across the planning table in the Cherry Dog lobby. "Ha. Ha."

"You have to be super careful with it," said Jaya.

"Hang on," said Marisa, "I'm not done." She looked back at Fang. "Ha." She looked at Jaya. "Okay, I'm done now."

Sahara gestured at the virtual model of the extracted djinni that sat on their table. Marisa hadn't modeled the blood on it, so it was pristine and glittering, like a pale ceramic star. "I can't believe you agreed to this. I should have gone with you."

"He insisted," said Marisa. "He said even if he had the skills to extract the data inside, he didn't have the equipment to do it, or anything with an internet connection to put it to use."

"They trusted you not to lose it?" asked Jaya.

"They threatened my entire family if I did," said Marisa. "So yeah, I'm protecting the ever-loving hell out of it."

"This is amazing," said Anja. "A gang lord's digital brain—I mean, the saved passwords to online accounts are one thing, but even just the photos have got to be amazing. The notepad. The GPS archive!"

"Don't touch anything he doesn't want you to touch," said Sahara. "She literally just said he threatened her life."

"It's like a bomb," said Marisa, staring at the delicate construct. "I don't even want to touch it."

"Maybe we don't have to," said Sahara. "What'd you girls find out about the creepy supermodel? Please tell me you have so many clues we don't have to ever think about this guy's djinni ever again."

"Pretty dang close," said Anja. She looked at Fang and Jaya. "Who wants to go first?"

"I will," said Jaya. She worked internal tech support for Johara, the largest telecom company in the world, so if she bent a rule here or there, she could access some pretty impressive things. "You're going to love this: so I ran her name and face through every recognition database I could access, and I found her. Ramira Bennett is an employee for—drumroll, please—ZooMorrow."

Marisa's eyes went wide. "ZooMorrow? Like, the gengineering company?"

"Exactly," said Jaya. "Have you ever seen a MyDragon?"

"Franca Maldonado has one," said Sahara. "ZooMorrow makes them?"

Jaya nodded. "Along with the HugMonkey, the SaniDog, and the Riddler."

"What's a Riddler?" asked Fang.

"It's a cat with wings," said Sahara. "I guess MySphinx was too hard to pronounce."

"Or it just sounds too much like MySphincter," said Anja.

"Gross," said Sahara.

"Isn't anyone going to make a joke about what my sphincter sounds like?" asked Anja. "I set you right up for it. It was perfect!"

"The models I listed are just their retail chimeras," said Jaya. "They have a whole industrial line, too, including a Ferrat—that's a rodent that's been gengineered to eat scrap metal—and something called a Plumber's Helper, which is kind of a snake-ish weasel thing that goes into toilet pipes and eats through clogs."

"That's revolting," said Marisa.

"*Now* can someone make a MySphincter joke?" asked Anja.

"I think I need a HugMonkey," said Fang with a grimace.

"The point," said Jaya, "is that ZooMorrow is a gengineering superstar—they do chimeras, human genhancements, the whole nine yards. Medical tech, fast-healing gene therapies, replacement organs, you name it, and they're literally on top of the industry, worldwide."

"Yay America," said Sahara.

"So Bennett works for them," said Marisa. "What does she do for them?"

"That's where it gets weird," said Jaya. "Her name and face show up all over the world, maybe five or six times a year, but only in police stations. Nowhere else—maybe on the streets, because there's no way I can search every storefront in every city, but in big buildings like hotels and office buildings there's nothing. Not even in airports. Johara hosts a facial recognition system called Aankh, which most of the big airlines use to track passengers, and she's not even in there—not her face, not her ID, nothing."

"So she travels around," said Marisa, "apparently in a private jet, going from police station to police station, just . . . what, confiscating evidence? Is ZooMorrow covering up crimes?"

"I don't think so," said Anja. "You remember statute Whatever-the-Hell?"

"That's my favorite statute," said Fang.

"It was in Mari's recording: federal statute 7o.3482," said Anja. "It's a law that governs intellectual property and proprietary technology. Which would only make sense—"

"If the hand was genetically modified," said Marisa eagerly. "If Zenaida had had some kind of gene therapy or genhancement, on her skin or her blood or whatever, then her arm would contain technology created by a gengineering company. But . . ." She paused. "Plenty of people have genhancements—way more than five or six a year. And I've looked up gengineering stuff before, back when we were thinking of buying me a biological arm instead of another cybernetic one, and the rights document they make you sign definitely doesn't give them ownership of your body. So how do they have the right to claim Zenaida's hand after she dies?"

"It's the proprietary part," said Anja. "If Zenaida had a genhancement that contained some kind of secret technology that hasn't been released yet, then they can claim the right to protect it as a trade secret—even if that secret shows up in an unrelated criminal case, like this one."

Marisa shook her head. "But why would a random woman in Mirador have proprietary gene tech? It doesn't make sense."

"She's rich," said Anja, whose family was also wealthy. "Rich people have all kinds of stuff we're not supposed to."

"Even if this is true," said Marisa, "it doesn't answer any of our questions. What happened the day of the accident, and what do I have to do with it?"

Sahara looked at her, scrunching her face into a frustrated grimace, and then shrugged. "Maybe you're a horrible freak of nature, grown in a lab with spliced-in DNA from a dozen different animals."

"Thanks," said Marisa.

"Have you tried eating a toilet clog?" asked Anja. "That would answer the question pretty quick."

Marisa blinked on the virtual reality's interface menu, asked it for a snowball, and then threw it in Anja's face. Anja staggered back, laughing, and the snow crystals disappeared into nothing.

"I think we've made some very good progress so far," said Fang, getting back to business. "Are you ready to be super confused now?"

"Oh boy," said Sahara. "What is it?"

"You're going to love it," said Jaya.

Fang smiled. "While Jaya was running the video of Bennett's face through recognition programs, I was deconstructing it in a virtual reality program."

"Why?" asked Sahara.

"Because I was bored, and she's super intimidating, so I thought she'd be perfect as a new Overworld avatar. But here's the thing: once I got in there, trying to re-create her face in VR, it turned out to be super easy because it's already VR. Or a hologram, technically, which is just real-world VR anyway."

"She's a hologram?" asked Sahara.

"Not all of her," said Fang. "Just her face. She probably had projectors built into her collar, or maybe just embedded right into her head, like Anja's cybernetic eye." Fang grinned. "So the beautiful face we all saw was completely fake."

"I couldn't tell a thing," said Marisa. "I was right there, just a few feet away from her, and I couldn't spot *a thing*."

"That must be one hell of an expensive holoprojector," said Sahara.

"No kidding," said Fang. "Lots of celebrities use holomasks when they go out in public, but you can usually tell it's a mask. We use them all the time in Beijing for festivals and stuff. But one that looks this realistic has got to be state of the art."

"So ZooMorrow has proprietary gene tech *and* cutting-edge holotech," said Anja. "How can they afford all that?"

"By protecting their tech with aggressive, hidden operatives," said Sahara. "We don't know how their genetic stuff got into Zenaida, but it did, and then when the police ran a DNA test to identify her body it tripped some alert, and out comes Hottie McGorgeousFace to get it back under control."

"So what's under the mask?" asked Marisa.

"Her real face," said Jaya. "Which for all we know no one ever sees. We know this mask, at least, is the one she uses for police, but she might have a dozen different ones, and the IDs to go with them. She could be a different person everywhere she goes. Solves the mystery of why she only pops up on the grid a few times a year."

"I've got a pretty cool theory," said Anja.

Sahara sighed. "Is it ridiculous?"

"More or less ridiculous than a faceless superspy stealing severed hands for a toilet-munching-weasel company?" asked Anja.

"I concede the point," said Sahara. "Whaddaya got?"

"What if Ramira Bennett *is* Zenaida de Maldonado?"

Marisa narrowed her eyes. "That . . . doesn't make any sense."

"I didn't say it made sense," said Anja, "I said it was cool."

"We have a lot to think about," said Sahara. "What we don't have is anywhere to go next. How would we even follow up on Ramira Bennett? Contact ZooMorrow directly? They wouldn't tell us anything."

"We could try to hack their private servers," said Fang.

"And maybe we will," said Sahara, "but that's going to take weeks, and we have to move on this sooner than that. I hate to say this, but . . ." She looked at Marisa and tapped the 3D simulation of Memo's djinni. "You're going to have to open this up."

SIX

"Olaya," said Marisa, sitting at her desk, "lock my door."

She heard a click, and then Olaya, the house computer, responded in her calm, disembodied voice: "Your door is locked. Would you like me to dim the lights?"

"No thanks," said Marisa, "I'm not going to sleep yet—but I need everyone to think I am, so fudge the data for me, okay?"

"I do not fudge data," said Olaya.

"Ugh," said Marisa, "I forgot to load your sidekick hacks. Olaya, run subroutine GooeyFudge."

Olaya could converse, but she wasn't a true AI—she wasn't a self-aware entity, just an interface that made using the house computer easier. And that meant she could be altered by anyone with coding expertise and sufficient access. Marisa had both. The voice was silent for a moment, then spoke again: "The data has been fudged. Don't forget to put a towel at the bottom of your door."

"Right," said Marisa, and jumped up from her seat. "Thanks." She always forgot the towel, so she'd added that reminder as part of her hack. Olaya was supposed to help run the home, keeping track of schedules and meals and such, but she could also tap into each family member's djinni data to report where they were, how they were, and what they were probably doing. Marisa had almost immediately suborned this feature: when GooeyFudge was running, Olaya would report that Marisa was in her bed, and that her heart rate and breathing were consistent with that of a person who was fast asleep. She gave Marisa the freedom to stay up and work in private, but unless she remembered to cover the base of her door with a towel, light would shine out under it and give her away. Some parts of hacking, she had learned, were surprisingly low-tech.

With her room safely secured, she walked back to her desk and sat down. Stacks of computers and banks of screens and tangled webs of cords and cables filled most of it, and almost the entire wall beyond, but in the center sat the new project: old homework printouts covered the surface to keep it clean, and on them sat the plastic container with a crime lord's bloody, digital brain. She made a face, and then popped it open. The lid came off with a slight sucking sound, and the djinni implant glistened in the light. She reached over and clicked on another lamp, shining an even brighter light on the gory object.

"I am detecting blood particles in the air," said Olaya. "Are you injured?"

"No!" said Marisa, and then said it again more softly, glancing at the door. "No, I'm fine, don't do anything. And don't tell anyone."

"I will not," said Olaya.

"Did you already tell someone?"

"I have not."

Marisa blew out a low whistle as she looked at the djinni. "Okay. Let's kill the antenna first."

The biggest obstacle to looking at the djinni was the one that Memo had been most afraid of: if she activated it and it connected to the internet, anyone who was looking could find its location and come straight to her doorstep. She was not in the mood to meet anyone who was actively looking for a gangster, least of all the police, so she had to start it up in a way that kept it inert and isolated. Memo had a Ganika 5 djinni, one of the most popular models, in part because they used the body itself as a signal booster—your entire skeleton basically became a secondary antenna, with the Wi-Fi and satellite signals resonating through the bones, which gave better service than a regular antenna and made more room for other hardware in the implant itself. On the other hand, it left the djinni's connectivity very easy to compromise. Marisa needed to disable only one tiny auxiliary antenna before she turned it on. She pulled on some plastic gloves, and with a tweezer in one hand and a tiny screwdriver in the other, she got to work.

Her phone rang suddenly, and she almost screamed in surprise.

"I'm sorry," said Olaya. "I didn't understand that. Could you repeat it?"

"It's nothing," said Marisa. The phone icon in her vision was bouncing, and the audio alert rang out again. "It's just my phone." She blinked to dismiss it, then paused. The call hadn't been given a custom icon, which meant it wasn't from any of her friends or family. Who else would be calling her this late? "Olaya, what time is it?"

"Eleven oh three p.m.," said Olaya. "Is your djinni clock malfunctioning?"

"No," said Marisa, "it says the same thing."

The audio alert sounded again, and the icon returned. She looked at it more closely this time, reading the name.

It was Omar.

Marisa looked at her hands, and the bloody djinni she was working on. Omar hadn't called her in years—he talked to her in public, but usually it was just a jibe or a snide remark. Their chat at the police station the day before had been the longest conversation she'd had with him in ages. What did he want?

The phone rang again, and she blinked to answer it.

"Omar?"

"Marisa," he said. He spoke slowly. "I'm . . . sorry to bother you."

"Did something happen?" she asked.

"Yes," he said. "Well, no. I don't have news from the police or my father or anything. And none of them are talking to me, so you probably know more than I do."

Marisa frowned, confused. "So . . . what happened?"

Omar didn't respond, and all she heard were shallow breaths, like he'd been running.

"Omar, are you okay?"

"She's dead," he said.

"Who? Your mom? We don't know that—"

"She's dead," he said again, "and it's not because of the hand. You can lose a hand and live through it—not that I need to tell *you* that. But now she's dead for sure."

"You—" She had too many questions, and not enough time to put her thoughts in order. "You haven't heard from the police, so who have you heard from? You—" She stopped again, a terrifying possibility rearing up in her mind. "Did you find her?"

"No," he said. "Yes, sort of. Marisa, she's . . ." He trailed off, and again she heard only ragged breathing. Whatever he was trying to say, it scared him.

"It's okay," she said. "You can tell me."

"I saw . . . ," said Omar. "I saw her . . . ghost."

What? "Her 'ghost'?"

"I know it sounds crazy," he said. "You have to believe me."

"But what—"

"I saw her again," he said. "Like in my dream. The same dream, really, but I wasn't asleep this time. I was here in my house, and I was awake, and suddenly she was here, looking at me and running down the hallway, and she was terrified. Of *me*. She kept looking over her shoulder, and trying to run away, and she got to the end of the hall and ran straight through the wall and she was gone. I called you because . . . because you know about the dream. And because I don't have anyone else I can talk to."

Omar had a father, and almost as many siblings as Marisa did, and a private army of housekeepers and cooks and gardeners and guards, and of course the whole group of Maldonado enforcers that patrolled Mirador and did everything Omar told them. And yet he didn't have anyone to talk to.

"Ghosts," she started, and then stopped. Was this really the best thing to start with, in this situation? "Even if you saw a . . . ghost, I don't know that it means for sure that she's dead."

"Why? Because ghosts aren't real?"

"Um, yeah?"

"We have spirits," he said, "and they have to go somewhere. People have been seeing them for centuries. Some of the most popular vidcasts in the world are about ghost hunters."

"That doesn't mean your mom is a ghost."

"Why not?" His voice was a fragile mix of anger and pain. "Why are the ghosts they see real, but my mom's isn't?"

"Omar," she said, and stopped again. Arguing wasn't helping. "You had a bad dream," she said, "and now you're exhausted and you were half asleep and you had the same dream again. And that sucks, because it's a rotten dream, and I'm sorry you keep having it—"

"My mom is not a nightmare."

"Your mom is a . . ." She searched for the right word. "A mystery. And your brain is trying to solve it."

"Don't patronize me," he snapped. "I'm not a child."

"It's not just you," said Marisa. "I haven't seen any ghosts, but I'm having plenty of bad dreams too, awake and asleep, and it's all I can think about." She looked at the bloody djinni. "And I'm trying to solve it, just like you. I'm going to find her, or find out what happened to her."

His voice was a sneer. "Marisa to the rescue."

"Why did you call me?" she demanded. "Why try to talk to me if you don't want to hear anything I have to say?"

"I don't know," he snapped back. "Maybe I just—"

He fell silent, and Marisa stewed in her thoughts, angry and sympathetic at the same time. He'd called her because he had no one else to call; he'd already said that. But he was still Omar, and acting like a blowhole was second nature.

"I only remember one time with her," he said softly. "I was three when she . . . left. I was here in the house, outside in the garden, and I was helping her plant flowers. I asked my father later, and he said that she loved working in the garden and always did it herself—the gardener maintained it, but she planned it and planted it and one time I helped. Maybe more, I guess, but I only remember the one."

He trailed off, and she asked a question to keep him going. "What were you planting?"

He laughed again, with slightly more life in it than before. "I barely know the names of those flowers today; I definitely didn't know them when I was three."

"Red? Blue?"

"Maybe orange?" he said. "I don't know; they were small, kind of low to the ground. I guess that's why she let a three-year-old help with them."

Marisa smiled. "What else did your mother do? Did she have a job?"

"Yeah," he said, "but I don't know what. Dad never talks about her, so I don't know what her degree was in. She might have done accounting or marketing or some kind of science. It was a science company, but that doesn't mean—"

Marisa sat up straight, at full and sudden attention. "Which science company?"

"Erm, why?" said Omar.

"Just tell me the name," she said.

"It was ZooMorrow," said Omar. "The MyDragon guys. Why?"

Marisa shook her head in disbelief, and then laughed out loud. "You're not going to believe this. You know that woman in the black suit? The one who took your mom's hand?"

"How am I going to forget her?"

"We looked her up," said Marisa. "She works for ZooMorrow, too."

Omar spluttered for a moment, then finally got a word out. "What?"

"Right?" she asked. "This can't be a coincidence."

"What else do you know about her?"

"Nothing," said Marisa. "She's practically a . . . well, a ghost—no pun intended, or whatever. We don't even know what she looks like, because that supermodel face was a holomask."

"You've been busy."

"Marisa to the rescue," she said.

"We need to know more," said Omar. "Why did she want the hand? Why did she even have a claim on it?"

"We found that out, too," said Marisa. "That statute she cited is about proprietary technology. Your mom's body probably contained some kind of unreleased genetic augmentation, which tripped a flag when the police did their blood test. Did your mom have any genhancements?"

"Not as far as I know," said Omar.

"But your dad would know."

"I told you, he never talks about her."

"But he told you about the ZooMorrow thing," said Marisa. "Obviously he talks about her sometimes."

"But he doesn't like to," said Omar. "Just superficial stuff, like how beautiful she was—everything else I know about her comes from late night rants when he's too drunk to stop himself."

Marisa raised her eyebrow. "So maybe we need to get him drunk."

"You don't want to see my father drunk," said Omar. "Even if we could guarantee he'd talk about her, which he never does."

"Then what about Sergio?" asked Marisa. "He was already a teenager when she died—he'll have to remember something."

"Sergio hates her," said Omar. "I don't even know why—as soon as anyone talks about her he just curses and leaves the room. Once I pressed him on it and he told me she was the worst person he'd ever known."

Marisa frowned. "Does anyone else remember her that way?"

"No one else who remembers her will talk about her," said Omar.

"Yeah, I know what that feels like," Marisa said, thinking back on every conversation she'd tried to have with her father about the night of the accident. She stopped, chewing on her lip as she thought. "There's got to be some way we can learn more. What about . . ." She tried to think: Who else knew Zenaida when she was alive, and was old enough to remember it? Omar's sister, La Princesa, had been five, which was probably still too young. And she hadn't been in the car.

But someone older had.

"What about Jacinto?" she asked. "He was nine. He probably remembers her pretty well."

Omar scoffed. "He doesn't like talking."

"You live in the same house," said Marisa. "You have to talk to him sometimes."

"He lives here," said Omar, "but over in what I guess used to be the guesthouse. He gets food delivered by nulis, or he just nukes frozen burritos and ramen. We literally never see him, sometimes for weeks in a row, and then only a glimpse."

"Why?"

"Most of his body was rebuilt and replaced after the crash," said Omar. "And it's not that he looks weird—you know my father; he wouldn't waste time on the cheap stuff. Jacinto has the best cybernetic body that money can buy, but I guess he just . . . maybe it's because it's not his, you know? Like he's a stranger in his own body, so he feels like a stranger everywhere else, too."

"That's awful," said Marisa.

"He mostly just lives online," said Omar. "If it weren't for the house computer tracking vital signs, we'd barely even know he was there."

"That's it!" said Marisa. "Your house computer. It's bound to have information about her."

"You want to hack my house computer to ask it about my dead mother?"

"We don't have to hack it," said Marisa, "it's yours—just ask it. You can do it right now."

"I don't have full access," said Omar. "I help my father with a lot of his business, but he still has a lot of secrets."

"Sounds like you all do," said Marisa with a sigh. She tapped her fingers on the table, staring at the djinni. "So I guess the question is: How badly do you want to know this one?"

Omar was silent again, and then started chuckling dryly. "Oh, Mari, Mari, Mari. You have no idea what you're asking for."

"I'm asking a mob boss's son to help me hack into his father's private server."

"You make it sound so easy," said Omar. "We have full biometric security these days—completely unhackable."

"So that's it?" Marisa said. "We're completely out of luck?"

"Not unless you want to come over and just plug into our mainframe."

"Why not?" said Marisa, not a hint of humor in her voice. "You get me through the biometrics, and I can crack everything else in . . . two hours, tops."

"And how am I supposed to get you into my house?" asked Omar. "Even if the old feud hadn't just been brought to the surface again, my father's not going to let any Carnesecas within three blocks of his house, let alone right inside and plugged into the mainframe. We're on high alert in here. It's an anti-Carneseca zone."

"That only makes me want these answers more," said Marisa. "What made them so mad? Do you think . . . okay, so what about this: Do you think my dad helped your mom fake her death? Maybe she wanted to leave, and this was the only way she could do it, and your dad found out about it just barely too late to stop them."

"Why would your dad do that?"

"How should I know? Get me into your house computer and let's figure it out."

"Let me think," said Omar. "How do I get Marisa Carneseca behind enemy lines?"

"I can spoof my djinni ID," said Marisa. "Make it read me as someone else."

"Really?"

"I'm amazing," said Marisa.

"You're a straight-up criminal," said Omar.

"Look who's talking."

"We can do this," said Omar. "If you spoof your ID, then I don't have to get Marisa Carneseca into the house, I just have to get a girl into the house—and that, I assure you, is one of my specialties."

"You're gross."

"It gets better," he said. "You still have that green dress?"

"Midcalf or midthigh?"

"Midthigh," said Omar. "Shorter if you can manage it. Spoofed ID or not, the enforcers know your face, and we need to make sure they're looking at something else."

"You're going to disguise me as my butt? Are men really that stupid?"

"I'm going to disguise you as one of several butts," said Omar. "I'm going to throw a party, and you're going to blend into a very scantily dressed crowd."

"You're right," said Marisa. "This is way grosser than I thought."

"It's just a party."

"It's a sex party."

"It is, at worst, an underage drinking party." Omar described it as if it were the most normal thing in the world. "No sex. In fact, I'll keep it all college girls this time, so it's not even 'underage,' just 'drinking.'"

"You and a bunch of girls?"

"And a bunch of guys," said Omar. "I'll invite my frat."

"Of course you're in a frat."

"All you have to do is doll yourself up a bit to get through the door," said Omar. "Once you're inside I can take you to a back room, plug you in, and run interference so nobody suspects anything. In a crowd that big, one girl isn't going to stand out. And I throw these parties often enough that no one will bat an eyelash at another one."

Marisa hesitated. Did she really want to do this? No. But she wanted the information.

The bigger question, though: Did she really trust Omar? No, but in this case she and Omar wanted the same thing, which was as much of an insurance policy as she could hope for. He might have been a dirtbag, but he was, at least for now, a convenient dirtbag.

"Fine," she said, "but you make sure it's a big enough party that two girls won't stand out. I'm not going into that lion's den alone."

"Don't bring Anja," said Omar. "She still hates me—she'll probably start breaking stuff."

"As fun as that would be," said Marisa, and looked down at the bloody djinni, "I'm going to give Anja this thing I'm working on, and bring Sahara to the party instead. How fast can you make this happen?"

"I'm already working on it," said Omar. "Tomorrow night at ten."

"Isn't that kind of late for a party?"

"Marisa," he said, "you've been going to the wrong kinds of parties."

SEVEN

"My fans are going to lose their minds," said Sahara. She and Marisa were wearing their tightest dresses and highest heels, and walking through the hot Los Angeles evening toward the Maldonado complex. Even at 10:00 p.m., the sky was only barely dark, and the two camera nulis were swirling around them in an eager dance: one filming in front of them, to show their faces, and one behind to show their other assets. Marisa hated this kind of exhibitionism, but Sahara reveled in it. "A college party in one of the most expensive houses I have ever seen—and not just any expensive house, the house of a notorious crime boss. We'll probably have half the police officers in LA watching the feed tonight, just to get a glimpse inside."

"Which is maybe not ideal considering our illegal infiltration," said Marisa.

"Relax," said Sahara. "The nulis aren't recording our voices right now, and as soon as we get inside I'll activate the algorithm that makes them avoid filming you—it'll be like you're not even there."

"So you'll keep all of the online attention on you," said Marisa. "Can you keep all the in-person attention on you, too?"

"Honey," said Sahara, "if I don't have every eye in that building focused solely on me, it'll be a downright insult."

"Well, heads up," said Marisa, and nodded toward the crowd on the street ahead of them. "Time to check out the competition."

The Maldonado estate was a full block, maybe eighty meters on a side, with a high wall around it that looked like red brick, but which Marisa knew was heavily reinforced with plastered armor. Mob bosses didn't mess around. The wall was almost two stories high, and only one of the buildings in the complex rose above it—the main estate, with a three-story tower and a roof of classic Southern California curved clay tiles. Marisa had been inside of it once before, when relations between their families had been . . . if not friendly, at least calmer.

She was suddenly struck by the thought that maybe she'd been here more than once, as a child. She'd been in Zenaida's car, after all—had she been in their home as well? How close had they been? She looked up at the walls as they approached, but felt no sense of welcome.

Only foreboding.

Standing in front of the high metal gate—not bars, but a solid sheet of armor—was a group of girls, each of them dressed every bit as scandalously as Marisa and Sahara. They noticed the two girls approach with only mild interest; they had their own agenda, and it didn't involve making friends with the locals. Cameron and Camilla weren't the only camera nulis hovering over the group; some girls were posing for selfie bots, others were monologuing to vidcast subscribers, and some were simply drawing focus in the background, subtly trying to be the center of attention in the other girls' pics and videos.

"You are among your people," said Marisa.

"I want to slap every one of them," said Sahara. "Is this what I look like to the rest of you?"

"They look like they want attention," said Marisa. "You look like you deserve it."

"I love you," said Sahara.

Marisa had worn her green dress—not the long one she wore to church, but the short, tight one she wore when they went dancing. The sleeves were long and the collar high, because Marisa had always tried to hide her old clunky metal arm, but then on her last birthday, when she'd upgraded to a gorgeous Jeon Generation prosthetic, Sahara had helped her to cut the left sleeve back to the shoulder, showing off the whole thing. Jeon limbs had a smooth robotic core, covered with rounded ceramic panels specifically designed not to look like skin: Marisa's were a faintly glossy white, almost opalescent, with a soft blue glow in the gaps and joints. Tonight Marisa had turned the glow green, accenting her dress; it made a stunning contrast to the hint of sparkles in the wrist-length fabric of her other arm and the burnished bronze color of her skin.

Sahara was dressed, as always, in a dress of her own design: tonight's was red and yellow and black, in not just the colors but the shape of a monarch butterfly. Thin layers of material fluttered around her, with the bottom slit high up the center and the top spreading out into two diaphanous wings. Tiny floating nulis, each barely the size an apricot, were strategically placed throughout the dress to hold it up, calibrated to Sahara's movement and controllable through her djinni—if she wanted the wings to flap, or the skirt to twirl, it would. The whole effect was otherworldly, like a faerie or a nature spirit walking among mortals.

The other girls looked stunning, and at any other party any one of them might have been the best-dressed person there. Tonight, Sahara outshone them all.

"You look amazing," Marisa whispered.

"I'd better," she whispered back. "I spent every last yuan on these tiny nulis. For this dress, at this party. If I don't get a ton of new subscribers to the vidcast, I . . . I don't know."

"You'll be fine," Marisa told her. "Go be amazing."

Sahara surveyed the crowd. "Looks like we have, what, twenty girls here? Twenty-five? They can't all be hetero."

Marisa stifled a laugh. "You think you can make it with one of Omar's party toys? These girls look custom-picked for frat boy fantasies. Some of them look custom-*built* for it. They're like MyDragons."

"O ye of little faith," said Sahara. "Watch the master at work."

She swirled off through the crowd, smiling and greeting each girl in turn, her dress floating behind her like a mermaid's hair. Marisa looked up at the gate again, then blinked to get the time from her djinni: 10:08. She could already hear music inside; had the party already started without them?

"First time?" asked a Korean girl by the wall. She wore a blue dress, textured like chain mail, that glistened in the streetlights almost like it was made of glass. "Don't worry, they always start late."

"Thanks," said Marisa. "You come to a lot of these?"

"When I can," said the girl. "Omar throws a good party." She extended her hand. "I'm Yuni."

"Nastia," said Marisa, giving her the fake name she'd picked for her spoofed ID. She leaned against the wall next to her, feeling the sunbaked bricks, warm against her back. It made her feel like a lizard, sunning itself on a rock. "So: Are these parties as crazy as I hear they are?"

"They can be," said Yuni. "Depends on what you're looking for."

"Dancing," said Marisa. "Fancy snacks on silver trays. Maybe some light physical contact, shoulders up."

Yuni laughed. "This might be a little more party than you're ready for."

"Sex and drugs and rock and roll?"

"That's closer to the mark."

Marisa shook her head. "Good old Omar. I ask him for a party, he gives me a gaggle of shallow idiots looking to score with rich boys."

Yuni looked at her a moment, then looked back at the girls. "You ever played Salad Bowl?"

"I love Salad Bowl," said Marisa. "I suck at the tomato level, though."

"Girl over there," said Yuni, pointing into the crowd. "Blond hair, black dress, seashell toggles on the side?"

"I see her."

"She wrote that game," said Yuni. "The girl next to her licensed it; together they're worth what I will subtly describe as a large amount of money."

"Wow," said Marisa, and then she realized the implications of what Yuni was telling her, and she felt her stomach twist into a knot. "Wow," she said again. "I was kind of a blowhole, wasn't I?"

"The women at this party are almost all from Omar's business program at USC," said Yuni. "You don't get into that program by being a shallow idiot." She looked at the girls a moment longer, and then grinned at Marisa. "But to be fair, some of them are very shallow geniuses."

"What do you do?" asked Marisa.

Yuni grinned. "You ever play Salad Bowl in a VR parlor?"

"Please don't tell me you own the VR parlor."

"Heavens no," said Yuni. "The overhead on a place like that is ridiculous. But I can almost guarantee that whatever parlor you go to, they bought their djinni cables from me."

"Here they come," said one of the girls, and pointed down the street at an approaching bus—wide and low to the ground, a party bus for hire.

"Sometimes I feel bad taking advantage of them like this," said another girl, and hiked up her skirt just a tiny bit more.

"I'm beginning to think that I grossly misjudged the power dynamic here," said Marisa, and Yuni laughed again.

"Go easy on them," she said. "Looks like Omar dragged them here from a club—they'll be half hammered already."

The party bus rolled up, and Omar leaned out the window with a whoop. The gate to the estate opened, and a pair of long-suffering security guards watched as the boys piled out of the bus and grabbed the girls—or were grabbed by them—and strutted into the estate. Marisa found Sahara and followed her in, waiting for the subtle ping that said the doorway scanners had read her ID. It came and went, and nothing happened. The deception had worked.

Outside the gate, the estate looked as plain and featureless as a warehouse, but on the inside it was a verdant wonderland. Flowers and trees of every variety seemed to crowd up from every patch of free space, and humidity hung in the air like a welcoming breath. Marisa had always seen the plants as a sign of opulence—they had money and resources to throw away on luxuries while the rest of LA struggled to survive—but now, after hearing Omar's story about his mother's garden, it looked different. It was still a staggering display of wealth, but it felt . . . almost sweet, in a way. Don Francisco had lost his wife, but he had kept her favorite thing alive and magnificent.

The group passed under the overhanging trees to a side door into the main house, where music was already blaring; through the branches Marisa could see the two other buildings in the compound, a guesthouse and a massive garage, but both were closed and dark. Sahara was moving her body in time to the music as they walked, feeling the beat in a way that Marisa was too nervous to emulate.

Try to look like you're enjoying yourself, sent Sahara.

This is my "enjoying myself" face, Marisa sent back. **Can't you tell?**

Is that also your "enjoying myself" body language?

If I throw up from nerves maybe I can pass it off as being drunk.

Omar was already behind the bar, passing out soda and shots and everything else people wanted to drink. Marisa watched his easy smile, and the mischievous wrinkles in the corners of his eyes, and wondered how he did it. He looked as happy and natural as anybody in the party, and yet just yesterday he'd been nervous and terrified and alone. How did he turn all of that off, and turn on this instead? It was like he was two different people.

Now that she thought of it, he was probably more than just two.

"Hola, morenita," said a young man approaching her. His breath reached her just behind the words, and she struggled not to make a face at the powerful odor of alcohol. "I don't think I've seen you here before, nena."

"How many of these things does Omar have?" asked Marisa. "Do you all know each other but me?"

"I know maybe half the girls here," said the boy, slurring his words just enough to raise the hairs on the back of Marisa's neck. He was holding a brown glass bottle, and gestured around the room with it. "And the ones I don't are hot as hell, but none of them are as hot as you."

He was too close, and Marisa didn't have any convenient routes of escape. She kept her face neutral, not smiling to encourage him but careful not to offend him either. She asked the least sexy question she could think of. "Are you in business school?"

"Machinzote," said the boy, flashing some kind of finger sign. "Making the yuan and getting paid. You like getting paid, nena?"

"You know what?" asked Marisa. "I need to go talk to some-body."

"You're talking to somebody right now." He took another pull on the bottle in his hand. "What's your name?"

"I need to go," said Marisa.

"That's a funny name," the boy slurred. "My name is I Want to F—"

Before he could finish his sentence he jerked upright, straighten-ing his spine so far it arched backward. Sahara had come up behind him, and was holding his arm in a tight, twisted hold that looked like it was straining every joint from his thumb to his shoulder.

"Hi," said Sahara. "My name's I Know How to Break This Hand Right Off at the Wrist. My last name is just you screaming."

"Get off me, bi—"

Sahara twisted his arm a little farther, and he bit off his com-ment with a grunt of pain.

"Get off me what?" asked Sahara. "It started with a 'bih' sound, like you were going to say 'big-time internet celebrity' or something. Was that it?"

"It was—ow!" She twisted again, and he winced. The rest of the room was so crowded and noisy, nobody even seemed to notice them. The boy groaned, then spoke again. "That was it," he said. "Big-time, um, internet—ow!—celebrity."

"That," said Sahara, "was very nice of you to say. It's always good to meet a fan. I'm going to let go of you now, and you're going to go to a different part of the room and leave my friend alone for the rest of the night, okay? And if you don't, I'm going to tell you my middle name, and you are really, really not going to like it."

"Yeah," said the boy, "I'll go."

Sahara released him, and he staggered away with an audible rush of breath. He turned back toward the girls, and took one step toward Sahara. She calmly raised her hand, palm up, and curled her fingers to beckon him forward. He stopped, thought better of it, and stumbled off into the crowd.

"Thanks," said Marisa.

"I keep telling you," said Sahara. "Self-defense classes."

"I shouldn't need to defend myself," said Marisa. "Boys should just . . . be better."

"How well did that dream of a better tomorrow protect you just now?"

"Point taken," said Marisa. "Thanks again."

"Any time, babe," said Sahara, and gave her a fist bump. "Cherry Dogs forever."

"How long do we have to wait?" asked Marisa. "The party's just to get us in the door; now that we're in here he's supposed to take us to the mainframe."

"He needs to achieve Full Party Stability first," said Sahara. "If he leaves too soon it will collapse without him."

Marisa searched the crowd again, and found Omar dancing with the Salad Bowl girl in the middle of the floor. The music was some kind of Korean-Cuban rap, and he moved like it was second nature to him; it was all in the shoulders and the hips, the arms and legs barely moving at all, but it was sinuous and rhythmic and powerfully masculine—

"Whoa," whispered Sahara. "You're staring."

"I'm what?" asked Marisa. "No I'm not."

"You are," said Sahara. "At *Omar*."

Marisa felt her face start to flush. "I'm just waiting for him to come over and take us to the mainframe."

"I think I know the difference between waiting and staring."

"Fine," said Marisa, "I was staring."

"Why?"

"Why?" asked Marisa. "What do you mean, why?" She looked at Omar, his shirt half-unbuttoned, his jeans tight around his hips, and then looked back at Sahara. "Are we talking about the same person?"

"I'm a lesbian."

"No one's that lesbian."

"You can't stand him."

"I can't stand the things he does," said Marisa. "It's not my fault he does them inside of a visually perfect body."

Sahara smiled. "I remember a time when the mere sight of him would make you fly into a rage."

"You're kind of gunning for that status yourself right now, Former Best Friend."

"Fine," said Sahara. "I'll stop talking about it."

"Thank you."

"Can I tell the other girls?"

"I will literally murder you."

Another voice intruded on their conversation, like silk dipped in venom. "Well, well, well."

Marisa looked up to see La Princesa, Omar's older sister,

standing in front of them with her hands on her hips. The iridescent purple MyDragon was perched on her shoulder, its tail wrapped protectively around her neck. Marisa did her best to sound polite. "Hello, Franca."

"I never thought I'd see the day," said Franca. "You can't tell me you're here as guests. Servers, maybe? Are you supposed to be taking drink orders?"

"Omar invited us," said Sahara.

"Then excuse me a moment," said Franca. "I have to send the devil a sweater."

"There are so many jokes I could make right now," said Marisa. "How do I pick just one?"

"Seriously," said Franca, "what are you doing here?"

"We're thinking of buying the place," said Sahara. "Tear it down, maybe build a very tiny theme park."

"I should have you thrown out," said Franca. "Do you know what my father would do if he knew you were here?"

"With like a little tiny roller coaster," said Sahara, "that only goes around in a loop." She drew a circle in the air with her finger. "Just one loop."

"That's called a Ferris wheel," said Marisa.

"We could put her face on the side of it," said Sahara. "Call it the Franca wheel."

"That's not even an insult," said Franca.

"No insult intended," said Marisa. "We're naming our imaginary Ferris wheel after you out of genuine admiration."

"We will need to buy your merchandising rights, though," said Sahara. "I assume they're still available?"

"That's about enough," said Omar, stepping quickly between the girls. "I saw you talking from across the room and I knew there was going to be trouble."

Franca looked at him like he was covered with mud. "You knew they were here?"

"Friend of mine is a big fan," said Omar. "Cherry Dogs forever, or whatever the slogan is. He's out in the garden, though, so I'm going to take them out for a quick autograph."

"And then you throw them out," said Franca. "You know what our father will do if he finds out you had a Carneseca in here."

"He'll do it to both of us," said Omar, "so cállate la boca, okay?"

"Don't talk to me that way."

"Cállate la boca," Omar repeated. "Keep this party going while I get rid of them."

"Fine," said Franca, and turned to leave, but took a final look at Sahara. "That dress is killer, by the way. Die in a fire and whatever, but: respect where it's due."

"Thank you," said Sahara.

Franca walked away, the MyDragon looking back at them with tiny golden eyes. Omar put his hand on Marisa's shoulder and guided her toward a hallway.

"I was really hoping she wouldn't notice you," he said.

"What will your father do if he finds out I'm here?" asked Marisa.

"Nothing to you directly," said Omar. "Probably. No promises, though. Maybe lean on your restaurant a little."

Marisa clenched her teeth and tried to look unnoticeable.

"What'll he do to you?" asked Sahara.

"Nothing you want to hear about," said Omar.

He opened a door at the end of the hall, leading them through a small kitchen where a pair of cooks were busily adding garnish to a series of refreshment trays. Omar put on his roguish smile, as quickly and easily as if he had put on a hat, and stole a sushi roll off one of the trays.

"Ay, qué feo," said the cook, swatting at his hand.

"Afilado," said Omar with a grin, and pushed open the door to take the girls outside. Sahara giggled girlishly, like they were doing something innocent and wicked at the same time, and then they were outside in the driveway, and the door clicked shut behind them.

Night had fallen more completely now, though the lights from the city were too bright to let any stars shine through. A vast web of flying nulis glittered across the sky in their place.

"Okay," said Omar. The charming facade was gone again, replaced by a grim set to his jaw. "Follow me."

Marisa and Sahara slipped off their high-heeled shoes and crept silently through the empty yard, following Omar's lead. Light and noise spilled out from the open windows of the main house, but the rest of the estate was dark, lit only by a scattering of lamps that shone dimly through the trees. Sahara's nulis stayed behind, taking footage of the party and, Marisa hoped, fooling the online audience into thinking they were still inside.

"Remember that time we snuck out of first grade?" Omar whispered.

"You thought you heard an ice cream truck," said Marisa. She smiled at the memory. "Turned out it was a cholo in a lowrider, blasting the bass."

"What kind of ice cream trucks did you have here?" asked Sahara.

"Awesome ones," said Omar.

He led the girls behind the garage, down a narrow walkway between the building and the armored outer wall, and then to a small back door on the guesthouse. It unlocked when it detected him coming, and the house computer greeted him with a soft, feminine voice when he opened the door.

"Good evening, Omar. Is there something I can do for you?"

"No thank you, Sofia," said Omar. He stepped inside, and when Marisa followed the lights dimmed, and a speaker in the wall started playing a slow, sultry song. Omar rolled his eyes.

"I think Sofia is coming on to me," said Marisa.

"He's alone in the guesthouse with two girls," said Sahara, stepping in and closing the door behind her. "Sofia knows exactly what that usually means."

"I have a full selection of beverages in the main bar," said the house computer.

"No," said Omar, "this is nothing like that—bring up the lights, shut off the music—"

"Wait," said Marisa, "this is good. One more layer of cover, right? Hey, Sofia?"

"Yes, Nastia?"

Marisa nodded; her fake ID was still working, and the house

was completely fooled. "Can you link our IDs to the bedroom?" she asked. "We want anyone who looks or asks to think we're in there together."

"Deception is contrary to my purpose," said Sofia.

"Do it," said Omar. "On my authorization."

"Yes, sir," said Sofia. Marisa smirked but said nothing. Apparently Omar had built a few backdoors into his house computer, just like she had. She hadn't known he had the skills to do it. There was apparently a lot she didn't know about Omar.

Omar led them through one hallway and down another, walking softly through the mood lighting and make-out music. "The second floor here is Jacinto's, and he almost never leaves it. Sofia, is Jacinto asleep?"

"Yes, sir."

"Good," said Omar, and looked at Marisa. "I don't know how happy he'd be about us messing around in his system. It's my father's server farm, but Jacinto built it—"

"Whoa," said Marisa, "a whole farm? Why do you need so much power?"

Omar shook his head. "That's a question for my father, not me. I know what we do, and I know how doing it makes us money, but I have no idea how much computing power it requires. Here it is." He stopped in front of a door at the end of the long hallway and tried the handle. "Sofia, can you open this for me?"

"I must remind you that your father is the admin account for my system," said Sofia, "and the mainframe room is a priority location. If you go inside, your father will be able to see it, no matter where I register your IDs."

"Is my father awake?" asked Omar.

"No," said the computer, though Marisa had no idea how anyone could sleep through all that noise in the main building.

"Then open it," said Omar. A small light over the keyhole turned green, and Marisa heard the lock click. Omar opened the door, and they walked into the room beyond.

"Holy crap," said Sahara.

The mainframe in most homes was small—a distributed network that tracked people, appliances, light switches, and locks, with no more hardware of its own than a scattering of palm-sized panels built into the walls. The Maldonado mainframe was four full towers of drives and processors, half of it majestically professional and the other half cobbled together from a mishmash of boxes and cables. They even had cooling tubes mixed into the spiderweb of wires and cords. It was far more computing power than they would need for even a three-building estate; they could run an entire corporation with this.

"Holy crap is right," said Marisa.

"Is this a lot?" asked Omar.

"Your cluelessness astonishes me," said Sahara. "Are you really so rich that you don't know what a normal person's house computer is?"

"My father doesn't do things halfway."

"Whatever," said Marisa, looking at the clock in her djinni display. "Plug me in and get me past the biometrics."

"Híjole," said Omar, frowning at the knotted cables. "Did you . . . bring your own cord?"

"Of course I did," said Marisa, sighing and pulling a long

white cord from her purse. "Just . . . give me a minute." She studied the towers closely, trying to guess what each of them did and which would be the best to plug into. Finally she shrugged and plugged the cable into a port on the cleanest-looking of the towers, and clipped the other one into the djinni port at the base of her skull. A welcome message appeared in her djinni display, offering her a variety of options; she blinked on the archive, thinking that was the best place to start looking, and a screen lit up on the side of the neighboring computer tower:

"Biometric Passcode Required."

Omar pressed his hand against the screen; it read his fingerprints, heart rate, and other vitals. It blinked again, asking for a retinal scan, and he held his eyes in front of the small camera at the top of the screen. A moment later the system blinked, and the screen shut off, and the menu in Marisa's djinni display unlocked.

"Got it," said Marisa. "This is just broad access, though; I'll need to work pretty hard on any files your father has sealed."

"How long will it take?" asked Omar.

"I don't know," said Marisa, focusing completely on the file system as it unfolded before her. The rest of the world seemed to fade away, and one by one a series of folders and databases blossomed open, stacked and nested and side by side. It wasn't virtual reality, but it felt like it—more immersive, somehow, than any filing system she'd ever seen. She shook her head, looking at the physical room again just to convince herself she was still in it. The server towers hummed and blinked, and Sahara's dress floated mystically on its flock of nulis.

"Everything okay?" Sahara asked.

"Yeah," said Marisa, though she frowned as she said it. "Just a weird filing system." She refocused on the files again. It was a custom-built system, she was sure—nobody bought something like this off the shelf. The folders seemed to surround her, but leaped to attention as she thought of each one, seeming to reorganize themselves in real time. She tried to search, and suddenly the search function was there, not a window or an entry field but a kind of movable bubble that was poised to envelop her, ready and almost eager to help her find the files she needed. She wasn't even sure how to use it—was it an AI? Another layer of Sofia, the house computer? She fed it the name Zenaida, and it whisked her off through the database.

A row of file names appeared in front of her, glowing faintly in the half-light of the server room. She blinked on each in turn, reading them carefully, but they included no real information—most of them were about completely unrelated things, like guest lists to old parties with Zenaida's name stuck in with the others, or long, archived email conversations that mentioned her in passing. She finished the list, and found nothing. Obviously the good stuff—the actual data about who Zenaida was and the important details of her life—was locked behind a security wall somewhere. But how could she find the files when she couldn't even find the wall?

A portion of the interface changed color, spiraling open like a glowing flower, and a chat name appeared.

Jacinto: Nastia Turón is a false identity.

Marisa widened her eyes in surprise. She'd thought her fake ID was pretty good. Of course, she'd also thought Jacinto was asleep.

The chat window—or flower, or whatever it was—had a space

for her to reply, but she didn't dare to give him her real name, and didn't know what to say to explain herself. Instead she appealed to the only authority she had:

Nastia: I'm here with Omar.

Jacinto: You're Marisa Carneseca.

Well, thought Marisa. *No point lying anymore.* Though the chat name was already locked in, so she kept using it.

Nastia: Can you see me?

Jacinto: I watch Sahara's show.

Jacinto: Sofia logged Omar, Sahara, and a third per-
        son named Nastia, but that ID's obviously a fake,
        and Marisa is the most likely person to be with
        her.

Marisa blinked, not on her djinni but simply in surprise. It was impossible to read emotions through a chat window, but he didn't seem angry. He hadn't demanded that she leave, or warned her that he'd summoned the guards. What was he playing at?

Nastia: Yep, it's me. How'd you spot the fake?

Jacinto: It's not like it's a great fake. You only
        scrubbed three levels of artifact code.

Nastia: Three levels deep is the law enforcement
        standard.

Jacinto: Three levels deep is where corporate secu-
        rity starts.

Marisa thought for a moment, then nodded. Fair enough. She looked at the filing system again, so clearly custom-made, and nodded as the situation started to become clear.

Nastia: You built this, didn't you?

Jacinto: Not much else to do.

Nastia: You live online.

Jacinto: Doesn't everybody?

Again, he had a point, but Marisa was sure that Jacinto's life was even more digital than most. The person who'd built this filing system was not some internet cowboy living a wild double life; he was a homebody, a shut-in, like an old man building bird feeders. But instead he'd built . . . this. He'd upgraded and customized and personalized the home computer until it was as much his home as the physical building that housed it.

Nastia: This file system is amazing. The software and
    the interface are . . . well, I mean, you could
    do this professionally, you know? Literally anyone
    would hire you.

Jacinto didn't respond for a long time, long enough that she worried she'd scared him away. Just as she looked back at the search bubble, trying to plot her next move, he answered:

Jacinto: Thanks, but I don't really talk to people.

Nastia: Well, thanks for talking to me.

Another short pause, and then:

Jacinto: You're trying to find my mother.

Marisa tensed, not sure if he was upset by this or not. There was very little emotion in anything he said. She didn't know what else to do, though, or how else to find the info she needed, so she carefully phrased a response, hoping to get him talking.

Nastia: I am.

Nastia: I'm trying to find—we're all trying find, me
        and Sahara and Omar—what might have happened to
        her.
Jacinto: And you think my father knows?
Nastia: I think your father knows about her past,
        maybe her job at ZooMorrow, and whatever happened
        to her might have something to do with that.

She waited for an answer, but none came.

Nastia: Jacinto?

Nothing. She waited a moment longer, wondering what she might have said to scare him off. Or had she offended him? She glanced at Omar, leaning against the wall with the unfocused eyes of someone deep in their djinni. Could she ask him? Would he know, or even care? He never seemed to take Jacinto seriously. She looked at the files again, and tried to think of some way to find the hidden ones. How would Jacinto have set up his interface to do it? She tried the search bubble, and poked around at it, testing to see what it could do.

Jacinto: Stop.
Nastia: I was only trying to find records about your
        mom's job.
Jacinto: No.
Jacinto: Someone's plugged into the system.
Jacinto: Not you.
Jacinto: this is someone else theres
Jacinto: someone else in the system theyre plugged in
        somewhere I cant see where the cameras are turned
        off someones here

It was still just text, scrolling across her display, but Marisa could tell that Jacinto was terrified.

Nastia: Is it someone from the party?

She didn't know who else would be plugged in, or why it would bother him so much.

Nastia: There's like thirty people here, it could be
    anyone.

Jacinto: Someone's plugged insomeones plugedin

Even his spelling and spacing were failing now—and since he probably wasn't using a keyboard, that meant the djinni interface itself was failing. That only happened when the neurochemicals were wildly thrown off.

"Omar!" Marisa shouted.

Jacinto: Find them plese you have tostop them I cant
    do it Icant do it

Marisa snapped her eyes open. Omar was standing up straight, startled at the sudden shout. "Someone's in your house," she said.

Omar must have seen something in her face, because he grew instantly serious. "What's wrong?"

"You're being hacked," said Marisa. "Not by me, by someone else—Jacinto! Can you hear me?"

"Jacinto?" asked Omar.

Jacinto: youhave to stopthem yu havto stop thm

"Listen to me," said Marisa, thinking out loud so everyone could hear at once. She was certain Jacinto had a security mic somewhere in the room that could listen in. "We can stop them, but you have to tell us where. Someone plugged in with a hard line and turned off the cameras to hide their tracks. Where in the system you built would be the best place for an attack like that?"

"What's going on?" asked Sahara. "There's another hacker?"

"Take a deep breath," said Marisa softly, casting her eyes around the room. "Think. Tell us where to go."

Jacinto: Main house.

Jacinto: Service closet, second floor, by the theater.

"Thanks," said Marisa, and ripped the plug from the jack in the back of her neck. The filing system disappeared, and she looked at Omar. "You have a theater?"

"Second floor," he said. "Main house."

"Get us there now."

Their shoes were already off, but the dresses were still constricting to run in. Omar outpaced them easily, and when Marisa reached the back door he was already propping it open with one hand, holding a small black pistol in the other. She reeled back when she saw it.

"Holy crap."

"You said someone's hacking in?" he asked.

"Yes," said Marisa. Sahara caught up to them, and the three raced outside and back through the garden. "Jacinto's scared senseless."

"He built this computer system," said Omar. "It's like his body. If someone's breaking in without his consent . . ."

The guards in the estate were already moving; either Omar had warned them, or Jacinto had sent out a general alarm. One of them saw Omar and angled toward him as they ran past the garage.

"Theater," said Omar. "Check the service closet, and block all the exits." The man sprinted toward the house, and Omar shouted after him, "And get the lights on out here! We don't want him to disappea—"

He stopped abruptly as a shadow passed overhead, sudden and silent. Marisa caught the vague outline of a thin human form as it leaped from the window above them, and then she ducked in fright as Omar and two of the guards raised their guns and started firing. The shape crossed the open space and vanished into the trees.

"Did you get him?" asked Marisa.

"I don't think so," said Omar. "He landed too smoothly—we would have heard it if he was injured."

The noise from the party stopped, the pounding music replaced by the hushed murmur of frightened voices.

"He's in the garden somewhere," said Sahara. "Down on the ground—none of the tree branches are creaking."

"Keep the guests in the house," said Omar, pointing to another guard. "And somebody get these pinche lights on!"

Sahara blinked, summoning her nulis, and they flew out of an open window and up toward the walls, patrolling from above. "His only way out is up," said Sahara. "Do you have any more camera nulis?"

"No," said Omar. He reloaded his pistol and crept toward the darkened garden. "Stay back."

Marisa ignored his command and moved up behind him, practically touching his back. Sahara paused for a moment, then jogged toward the open window.

"Ladies!" she shouted. "I need everybody's selfie nulis outside.

Now. Set them to patrol the upper walls."

"Mine's not automated," said one of the girls.

"Then guide it remotely," said Sahara. "We have an intruder, and the clearest photo anyone takes of him gets a cash reward." She looked back at Omar with wild eyes. "Come on, man. With this crowd, you've got half the mobile cameras in Mirador at your disposal."

A swarm of smooth-sided nulis flew out from the party room, each of them no larger than a deck of cards, tiny rotors whirring almost whisper-soft in the night. As if that was the cue, the intruder in the garden leaped up and ran, bushes rustling and distant lamps winking in and out as the runner passed in front of them.

"Hold your fire!" shouted a guard. There were too many of them, aiming from too many angles, and the threat of cross fire was too high. "Get to the walls!"

Omar ran, and Marisa followed after him, dodging through the garden in hot pursuit. A gun fired, and Marisa shrieked as Sahara dragged her to the ground.

"We care about cross fire," said Sahara. "She doesn't."

"She?" asked Marisa. "How do you know it's a woman?"

"The silhouette," said Sahara, and then, in unison with Omar: "Hips."

"Couple of one-track minds," muttered Marisa. She could barely see anything from where she was, facedown in the weeds, so instead she blinked on her djinni and tapped into Sahara's camera feeds. Suddenly it seemed as if she was up in the air, floating above the compound; they had basic nightvision, amplifying the ambient light into a grayscale tableau, but she could only identify some guards in the driveway and on the periphery. Everyone else was either inside a building or under the trees.

"She ran toward the guesthouse," said Omar. "If she goes right, she'll pass the pool, which has a lot of open sight lines, so she won't go right. That means left, to that path we took behind the garage." He blinked, opening a voice channel, and directed the guards to surround the intruder. "Cap the ends of that path, and get someone into the garage so she can't leave that way. She'll have nowhere to go but up."

Sahara directed one of nulis toward the roof of the garage, and Marisa looked down through its camera as it hovered closer to the dark black walkway behind it, a thick swath of darkness against the outer wall. The intruder had killed the lights; there was nothing for the nightvision to amplify.

"Ramón," said Omar, guiding the guards through his djinni, "you take the lead. Nonlethal rounds; I want to ask this pendeja some very detailed questions."

Marisa watched the darkness, and jumped at the sudden sound of gunfire. Muzzle flashes lit the dark pathway, showing brief, staccato images of a slim figure firing at the guards; she barely seemed to move, merely to appear in different places and positions every time it was bright enough to see her. Each flash of visibility showed her higher up the wall, as if she was running up the side, or maybe kicking back and forth between the building and the outer wall, and then suddenly she was over it, sailing out of the compound and into the street. She was visible to the nuli for almost three full seconds, and Marisa prayed they could capture a good still that showed her face. A final shot from one of the guards grazed her neck, and Marisa gasped at the spray of liquid that erupted from the impact. The woman lost her balance and started falling gracelessly toward the street below, arms flailing, and one incongruous detail stood out so starkly Marisa felt her jaw fall open.

"Holy crap," said Sahara. "Did you see that?"

"Yeah," said Marisa. "She's . . . not wearing shoes."

Marisa thought the woman was dead or dying in midair, but at the last moment she managed to right herself, and landed in a roll so perfect that she was up and running before anyone could react. A guard on the street ran toward her, but she dropped him with a shot from her pistol and sprinted across the street. The camera nulis followed, but she jumped on a motorcycle and turned it on with a roar, speeding away so fast the little nulis couldn't keep up.

Omar stood with a snarl, cursing loudly. "She got away!"

"We couldn't stop her, sir," said a guard, running toward them. "She's too fast."

"You hit her once," said Omar. "Get a blood sample, and get me a DNA identification by morning."

"That's the thing, sir," said the guard. He looked uncomfortable, as if he didn't want to say what he was about to say. "It . . . it wasn't blood, sir."

"What was it?" asked Marisa.

The guard hesitated, then spoke: "Acid."

EIGHT

"Acid?" asked Jaya.

"Acid," said Sahara.

Jaya's VR avatar had her jaw hanging open. Anja reached over with a single finger and pushed her mouth closed.

"That's the most baller thing I've ever heard," said Fang. "She has acid blood?"

"And no shoes," said Marisa. "I almost think the shoe thing is creepier, because why on earth would you not wear shoes?"

"We've worn shoes literally every time we've broken into a building," said Anja. "And while that's a small sample size, it is nonzero, so I'm very proud of us." She spread her arms wide. "Group hug. Bring it in."

The other girls ignored her, staring at Sahara as she continued to recount the events of the previous night. "It's not her blood," she said. "People don't have acid blood. I showed you the video—it hit right at the back of the neck, where a djinni port would be, but we can't actually see the point of contact because it's covered by her hair."

"An acidic djinni port?" asked Jaya. "That's not a technology I've ever heard of."

"If it was blood," said Marisa, "she would have been more hurt by it. Obviously it hurt a little, but she still lands on her feet, runs across the street, and rides away on a motorcycle. You can't do any of that with a bullet hole in your neck."

"Maybe *you* can't," said Anja, "but you're not an acid-blood monster person."

"She's not a monster person," said Sahara.

"Why not?" asked Fang. "We already have a ghost."

Sahara looked at the ceiling. "No, we don't. Why do I have to keep stating the obvious boundaries of the known universe?"

"Ghosts are totally real," said Fang.

"I thought you were an atheist," said Sahara.

Fang raised her avatar's eyebrow. "What does that have to do with it?"

"Let's get back to the basics," said Jaya, reining in the discussion. "Ghosts and monsters aside: Did you get the data you needed from the mainframe?"

"No," said Marisa, and grimaced at her failure. "I should have stayed in the system and let the others deal with the intruder, but . . . it's just that Jacinto was freaking out. Like: *freaking out.* I couldn't just sit there, you know?"

"I know," said Jaya. "It's okay."

"Doubly okay," said Anja, reaching into her avatar's jacket, "because I have succeeded gloriously in my part of the night's festivities."

"And by 'festivities,'" said Sahara, "you mean 'prying apart a gore-soaked neural implant.'"

"Stop," said Anja, "you're turning me on." She still had her hand hidden dramatically in her jacket. "But yes: I cracked open the djinni and found the data we need."

"I knew you would," said Marisa. "You're way better at hardware than I am."

"Stop teasing and just pull it out!" said Jaya, practically clapping her hands. She was older than the others by several years—early twenties to their late teens—but was often the most childlike member of the group.

Anja smiled wickedly and pulled out a rabbit.

"That's a rabbit," said Sahara dryly.

"Yes it is," said Anja. "Ten points to Gryffindor." She set it on the table. "Come on! We're in a virtual space: I can make the data look like whatever I want, and obviously I'm not going to waste my time programming a detailed virtual image of a piece of paper." She pointed at the animal's back. "Look: it's written in the spots on his fur."

"It's adorable!" said Jaya.

"It's an ID tag," said Sahara, reading the pattern in the fur. "A rabbit's not the way I would have presented the ID of a chop shop gangster, but: okay. We've got it. Now we just have to find . . ." She read the name: "Braydon Garrett."

Jaya looked more closely at the numbers in the ID tag. "This isn't a Johara ID, so I can't just look it up in our database."

"So we have to hack another service provider?" asked Fang. "That's going to take months."

"Weeks, if we do it right," said Anja, "but yeah. Sorry. I was hoping maybe the bunny rabbit would soften the disappointment."

"We don't need to hack a provider," said Marisa, staring closely at the code. She looked up with a sly smile. "Who else keeps track of location data? Even more closely than the service providers?"

Fang laughed. "Tā mā de, you're right! Advertisers."

"You can't walk five feet in this city without getting your ID scanned by a storefront or a billboard," said Marisa. "Service providers have airtight security, but some mom-and-pop taco truck is barely going to have any security at all."

"One taco truck won't give us everything," said Sahara. "We need the central server. Most of these little shops sell their customer data to advertising co-ops: you visit a storefront, it logs you, and then every other storefront in the area knows you're nearby. We need that co-op."

"We use one of those at the restaurant," said Marisa.

"Shopping preferences aren't going to help us find him," said Jaya.

"The location data will," said Fang. "If enough of the places he visits use the same central adware server, all those logged visits will draw us a map of where he's been in the city."

Sahara smiled. "Spend enough time with that kind of data and we can probably pinpoint his house, let alone what neighborhood he lives in." She gestured at the massive wall display. "Mari, mirror your djinni to the main screen, and pull up a map."

"Wait," said Jaya. "Tell me first what our plan is: we track down this chop shop guy and . . . then what? Turn him over to the police?"

"Turn him over to La Sesenta," said Anja. "He still gets executed, but he suffers more first."

"I don't want to hurt anyone," said Marisa.

"We're just trying to find Zenaida," said Sahara, and looked pointedly at Fang. "Who is *not a ghost,* and thus might still be alive. Braydon might know where she is—at the very least he'll know where her hand came from."

"You're not going to talk to him," said Jaya. "It's too dangerous."

"Not in person," said Anja. "But we could spy on him. Get one of the nulis close enough while he's talking to the rest of the chop shop, and we could learn all kinds of things."

Marisa blinked, linking her Overworld program to an outside internet line, and then linked that to the wall display. A map of Los Angeles appeared; the city was massive, larger than some of the smaller US states, and covered almost edge to edge in streets and buildings. She whistled. "That's a lot of space to cover."

"We can narrow it down pretty quickly," said Fang. "We already know the exact address of the shootout where they found the hand."

"We'll start there," said Marisa, and fed the address into the map program. Instantly a street corner appeared, including an overhead view, a street view, and an option for a live camera feed. Marisa blinked on the option to show nearby stores, and suddenly the map was covered with little colored dots, like a digital garden blooming in a single second.

"Holy crap," said Anja, "this neighborhood has a Yorma's."

"What's a Yorma's?" asked Jaya.

"Delicious," said Anja. "I thought they were only in Europe."

"Does Yorma's do a customer loyalty program?" asked Marisa, blinking on the name. It looked like some kind of fast food bratwurst place.

"Deliciousness is the only customer loyalty program they need," said Anja. "Let's go right now."

"We need a digital list," said Marisa. "If we get lucky, some of these places we won't even have to hack, they'll just display—ha! There's one." She blinked on another orange dot, and the map zoomed over to a coffee shop called the Crowe's Nest. "Crowe's always keeps a list, like a leaderboard in a video game, to show who's bought the most coffee at each location. We'll just check Braydon Garrett's ID against it, and . . . eso." The name popped up on the screen, highlighted in the middle of the coffee list. "Braydon Garrett is the 2,137th most frequent customer at that location. So he doesn't spend a ton of time there—it's not his neighborhood coffee shop—but he is there occasionally."

"Crowe's is too big a chain," said Sahara. "They'll have corporate security, and they'll sell to a big ad company with probably pretty good security of their own. We want the weak link—what's nearby and looks super crappy?"

"The noodle store next door," said Fang. "It's called Noodle Bam, followed by the Chinese characters for horse, depression, and soap. There's no way that's owned by a big company."

"Never underestimate stupidity," said Sahara.

"They're right next door, though," said Marisa, "and any ID that goes to the one will be close enough to get read by the other.

Garrett's definitely on both, so we just need to find out which ad company Noodle Bam sells their data to." She connected to the Noodle Bam computer and blinked through the menu, looking at the layout. "This is a prefab website, which means it came with a built-in password. If they didn't change their factory settings, we should be able to log in to the admin section and find everything we need." She studied the layout more closely, trying to guess which prefab company had made it. "Probably . . . Merchazoid?"

"CoinPress," said Sahara. "I used to use them for my vidcast, and I recognize the menu."

"I'm already on Lemnisca.te," said Jaya. "They've got a whole subthread about CoinPress, including a list of preset passwords. Ready?"

"Ready," said Marisa. Jaya read her the passwords one by one, but none of them worked. "Crap."

"I hate it when people protect their technology wisely," said Fang.

"Hold up," said Sahara, and pointed at the screen. "There's an ad on the sidebar of their menu."

"Santa vaca," said Marisa. "Why didn't we just blink on the ad?" She blinked on it now, and it routed her through a series of rapid connections before arriving at an online T-shirt vendor. She traced the path and found the name of the ad company. "Vesch Networks," she said. "Let's see how hard they are to break into."

"Slow down," said Anja. "Maybe I want to buy a T-shirt?"

Sahara sighed. "Anja . . ."

"Just kidding," said Anja, and blinked on something on her djinni. "Really I'm just going to buy some ad data."

"That sounds expensive," said Marisa.

"It's my dad's money," said Anja, "and he's rich, so what do we care? Looks like ¥90. That's, like, a prom dress."

"Yeah," said Marisa, "and prom dresses are expensive."

"Done," said Anja. She took control of the wall screen, and filled it with a rolling cascade of names and columns. She blinked again to search, and soon they had Braydon Garrett's entire life arrayed before them: every store he'd visited, every website he'd bought from, and every ad he'd blinked on. Every day for more than a year.

"Wow," said Fang. "Now I get why Bao doesn't have one of these."

"And why La Sesenta are having theirs removed," said Jaya.

"I'm kind of creeped out," said Marisa.

"Privacy is a myth," said Sahara. "I live stream my entire life because anyone who wants to can find all of this stuff no matter what I do to stop them. You go outside, people see you with their eyes; you go online, people see you with this stuff—ID readers, location data, ad blinks. You can't just never go anywhere, so this is the life we accept."

"Now I'm creeped out and depressed," said Marisa.

"Look for patterns," said Sahara. "The same store popping up over and over, or a specific store that he walks past every day at the same time—that kind of thing."

"And start with big blocks of time," said Jaya. "Maybe a restaurant or a train car or—"

"Or a dance club," said Marisa, pointing at an item on the list. "Three hours last Saturday night." She blinked through the list, scrolling to the previous week. "And three and a half hours the Saturday before." She kept scrolling, looking at every Saturday in turn. She grinned. "Foxtrot City, in a neighborhood called Athens. Same place, same time, every single week."

"Dude likes to dance," said Anja.

"Or it's a convenient meeting place," said Sahara. "Maybe he lives nearby, or his boss does. And a dance club is the perfect place to spy on them, because we'll blend right into the background."

Marisa touched her left arm. It wasn't metal in this VR simulation, but the dance club was in real life. Detective Hendel had said that the chop shops targeted prosthetics—would they target her? Her family had saved for years to buy that arm; it cost thousands of dollars, and Marisa was suddenly, terrifyingly conscious of how many people might want to steal it, and how easy it would be to do so. She would never walk around with thousands of yuan in her purse or her pocket, and yet here she was, with a lump of tempting, resellable treasure hanging off her shoulder, ready for the taking for anyone with a machete and a dark alley. A shady dance club full of chop shop goons was the last place she wanted to go right now.

We can find Zenaida, she told herself. *We can end my dad's stupid feud. I can do this.*

"Tomorrow's Saturday," she said out loud. "If the pattern holds, they'll be there."

"These are the times I'm glad I live on another continent," said Fang. "I hate clubbing."

Anja stroked the rabbit's fur and sighed happily. "I friggin' love it."

* * *

Foxtrot City was a large club, built into what looked like used to be a rec center. The walls outside were covered with digital screens with old-timey dancers in tuxedos and flapper dresses, projected in glacial black and white; inside it was a riot of color that looked more or less like every other dance club Marisa had ever been to. She felt fairly confident that no one had ever done the foxtrot in that building at any point in its history.

"Fan out," said Sahara as the bouncer at the door let them in. She was dressed more simply than the other night—they'd barely been able to run when the chase broke out with the mysterious intruder, and they weren't making the same mistake again. Sahara was wearing a yellow minidress with a black collar and no shoulders; pretty standard club clothes, except for her black flats. If they had to run, she was ready. "Get a sense of where everything is, where the doors are and the restrooms, and any private rooms Braydon Garrett might be meeting in. Don't actually look for him, though—let the nulis do that. If we're lucky they can do all the eavesdropping, too. The farther we stay from these chop shop psychos, the better."

"Check," said Anja. In contrast to Sahara's elegance, Anja was wearing a pair of shredded black vinyl pants that showed more skin than vinyl, incongruously matched with a lacy cream-colored top and her long blond hair—half shaved off—dyed a deep, rich purple. The other half of her head was bald, right down to the eyebrow, leaving Anja's cybernetic eye to draw even more attention than usual.

Marisa merely nodded and rubbed her arm nervously. She'd

always been self-conscious about her missing arm, especially back when she'd had a cheap, clunky SuperYu prosthetic. The new Jeon one had helped her feel confident again, even beautiful, but now it just made her feel vulnerable. She wasn't even wearing a dress, just black jeans, a black T-shirt, and a black leather jacket. Just like the green dress, the jacket had the left sleeve removed—she'd modified all of her clothing to show the arm off, and now cursed herself silently for it. She looked around for other cybernetic limbs in the club, and spotted a couple. So she stood out, but not much. She told herself it was fine, but put her hand in her jacket pocket and gripped her lipstick-sized pepper spray tightly.

Anja winked at her, mouthing "You've got this" before raising her hands in the air and diving into the crowded dance floor with a whoop, bobbing her head—her entire body—to the driving beat of the music. It was a Nigerian reggaeton band that Marisa knew she'd heard before, but she was too distracted to focus on it. Anja disappeared into the throbbing mass of dancers, and Marisa was alone. She skirted the edge of the dance floor and looked for somewhere to sit.

Sahara's camera nulis, Cameron and Camilla, had been programmed with a variation of Sandro's nuli algorithm from the science fair: instead of seeking out sick trees, they were nonchalantly skimming the crowd and scanning for Garrett's ID. When one of the nulis found him—which might take a while, as their scanning range was relatively limited—it was programmed to alert the girls and move on. If the girls could find a nice hiding spot nearby, they'd send one of the nulis back in, with its microphone primed to listen in on whatever Garrett was saying. If they couldn't, and there was no way to get the nuli close enough without being seen, then the girls had to move in themselves, sitting nearby or even—as a last-ditch effort—trying to turn on the charm and join the group.

Marisa desperately hoped that the nulis could do it by themselves. A part of her was even wishing that the nulis wouldn't find Garrett at all.

Not a bad club, sent Sahara.

I prefer clubs less full of murderers, Marisa sent back.

There's probably ten murderers here at most, sent Sahara. **And now that I'm thinking about it, that's probably true of most clubs we go to.**

You're not helping.

Get a drink, sent Sahara. **Something with way too much sugar and caffeine—it'll pep you right up.**

Marisa found a row of couches and low tables, and sat carefully near the edge of one: out of the high-traffic zones, but with plenty of escape routes if somebody tried to bother her. Chop shops were only one of the dangers in a club like this. The table included a touch screen menu, and she ordered a Lift; a waiter nuli brought it almost instantly, and she nodded at the service. Usually they weren't this fast. She looked around and nodded again, realizing that there were far more nulis than normal buzzing back and forth overhead. That was good; it would help keep Cameron and Camilla inconspicuous.

A movement caught her eye, somehow, in a room full of flashing lights and jumping dancers. She stared hard into that corner of the club and saw it again: something small and sinuous, completely out of sync with the rest of the party. It was another ZooMorrow chimera, a miniature lion no larger than a young house cat, prowling anxiously back and forth across a flat stretch of table. Its fur shone gold in the light, and its wide, bushy mane seemed to sparkle. The humans beside it, probably its owners, weren't paying any particular attention to it; a narrow leash ran down to its neck, and with that to keep it from straying, the breathtaking miracle of science and nature was allowed to wander freely, unheeded by the people who must have spent thousands of yuan to get it.

Marisa stood up, curious, but before she could move any closer, a text message appeared from Camilla:

Found him.

Hot damn, sent Anja.

Marisa blinked on the map icon at the end of the nuli's message, and it showed her a basic floorplan of the club, with Garrett's position marked in red. Not as sophisticated as an Overworld mini-map, but not too shabby, either. She blinked again, and the map was replaced by a soft blue arrow through the crowd. It pointed to the opposite side of the room, far away from the bonsai lion.

Camilla's filming me now, sent Sahara, **and I've got Cameron moving in to take a look at the chop shop.** Keeping one camera "innocent," separate from their intrigue, helped keep Sahara's vidcast going; it continued the pretense that they were just here for a fun night out. Sahara paused a moment, then sent another message: **It's going to be tough getting close.**

Marisa blinked into Cameron's video feed, and grabbed a nearby pillar as a wave of vertigo swept over her. The nuli was flying over the crowd, high up where it wouldn't be noticed, with its camera pointed straight down. A group of men, mostly middle-aged, sat around a table by the wall, deep in conversation.

No good place to hide a nuli, sent Sahara.

And no arm candy, sent Anja. **These boys are all business.**

All the more reason we have to hear what they're saying, said Marisa.

The nuli passed over, and they lost their view. Marisa grabbed the pillar again as the room suddenly reoriented itself—the nuli camera had swiveled ninety degrees up, so that down was now sideways. **I'm taking another pass to look at the wall and ceiling,** said Sahara. **If there's a place Cameron can grab on to, I might be able to boost the gain on the microphone and hear what they're saying.**

How good is your directional mic? asked Anja.

Not great.

Then boosting the gain isn't going to help you, sent Anja. **You'll just make the background noise louder. We need to get close.**

Don't, sent Sahara, but Anja's only response was an animated picture of kissing lips. **Arg,** sent Sahara.

Cameron's second pass turned up nothing—just like Sahara had thought at first, there was no good place to park the nuli.

Remind me what model nulis you use, sent Anja.

Arora Shutterbug 47s, sent Sahara. **Why?**

Good, sent Anja. **That's the kind where you can fold in the rotor arms.**

Marisa's eyes widened. **Don't do it.**

It doesn't hurt them, sent Sahara, they're designed to fold.

It's not that, sent Marisa, it's her plan. She wants to make one of the nulis as small as possible and then plant it nearby, like a surveillance bug or something.

I just walked through the area, sent Anja, and there's a great place behind a trash can but it won't fit there with the rotors extended. That means it can't fly itself into place, so I'll have to do it manually.

And then recover it manually, sent Marisa. That's two chances for them to see you doing something very suspicious, and I guarantee they won't be happy when they do.

We can distract them, sent Sahara. Get them all to look the other way and then shove the nuli into place behind them.

Too risky, sent Marisa.

Move right here, sent Anja, and another map icon appeared by her message. It's the perfect spot, and with that sleeve of yours cut off I guarantee you'll get their attention.

"Like hell," snapped Marisa, muttering the words out loud. She took a breath, and then sent a more measured response. I'm not getting anywhere near them. She remembered the Foundation doctor, sneering and calling her a golem, and she shuddered.

I'll do it, sent Sahara. Cameron's on his way to you, Anja, so get out of sight before the whole group of them watches you catch and fold up a nuli.

Marisa stared across the room in the direction of the glowing blue arrow, barely daring to breathe. She couldn't see Garrett and his cronies, or even Anja or Sahara, but she couldn't look away. She gripped her pepper spray tighter, and then blinked into Camilla's video feed.

Sahara was sashaying across the floor, smiling like a movie star and swaying her hips like a runway model. She looked stunning, and Marisa gasped out loud when she saw what her friend was doing: she walked straight toward the circle of chop shop gangsters, leaned over the back of one of their chairs, and purred a greeting.

"Hello, boys."

"No hookers," said Garrett, dismissing her with a wave. "We're busy tonight."

Marisa clenched her teeth in silent fury.

Stall, sent Anja.

"I'm no hooker," said Sahara, keeping her voice sultry. "My friends and I saw you over here and thought you might like to buy us a drink."

"What are you, fifteen?" asked one of the men. "Is this a sting?"

Sahara smiled. "Do you want it to be?"

"Beat it," said a third man, and looked at one of the others. "Braydon, can you convince this girl we're not interested?"

One of the men stood up and Sahara backed away, holding out her hands in a placating gesture.

"Fine," said Sahara. "You're not interested, you're not interested. I can do better anyway."

Got it, sent Anja. **Get out of there.**

Sahara turned to leave, and Camilla swung around to film

her from the front—giving the vidcast viewers a perfect look at Sahara's smirk, and giving Marisa a chance to look over Sahara's shoulder at the menacing thug beyond.

He's not following you, sent Marisa. She sat down at an empty table, and blinked to send the other girls her position. **Join me over here. We can listen from a safe distance.**

I feel dirty, sent Sahara.

You should, sent Anja. **Did you offer to fake a police sting for them? That is a fetish I was not aware of.**

I didn't know what else to say! sent Sahara. **I don't usually get shut down that hard.**

Anja appeared out of the crowd and sat down next to Marisa. "It's got to be a thing," she said out loud. "Make it with an underage girl while some authority figure watches? That's too sick to not be real."

"Shut up," said Sahara, sitting down across from her. "It worked. Camilla's audio feed is turned off, and Cameron's is already coming in."

Anja and Marisa both blinked on the audio, and all three girls listened intently as the chop shop circle got back to their discussion.

"—later," said a deep voice. "Think she'll still be around?"

"Stop thinking with your dick," said another. "She had a camera nuli following her; one of those vidcasters. We don't need that kind of visibility."

"Damn it," muttered Sahara. "That's two steps away from them finding me if they ever decide to look."

"She's no good for organs, either," said another of the men.

"People are going to notice if a vidcaster goes missing."

"I take it back," said Sahara. "Three cheers for camera nulis."

"No kidding," said Marisa. "I'm buying one tonight."

"All of you shut up," said another voice. Without a video feed to go along with the audio, Marisa couldn't keep track of which speaker was which, or if the same person had spoken more than once. "We got another order, and we can fill most of it with the stuff we've got in storage, but this is a hospital and they need organs. We're one heart shy."

"Specs?"

"Vanilla is fine. Anything too nice and a hospital will start asking questions."

"That's why we need to stop selling in bulk and stick to the specialty market—cybernetics, genhancements; rich clients with expensive tastes. It's less work, it's less inventory, and that means less risk for us."

Marisa felt her throat constrict. "I'm going to be sick." Sahara grabbed her hand and squeezed.

"We'd be stupid to cut our audience in half," said one of the men. "We can sell bulk *and* specialty, and we need everything we can get with that bastard trying to undercut us. Now: Which of your boys is going to get the heart?"

"I'm calling the police," said Sahara.

"We still don't know about Zenaida," said Anja. "Isn't that why we're here?"

"They're plotting a murder," said Marisa.

"So we stop them," said Anja, "but if we don't let them talk first, we don't get any of the info we need."

Marisa's response was cut off almost instantly by an excited squeal.

"It's her! See, I told you she was here—I recognized the club on her feed! That's her, that's Sahara!"

"Wut," said Anja.

The three friends looked over to see a group of girls standing about ten feet away, clutching their hands to their chins; when they saw Marisa looking at them they giggled and blushed.

"Please no," muttered Sahara.

"Hi," said the lead girl. She had limbs like sticks, and was dressed in a shapeless blue bag that barely covered her from armpit to inseam. Marisa got the impression that it could inflate, leaving the girl in the middle of a dark blue sphere. She held the bonsai lion in one arm, and her grin stretched from ear to ear. "Are you Sahara Cowan?"

Sahara put on a stately face and smiled back kindly. "Yes I am."

"Oooh!" said the girl. "And that's Marisa and Anja. Holy gods, I love you so much. I watch your show all the time."

"So do we!" squealed another girl beside her. The skinny lion girl glared at her.

"Shut up, Feather, you're making us look like idiots." The girl smiled at Sahara again. "Sorry about Feather, she's kind of a horkus."

The girl named Feather tried to frown and smile at the same time. "Sorry, I'm just . . . you're right here. You're real!"

Anja leaned back in her chair and nodded her chin at the embarrassed girl. "What's the matter? Never seen a great woman before?"

"And I'm sorry about my friend," said Sahara. "It's nice to meet you, though; thanks for watching." She turned back toward the center of the table, away from the giggling girls, but the lion girl stepped forward and kept talking.

"What I really love is how *real* the show is, you know? Like, how you really get to see poverty, up close and personal, and the lives of the people who face it every day."

"And here we go," said Anja.

"We're trying to have a low-key night," said Sahara, and turned her back again.

"Oh, I totally get it," said the lion girl. "My name's Pendant, by the way. Like the necklace?" She put the bonsai lion on the table and sat in the empty fourth chair. The lion yawned. "Like you: Marisa, right? Your family's restaurant is barely scraping by, but you all stick together anyway. We see you on the vidcast all the time, and you're, like . . . real. You know? But you're out here trying to get away from all of that, and I totally get it."

Anja sent a text message: **Don't kill them.**

The girl named Feather inched forward. "Can I . . . have your autograph?"

Marisa looked at Sahara. "Does this happen to you a lot?"

"Not really."

"And I love how humble you are," said Pendant. "I just want to lick your face."

"I think we're done here," said Sahara.

More people are starting to look at us, sent Anja. **We're attracting attention.**

Marisa sent a warning back: **If Discount Arms sees us attracting attention, they will definitely look up Sahara. We want them to forget about us, not follow us online.**

"Here," said Feather, and shoved a notebook in Sahara's face. "Just write, 'To Feather.'"

"We have to go now," said Sahara, and stood up. Marisa stood as well, looking around warily at the faces watching her from the crowd, hoping none of the chop shop men were there—

—and then she froze, staring at a woman's face.

The woman stared back at her, eyes wide with fear.

"No," said Marisa.

"You okay?" asked Anja.

"Don't you see her?" asked Marisa.

"Who?"

Marisa pointed. "Zenaida de Maldonado."

In the middle of the crowd, a terrified Zenaida turned away and started running—straight through the people, straight through the chairs and the benches and the bars. Marisa shouted and ran after her, pushing her way through the crowd, until Zenaida reached the wall.

And ran straight through it.

NINE

"We have to go," said Sahara.

Marisa felt frozen to the floor. "I can't believe it. I saw a . . . a ghost."

"And the whole club saw you," said Sahara, hissing through clenched teeth. "We have to go now, unless you want the chop shop's full attention?"

Marisa stared at the spot in the wall where Zenaida had disappeared, reeling from a turbulent mix of shock and fear. She couldn't move on her own, but let herself be hurried out of the club by Sahara on one side and Anja on the other.

"I've called an autocab," said Anja.

"We never should have tried to do this ourselves," said Sahara. "They know who I am now—they could follow us anywhere."

"Only if they care," said Anja. "If we're lucky, everyone back there is laughing about the girl who got high and freaked out."

"I saw her," said Marisa. "Zenaida. She was right there. Just like Omar said."

"You imagined it," said Sahara. A cab pulled up next to them and opened its door with a gentle hum.

Marisa shook her head. "It was real."

"Maybe you really were high," said Anja, maneuvering her into the cab. "What was in that drink you ordered?"

"It was Lift," said Marisa. Sahara got in after them, and the cab closed its door and merged smoothly into the traffic. "Just caffeine—I'm not high or drunk or anything else. I saw her."

"I can't believe I seriously have to say this," said Sahara. "Marisa. Ghosts. Aren't. Real."

"I know," said Marisa, trying to convince herself. "I know. But then . . . what else could it be? Because I saw her."

"Maybe it was a hologram," said Sahara.

"Projected by what?" asked Marisa. "Or by who? And why couldn't anyone else see it?"

"Or it might have been . . ." Sahara hesitated. "I don't know. A hallucination."

Marisa glared at her. "You think I'm crazy?"

"I think you just chased a figment of your imagination across a crowded bar," said Sahara, "so yeah, maybe a little."

"We left Cameron behind," said Anja.

"I can get him later," said Sahara. "Not really a concern right now, all things considered."

"No," said Anja, "I mean it's still there, transmitting, and I've been listening. The chop shop didn't say anything about us."

"Hallelujah," said Sahara. "Did they say anything else?"

"Not really," said Anja, "but I think I know which ID belongs to the guy they sent out to steal a heart. Someone named Brayden Clay left early."

"You mean Braydon Garrett," said Marisa.

"There's two Braydons," said Anja, and then paused, reading the list of IDs on her djinni. "Strike that, there's actually four Braydons. Four of the six chop shop guys are named Braydon." Her face broke into a wide smile. "Oh man, and they're all spelled differently. Braydon, Brayden, Braiden, and Braden. If this whole chop shop thing doesn't work out, they could probably start a boy band."

"They were all in their forties," said Sahara. "Born in . . . 2008? 2009? Everyone back then was named Braydon."

"Can we try to focus?" asked Marisa. "The cult of evil Braydons is going to *kill someone,* and I saw *a pinche ghost.*"

"You told me that was a bad word," said Anja, and grinned. "High five."

"Send Hitman Brayden's ID to La Sesenta," said Sahara. "Memo is expecting results, so it's about time we give him some."

"Fine," said Marisa, "but send the same ID to the cops. Memo will be grateful, but the police can probably track the guy fast enough to stop him before he kills someone."

"Done and done," said Anja. "What next?"

Sahara tapped her fingernail against her teeth, thinking. "One of the things we overheard tonight is that they keep an *inventory* somewhere—which is horrific, but—if the Braydons killed Zenaida there will be evidence, and that's the most likely place. We need to find it."

"That's another thing the police can do for us," said Marisa. "Send them all the other Braydon IDs and let them hunt the chop shop down. We won't get the info ourselves, but we'll find out if they find Zenaida's body, which is the whole point."

"If the cops find anything on Zenaida, there's no way we'll find out anything about it," said Anja.

"They'll tell Omar what they find," said Marisa. "And he'll tell us."

"I'm confused about your sudden pro-Omar policy shift," said Sahara.

Marisa slumped down in her seat. "Ay, Dios, so am I. He's still a bastard, but he's . . . in pain? Does that count for anything?"

"You're a healer in Overworld," said Anja. "You don't have to be a healer everywhere else, too."

"Whatever, whatever," said Marisa, closing her eyes. "I'm not thinking about it. We're trying to find Zenaida. What's our next step?"

Sahara sighed. "Back to the basics, I guess. I'm going to research old news items from back at the time of the crash. Maybe there was something else going on, with ZooMorrow or with any of these chop shop dudes, that we missed before because we didn't know about them yet."

Marisa nodded, and closed her eyes. She'd seen a ghost or a hallucination or a hologram or who knows what it was, and it had freaked her out. And she barely knew the woman—how shocking must it have been for Omar to see his own mother, terrified and running away from him?

And now I'm thinking about Omar again, she thought. *Stop it!*

But that look on Zenaida's face: absolute fear, and . . . something harsher. Anger, maybe, or disgust. Did she give the same look to Omar?

Why did she give it to Marisa?

Marisa took a breath, stretching her legs and toes, and then cracked her neck and sat up straight. Time to get back to business. She blinked onto the internet, connected to Lemnisca.te, and opened a search.

And saw a message icon, blinking in the corner of her vision.

She frowned at it. She had a few contacts and acquaintances on Lemnisca.te, but it was a darknet site—a deep, inky ocean full of incredibly secretive people, and none of them were easy to get close to. She'd rarely ever had a personal message from any of them before. She looked at the username of the sender:

BeowulfsBuddy.

"Grendel," she said out loud.

"What?" asked Sahara.

"I just got a message from Grendel," said Marisa. "He just . . . contacted me, out of the blue." She looked at the private mail in trepidation, barely daring to touch it. "I guess all those messages I left for him finally worked."

"What does it say?" asked Anja.

"I haven't opened it."

"Scan it first," said Sahara. "Who's knows what kind of bonkers malware that guy's attaching to his messages."

Marisa nodded, and blinked. Lemnisca.te's users were endlessly paranoid, but that was one of the things she liked best about them. Their malware scanners were amazing. The scan came up clean, and then she hit it with her own scanner, just in case. Same result. She looked at Sahara and Anja, took a breath, and opened the message.

Gonzalo Sanchez.

Ricardo Guzmán.

Ingrid Castañeda.

"That's it?" asked Sahara.

"That's it," said Marisa. "Three names."

"This guy is so weird," said Anja.

"Let's look them up." Marisa pointed at each girl in turn. "One, two, three. See what we can find." She'd assigned herself Three, so she opened a general search window and plugged in "Ingrid Castañeda." It spat back a massive list of results, so she tried to narrow the search a bit; she combined the name with "Maldonado" and still got tens of thousands of results. Maybe if she combined it with "ZooMorrow"? Nothing. "Marisa"? Too many results. She frowned, and decided to try a few more just to see what worked. "Carlo Magno Carneseca"? Nothing special. "Omar Maldonado"? Nothing special. The date of the car crash?

Boom.

"I found something," she said. "Ingrid Castañeda died the same day Zenaida did—or, I guess, the same day we *thought* she did. The day of the accident. Gunshot wound."

The other girls looked up, then refocused their eyes on their djinnis. A moment later Anja nodded.

"Yup. Gonzalo Sanchez, too. Gunshot."

"And Ricardo Guzmán," said Sahara. "Same day, same cause of death."

"That's either a hell of a coincidence," said Marisa, "or Grendel's trying to tell us something."

Sahara held up her finger. "Some of these news articles I'm looking at talk about a turf war—Don Francisco was already powerful even back then, but he didn't have Mirador locked down yet. He was fighting for control with a rival crime family: a Russian group called the Severovs. Maybe there was a coordinated attack on the day of the crash—maybe these three were all Maldonado enforcers, and the Severovs came after them."

"That could explain why Zenaida was in the car," said Anja. "She was trying to get away from a rival hit squad, so she got in the car, and then maybe they . . . hacked her car's navigation? So she turned off the autopilot and tried to drive herself."

"Maybe," said Marisa. It was a good theory, and it meshed with a lot of her own thoughts, but it wasn't perfect. "That doesn't explain why I was in the car, though, or what my dad had to do with it. There's no way he was a Severov gunman."

"Maybe he was a Maldonado gunman," said Anja. Marisa shot her a withering glance, but the girl only shrugged. "That's not completely ridiculous, right? Francisco and your dad obviously knew each other. What's the whole mystery—that the Don has an old beef with your dad but also protects him? Or something like that?"

Marisa nodded, but sighed at the same time. "In part, yes."

"So maybe your dad was Zenaida's bodyguard or something—he could have been in the car too, for all we know. Don Francisco never forgave him for failing to protect Zenaida, but your dad did save Omar and Jacinto's lives, so the Don, like, owes him."

"Maybe," said Marisa. She didn't want to think of her father as an enforcer, though.

And yet . . .

Was that why he always refused to talk about it? Because he didn't want his children to know that he used to run with a gang?

Was that why he fought so much with Chuy over being in a gang himself?

An icon appeared in her djinni, accompanied by a soft audio alert. "I have a phone call," she said.

Sahara looked at her warily. "From who?"

Marisa grimaced at the icon. "Detective Kiki Hendel of the LAPD." She hesitated, then blinked to open the call. "Hello, Detective."

"Marisa," said Hendel. "Are these messages from you?"

Marisa looked at Anja. "No, ma'am, I haven't sent you any messages. What messages have you gotten?"

Hendel ignored the question. "Have you been doing anything related to the chop shop we talked about?"

Marisa gritted her teeth, then shook her head and tried to make her voice sound as innocent as possible. "No, I haven't, why do you ask?"

"We have you and your friends on surveillance footage in the Foxtrot City dance club barely half an hour ago," said Hendel. "We know the chop shop was there as well because that's why we were surveilling the club in the first place. And then mere moments after you left the club, we started getting anonymous messages about a member of the chop shop heading off to kill someone."

"That," said Marisa, "is a startling string of coincidences."

"You have to stay away from this," said Hendel. "Those men are dangerous in the extreme—especially for someone with a cybernetic arm. I am sick of finding hands in alleyways, and I don't want yours to be next."

"Wait," said Marisa, sitting up straighter. "You said 'hands,' plural. Did you find another hand?"

"We did," said Hendel. "Zenaida's. Again."

Marisa recoiled at the thought. "Ugh, qué asco. What's next, a foot? Her head? Are they scattering her body over the entire city piece by piece?"

"You don't understand," said Hendel. "I'm not sure I do either. We didn't find Zenaida's other hand, we found the same one again. Her left hand, severed at the wrist."

"The ZooMorrow lady lost it?" asked Marisa.

"It's not the same one," said Hendel. "Same wound, same DNA, different fingerprints. We don't know what's going on, but we know that it's dangerous, and we know that Discount Arms is in the middle of it. Stay away from them, Marisa. You don't have that many hands to lose."

TEN

"Salad Bowl is a really weird game," said Fang.

"I know," said Marisa, flicking a cucumber off to the side of the bowl. "But I don't think I can handle Overworld right now."

"They have the universe at their fingertips, the entire spectrum of human imagination made possible by the limitless power of bleeding-edge virtual reality technology—and they used it to program a giant bowl of salad."

"And then they make you collate it," said Jaya. "It's like paperwork, only . . . healthier."

Marisa flicked a leaf of lettuce toward the cucumber, and then another leaf toward a different spot on the other side of the bowl. A giant fork started descending toward a crouton, and she ran toward it and kicked the crouton in a diving leap, sending it gliding toward the pile of lettuce and cucumber she'd already started building. She overshot, and the crouton hit the side of the bowl and bounced away in a new direction.

"Nice," said Anja.

"She missed," said Fang.

"But she got it away from the fork," said Sahara. "Show some solidarity. Whoo!" Sahara clapped, cheering from her perch on the lip of the giant bowl. "Good job kicking that crouton! Give it up for Mari!"

"I don't need your pity," said Marisa, though the silly applause did make her feel a little better.

"So you're trying to turn the one big salad into a bunch of little, evenly distributed salads?" said Jaya.

"Yeah," said Marisa, knocking another cucumber into a pile just in time for a fork to spear the whole stack. "This is only level one—the tomatoes make it way harder, but they're, like, level ten."

"I take it back," said Fang. "This game isn't weird, it's stupid."

"Okay," said Sahara. "Let's get back to the business at hand. Also: I just realized that that's a pun, and I'm very sorry for it."

"You never do puns," said Anja.

"Puns are the worst form of language," said Sahara.

"The hand business at hand," said Marisa, stacking the final bits of lettuce, "is to figure out why there are two hands." A fork came down, stabbed the final pile, and a shower of ranch dressing proclaimed that she had won the level.

"Gross," said Fang.

"The obvious first guess is a clone," said Jaya. "Human cloning is illegal, but ZooMorrow presumably has the technology."

Sahara nodded. "And if they're running some kind of illegal

cloning operation, it would explain why they were so eager to get the hand back under their control instead of out where the police could study it."

"The problem with that theory," said Anja, "is that it only makes sense if ZooMorrow cares what the cops think. As we saw the other night, they have absolutely no reason to. There's virtually no law enforcement agency that has any real authority over the megacorps—they kind of regulate each other through competition, but that's it."

"So maybe they wanted to get the hand off the streets before another megacorp found out about it," said Marisa. Level two began with the salad bowl becoming instantly clean, and a rain of new ingredients tumbling in: lettuce, cucumbers, croutons, and now some shaved carrots. She started punching the food into piles. "Maybe there's a rival gengineering company trying to perfect the same sort of cloning tech ZooMorrow is working on, so they're trying to keep it secret? ParaGen, maybe?"

"But why clone Zenaida?" asked Jaya.

"The person they need to clone is that thief from Omar's party," said Anja. "In fact I bet you anything she's a ZooMorrow agent."

"We're forgetting the other obvious answer," said Sahara. "What if Zenaida's a natural clone? What if she was a twin, or even a triplet? Hendel said they have different fingerprints. The one Mari knew died in the car accident, but the others might still be out there—or they used to be."

"I already looked," said Marisa, throwing slim darts of carrot into piles around the edge of the bowl. Some of them landed askew, and when the fork speared the pile the carrots fell off. "Demonios."

"How do you say carrots in Spanish?" asked Fang.

"Zanahoria," said Jaya.

Fang shook her head. "That is such a weird language."

"What is it in Mandarin?" asked Anja.

"Better," said Fang.

"Luóbo," said Jaya.

"See?" said Fang.

Marisa knocked the last few bits into a pile—featuring a lot more carrots than was strictly ideal—and was rewarded with another shower of salad dressing when she won the level. Her lower score only got her a B rating, so it was Thousand Island.

"Zenaida's not a twin," she said, "or a triplet or anything else. And she's not a clone, either. Hendel said the hand was identical to the first, right down to the wound. They can't figure out what caused that wound, by the way." Level three tried to start, but she paused it with a blink; salad ingredients hung in the air above her, frozen in time. "That's because it's not a wound."

"Oh snap," said Anja. "Marisa already figured it out."

Jaya frowned. "I thought we were playing the ridiculous salad game because she hadn't figured it out? Because she needs to think?"

"This isn't about thinking," said Marisa, "it's about frustration. I think I figured out what's going on, but I haven't figured out what to do about it yet."

"Zenaida's hand is not connected to her body anymore," said Fang. "That's called a wound, right? You didn't suddenly change all the rules of English vocabulary without telling me?"

Marisa smiled slyly. "If there was only one hand I don't think we ever would have solved it, but there are two. More than that, we heard Discount Arms practically give the whole the solution away, but we weren't paying attention."

"That they were talking about killing somebody," said Sahara. "That has a way of drawing focus."

"Yes," said Marisa, "but there was another part of their conversation, so fast I almost missed it: they said someone was trying to undercut them. The chop shop is losing business, and their business is replacement body parts, so: What one technology answers all our questions at once? The multiple hands, the weird wounds, the ZooMorrow meddling, *and* the replacement organ market?"

Sahara's mouth fell open. "Bioprinting."

Marisa pointed at her. "Ándale."

"Bioprinters have been making limbs and organs for years," said Jaya, smacking herself in the forehead. "Why didn't we think of this before?"

"Because until we found a second hand we had no reason to," said Marisa. "Look: we already know ZooMorrow had Zenaida's DNA on file, because it tripped an alert when the police ran a test on the hand. And we know there's proprietary gene-tech in her DNA, so you'd have a lot of interested buyers. So: if that DNA got out somehow, and someone started printing cheap, genhanced replacement organs to sell on the black market, who are the two groups you're going to piss off?" She held up her fingers, and counted off as she spoke: "The company you stole the DNA from, and the chop shop you're stealing the sales from."

"Brilliant," said Anja. "I knew I liked you."

"So Zenaida's probably still dead," said Jaya, "just like we thought."

"Exactly," said Marisa, and felt her triumph deflate at the thought. "Exactly."

"This answers a lot of our questions," said Sahara, "but we're still missing something: a dead bioprinter."

"The machine?" said Fang.

"No, I mean somewhere out there is a criminal entrepreneur who owns one," said Sahara, "and who pissed off at least two groups of very powerful, very dangerous people. And since the hands are still showing up, and since we have yet to see any news stories about a black-market bioprinter shot dead in a gang war, that means the bioprinter is still alive."

"Then we have to find him," said Marisa. "He's the only one who knows for sure where that DNA came from. Maybe she really has been dead for fifteen years, but . . . I want to know for sure." She stared at the bottom of the bowl for a moment, then unpaused the game and started smacking bits of onion around with furious energy.

"So the bioprinter is our only link to the DNA," said Sahara. "And the chop shop is our only link to the bioprinter."

"And you've already tried following them," said Jaya. "It's too dangerous."

"Following them didn't work because it was all on their turf," said Anja. She jumped down into the bowl with Marisa and slapped a cucumber with all her might, caroming it off the side of the bowl so hard it bounced two more times before slowing. She looked up at the other girls with a devilish grin. "All we have to do is reverse it: set our own terms, and get the chop shop to follow us."

Marisa paused the game again.

"You're nuts," said Jaya.

"You're dangerously, stupidly nuts," Sahara added.

"We can do this," said Anja.

"I'm not bait," said Sahara. "Just because they already know who I am doesn't mean I'm going to wave myself in front them like a free pot sticker."

"Of course not," said Anja. "We can't let them know who we are—we need to trap them and interrogate them in such a way that they can never trace it back to us."

"Normally I like the really crazy plans," said Fang, "but this is too much even for me."

"They want to cut my arm off," said Marisa. "Anja, you have a cybernetic eye—they'll want to cut that out, too, and probably our djinnis, and any interior organs that still work, and that's not even counting what they'll do to us *before* they start cutting."

Anja was still smiling, as if everything the rest of them said was meaningless. "Taser nulis," she said proudly. "We buy some cheap little flyers, load them up with a charge big enough to drop a guy, and then fill a room with them. If we can get even one of the Braydons into that room, boom goes the dynamite. We wait till they're all down, then we tie them up and put some bags on their heads. Slicker than snot on a doorknob."

"I don't understand that last part," said Fang, "but I am totally back in on this plan."

"It's too expensive," said Jaya.

"I'm rich," said Anja. "Next question."

"How do we lure them without letting them know who we are?" asked Sahara.

"That's the easiest part of the whole plan," said Anja. "We already have a lure that they are actively searching for, and that has nothing to do with us." She shrugged. "All we have to do is turn it on."

Marisa stared at her a moment, then nodded when she figured it out. "Memo's djinni."

"Memo's djinni," said Anja, pointing at her. "That's the whole reason they're in hiding. We take that djinni to a big empty building, fill it full of targeted nulis, and turn on the power. The evil Braydons will arrive within the hour, and we'll have the bioprinter's name within an hour of that. Then we walk away, and no one knows anything."

"I don't think it's going to be as easy as you say it is," said Sahara.

Anja grinned wolfishly, showing her teeth, and bounced her eyebrows up and down. "But you're going to do it anyway, right?"

Sahara sighed. "Yeah, I think we are."

"Heaven help us," said Marisa.

Anja and Sahara got to work on modifying the nulis, but Marisa had to go to work.

San Juanito was a pretty successful restaurant, all things considered; it had been a steak place, back when beef was still affordable for the average consumer, but twenty years ago Marisa's parents had taken out a loan, bought the place, and rebranded it as a homey "just like mi abuela used to make" northern Mexican restaurant. Marisa's actual abuela had even helped in the kitchen, because they'd all lived in the tiny apartment on the second floor, and they'd lived on too small of a budget to afford any other help. When Chuy had gotten old enough to carry trays, they'd put him to work memorizing table numbers and hauling food out to the guests, and a few years later Marisa had started doing the same. Most restaurants these days used nuli waiters, but even when the restaurant started paying for itself—even when they grew so successful that they bought a new house and rented the old apartment to Sahara and let Marisa's abuela stay home—they never used nulis. It was part of the old homey feel, and as long as they still had children to work for free, they could save money.

Marisa hated working in the restaurant, but times had gotten tough, and if the alternative was losing their house and moving back into the tiny apartment? She could wait a few tables.

She held the tray carefully while she laid each plate in front of its customer. "That's one corn enchilada for you, one tofu enchilada for you, and one side order of jalapeño lo mein."

Okay, she thought, *so it isn't exactly like mi abuela used to make.*

The customers tucked into their food without so much as a thank-you, though at this point that hardly fazed Marisa. Restaurant customers were the worst. She smiled anyway, stopped at a nearby table to ask if everything was okay, and then hurried back into the kitchen to wash off the tray for the next load of food.

"Table twelve is almost up," said Carlo Magno. He was seated on a makeshift stool in front of the stove, frying vegetables and mushrooms with one hand while chopping a slab of sautéed

Chikn™ with the other. It didn't taste as good as the TastyChick™ they used to use, but it was cheaper, and with enough salsa you couldn't tell what it tasted like anyway. Plus it came with the grill lines already printed on it.

"Table four is getting impatient," said Marisa. "They've already mouthed off to Gabi once tonight."

Carlo Magno glowered. "Tell them if they try it again, les echo por la calle."

"Your heart rate is approaching the upper end of its normal range," said Triste Chango, lurking under a preparation table nearby. "You should take a break."

"Here's the last of twelve's fajitas," said Carlo Magno, sliding the protein and vegetables onto a plate. "Garnish 'em up and get 'em out of here, and then do me a quick favor and chop this nuli into pieces with an ax."

"You got it," said Marisa. She gathered table twelve's plates onto her tray, added scoops of rice and beans and pico de gallo, and bustled back out into the dining room.

"Four's getting sassy again," said Gabi, passing her on the way.

"Grabby or just antsy?"

"Antsy."

"Don't tell Papi," said Marisa, "just tell him to hurry it up."

Gabi ducked into the kitchen, and Marisa brought the tray to table twelve. "Here we go, listen to that sizzle! Chicken fajitas, tacos de chapulín, tacos de hongo, and a General Tso's burrito smothered with our own chile verde."

"I'm trusting you on this," said the man, winking as he did. Marisa gave him a flirty smile.

"You'll love it," she said. "It's literally my favorite thing on the menu."

He raised his eyebrow in playful disbelief, and Marisa giggled just long enough to get out of earshot. If he didn't tip well . . .

"Oye," said Marisa's mother, summoning her to the side with a single finger. She was a large woman, thick and solid, like a tree trunk. She was also a full head taller than Carlo Magno, but all that height had apparently gone to Chuy and Gabi; Marisa and Sandro weren't short, necessarily, but they'd inherited their father's compact size. Pati could still go either way, but Marisa expected her to sprout like a weed sometime in the next year.

Marisa walked quickly to Guadalupe, who pointed to table fifteen. "Just seated them," she said. "Seven was open, but they're already kind of drunk so I made them wait a bit and put them in your section."

"Gabi can handle it," said Marisa.

"Gabi's got her hands full with four," said Guadalupe.

"Frakkin' four," muttered Marisa.

"We can't afford to lose any customers tonight, okay?" said Guadalupe. "Don't tell your father or he'll throw them out."

"I won't," said Marisa, and handed her mother the tray. "Take this in the back for me?" Guadalupe took the tray, and Marisa grabbed a handful of menus on her way to table fifteen. "Welcome to San Juanito's," she said, handing out the menus. "I'm Marisa, I'll be your server tonight. Would you like to order some drinks or should I give you time—"

"You have Mexican beer?"

"Corona, Tres Equis, and Gusanito," said Marisa. "Would you like a round for the table?"

"Gansitos for everyone!" said the man, and Marisa smiled. Her mom was right: these guys were already pretty drunk. She walked back into the kitchen and went straight to the fridge.

"Table two is almost up, Gabi," said Carlo Magno.

"I'm Marisa," said Marisa. Two was in Gabi's section.

Carlo Magno glanced at her, then back at his grill. "Sorry. Busy."

Marisa pulled out beers and started popping off the lids with a bottle opener. "One of my tables just ordered a round of Gansitos—should I run to the corner store for snack cakes, or should I just give them these Gusanito beers instead?"

Carlo Magno smiled at her. "Gringos or Japanese?"

"Latinos," said Marisa with a wink. "But they're drunk."

Gabi stuck her head in the door. "I need four!"

"Take two!" shouted Carlo Magno.

"I don't have time for two!" shouted Gabi, and closed the door with a whoosh.

"Mari, just take two," said Carlo Magno. "I'm drowning here, I don't even have space to plate anymore."

Marisa shoved lime wedges into the mouth of each open bottle. "So buy some nulis."

"That is the last possible thing I want to hear from you right now, mija."

Marisa looked up, halfway to the giant bag of tortilla chips looming high in the back corner. "Not the last thing." She put her metal hand on her hip. "Tell me about the accident."

"Your heart rate has gone above your normal range," said Triste Chango. "You should take a break."

Carlo Magno turned on his stool and pulled a plate of enchiladas from the oven; the molten cheese on top of it bubbled and hissed. "You say that one more time," he said, "and I will bolt a tray to the top of your head and make you wait tables."

Marisa frowned. "You talking to the nuli or me?"

"Take your pick," said Carlo Magno. "And get this table two order out of here before I throw it on the floor!"

Marisa scooped a bowl full of chips, ladled a smaller bowl of dark red salsa, and put them on a tray with the beers. Then she grabbed a second tray, wiped it down, and started loading up table two's plates.

"You can't take two trays at once," said her father.

"Want to bet?"

"I was talking about permission, not ability."

"Here's the deal," said Marisa, and picked up a tray with each hand, balancing them carefully on her arms. "I get this out of your way, and when I come back, you tell me who the Severovs are."

"I don't know any Severovs."

"Yes, you do," said Marisa. "I'm talking about *those* Severovs. Don Francisco's old rivals, from back in the day. You remember them?"

"Mari—"

"Or I could leave this here," said Marisa, starting to put the tray back down. "Your choice."

"I'll fire you."

"Don't I wish."

"I'll give you extra shifts, then."

"You'll punish me for asking a question?"

"Some things you just have to let go, okay?" He finished rolling another burrito, slapped it on a plate, and covered it with red sauce and cheese. "The past is past. It's gone. Nothing we do now is going to change it, so we keep our heads high, and we look to the future."

"I'm not even kidding about this tray," said Marisa, moving to set it down. "I'll leave it right here. Maybe all night."

"Take it," said Carlo Magno. "We'll talk when you get back."

Marisa smiled and lifted the tray again, maneuvering expertly through the swinging door and out into the dining room. She gave fifteen their chips and beers, and worked her way over to two.

"Chiles rellenos—my personal favorite—some enchiladas, and three different orders of tacos." She waited for hands to go up, identifying who ordered what, and sorted them all out. From the corner of her eye she saw Gabi talking to table four, trying to mollify the group of unruly twentysomething men. She couldn't hear what they were saying, but watched as one of the men reached out and grabbed Gabi's butt.

Marisa handed out the last plate of tacos and stalked straight to table four, her hands gripping the tray like a club.

Gabi stopped her, eyes wide, and leaned in to whisper: "Don't tell Papi."

"I don't have to tell Papi," Marisa whispered back, "I'm throwing them out myself." She handed the tray to Gabi, just to be sure she didn't smack anyone with it, and planted herself next to the table. "All right: you're gone."

164

"What?"

"You're gone," said Marisa. "Out. Afuera de aquí. Chūqù."

"You can't just throw us out," said one of the men. "We've been waiting for, like, fifteen minutes!"

"Look around," said Marisa, gesturing at the full restaurant. "We're kind of busy. Now hit the road so we can give this table to someone who deserves it."

"Bring us food or we'll sue you!"

"You grabbed my sister's ass!" shouted Marisa. "Get out in the next thirty seconds, or I call Maldonado's enforcers and tell them we have a child sex predator here!" The men stared at her, but obviously the threat meant something because they started gathering their things. "You know what the Maldonado family does to child sex predators?" she asked, watching them slowly stand up. "You know how long it takes them to do it?"

"Perra," said the man, and as he walked away from the table he picked up a glass and threw the water in her face. She put up her human hand and blocked some of it, but she and the two customers behind her still got soaked. She stood still as a statue, watching the men until they left, and rolled her eyes when the other customers gave her a round of applause.

Marisa turned to the people behind her, pulling a towel from the waistband of her apron and helping to sop up the water on their table. "I'm so sorry about that," she said. "Your dinner's on me tonight, okay?"

"Don't worry about it," said the man. "I saw what he did to her. You're a hero."

"Thanks," said Marisa. "But next time you see a fourteen-year-old girl getting groped, don't wait for a seventeen-year-old girl to step in and save her." She spat the last few words with more venom than she expected, and walked back into the kitchen to another smattering of applause.

"Four's almost done," said Carlo Magno, then looked at her and stopped. "Why are you wet?"

"You didn't hear the applause?" snapped Marisa, hunting through a side closet for a dry towel. "We had a wet T-shirt contest."

"She threw out table four," said Gabi, barging into the room with a sneer. "I needed those tips, Mari."

"You can have mine," said Marisa, dabbing the towel at her hair.

"They got out of line?" asked Carlo Magno, standing up with an angry grunt. "Grabby or antsy?"

Marisa and Triste Chango said the line in unison: "Your heart rate is reaching dangerous levels. You should take a break."

"I can take care of myself," said Gabi.

"Then start doing it," said Marisa. Gabi rolled her eyes and left the kitchen. Marisa stared at her father, who stared back in silence, until finally she broke it by throwing the wet towel across the room. "I know, okay? I know we can't afford to lose any customers."

"You did the right thing," said Carlo Magno, and sat back down with a grimace. "Thank you for watching out for your sister."

Marisa stared at him a moment longer, not sure what to say, then nodded and grabbed another towel. "You're welcome." She grabbed a pair of menus, ready to take them sheepishly to the table in the splash zone and offer to comp their dessert as well as their meal, but her father stopped her with a sentence:

"The Severovs were a crime family," said Carlo Magno.

"Russian mob, but they'd only just moved into LA so they were more or less evenly matched against this upstart Mexican gang trying to push them out of their territory."

Marisa turned around slowly, almost as if her father were a deer or a squirrel, some fragile forest animal ready to bolt into the trees if she made any sudden moves. She looked at his chest, and then, in a burst of courage, his eyes. He stared back, and didn't stop talking.

"It got bad," he said, "the hits got bad, and the level of 'I can't believe this is happening' got higher and higher until everyone in Mirador feared for our lives."

"Were you a part of it? This . . . war?"

He scowled. "What kind of question is that?"

Marisa nodded. "But Zenaida was in the middle of it."

Carlo Magno nodded slowly. "Lav came after her—Lavrenti Severov, the leader of the Russian group. Don Francisco stopped him—was furious they'd come after his family. Hit back, hard. Lavrenti lost both of his children."

"Santa vaca," breathed Marisa.

"The Severovs were pretty much done then, but they broke everything they could find on their way out. We were rebuilding this neighborhood for years after that—do you remember the upstairs hallway window?"

"I remember it had a sheet of plastic over it when I was little."

"Severov thugs broke every window we have—that was the last one, and we couldn't afford to fix it for a while."

Marisa spoke hesitantly, not wanting to break the spell. "Is that who caused the car accident?"

Carlo Magno stared at her a moment, then shook his head. "No. That was a few months later. I guess I can tell you that much."

"You can tell me more."

"No, I can't," said Carlo Magno, and the spell broke. He turned back to the oven, saved a pan of almost-burning Chikn™, and dumped it on a plate. "Back to work."

ELEVEN

When her shift ended, Marisa went straight to Sahara's house, pausing only to wave at her father through the door of the San Juanito kitchen. "Hey, Papi, I'm going upstairs."

Carlo Magno was frying green chiles on the big flat griddle. "Homework?"

"Lots. I'm going to stay the night, okay? There's a big project we're working on."

"You're supposed to ask permission," said Carlo Magno, flipping a chile with calloused fingers. "Not just tell me things."

"I never ask permission for anything," said Sandro, ducking through the kitchen to grab a bowl of salsa. It was his turn to wait tables.

"Because you never do anything I disagree with," Carlo Magno shouted after him, but Sandro was already gone. Carlo Magno looked at the swinging door, then looked back at Marisa.

"He never does anything I disagree with."

"Good thing you have me, then," said Marisa, and slipped in to grab a grapefruit soda from the fridge. She kissed her father on the cheek and jogged back to the door. "You'd be so bored without me."

"Be good!" he shouted.

"I will!" she shouted back, and pounded up the stairs to Sahara's apartment. The house computer recognized her and unlocked the door, and a slight imbalance in the old hinges caused it to swing open about five inches. Marisa let herself in and closed it behind her. "Hey, Diggs."

"Hello, Marisa," said Sahara's house computer. Marisa didn't know how much Sahara had paid for the voice module, but it was smooth as silk. "You look lovely today."

"Marry me," said Marisa, and walked back into Sahara's bedroom. "Ready?"

Sahara turned around, holding up two different outfits: both black, but one was made of faux leather and the other was covered with hundreds of tiny rubberized scales, like dragon skin. "Which is better for trapping and interrogating a group of murderers who sell body parts? Classic, or techy?"

"Which is which?"

"You're the worst friend ever."

"I'm also the worst daughter," said Marisa, and blinked into her djinni's GPS settings. "I just told my dad I'd be good, and now it's like forty seconds later and—" She blinked, activating a program. "I've just spoofed my djinni's GPS signal onto Cameron." The camera nulis would be staying behind, looping old footage of the girls doing homework at Sahara's beat-up kitchen table.

"I'm already spoofed to Camilla," said Sahara. "They'll think we're here all night long. And Diggs won't tell, will you?"

"Anything for you, baby," said the computer.

Marisa widened her eyes. "I feel like maybe that's a little inappropriate."

"You're just jealous."

"Always," said Marisa. She dropped her backpack and picked up a carrying case filled with modified nulis. "Let's do this."

Chuy had chosen their ambush site: Bao's shantytown, built inside of another abandoned construction project, though this one was above the ground instead of below it. A ten-story hotel, with a foundation and a metal frame and enough concrete to act as floors and ceilings and stairs. A handful of interior walls were finished as well, but the company had run out of money before completing anything else. The lower floors were full of squatters, an entire miniature city living in the ruins of one company's tiny apocalypse, but the top three floors had long ago been claimed as La Sesenta territory, and even with the whole gang in hiding, the locals respected their rule.

"Don't worry," said Chuy, "we'll be a few floors up from the civilians, so no one will get hurt."

"Can't we do this somewhere with fewer people?" asked Marisa.

"This is Los Angeles," said Chuy. "Anywhere we go will have people in it."

Marisa frowned, but she couldn't disagree.

"Watch out for the elevator shafts," said Bao, leading the group past a row of tents and blankets toward the stairwell. "The hotel has two basements, so they're basically twelve-story death pits."

Marisa peered into one as they passed it; even on the ground floor it made her shiver to look into the inky black holes.

"We've walled them off on the other floors," said Bao, "so nobody accidentally falls in, but we keep this one open as a warning, and La Sesenta kept theirs open for . . . I shudder to think."

"Persuasion," said Chuy. Marisa didn't like the sound of that at all.

The stairwell was enclosed in cement walls, so they trudged up in relative safety in a somber single file: Chuy, Marisa, Bao, then Anja, with Sahara bringing up the rear. Chuy had wanted to bring more, but Marisa insisted; she didn't want this to turn into a bloodbath, just a fast ambush and interrogation. Too many trigger fingers made her nervous. Even so, they weren't completely unprepared. They had their modified nulis, ready to knock out each attacker's sight and hearing, and they were all armed with stun guns. Chuy was armed with a real gun—a Cirrus-7 handgun with magnetic accelerators. If all else failed, he could shoot straight through a concrete wall.

It occurred to her that the chop shop boys could probably do the same. She swallowed nervously, and thought about happier things.

Because of the stairwell walls, they didn't get a real sense of the height until they stepped out on the ninth floor and caught their first glimpse of the city: the sky still barely lit by sunlight, but the early evening dark enough that most of the lights were on. Los Angeles stretched for hundreds of miles in every direction, having swallowed city after city into a single massive metropolitan area. Even the ocean held rows of metal wharves and docks and fueling stations stretching far out from the shore. The city covered the hills and valleys like an endless carpet of concrete and palm trees; ten-story buildings like this one were an anomaly, and aside from the occasional downtown center or business park, most of the city was only a few stories tall.

"I love this view," said Marisa.

"Looks like the view from my house," said Anja.

Bao winked. "And we didn't even pay a couple million yuan to get it."

"Only a couple?" asked Anja, raising her eyebrow in mock offense. "How poor do you think we are?"

"This staircase is a perfect bottleneck," said Sahara, focusing them back on the job. "Is this the only one?"

"There's another on the far side," said Chuy, gesturing to the other end of the hotel.

Sahara looked around the space. Most of it was flat and open, with only a forest of half-completed water pipes to mark where the hotel's rooms were supposed to be. A scattering of furniture and trash showed that La Sesenta hadn't taken everything when they'd left. The three elevator shafts had been roped off—two for guests, and a wider one for service and laundry—and next to the service elevator stood a finished room with concrete walls. "What's that?"

"Laundry room, I think," said Chuy. "Some kind of service room, at least. Memo used to use it as his headquarters."

"Then that's what we'll use it for again," said Sahara. She nodded at Anja, who smiled and pulled the blood-crusted djinni from its plastic container. "We'll scatter the nulis around the outside and put the djinni in there. When they come for it, no matter which staircase they use, they'll group up here and the nulis can zap them."

"I don't want to be trapped in that room if something goes wrong," said Bao.

"Amen," said Chuy.

"We don't have to be anywhere near that room," said Sahara. "The nulis all have cameras—we'll go one floor up, wait to see what happens, and watch the whole thing in safety and high-def."

"And if they have rail guns like Chuy?" asked Marisa.

Sahara winced. "Good point. Maybe we'll go up two floors, and wait on the roof."

They opened the carrying case and pulled out the nulis—one keyed to each ID tag they'd identified at the dance club, and four more with tasers that they could pilot remotely, just in case. They came online with an almost inaudible hum of tiny rotors, and Sahara guided them to hiding places in piles of garbage, or perched on the ceiling. Anja placed Memo's djinni in the exact center of the service room, sitting on a table, so that anyone tracking the signal would have no doubts about where it was, and then with a set of long, needle-thin tools, she turned it on.

"It's connecting to the net," said Anja. "I don't know how long it'll take for the Braydons to find the tag and come after it, but they can now."

"Time to go upstairs and wait," said Sahara. "We'll split into groups to watch the top of each staircase: Anja with me on the north side, Mari and Chuy on the south."

"What about me?" asked Bao.

"You're—" Sahara stopped mid-sentence, her mouth hanging open, then shook her head and laughed. "Holy crap. You're the Jungler."

"What?" asked Chuy.

"I just now realized that I've been planning this whole thing like an Overworld match," said Sahara. "Me as General with Anja supporting, Chuy as Sniper with Mari supporting, and Bao running around on his own." She looked at Bao. "I didn't make a plan for you because I never make one for Fang."

"Awesome," said Anja.

"This is not a game," said Chuy.

"I know that," said Sahara. "I know that, I just . . . I just fell into the pattern. Bao, you stay with me and Anja."

"You know, it's not a bad idea to keep me separate," said Bao. "I'll go a few floors down, buy some pho, and hang out in a corner somewhere. I don't have a djinni, and they've never seen me with you. If the nulis take care of everything, we're good, and if they don't, I can flank them."

"That sounds dangerous," said Marisa.

"If the nulis don't work we're boned anyway," said Bao. "Better to have someone they're not expecting with an attack angle they're not planning on, right?"

"He's right," said Anja. "And also this is awesome. I want to use call signs."

"This is not a game," said Chuy again. "They could kill us."

"That's just how Anja is," said Marisa, pulling on his arm. "Look, the plan hasn't changed, we're just . . . doing it the way we know how, right? We're good at this."

"You don't come back to life in this version," said Chuy. "Take it seriously, because I guarantee they are."

"We are," said Sahara. "The plan is sound—now go to your places and wait. We might have hours or we might have just a couple of minutes. And, um, take a taser nuli with you, just in case."

"Come on," said Marisa again, pulling Chuy toward the south stairs. She blinked to find their web of nulis, and told one of the tasers to follow her. Bao waved and went downstairs, and Sahara and Anja went up. One of the little taser nulis followed them as well.

"I don't like this," said Chuy, picking his way across the abandoned floor.

"Did you like it before?" asked Marisa.

"No."

"Then nothing's changed," she told him. "Relax. Ninety-five percent chance the nulis do everything without us lifting a finger anyway."

"That's one chance out of twenty that we get murdered by a chop shop," said Chuy. "I don't like those odds."

A message popped up in Marisa's djinni: a group message from Anja. **Chuy's call sign is Baconator. Bao can make up his own.**

You're lucky Chuy's not reading this, Marisa sent back. **The man is Not Amused.**

Why does he get to be Baconator? asked Bao. His responses were slower than the girls', because he was typing them into a phone instead of thinking them into a djinni. **My name is literally three of the first four letters in the word bacon.**

Because bacon is chewy, sent Anja.

Bacon is crispy, sent Sahara.

My letters are even in the right order, sent Bao.

Only overcooked bacon is crispy, sent Anja. **The good stuff is chewy.**

What kind of monster prefers chewy bacon to crispy bacon? asked Sahara.

Now I'm even happier that Chuy's not reading this, sent Marisa. **He'd shoot you himself.**

I want my call sign to be Smug Bastard, sent Bao. **Ask me why.**

No, sent Sahara.

Why? asked Anja.

Because you're stuck on the roof, sent Bao, **and I just bought pho from a food cart.**

No fair, sent Marisa. **Home court advantage.**

I've got my sisters with me, too, said Bao. **If anyone comes up either staircase, we'll see them.**

Say hi for me, sent Marisa. She didn't see Jin and Jun very often, but she'd always liked them. **And whatever you do, do not approach these guys. At all.**

Playtime's over, sent Sahara. **Time for silent waiting.**

Yes, Mother, sent Anja.

Marisa couldn't see them from her side of the roof, but she imagined Sahara punching Anja in the arm, and laughed.

"What?" asked Chuy.

"Tell you later, Baconator," said Marisa. She set the nuli to wait in a shadowed corner of the stairwell, and pulled out her taser. "Now we just . . . aim our guns at this doorway and wait?"

"Pretty much," said Chuy, and pulled her toward a discarded crate and a pair of chairs. "But let's do it from cover."

They lay on their stomachs, guns trained on the doorway, and waited.

The first Braydon showed up almost two hours later.

I take it all back, sent Anja. **This is the most boring game of Overworld ever.**

Quiet, sent Sahara. **We've got one.**

Marisa blinked into the web of modified camera nulis, and watched as a man's face peered out from one of the stairways. **That's south,** she sent, and a shiver of fear ran through her. He was one of the chop shop boys, and he was barely thirty feet away from her. Even with two concrete floors between them, it freaked her out.

"Stay calm," whispered Chuy.

"They're here," Marisa whispered back.

Chuy nodded, and adjusted his grip on his gun.

Two more, sent Bao. **No, three. Four total, two per stairwell. They're being cautious and trying to blend in.**

The man visible on camera pulled a large gun from his jacket, some kind of submachine gun that Marisa could recognize but not identify. He pointed it out of the stairwell door, scanning the room carefully before stepping out and beckoning to someone behind him.

Everyone stay quiet, sent Sahara. **Let them take the bait.**

"Four men," Marisa whispered to Chuy.

"You're shaking," whispered Chuy, and put a hand on hers.

"I can't imagine why."

"Your plan is good," Chuy whispered. "Take your finger off the trigger."

Marisa realized that she was almost squeezing the stun gun's trigger, and eased off, moving her finger to the side of the weapon. "Thanks."

I see two more, sent Sahara. **And there's the fourth. They're converging on the service room.**

No one's following them, sent Bao. **Or if they are, they're playing it cool as ice down here in the tent city. I'm pretty sure we'd recognize anyone out of place, but . . . maybe not?**

So they may or may not have secret backup, sent Anja. **I am getting so turned on right now.**

Quiet, sent Sahara. **They're moving in.**

Marisa watched through her djinni, blinking back and forth between various nulis as different ones gained a better view.

The nulis are go, sent Sahara.

Anja sent a series of messages: **Activating seeker droids in three.**

Two.

One.

The video feeds swirled abruptly as four of the nulis jumped up, flew through the air, and made a beeline for their targets' heads. Marisa held her breath, watching the other feeds, as each of the four men collapsed to the ground when the tasers hit them.

It was over in less than a heartbeat.

Holy what? sent Sahara.

"Did it work?" whispered Chuy.

"I . . . think so?" said Marisa.

That was the greatest thing I've ever seen, sent Anja. **General: I request permission to strike a superstar pose. And to shout "Superstar!" at the top of my lungs.**

Denied, sent Sahara. **Bao, any reaction from hidden backup?**

Nothing, sent Bao. **Did this really just work?**

Don't sound so surprised, sent Sahara.

Anja's voice echoed across the roof. "Superstar!"

"Let's get down there," said Chuy, climbing to his feet. Marisa followed, stun gun up, and sent the nuli ahead to look for traps or ambushes. It found nothing, and she sent it down two more floors. There was a shape silhouetted in the seventh-floor doorway, but as the camera flew in close she could see that it was only Jun. Or Jin? They were identical twins who went out of their way to look as similar as possible, and on a grainy camera of a mininuli she couldn't spot any of the usual giveaways. The girl looked into the nuli's camera and shrugged; there was no one else. Marisa left the nuli perched in the corner, watching for movement.

Why would they come without backup? sent Sahara.

Chuy and Marisa reached the ninth floor and peered out carefully; Marisa had a quick flashback to watching the chop shop guy peek out of the same door in the same way, and shivered at the similarity. She saw nothing, and blinked to activate her night-vision mod—it wasn't military grade or anything, just a cheap app she'd picked up, but it lit up the ninth floor in soft greens that made it easier to see in the post-sunset gloom. Still nothing. She followed Chuy forward, picking their way through the pipes and rubble, and met Sahara and Anja near the door of the service room. The four Braydons were still on the floor, unmoving.

"Nothing," said Marisa.

"Nothing," Sahara agreed, shrugging. "Guess we lucked out."

"Start dragging them in here," said Chuy, and leaned down to grab one of the men by the wrists. He pulled him into the service room, propped him in a metal chair, and patted him down for weapons: he had a handgun, a plasteel syringe, and two wicked-looking combat knives. He placed them on the table next to Memo's djinni and then starting strapping the man to the chair with zip ties. Anja and Sahara got to work on the others, while Marisa followed Chuy and helped tie the first man to the chair.

Whoa, sent Bao. **Did you see that?**

Marisa jerked up. **See what?**

Something moved, he sent. **Camera six.**

I didn't see anything, sent Anja.

Who got past you? sent Sahara.

No one did, sent Bao. **With me and Jin and Jun, we've got both stairwells completely under surveillance. Nobody's gone up.**

Maybe it was a bird, sent Marisa, though all she could think about was Zenaida's ghost, running through the walls.

Bao denied it almost instantly. **Whatever I saw was bigger than a bird. I'm coming up there.**

Chuy slapped the Braydon's face, then pulled a black bag down over it to cover his eyes. He looked up, saw Marisa's face, and immediately put his hand to the rail gun pistol on his hip. "What's wrong?"

"Bao thinks he saw something," said Marisa. "There was a shadow on one of the cameras."

"What do you think it is?" shouted Sahara, dragging a second Braydon into the room.

"Probably another squatter," said Chuy, standing up. "We didn't see anyone when we got here, but this is a big floor, and La Sesenta hasn't been here to throw people out in over a week. Someone moved in."

"That makes sense," said Marisa, nodding her head. As long as it wasn't a ghost, she was happy.

"We'll check it out," said Sahara, leaning the second Braydon against the wall. She pointed at the first Braydon. "Slap him awake so we can interrogate him and get out of here."

"*I'll* check it out," said Chuy. He handed Sahara the rest of the zip ties and then pulled out his handgun. "Get these fulanos tied up before they come to." He strode out of the service room, and Marisa looked at Sahara, sharing an uncertain glance.

"Probably just another squatter," said Sahara.

Marisa nodded. "Yeah." She shook the man in the chair again, trying to wake him.

Sahara put a bag over the second Braydon's head and started tying his wrists and ankles.

"Never," the Braydon in the chair mumbled. He was slowly coming to.

Eight, sent Bao. **There it was again, on eight, did you see it?**

Marisa remembered the image of Zenaida's ghost, burned into her brain, and gripped the mumbling man's arm for support. She remembered just as quickly that he was a chop shop murderer, and backed away as far as the djinni cable could reach.

"Who's out there?" shouted Anja. Her voice echoed in from beyond the service room door, half open in the darkness. "We come in peace. Take me to your leader."

"Never get me," muttered the Braydon in the chair.

Marisa gritted her teeth, feeling her heart pounding in her chest. Was Zenaida back?

What could a ghost do to a person, anyway?

Suddenly she remembered that Bao had said he was coming upstairs. Shouldn't he have been here by now? **Bao?** she sent. **Did you come upstairs?**

She waited for his answer.

And waited.

"You got the rest," muttered the Braydon, "but you'll never get me."

"Damn it," said Sahara, looking up at the door. "Where is he?" She glanced at Marisa again, sickly and pale in Marisa's green nightvision. She pulled out her stun gun. "Bao!"

"I didn't see him," said Anja, pulling the third Braydon into the service room. He groaned as she dropped him on the cement floor. "I don't like this."

"He might just not be answering," said Marisa. "He's on a phone, not a djinni, so anytime he uses the screen it glows. If he's trying to sneak around, he might be ignoring us to stay hidden."

"Everybody stay calm," said Sahara. "We're down one Jungler—that's nothing we haven't dealt with before—"

"That's Bao," snapped Marisa, "and this is real."

"And staying calm is priority one," said Sahara forcefully. "We have to think: whoever's out there knows where we are, so we either move or we defend. We can't move, so we defend."

"Chuy's alone," said Marisa. "I'm his support—I need to go help him."

"You need to wake up this blowhole and get the info we need," said Sahara. She tapped her temple and blinked, her eyes unfocusing as she looked at her djinni display. "I've got six nulis to help support Chuy. Nightvision engaged. Anja, get the last man and tie everyone up."

"On it," said Anja, and slipped back outside.

Marisa looked at the man in the chair, who was slowly starting to twitch his head. She ran to the third Braydon, covered his head, and started tying him up.

"Hey," said the Braydon in the chair. His voice was slurred, and muffled by the bag. "Where am I?"

Marisa stood and faced him. "Who's your backup?" she asked. "Who's with you?"

"No backup," the Braydon muttered. He was awake but still groggy. "Just four of us left."

"I can't find Chuy," said Sahara.

Marisa glanced at her, sitting cross-legged behind the room's one table. She looked like she was meditating as she focused on driving the drones. "What do you mean you can't find him?"

"What do you think I mean?" Sahara snapped.

"Where's Memo?" asked the Braydon.

"There were six of you before," said Marisa, steeling her resolve and returning to her interrogation. "Plus who knows how many others. Why are there only four here now?"

"She got them all," the man mumbled, trying to shake himself awake. "That's why we need to find Memo."

"Who got them?" Marisa demanded. The ghost of Zenaida loomed large and deadly in her thoughts. "Who are you talking about?"

"She's here," the man said. He sounded more lucid now. "We thought we could get help from La Sesenta, because she's after them, too, but I don't see Memo. My tracker app tells me he's here, so I assume this is a trap. Which means we're all dead: my team and yours."

Marisa stepped toward him. "Who's here? The other person moving around in the darkness—who is it!"

The man glowed a nauseating green in the nightvision filter, and his voice shook with fear from inside the bag: "The witch."

"Chuy's down!" shouted Sahara. "Camera nine! I can't tell if he's unconscious or dead—"

Another Braydon moved, and Marisa screamed for Anja: "Anja! Get back in here now!"

"It's too late," said the Braydon in the chair. "I had a gun in my waistband. Whoever you are: pick it up, and shoot the next thing that comes through that door."

"My friend's still out there!" shouted Marisa.

"Tā mā de!" said Sahara. She leaped to her feet, stumbling into the table and knocking it over. Weapons and Memo's djinni scattered across the floor. Sahara looked wildly around the room, struggling to refocus on the real world, and then stumbled toward the door, slamming it closed with a reverberating clang.

Marisa shouted at her: "Anja's still out th—"

"No she's not," said Sahara. "I just saw her go down." Marisa was stunned into silence. Sahara fumbled for a lock, but there wasn't even a knob. She backed away from the door, then turned and scrambled on the floor for the weapons Chuy had taken from the chop shop boys. She pulled up a thick black handgun—not accelerated like Chuy's was, but with a wide barrel that hinted at a massive-caliber bullet—and pointed it at the closed steel door. "It's her."

"I told you," said the Braydon.

Marisa pulled out her stun gun, increasingly terrified that it wouldn't be any use at all. "Who?" She gulped. "Zenaida?"

"Zenaida's dead," said Sahara. "This is the woman from Omar's house—the hacker."

"The ha—"

"At least I think so," said Sahara. "She's barefoot, and she has the same silhouette, but I . . . I saw her eyes this time." She glanced at Marisa, but only for a second, and then she looked straight back at the door, the heavy pistol shaking in her hands. "She's not human."

Marisa gripped her stun gun tighter, her jaw hanging down. "What is she?"

"Hell if I know. Some gengineered banshee."

"She must be searching for Memo, too," said Marisa. "Right? His djinni is a beacon to anyone looking for him."

"She might be after Memo," said Sahara, jerking her head toward the Braydon. "Or us, even."

Marisa shook her head. "She's looking for Zenaida. Just like everyone else."

"Who's Zenaida?" asked the Braydon.

"You cut off her hand," said Marisa.

"I don't know what you're talking about," said the Braydon.

"Twice," she snarled.

"I've never cut off anyone's—"

Marisa heard a puff of air, and Sahara collapsed to the floor. The gun clattered away from her limp fingers, and Marisa barely had time to look up at the door before it burst open and a woman stepped in, a wraith in the green nightvision, her pistol raised in front of her. She fired, and Marisa twisted, and she felt the impact against her cybernetic arm with a soft, metallic clink. She looked down, seeing a tiny dart dangling from the fabric of her sleeve, and thought: *a tranquilizer.*

She made her decision in a split second, hoping it was the right one, and sank to the floor behind the Braydon's metal chair, draping her arm across her face and pretending she was unconscious. She tried to breathe as lightly and as evenly as possible.

The woman looked at her for a moment, and Marisa looked back through the tiny crack between her eyelids and arm. The woman was dressed in black, with the hint of a shimmer that suggested it was some kind of stealth fabric—a chameleon suit, maybe, or a thermal dampener to hide from infrared. Her feet and hands were bare, which struck Marisa just as oddly tonight as it had the other day, and her skin, up close, was somehow odd, but in the nightvision green, she couldn't tell exactly how so. The worst part, though, was just what Sahara had said it was: her eyes. Instead of a white and an iris and a pupil, each eye was a single iridescent mass, with a stripe across the middle and three vertical irises running in perpendicular lines. Marisa had seen plenty of cybernetic eyes—even Anja had one—but these were organic. The woman's face was smooth and beautiful, and hauntingly familiar, but those eyes . . . They looked almost like compound eyes, like an insect's eyes, and the contrast of those eyes in a human face nearly shook Marisa with a wave of revulsion. It took all of her self-control not to gasp out loud at the sheer alienness of it.

Who was she?

What was going on?

The woman looked at Marisa for what seemed like an eternity before finally looking away. The Braydons against the wall were struggling, still blind and deaf but nearly awake, and she shot each with a tranq dart from her pistol. They collapsed, motionless, and she retrained her gun on the Braydon in the chair.

"Where is he?" she hissed.

Marisa knew that voice. This was the woman from the police station—Ramira Bennett. The ZooMorrow agent. What was she doing here? And why did she look so strange?

Marisa suppressed a shiver. At least now she knew why Bennett usually covered her face with a holomask.

"You're looking for Memo, too?" asked the Braydon. "He's a popular man."

"His djinni signal is here," said Bennett, "but he's not. I assume this is a trap?"

"Meant to catch me," said the Braydon. "They're looking for someone named Zenaida."

Shut up! Marisa thought. *Stop telling her everything!*

Bennett nodded. "Zenaida Padilla Lozano de Maldonado."

"Maybe?" said the Braydon. "I only heard a little before you took them out. But you don't have beef with me, and I don't have beef with you, so let's just walk away, okay?"

"I wasn't asking, I was telling," said Bennett. She looked away from him for a second, taking in the rest of the room, and Marisa used the moment to blink, turning off her nightvision app. It was much darker without it, but there was still enough moonlight to see. Marisa nearly gasped again at the sudden change—or rather, at the part that didn't change. The tinted glow of the nightvision was gone, but the woman's skin didn't change.

She had *green skin*.

Bennett's insectile eyes found something against the back wall, and Marisa did everything she could to stay motionless while the woman walked forward and stepped over her. As soon as Bennett was behind her, she risked a tiny glance around the room, and saw that one of Braydon's combat knives was barely inches from her hand. She could grab it, but what could she do with it? Farther away, but still in arm's reach, was the handgun Sahara had picked up. She could do some damage with that. Though as fast as this woman moved, she might not even get a shot off.

"You're going to let me go, right?" asked the Braydon again. "Now that you know Memo's not here, you can just—"

"This is his djinni," said Bennett, walking back across the room. Marisa had just a few seconds before Bennett could see her face again—if she wanted to do something with her djinni, she had to do it now. A message to Fang or Jaya? But what could they do? Maybe the police? Maybe Omar? But she needed someone here—someone who was close enough to help *now*. Could she control one of the taser drones? Not with a single blink, and that's all she had time for. She had one chance left: Had the woman already taken out Bao, or was he simply hiding, like Marisa had guessed? She gambled everything on a single message, and sent it: **Make her turn around.**

Bennett stood in front of Braydon again, and held up the bloody djinni. "This is how they baited us here—you and me both, though I don't think they were expecting me. They turned on Memo's djinni, and waited for you to track the signal."

"Yes, yes, okay," said Braydon. He spoke like he didn't know why he was still alive, and was trying to be as agreeable and helpful as possible before she changed her mind and shot him. "We can usually tell if it's a spoofed ID tag, but this looked legit. I guess it was."

"Do you know who they are?" asked Bennett.

"Girls," said Braydon eagerly. "They look familiar, though—"

"Girls," said Bennett, examining the djinni curiously. "They didn't steal this against Memo's will, and the man outside has La Sesenta tattoos, which means that whoever these girls are, they know where Memo's hiding. My toxin wears off in about half an hour, so: you have thirty minutes before they wake up to tell me what I need to know. After that, I won't need you anymore."

"But—you're not going to kill me, right?" asked the Braydon.

"You work for a chop shop," said the woman. "Give me a reason to leave you alive."

"But—" said the man, though before he could finish he was interrupted by a loud clang from the doorway, and a sudden shout:

"Hey, guys, whatcha doin'?"

The woman spun toward the doorway, firing tranq darts from her pistol, and in that instant Marisa lunged for the gun on the floor. Bennett saw her, and started to swing her pistol back, but a drone flew in from the doorway, distracting her again—it wasn't flying straight, just spinning end over end, like it had been thrown. Bennett hesitated, and Marisa brought up the gun, clicked off the safety, and fired. The boom was deafening in the concrete room, and Marisa screamed at the shock of it, and the barefoot killer with the alien eyes clutched Memo's djinni tight in her hand and ran out the door. Marisa staggered to her feet and ran after her, blinking to call back her nightvision, but when she came out of the room all she saw was Bao, waving his arms and shouting silently.

Silently? She wondered for half a second, but of course she couldn't hear him—the gunshot had been literally deafening, at least temporarily. She sent him a message:

I can't hear anything. Where is she?

Bao frowned but looked at his phone, and then ran around the corner to the far side of the concrete room. Marisa followed him, but he pulled her back sharply; she looked down and saw the deep black pit of the elevator shaft yawning barely an inch in front her.

And down inside of it, two floors away and scuttling on the wall like a spider, was Ramira Bennett—a green-skinned monster with inhuman eyes. She clung to the brick walls with her fingers and toes, and as she looked back up at Marisa her eyes flashed, reflecting some shaft of ambient light. Marisa was too unnerved to fire again, and the woman scuttled away, straight down the wall into the darkness below.

TWELVE

Bao's message popped up in Marisa's vision: **What the hell was that?**

She's a ZooMorrow agent.

Are they hiring nightmares now? Bao sent back.

Find Chuy, sent Marisa. The heavy silence in her damaged ears was slowly turning into a high-pitched ringing. She ran to Anja, lying slumped on the floor about ten yards away, and checked her pulse; she was alive. Whatever tranquilizer Bennett had used on Sahara and the Braydons, she'd apparently used the same thing on Anja. Had she tranqed Chuy as well, or was he dead? She didn't wait for Bao to come back; she jumped up and ran through the empty concrete room toward where he was struggling with Chuy's body. Bao looked up, let go of Chuy's arm, and gave a thumbs-up: he was alive too. She nodded, and helped him drag her older brother back toward the others. Soon Jin and Jun joined them, and together they got both Chuy and Anja toward the service room.

"She said it wears off in thirty minutes," said Bao. Marisa's hearing was almost back to normal. "They'll wake up, and we can get out of here."

"She could have killed us," said Marisa.

"She didn't," said Bao.

"She'll come back," said Marisa. "She wants Memo, and she knows we know where he is. We caught her by surprise, but she'll come back."

"Maybe not," said Bao. "She took Memo's djinni, and there's probably enough data in there to lead her straight to him. She doesn't need us anymore."

"Great," said Marisa. "Then La Sesenta's going to kill us instead of ZooMorrow. I don't know how much better off we are."

Back in the service room, the Braydon in the chair had knocked himself over, and was awkwardly crawling across the floor, chair and all, trying to reach the fallen weapons. Marisa shouted, "Stop moving, and tell me everything you know."

He froze, still lying on his side. "I don't know anything!"

Anja coughed, and Marisa knelt by her side and helped her sit up. "Hey, babe, are you awake?"

"Awake or dead," mumbled Anja. "Is this hell? Which religion was right?"

"You're alive," said Marisa. "You got tranqed by that ZooMorrow agent we saw at the police station."

"She's here?"

"Not anymore."

"Good," said Anja. "I need to lie down again. My head feels like someone beat it with a hammer." She lowered herself back to the cold cement floor. "Wake me up if I die."

"Okay, wow," said the Braydon in the chair. He was still on his side. "Did you just say that woman works for ZooMorrow?"

"We need to stop saying things in front of you," said Marisa.

"You need to stop saying everything," said Chuy. He was sitting up, rubbing his head with his hands. "This entire thing se fue a la mierda."

"Technically we're supposed to be interrogating you," said Bao, looking at the Braydon pointedly. "You're supposed to tell us . . . crap, what was he supposed to tell us?"

"A bioprinter," said Marisa, her ears still ringing. "A black-market bioprinter who sold organs made from illicit DNA. I need his name."

"Look, I know a lot of bioprinters," said the Braydon. "They can be handy for cheap merchandise in a pinch, or . . . they can be bad for business." He seemed as eager to help her as he'd been to help the ZooMorrow agent. "Narrow it down for me."

Marisa shrugged, helpless. "He . . . had a woman's left hand?"

"Ugh" said the Braydon, wrinkling his nose. "That guy? Really?"

"You know him?" asked Chuy. He pulled himself to his feet, bracing his hand against the wall as the world spun around him. Marisa stood as well, and tucked herself under his arm to support him. "Who is he?"

"His name's Song," said the Braydon. "Andy Song. I can even give you his address."

"If you know where he lives," asked Marisa, "why is he still alive?"

"Haven't you been listening?" asked the Braydon. "That bug-eyed monster person has been trying to kill us. When are we going to have time to take out a bioprinter?"

"Give us the address," Chuy repeated.

The Braydon blinked, tagging Marisa's ID and sending a message. "Done. Now let me go."

"Sure thing," said Chuy, and grabbed the back of the man's metal chair, standing him up and dragging him out of the room.

"Whoa," said the Braydon. "Please don't tell me you're going to chuck me down the stairs."

"Close," said Chuy, and shoved the chair over the ledge of the elevator shaft. Marisa shouted, but it was too late. The man screamed and tumbled out of sight. Three agonizing seconds later, the screams stopped abruptly.

"What are you doing?" Marisa smacked Chuy in the arm, and when he turned to face her she punched him harder. "Are you crazy? Are you insane?"

Chuy frowned. "What did you think was going to happen?"

"He helped us!"

"He's a kidnapper and butcher," said Chuy calmly. "You knew we were going to kill whoever we caught here tonight."

"I'm not a killer!" shouted Marisa.

"I am," said Chuy.

"What's going on?" asked Sahara. She was leaning on Anja's arm, staggering out of the service room, still groggy from the tranq.

Marisa shook her head, still furious. "This chundo just murdered one of the Braydons!"

"Too bad," mumbled Sahara. "Can't have a self-respecting boy band with just three of them."

"This isn't a joke," snarled Marisa.

"No it's not," said Chuy. "And it's not a video game, either. We're not fighting them because they got matched against us in a tournament bracket—we're fighting them because they are human predators, who kidnap and kill and maim people in our neighborhood. How did you think this was going to end? You wanted to capture a bunch of murderers, get the name you needed, and then what? Just put them back out on the street?"

Marisa had never wanted anyone to get hurt, on any side, but she'd also known . . . well, she'd known that people would. She just hadn't let herself think about it. Until it was too late not to.

"The police," she said softly. "Detective Hendel. We could have left them tied up here and then called her to come and get them. An anonymous tip."

"They'd be back on the street in a year," said Chuy. "Assuming she had enough evidence to get them convicted in the first place."

"Then I guess we'll see," said Marisa, folding her arms. "Because that's exactly what I'm going to do with those other three."

"Not a chance," said Chuy. "You lost Memo's djinni, and the person who has it is going to find him and kill him. Those three chop shop thugs are the peace offering that's going to keep you alive when he finds out how badly you messed this up."

"He's got a point," said Sahara. "It's not like these blowholes deserve any better."

"We are not executioners," said Marisa. "We're not the law."

"Nobody is, these days," said Chuy. He walked wearily back toward the service room, pulling a small handphone from his pocket. "If your conscience really doesn't want you to let these monsters die, console yourself with the knowledge that there's nothing you can really do to stop me." He sent a message and put the phone away. "La Sesenta's on their way to interrogate these guys. You don't want to be here until after I've had a chance to explain everything."

Marisa stared at him, not even knowing why she was fighting so hard for the lives of people so vile.

Because it was the right thing to do.

She blinked, sending a message of her own, and then looked Chuy square in the eyes. "Now Hendel's on her way, too. I guess we all just do what we have to."

"Damn it, Mari!" Chuy turned and ran into the service room, clattering things around as he struggled to salvage what he could of the situation.

"Come on, Marisa," said Bao. "Let's get out of here."

"We have the bioprinter's name and address," said Sahara. "The situation here is only going to get worse, so let's get out of it while we still can. It's barely midnight—we can visit this bioprinter and still get home before anyone misses us."

Marisa didn't move.

"Come on," said Sahara. "All we need is his contact—where did he get Zenaida's DNA? He's the last link in the puzzle." Sahara took a step toward her and put a hand on Marisa's metal arm. "We'll find out what happened in that accident. We'll find out the truth."

Marisa felt sick and tired and drained of life and energy, but eventually she nodded. "Let's go."

Marisa closed her eyes as the autocab rolled them silently through the city. Sahara sat beside her, holding her hand, and across from them, on the opposite bench, Anja and Bao speculated about Ramira Bennett.

"Obviously she has some kind of genhancements," said Anja. "Those eyes weren't cybernetic."

"I didn't realize they did genhancements like that," said Bao. "Heightened metabolism, boosted muscle mass—any pro football player has that kind of stuff. But . . . freaky alien eyes?"

"Not alien," said Anja. "Mantis shrimp."

"What?" asked Sahara.

"I ran an image search," said Anja, "using Marisa's description: compound eyes with a stripe and three irises. I figured maybe I could find some bootleg photo of her, or some sign of where she's been or what she's done, but instead it gave me picture after picture of something called a mantis shrimp. Marisa—is this what you saw?"

Marisa opened her eyes to see that Anja had synced her djinni to the windows of the cab, and was displaying a series of images of what looked like a psychedelic lobster. The body was mostly green, and the legs were mostly red, but mixed in and around those was every other color in the rainbow; blues and yellows and purples and more. The eyes were up on stalks, like pale lavender mushrooms. "Show me the eyes in close-up," she asked, and Anja blinked. A new set of images replaced the others, and Marisa gasped when she saw them. "That's it. Those are her eyes."

Sahara grimaced in disgust. "She's a mantis shrimp?"

"At least her eyes are," said Bao. "Most of her's human—she probably started as all human, unless ZooMorrow's started building people from scratch now—but they've gone in and messed with her DNA, mixing in mantis shrimp and who knows what else." He looked at Anja. "I assume mantis shrimp have some crazy amazing eyes?"

Anja's own eyes were unfocused, reading something on her djinni. "According to this article, yes. A human eye has three cones—blue, red, and green—that let it distinguish about a million different colors. A mantis shrimp eye has sixteen cones, and scientists think they can see colors we can't even comprehend. They can see in infrared and ultraviolet, and those three irises give them a better sense of 3D and depth perception than any other animal on earth, including humans."

"What's with the stripe?" asked Marisa.

"That's part of the UV thing," said Anja, still reading the article, "and also polarized light, whatever that is. There's some speculation that they can see electrical signals."

"She saw Memo's djinni from across the room, in the dark, behind some rubble," said Marisa. "I guess if she can see electricity, that's pretty awesome."

"What on earth do mantis shrimp need all this crap for?" asked Sahara. "Do they get attacked by . . . invisible alien bounty hunters? What possible evolutionary pressure created something so advanced?"

"The article doesn't say," said Anja. Her eyes refocused on the real world. "Kind of a nice thing to have around, though, when you're a gengineering company looking for some naturally occurring superpowers to give your secret agents."

"Is that why her skin was green?" asked Marisa. "Is she, like, half mantis shrimp?"

"Maybe," said Bao. "Or maybe the skin is something else. She goes barefoot, and she doesn't wear gloves, which are both pretty weird things for a secret infiltrator to do. That implies that her skin has some other dope superpower that's more valuable than wearing armor or avoiding fingerprints."

"You said she crawled down a sheer wall, right?" asked Sahara. "I'll bet she has gecko toes."

Anja blinked, and a moment later the window displayed several images of little green lizards, along with some close-ups of some five-toed lizard feet. The toes were covered in narrow flaps running from one edge to the other, like little bands of skin.

"I studied these in school," said Sahara. "Each of those little bands is covered with hairs, and each of those hairs is covered with smaller hairs, and down and down until the tiniest hairs are measured in nanometers. They're not sticky to the touch, but they can walk on any surface." She looked at Marisa. "If I was giving my supermodel assassin crazy animal powers, I'd definitely give her some gecko toes."

"That explains how she got up there," said Bao. "We were watching the stairs, but she just wall-crawled right past us like Spider-Woman."

"I would read the hell out of a comic book called *Mantis-Shrimp-Woman*," said Anja.

"They work using something called the Van der Waals forces," said Sahara. "Very tiny electrical attractions between molecules. It's a super weak force, but when you get five zillion little hairs and microhairs and nanohairs all exerting that force at the same time, it works. Geckos can walk on anything."

"If she has a bunch of genhancements," said Marisa, "maybe that explains the acid blood we found at Omar's house?"

"More likely some kind of biotoxin," said Sahara. "Maybe she's got poison sacs, like a toad? Hidden under her hair, or inside her mouth?"

"Note to self," said Bao. "Never kiss a green woman with mantis-shrimp eyes."

"Is that the kind of thing that really requires a note?" asked Marisa.

"I'm just saying that if things were different, and we ran into each other in a club—"

"I would definitely hit that," said Anja. "Also, the cab says we're here. Autobots roll out."

The cab came to a stop outside of a small apartment building—not as small as the one where they'd gone looking for Chuy, but just as dingy. The door opened, and Marisa stepped out. A group of guys leaning against the wall whistled softly as the other girls joined her on the sidewalk, and Marisa heard at least one whispered "Ay, morenita," but she ignored them and looked at the apartments. The building was three stories tall, built like a U, and looked to have at least six units on each floor.

"Andy Song," Sahara whispered. "Number 216." They hiked up the stairs, found the door, and checked their stun guns one last time. "Let's do this," said Sahara, and knocked on the door.

Something crashed on the other side; whoever was in there had heard them, and was either running or trying to hide something. A few moments later he opened the door, though it stopped after only two inches, caught by a metal chain.

"Who are you?" asked a strained voice. "Are you cops?"

"Do we look like cops?" asked Sahara.

"No," said the man. "You're not like a hookergram or anything, right? Chinese dude's not your pimp?"

Bao rolled his eyes.

"Do we look like hookers?" asked Marisa, starting to get offended.

"Not really," said the man. "I don't know, do a dance or something, let me get a better look."

"We're looking for a man named Andy Song," said Sahara.

Marisa heard something in the background, and leaned closer to the open door. It sounded like a 3D printer. She wasn't certain what a bioprinter sounded like, but she imagined it was similar. If he was printing organs right at the moment, it was no wonder he didn't want to let anybody in. But then why open the door at all?

She was starting to grossly doubt the competence of Andy Song.

"I might know him," said the man behind the door. "Who's asking?"

"Customers," said Anja. "We're in the market."

"I don't sell Krok anymore."

"Not drugs," said Sahara. "The . . . other stuff."

The man sounded wary. "What other stuff?"

"The stuff you're printing right now," said Marisa. "We can hear it from out here."

"Balls," said the man, cursing and slamming the door. Marisa thought they'd scared him away, but a second later she heard the chain scrape through its housing, and he opened the door wide. "Get in here before the whole neighborhood hears it."

They filed in quickly, and Andy Song shut the door behind them. He looked about thirty years old, Asian, wearing shorts and a sleeveless T-shirt. The apartment was a cluttered mess, and Marisa wrinkled her nose at the smell of BO and old food. The bioprinter took up a surprisingly large space in the small living room, about the size of a two-seat futon. It was humming with activity, but with the bay door closed Marisa couldn't see what it was making.

"I wish I'd never bought this stupid bioprinter," said Song. "Nothing but trouble." He pointed at them. "Nothing!"

"We not looking to buy," said Sahara, "we just want information."

Song frowned. "You said you were customers!"

"Then sell us the information," said Anja.

"You printed two left hands—" said Marisa.

"Two?" asked Song, interrupting her before she could finish. He narrowed his eyes at her, then folded his arms smugly. "Yes, well. You found both of them, did you? Some of my best work." He eyed Marisa's cybernetic arm. "You're in the market for hands?"

"Those hands were found at a crime scene," said Marisa. "Which means their DNA was tested, which means the cops started asking questions about a . . ." She hesitated over the word. "A friend of ours. And don't worry, we're not with the cops; we just want to know where you got that DNA."

Song looked at her, nodding absently, then suddenly started shaking his head with dramatic emphasis. "Absolutely not. No. Not a chance in hell. You think I'm going to give her up? She'll kill me in a heartbeat."

Marisa closed her eyes. "Oh, for crying out loud."

"Wait," said Sahara, "it was her again? Crazy supermodel assassin?"

"That doesn't make sense," said Bao. "Why would she be trying to get all the DNA back again if she was the one who sold it in the first place?"

"There's no way she was selling it to someone like this," said Anja, and glanced at Song. "No offense."

Song glared back at her. "You can't just say 'no offense' after saying something offensive. They don't cancel out."

"So she was probably trying to make some money on the side," Anja continued. "Then the two gangs started fighting over turf, and the hand ended up in a police DNA lab, and word got back to Wonder Mantis Headquarters that the game was up. Now she's running around trying to destroy all the evidence before ZooMorrow hears about it."

"Maybe," said Marisa. "But how does that explain Memo? Why is she looking for him?"

"And why would she break into Omar's private database if she wasn't looking for Zenaida?" asked Sahara. "If all she needs is Zenaida's two recently printed hands, the Maldonado database is useless."

"Don't worry about them," said Bao, smiling cheerfully at Song. "They talk like this in front of *everybody*."

"Hold up," said Marisa, and pointed at Song. "How many other organs have you printed with that DNA?"

"Just a . . . few?"

"That doesn't sound very believable," said Anja.

"What about other DNA?" asked Sahara. "How long have you been bioprinting?"

"I just barely started," he said. "I didn't even have the printer until my uncle sold it to me used, and that was just a few weeks ago! So I went on the darknet, to some gene-tech forum full of underworld badass lunatics, and found a hacker willing to sell some cheap DNA templates. Good genhancement stuff, so I could get a good price on the street—the protein for the printer isn't cheap. So I went all in. And then those frigging hands—"

The bioprinter dinged, almost disturbingly like a microwave, and the bay door opened. A little tray slid out, tipped, and dumped a left hand into a little plastic basket. The tray retracted, the door closed, and the printer started humming again.

"A curse on all your microchips!" Song shouted at the machine.

"What on earth . . . ?" asked Marisa, staring openmouthed at the new hand. She tried to speak again, but her jaw simply moved noiselessly. Finally she looked at Song. "You made another one?"

"That's all it makes!" Song shouted.

"You said you made two hands," said Anja. "How many is it really?"

"My uncle cheated me," said Song. "He said this thing worked fine—a little used, but still fine! And so I hook it up and dump in the protein mix and what does it do? Five or six kidneys and a couple of livers and then it gets stuck on the left hand! All it makes is left hands!"

"How many?" Sahara demanded.

Song looked nervous. "Four?"

"Why don't I believe you?" asked Bao.

"Why don't you turn it off?" asked Marisa.

"And waste all that protein mix?" he asked. "If I shut off the power, I lose the refrigeration unit, and my entire investment rots away. Better to keep it going and try to find a market for all this fèiwù."

Sahara shook her head in disbelief. "So you tried to make money selling organs to hospitals and whatever, but then all it makes is hands and you thought maybe at least a chop shop would buy them."

Song backed up, suddenly wary. "Are you from Discount Arms? Because I kept my promise—I'm not selling them anywhere else, I'm not helping any of their competitors, and there's literally no reason to kill me or anything to be gained from doing so. Look at me!" He grabbed his hefty stomach. "Nobody wants my organs, they barely work—"

"We're not from the chop shop," said Sahara. "Though my urge to hurt you is definitely rising."

"What are you going to do with it?" asked Marisa. She nodded toward the hand.

"I'll keep it on ice," said Song. "I've found another buyer, and it'll go to a good home—"

"You just said you weren't selling them to anyone," said Bao.

Song threw his hands in the air. "I thought you were here to kill me, what was I supposed to say! Listen: just give me the hand, and I'll take care of everything."

"Yeah," said Anja, "I definitely trust this guy to take care of everything."

"Let's at least put it in the fridge," said Marisa. "That'll keep—"

"No!" screamed Song, and then he smiled sheepishly. "My fridge is a mess. I didn't know I'd be having company." He reached for the hand. "Seriously, just give it to me and be on your way—it's a little old lady! The hand is going to a little old . . ." He looked at Marisa. ". . . Mexican lady, with . . . three orphaned grandchildren, and she's their only source of support because their parents died in a . . . a . . ."

"Just shut up," said Sahara. "You're the worst liar I've ever met."

"Oh, come on," said Anja, "I wanted to see where that story was going."

"A granary fire!" said Song. "They died in a granary fire."

Anja frowned. "That was the best you could come up with?"

"I was hoping for a circus accident," said Bao.

"I'm putting it in the fridge," said Marisa, and walked past him to the apartment's tiny kitchen. Food covered the counters, and she wrinkled her nose again at the smell. Take-out boxes and dry-skinned oranges and a jug of half-drunk milk—

"Wait," said Marisa. She froze in her tracks and stared around at the kitchen. "Literally everything that should be in the fridge isn't." She turned her head slowly toward the refrigerator, feeling her heart sink and her nausea rise. "And it's been way too long for you to only have five hands." She swallowed. "Andy?"

"Yeah?" He sounded defeated.

"How many hands am I going to find when I open this fridge?"

"Probably more than you want to."

"This I have to see," said Anja, and walked into the kitchen. Bao and Sahara followed. They glanced at Marisa, and Marisa cringed as she opened the fridge.

"God in Heaven," said Sahara.

The refrigerator was crammed full of hands—front to back, top to bottom, every spare inch of every shelf and drawer was brimming over with Zenaida de Maldonado's left hand. The fingers curled like limp worms, or draped over each other in sickening intimacy, or twisted into horrible shapes where Andy Song had wedged them into nooks and corners to make room for more. It smelled like rotting meat. Anja opened the freezer, only to reveal a white, frost-covered version of the same horrific scene. She closed the freezer door without a word, and then took the fridge door from Marisa's limp grasp and closed that as well.

"I take it back," said Anja. "I did not have to see that."

Bao grimaced. "I'm going to have nightmares about this for the rest of my life."

"I need hugs," said Marisa. "I think I need all the hugs in the entire world."

"I told you not to open it," said Song sadly.

"What were you saving them for?" asked Marisa. "Did you even have a plan?"

"Well, I couldn't just throw them away—"

"You totally could have," said Sahara, and turned to face

him. "But you didn't want to lose your frakking protein mix, so . . . what was your plan? Fertilizer?"

"Dog food," said Song, and flashed a guilty smile. "They . . . need a lot of protein?"

"I'm calling the police," said Marisa, struggling to contain her sudden rage. "I'm reporting to Detective Kiki Hendel that we have found the source of the mysterious hands." She blinked on her djinni to send a message. "And if they don't get here soon, I have the feeling I'm going to have to report a fairly vicious assault and battery."

Sahara picked up a kitchen chair and started walking. Song flinched back, covering his face with his hands, but Sahara walked past him toward the bioprinter, raised the chair high over her head, and smashed the humming machine over and over, beating it with the metal chair until both printer and chair were bent and broken and still. She dropped the twisted wreckage and turned toward Song, brushing off her hands.

"I turned off your printer."

THIRTEEN

"That was our last lead," said Marisa. She was sitting in the police station again, staring at the same bare wall, though this time at least Sahara was with her. Bao and Anja had left before the police arrived: Anja because she didn't want her father or his company dragged into this mess, and Bao because he simply didn't want to be recognized by any cops. He lived fairly far outside the law.

Marisa was starting to realize that she did, too.

"The bioprinter was supposed to lead us back to the source of the DNA," said Sahara, "but all he led us to was ZooMorrow again, and I don't know where to go from here." She stuck out her lip, thinking, and then shook her head. "I know there's more to find, I just . . . don't know how to find it."

"I don't want to have to tangle with Ramira Bennett again," said Marisa. "And I definitely don't want her to tangle with me."

"The Wonder Mantis," said Sahara.

"The WoMantis," said Marisa.

"The Mantissassin," said Sahara.

"Nice," said Marisa.

"You know, you might not have a choice about seeing her again," said Sahara, and cast her a sidelong glance. "If she can't find Memo on her own, she's coming straight back to us."

"Thanks," said Marisa, some of her giddiness draining away. "That was exactly the chipper pick-me-up I needed right now."

They sat for a while in silence, waiting for Detective Hendel to excuse them. They'd already given their statements about Andy Song, and now Hendel was questioning Song for his side of the story. It was nearly two in the morning, and Marisa was exhausted. She closed her eyes, thinking about Fang—she never seemed to sleep at all. How did she do it? Though of course it was only five in the afternoon in Beijing right now.

Marisa's eyes snapped open. "It's afternoon in Asia."

"Lucky them," said Sahara, and yawned.

"Five in the afternoon in Beijing, and . . . what do you think in Moscow? Two? Earlier?"

"What does Moscow have to do with anything?" asked Sahara.

"Because Andy Song wasn't our last lead," said Marisa, and smiled for the first time in hours. "Lavrenti Severov is."

Sahara sat up straight. "Holy crap. I forgot about Severov."

"Grendel sent me those three names," said Marisa. "Those three Maldonado enforcers who died the same day as Zenaida. My dad said the gang war ended a month earlier, and Severov fled back to Russia, but what if he struck back one more time from across the ocean? Sent some hitmen or an assassin or something."

"A Mantissassin?"

"Maybe?" said Marisa. "My dad told me that Severov tried to kill Zenaida. Maybe he tried to do it again, and those were the three he had to get through in order to do it." She grinned mischievously. "We won't know until we call him."

Sahara's eyes widened. "You can't just call a Russian mob boss."

"Not with that attitude," said Marisa. She was feeling drained and reckless. She blinked to open a search window and typed in the name: Lavrenti Severov.

"He'll trace us."

"So we'll route the call weird and hide our trail."

"We're in a police station."

"I think Russia's a little out of their jurisdiction." She ran the search, scrolled through the list, and stopped in surprise.

Sahara raised her eyebrow. "Find something?"

"I found the end of the list," said Marisa. "That's literally the whole thing—a single page of results."

"That's like finding a unicorn."

"One of these has got to be him," said Marisa, and started reading each entry more deeply. "My dad called him Lav—which is suspicious by itself, right? That he would be on a nickname basis with this guy?"

"Maybe it's like we guessed before," said Sahara. "Maybe he worked for one of them."

"He seemed super offended when I brought that up."

Sahara shrugged. "Doesn't mean it's not true."

"Most of these are in Russian," said Marisa. "I don't have a

Cyrillic translator installed."

"Just look for a directory," said Sahara. She blinked, and ran the search herself. "I can't read most of these, but I can tell which ones are not what we want. Video site. Video site. Wiki site. Social media site. Here: phone directory."

"Give it to me," said Marisa, and Sahara blinked to text her the link. It popped open in Marisa's djinni, and she scrolled down the list of names. "Only three Lavrenti Severovs." She shrugged. "Well, it's late and I'm making poor choices. Let's do this."

She mirrored her audio feed and shared it with Sahara so she could listen in; routing the call to a speaker would be easier, but then the entire police station would be able to hear them. She ran an app she used to hide the origin of a phone call, and then just to be safe she spoofed her ID as well. Her djinni dialed the first number in the list, and it rang twice before a man answered: "Da?"

"Hi," said Marisa. "Do you speak English?"

"Yes," said the man, though his accent was thick as armor. "What do you want?"

"This may seem like a weird question," said Marisa, "but have you ever lived in Los Angeles?"

"Los Angeles?" he asked. "United States?"

"Yes," said Marisa. "Da."

"Never," said the man. "Who is this? What do you want?"

"I'm looking for a Lavrenti Severov who used to live in my neighborhood," said Marisa. "Is maybe your father also Lavrenti? A cousin?"

"No United States," he said. "No Los Angeles. Who is this?"

"Sorry to bother you," said Marisa, and hung up. She looked at Sahara. "Not a mob boss."

"At least, not our mob boss," said Sahara.

"Fair enough." She blinked again, and dialed the next number. "Da?"

"Hi," said Marisa. "Do you speak English?"

"Ya uzhe govoril tebe!" the man shouted. "Ya ne khochu vashey Biblii!" He hung up, and Marisa stared at Sahara with side-eyes.

"I don't know what that was about," said Marisa, "but I'm going to guess he never lived in LA before."

"One left," said Sahara.

Marisa dialed the final number, and waited.

"Da?" said a woman.

"Hi," said Marisa. "Do you speak English?"

"Yes," said the woman. "Are you calling for Teofilo?"

Marisa glanced at Sahara. "Actually, I was calling for Lavrenti."

"Oh, wonderful," said the woman. "Lav so rarely gets calls anymore. Let me get him."

"Well," muttered Marisa. "I guess everyone calls him that?"

"More importantly," said Sahara, "holy old technology, Batman. Are you connected to a landline?"

"Do they even have those anymore?" asked Marisa.

"Apparently in Russia they do," said Sahara. "Or maybe it's a secretary's line? To filter calls?" They waited, and after a moment the call chirped and cut out, and then reconnected to a new host.

"Secretary's line," whispered Sahara. "Whoever you called is important."

"Great," said Marisa. Any last remnant of her giddiness

drained away, and she realized for the first time the gravity of talking to a mob boss.

An old man's voice spoke in a heavy Slavic accent.

"This is Lavrenti Severov."

"Hi," said Marisa. "I'm . . . really sorry to bother you. I hope you won't think it's too . . . forward of me to ask you a question."

The old man paused a moment before answering. "I suppose that depends on the question."

"I guess it does," said Marisa. "I was, um, wondering if you've ever lived in the United States before? In, uh, Los Angeles?"

"Who is this?" asked the man.

"I'm . . . ," said Marisa, and then stopped. She didn't know how to proceed without offending him, or giving away too much information, or just looking like an idiot.

"My assistant has traced this call to a translator satellite operated by an independent nation in international waters," said the man, and Marisa felt her heart begin to sink. She almost closed the call right then, but if they'd only traced as far as the pirate satellite, she still had time. She stayed silent, and listened as he continued. "Usually, when someone does this, it's because they don't want me to know where they are, but you are very clearly in Los Angeles, based both on your accent and the bluntness of your question. I can only assume, then, that you know who I am, and what I used to do, and that you bear some kind of connection to it. Am I correct?"

"You run a crime family," said Marisa. "Or you used to. You controlled territory in a neighborhood called Mirador, and you fought for that territory with a man named Don Francisco Maldonado."

"And now I know that you live in Mirador as well," said Severov. "No one else calls him Don Francisco."

"Sounds like I've got the right Lavrenti Severov," said Marisa. "May I please ask you a couple of questions?"

"I don't do that kind of thing anymore," said Severov. Marisa didn't believe him, but she had the good sense to play along.

"Maldonado's wife died a month or two after you left Mirador," said Marisa. "You're well beyond the reach of what passes for our law enforcement system, so I hope you don't mind answering this because I have to know: Did you kill her?"

"I rejoiced when she died," said Severov, and he said it with such relish that Marisa and Sahara almost shivered as they listened. He paused, and Marisa felt like she couldn't breathe, and then at last he finished: "But I didn't kill her."

"Do you know how she died?"

"A car accident, I heard," said Severov. "Those were rare, even fifteen years ago, but not unheard of."

Marisa felt her hope begin to sink. Did he really not know anything? "But you didn't, like, cut the brakes or anything? Hack the steering system? Plant a bomb in a . . . car thing? I'm sorry, I don't really know much about cars."

"Only pirate satellites," said Severov.

"Do you remember a man named Carneseca?" she asked. "Carlo Magno Carneseca?"

He hesitated a moment before answering. "I don't believe so. Why, was he involved?"

"I was hoping you could tell me," said Marisa. She blinked up the list of names Grendel had sent her, and read them off. "How about Gonzalo Sanchez?"

"No."

"Ricardo Guzmán?"

"No."

"Ingrid Castañeda?"

"Was she . . ." He paused. "One of his enforcers?"

"She was," said Marisa. "They all were. Did you have any of them killed?"

"Probably," said the man. "It was a very bloody war. But you can't expect me to remember every soldier who died in it."

"These three died on the same day as Zenaida de Maldonado," said Marisa. "We wondered if maybe you'd taken them all out in a coordinated attack."

"I left Mirador with my tail between my legs," said Severov. "It was all I could do to keep my own backers from executing me for my failure. I longed to destroy Maldonado and his family, and I long for it to this day, but I left and I never looked back. The deaths you describe certainly sound like a coordinated attack, but I was not the author of it."

Marisa sighed. "So you have no knowledge of any of these people, or anything that happened to them?"

Severov's next question sounded more . . . hungry than Marisa was expecting: "Why are you so interested in the past?"

"It's a local legend," said Marisa, glancing at Sahara. "With a lot of unanswered questions. I'm just curious about what really happened."

"And what would you be willing to do to find out?"

Marisa made a face, feeling suddenly dirty at the direction the conversation had taken. "Nothing illegal."

"You've already done something illegal by bouncing your phone signal through some of these unlicensed carriers," he said. "Pirates, Nigeria, Croatia—that one's an embargo violation, that's very serious—"

"Let's just say I have a casual relationship with those sorts of laws," said Marisa, feigning confidence, but she looked at the hang-up icon again, ready to sever the call in the literal blink of an eye.

"Ha!" said Severov. "In that case, for now, at least, we are still allies."

"I don't like the sound of that," whispered Sahara.

"Francisco Maldonado killed my children," said Severov. "The pain of that wound is as fierce today as it was fifteen years ago. I want to hurt him, and from the direction of your questions I can tell that you hold no special love for him either, so it seems that we share not only a common enemy but a common goal."

"I really need to stop talking to mob bosses," said Marisa.

Severov laughed, with more humor than she'd expected. "I like you," he said. "I sincerely hope that we can remain allies, because I would hate to become your enemy."

"Thank you?"

"In the last fifteen years, I have reestablished my base of power, and . . . outlived some of my rivals. I don't control Mirador, but I have people in Los Angeles who answer to me. I would love to give them a target."

Marisa swallowed. "I'm glad we're such good friends, then."

"So am I," said Severov. "I suggest that you do what you can to keep us that way."

"Great Holy Handgrenades," breathed Sahara.

"Okay," said Marisa.

"I'll talk to you soon," said Severov, and closed the call.

Marisa stared at the wall for a moment, and then hurriedly blinked into her djinni and scrubbed the trail she'd used to hide her identity. How far had he traced her?

"That's really not how I wanted that to go," she said.

Sahara smirked. "Did the way you wanted it to go have any bearing on reality?"

"Probably not." Marisa groaned and covered her face with her hands. "That's the last time we make important life decisions at three in the morning."

"Amen to that."

"And it didn't even give us anything," said Marisa, uncovering her face. "He was our last lead, and instead of telling us something valuable he just threatened to kill us and tried to draft us into the Russian mob."

"Oh, but he did give us something," said Sahara. Marisa looked at her, confused, and Sahara shrugged. "He told us we were wrong about a clue. That's like getting the whole clue back over again. Fresh slate."

Marisa shook her head. "Losing him as a suspect doesn't count as a fresh slate unless we replace him with somebody else."

"But that's the thing," said Sahara. "Severov was *never* the clue—the three names from Grendel were. We thought they pointed to Severov, but they didn't. They have to point somewhere else. So: If they weren't killed by Severov, who were they killed by?"

"Maybe Memo," said Marisa. "Or La Sesenta in general. People keep looking for Memo, so there's got to be a reason why. And he's old enough that he could have been out shooting people fifteen years ago, maybe. His older brother Goyo definitely could have."

"That fits some of the puzzle pieces," said Sahara, "but not all of them. Even if Memo killed Zenaida, that doesn't explain why ZooMorrow's after him."

"True," said Marisa. "Unless . . ." She turned to face Sahara, laying out a new theory. "The other day we figured out that Zenaida probably had ZooMorrow genhancements—that's why ZooMorrow was able to claim that hand from police custody, because her DNA had their proprietary tech in it. So: What if Zenaida was a ZooMorrow agent, kind of like Bennett but not as . . . advanced . . . and then Memo killed her, and now they want revenge?"

"Why now, though?" asked Sahara. "Why not fifteen years ago?"

"Because . . . I don't know because," said Marisa. "Because it got lost in the shuffle, and Zenaida's DNA popping up in a police registry reminded them that oh yeah, we need to go kill that one guy."

"That's pretty flimsy reasoning."

"It's three in the morning," said Marisa. "What do you want from me?"

"I want to connect these three other deaths to Zenaida's," said

Sahara. She slumped down in her chair and stared up at the ceiling. "You think Memo would just tell us if we asked?"

"If he even remembers?" asked Marisa. "If he doesn't shoot us on sight for losing his djinni?" She slumped down next to Sahara, resting her head against her friend's, and stared at the ceiling with her. "Let's look at this from a different direction: We know that Zenaida had ZooMorrow genhancements, right? No Mantissassin eyes, but something. Enough that ZooMorrow's trying to protect it, and cutting-edge enough that they still consider the tech to be a proprietary secret fifteen years later. So: What if she stole it from them?"

"That doesn't seem very smart," said Sahara. "They have creepy Mantissassins to come and kill people who do that kind of thing." She thought about it for half a moment, then sat bolt upright in the waiting room chair, sending Marisa sprawling to the side. "Holy crap. ZooMorrow has assassins."

"Exactly!" said Marisa, pulling herself back to a sitting position. "Assassins who are more than capable of killing three gang enforcers all in the same day—if they had a reason to. And since their primary reason for doing anything seems to be protecting ZooMorrow's interests, what if they killed the Maldonado enforcers for having the same technology Zenaida did?"

"Wait," said Sahara, "you lost me. What does this have to do with stealing?"

"Sorry," said Marisa, "these pieces came together a weird way in my head, so I'm retelling them to you in the order that makes the most sense."

"No you're not."

"Okay," said Marisa, "think about it like this: Zenaida had a job at ZooMorrow, as some kind of scientist, so maybe she had access to the tech and started stealing it to help soup up the Maldonado soldiers for the war with the Severovs. They were desperate—they'd do anything to win, and to protect their family from a rival attack. And then they won the war, but ZooMorrow figured it out and came to claim their proprietary tech. In a police station they can just take it, like Bennett did with the hand, but out there on the street, especially against a trained fighter, they had to ask more forcefully. ZooMorrow sent in the brute squad, Zenaida knew they were coming, and she tried to run."

"This . . . actually works really well," said Sahara. "I think you're onto something."

"Thanks," said Marisa. "I have all my best ideas at three a.m."

"We need to verify it," said Sahara. "And we're in exactly the right place—the police keep files of every murder they investigate, including the DNA tests of the corpses. All we have to do is . . . damn it." She closed her eyes. "All we have to do is hack into the frakking police station, which we've already tried and failed at how many times?"

"We could just ask," said Marisa. "We're right here."

"And they're going to show them to us why?" asked Sahara. "We're teenagers, not detectives."

Marisa blinked to open a search window. "I bet I could register us as private detectives inside of five minutes, tops."

"And the police still won't care," said Sahara. "We don't need legitimacy, we need . . . influence. Money or power or . . . Anja. We need Anja."

"Tapping into Anja's power and influence means using Anja's dad," said Marisa. "He doesn't like us, and he especially doesn't like us when we drag his daughter and/or his company through a police station. He'll never agree to help us. But there's someone who might. . . ."

"Ugh," said Sahara, rolling her eyes. "Don't say Omar."

"Omar," said Marisa. "He's gotten us info before, including from the police. We know he can do it, and we know he's motivated."

"We're calling on him too much," said Sahara. "*You're* calling on him too much. The only reason he's not the single most untrustworthy person we know is because we also know the rest of his family."

"He'll help us," Marisa insisted. "He wants to find out what happened to Zenaida even more than we do."

"So call him," said Sahara, "but I want it on the record that I oppose this."

And that's where Marisa hesitated. Talking about Omar's help was one thing, but actually asking him for it was another. Their goals were aligned, but he was still miles away from sympathetic. Let alone trustworthy.

And yet . . .

She wrote a quick email message, explaining the DNA records and why they wanted to see them, and sent it with a blink.

A moment later Detective Hendel opened the door to the interrogation room, and held it open while a pair of uniformed officers led Andy Song down the hall toward the overnight cells. She let out a sigh, then walked toward the girls.

"Looks like you can go," she said. "He wanted to press charges for breaking and entering, but his house computer shows that he invited you in, so . . . you're good."

"What did the house computer say about the smashed bioprinter?" asked Sahara, looking perfectly innocent.

Detective Hendel smirked. "Nothing, and neither did Song. Turns out that that particular device was reported stolen about six weeks ago, and Andy claims never to have seen it before in his life." She shrugged, and added airily: "I guess we might never find out who smashed it."

"It was already smashed when we got there," said Sahara. "I'm pretty sure."

"So," said Hendel. "You've given your reports, we've taken your statements, and you're done. The city of Los Angeles thanks you for your help in solving this crime. I can get a squad car to drive you home if you want."

"We have a question first," said Marisa. "And I know it's a weird question, but: we need to look at the DNA files of three people who were murdered fifteen years ago."

"Are you kidding?" asked Hendel.

Marisa smiled as sweetly as she knew how. "No?"

"I can't release police records to just anyone off the street," said Hendel.

"They relate to this case," said Sahara.

Hendel shook her head. "This case is closed."

"Are *you* kidding now?" asked Marisa. "We still don't know who killed Zenaida!"

"A car accident killed Zenaida," said Hendel. "Fifteen years ago."

"But—"

"This case," said Hendel, cutting her off, "was about a severed hand. We thought it was a murder, but it was an unlicensed bioprinter. Case closed, job done."

"But I saw—" This time Marisa stopped herself. Claiming to have seen a ghost, or whatever it was she'd seen, would only make Hendel trust her less. "There are still too many loose ends," she said instead. "Why did ZooMorrow take the hand out of your custody? How did the world's most inept black-market bioprinter get hold of fifteen-year-old-corpse DNA?"

Hendel leaned in closely, lowering her voice to a distinctly conspiratorial pitch. "Yes, I know there's more to this," she said, "but what do you want me to do? We're barely functioning as a law enforcement agency as it is; megacorps have all the real legal power, and they've put substantial pressure on my bosses, who have put that pressure on me. A murder I can investigate, but thanks to Andy Song, this is no longer a murder investigation. It's out of our hands."

"Who put pressure on you?" asked Marisa. "ZooMorrow?"

"I'm not at liberty to say."

"They're probably the killers," said Sahara. "They can't just stop you from investigating them."

"If there's something to find, I'll find it," said Hendel. "But this case is closed. Go home and go to sleep."

A message popped up in Marisa's vision, bouncing cheerfully for her attention. Omar. She blinked on it, and found six short words:

Done. Tell me what you find.

What had he done? She hadn't even known he was awake.

"I'm looking for a Ms. Carneseca," said a voice. Marisa looked up, bewildered, and saw a police officer standing next to her with a clear glass tablet.

Sahara pointed at Marisa. "Right here."

"I've been instructed to give this to you," said the officer. "Three murder files: Gonzalo Sanchez, Ricardo Guzmán, and Ingrid Castañeda."

Marisa smiled.

"Hold up," said Detective Hendel, putting her hand on the tablet. "Whose orders?"

"Straight from the top," said the officer. "Chief Grace."

"Thank you," said Marisa, and took the tablet from him, gently pulling it away from Hendel's hand and tapping on the glass to wake it up. It was a standard data slate—low onboard memory with a rechargeable battery, designed for on-site collaboration. The police didn't want to send old files to anyone's djinni, where they could make or edit a copy, so they shared it temporarily through devices like this. The screen showed three files, and Marisa tapped one. It opened into a giant cascade of data, and she bit her lip in confused frustration.

"Do you actually know how to read a police file?" asked Hendel.

"I do not," said Marisa, staring at the numbers and fields and abbreviations. "I can't even see the guy's name."

Hendel sighed. "I don't know how you did it, but fine. You got your files. Come into my office and let's at least make sure you use them correctly." They followed her down the hall to the same office Marisa had sat in before, and Marisa laid the data screen on the desk.

Hendel sat behind it, tapped it quickly in a few key places, and looked at them expectantly. "What do you want to know?"

"The DNA records," said Marisa. "We're looking for any kind of genhancement or gengineering or anything like that."

"From ZooMorrow?" asked Hendel. Sahara nodded, and Hendel looked down at the slate. Her fingers practically danced across it, tapping and swiping and moving the data around. A moment later she furrowed her brow, frowning at the screen, and her tapping became more intense. She paused on something, read it intently, and looked up at the girls with an impressed nod. "Well then. This is the first of the three records—Gonzalo Sanchez—and portions of the DNA information have been redacted, under, believe it or not, federal statute 7o.3482. The same one Zoo-Morrow claimed when they took Zenaida's hand. Protection of proprietary technology. So this doesn't prove Sanchez had genhancements, but it's pretty hard to read it any other way."

"Check the other two," said Marisa. She didn't dare to say more, worried that the spell would break and the detective would stop helping them.

Hendel looked back at the screen, tapping her way through the reports. "Second says the same thing," she murmured, and then a moment later: "Yeah. All three." She looked up. "Who are these people?"

"Enforcers in the Maldonado crime family," said Sahara. "As I'm sure you noticed, they all died on the same day as Zenaida."

"Yeah," said Hendel. "That's pretty suspicious, isn't it?"

"Can you look up accidents as well as murders?" asked Marisa. "Can we see if Zenaida's DNA had the same redacted info?"

"We're in this far," said Hendel with a shrug. "May as well keep going." She turned to her own computer screen, directly tied to the LAPD database, and called up the records of Zenaida's fatal car accident. She studied them for a moment, then shook her head. "Nothing. Which . . . makes no sense. Hang on." She tapped again, searching for another set of records, and then another, and displayed all three side by side. "Look: the DNA tests from the severed hands—or I guess the bioprinted hands—are redacted, just like those other three. ZooMorrow did it at the same time they took the hands away. But this old DNA test from Zenaida's car accident isn't even touched."

"Does it have any genhancements?" asked Marisa.

"No," said Hendel, "but it's more than that. They're not the same DNA." She tapped a few buttons. "See? The comparison software doesn't even think they're the same person."

"Maybe they're not," said Sahara. "Do you have anything you can compare this to? Like a . . . I don't know, one of Zenaida's old hospital visits or something?"

"I can get one," said Hendel. She swiped the three DNA tests into the corner of her screen, and then went online to connect to a hospital. She smiled as she typed. "Police don't have a lot of authority anymore, but we've got plenty of access. These records are sealed, but with the right authorization . . . Got it." Another file opened on the screen, and she clicked her teeth idly while she read it. "Postpartum checkup from three years before the accident. Mommy Zenaida and Baby Omar are perfectly healthy, and this DNA test . . ." She tapped it, bringing it alongside the other three, and then ran a comparison of all four together. It cycled for a moment, then beeped and lit up in bright green and red.

"Even I can read that," said Marisa, looking at the screen. "The DNA from the hospital visit matches the DNA from the two hands. That's the real Zenaida. The DNA from the car accident is someone else."

"But that's ridiculous," said Sahara. "How can the police not know who died in a car accident and who didn't?"

"You have to consider the situation," said Hendel, hiding the other files and focusing on the accident. "First, this was fifteen years ago. Standardized DNA testing was common but it was still new; we probably didn't have anything from Zenaida on file at the precinct. On top of that, the actual identification of the corpse was done at the hospital, not by the police; they probably just ran the DNA and filed the test away without looking at it, because see this? It says she was dead on arrival. There was nothing they could do, so they didn't do anything."

"Then why did they say it was Zenaida?" asked Marisa. "Somebody else died in that car accident, and we've thought it was the wrong person for fifteen years."

Hendel pointed to an entry field in the report. "It says the identity was determined visually. See here? Two people."

Marisa held her breath.

"Who?" asked Sahara.

Hendel turned to face the girls. "Francisco Maldonado and Carlo Magno Carneseca."

FOURTEEN

"So . . ." Sahara stared at the computer screen. "Is Zenaida alive or not?"

Marisa was too stunned to say anything.

"I don't have enough evidence to say," said Hendel. "We know that she didn't die in this car crash, but beyond that? We have no information to work with."

"But if you had to guess," said Sahara. "I mean, she must have gone into hiding, right? How else could you interpret this?"

"That's a *big* leap of logic," said Hendel.

"No it's not," said Sahara, leaning forward. "ZooMorrow was trying to kill people who were using stolen genhancements. Zenaida was the one who stole them, and obviously had some herself, so she had to go into hiding to stay alive. Carlo Magno and Don Francisco covered for her, identifying someone else's body as hers so that ZooMorrow would stop chasing her."

"That answers a lot of the questions we're finding," said Hendel, "but we have no evidence for it."

Sahara's eyes widened in disbelief. "Then how do you explain it? Any of it?"

"I can't yet," said Hendel.

"This is the only way that makes sense," said Sahara. "ZooMorrow gave up looking for her, and everyone thought it was over, until somebody stole her DNA data and sold it to Andy Song, who let it get out and it ended up at a crime scene and you ran a test and boom: ZooMorrow knows she's still alive and all hell breaks loose."

"You might be right," said Hendel. "It's a fine theory, given all the data we have. But 'fine' is a long way away from 'solid,' let alone 'actionable,' and I have to do things by the book. And you shouldn't be doing things at all, no matter what strings you can pull to get a look at our files. I'll investigate more, when I can, but you're just kids, and you're kids I already told to go home and go to sleep."

Marisa shook her head. "But if Zenaida's still out there—" She stopped suddenly, interrupted by a message from Omar. She blinked on it:

Sergio knows I called the police, and he's mad as hell. He must have an informant in the station. Get out now.

"Mierda," said Marisa.

"What's wrong?" asked Sahara.

Marisa's eyes went straight to the door. "Sergio Maldonado's on his way here."

"The Mirador police chief?" asked Hendel.

"He's Don Francisco's son," said Marisa. "He found out that Omar pulled some strings to release those DNA files."

"He has no authority here," said Hendel. "This is South Central. Though if he's got ears inside my station . . ." She grumbled angrily and stalked to the door. Marisa and Sahara followed, and heard angry shouting before they were even halfway down the hall.

". . . doesn't matter," said a male voice. "This is out of your jurisdiction—"

"She's my mother!" shouted Sergio.

"What's going on here?" demanded Hendel. They rounded the corner and found Sergio in a rumpled uniform, yelling at the officer at the front desk. "Maldonado, is there something I can help you with?"

"What's she doing here?" asked Sergio, pointing a finger at Marisa. "She has no right to look through those files."

"I agree," said Hendel, calm but firm. "I told her no, but the order came from the top of the chain. Chief Grace herself."

Sergio sneered. "Because my idiot brother said the family wanted her to have them."

"Then it sounds like you should take this up with your brother," said Hendel, "not yell at my officers."

"I don't know how you do things down here in South Central—" said Sergio, and Detective Hendel cut him off before he could finish.

"We do them the right way," she said.

Sergio continued as if she hadn't interrupted: "But in my precinct, we look out for each other. You should have called me."

Hendel stared. "To get your approval on something the head of the LAPD already approved?"

"As a professional courtesy," said Sergio.

"Oh, grow up," said Marisa. She was too tired, and too scared, to have any filter on her words. "There's a world outside of Mirador, and you're not in charge of it."

"You watch your mouth," snapped Sergio.

"Why?" asked Marisa. "Out of respect for the half-dressed chango screaming about how he doesn't get everything he wants?"

"Easy," whispered Sahara, tugging gently on her arm.

"That is no way to speak to an officer of the law!" shouted Sergio.

"I'm not speaking to an officer of the law," shouted Marisa, "I'm speaking to a mobster in a uniform!"

Sergio stepped toward her, but Hendel planted herself between them. "Everybody calm down!" she roared. "This is my precinct!"

"You're a whore," said Sergio, growling at Marisa over Hendel's shoulder. "You and your damn father."

The front door slid open, and Omar was shouting at Sergio before he even entered the building. "What have you done?"

Sergio never took his eyes off of Marisa. "Not now, Omar."

"Father's on his way here," said Omar, stepping inside. The door closed behind him. "Spitting nails. You've stirred up a whole chingado hornet's nest, Sergio."

Sergio whirled on him. "If he's coming, then I'll talk to him in person," he said, "not his jumped-up little mini-me."

"Are you sure that's what you want?" asked Omar. "Because it is not going to be pleasant for you."

"Why's he mad at me?" asked Sergio. "I'm the one trying to protect this family while you're out telling our secrets to every little slut with a nice pair of—"

"You will speak with respect in my building," boomed Hendel. Her voice echoed so loudly through the foyer Marisa thought she must have amplified it somehow. Maybe with a hidden implant.

"I'm sorry," said Omar, and he turned on his charm as he walked toward Hendel. Even at four in the morning his smile could stop a freight train. He stuck out his hand. "It's good to see you again, Detective. I'm sorry that you've gotten caught up in this."

"I'm delighted by it," said Hendel dryly. She shook his offered hand. "Before tonight I didn't realize how easily the Maldonados could go over my head." She shot a glance at Sergio. "Or how thoroughly they'd infiltrated my own department."

"We have nothing but the utmost respect for the LAPD," said Omar, "and for the brave work you do every day enforcing the law."

"What little of it we're still allowed to enforce," said Hendel. "How much longer before your family incorporates fully, and starts making and enforcing your own set of laws?"

"They've been doing that for years," said Marisa.

"And you're not going to be in her station forever," said Sergio. "Remember where you live."

"Is that a threat?" asked Marisa.

"It's not a threat," said Omar.

"It sounded like a threat," said Hendel.

"Detective Hendel," said Omar, trying to regain control of the conversation. "I called Chief Grace to get those files released, and when my brother found out about it he called my father, who is now on his way here. Frankly, I don't know whose head he's going to cut off."

"Yours," said Sergio.

"Possibly," said Omar. "It is my recommendation that none of us be here when he arrives."

"And let Officer Diamond take the brunt of Don Francisco's rage?" asked Hendel, gesturing at the officer still standing behind the front desk. "I don't think so. If something needs to be hashed out, let's hash it out."

"You won't like the way my father hashes things," said Omar.

The front door opened, sensing an approaching figure, and Marisa heard a programmed voice drifting through the night air: "Your heart rate is approaching dangerous levels. You should rest."

"Triste Chango," said Sahara.

"Papi?" whispered Marisa.

Carlo Magno came puffing through the door, wearing loose hospital scrubs and leaning heavily on his cane. "Marisa Carneseca Sanchez!"

"Papi!" shouted Marisa, running toward him. "What are you doing here? You're going to rip your stitches!"

"Then I'm going to take you down with me," said Carlo Magno. "You told me you were doing homework tonight! You promised me! And now I find you in the police station! Qué no me vengan las maldiciones de una hija tan malcriada!"

"Why are you even here?" asked Marisa. "How did you know?"

"My father called him," said Omar.

"And I'm twice as angry as he'll be," said Carlo Magno, and roared at Marisa: "This is the second time I've had to pick you up from a police station in the middle of the night! What do I have to do to get through to you?"

"I'm here reporting a crime," said Marisa, "not committing one."

"And that means you didn't lie to me?"

"We caught the guy who had the hands," Marisa shouted. "And he wasn't even dangerous, he was just a bioprinter! Detective Hendel can tell you!"

"I told you seventeen times tonight that you shouldn't have been out," said Hendel, "and I've tried to send you home seventeen more."

"Thanks for the support," muttered Marisa, and pulled her father toward a chair. "Sit down before you fall apart. I don't want to have to catch your liver when it tumbles out of your gaping, unhealed surgery hole."

"It is called an incision," said Triste Chango, pressing in close and extending a servo arm with a hypodermic syringe. "Please hold still. You need medication."

"I know what it's called," muttered Marisa.

Her father swatted at the syringe. "Get that away from me."

The medical nuli switched targets, from Carlo Magno's chest to his hand, and managed a solid hit with the hypodermic syringe. It let out a loud puff of air, applying a contact medicine directly to his skin. He gasped at the touch—hypodermics didn't prick your skin, but they still stung—and Marisa finally managed to sit him down in a chair.

"You're going to put yourself back in the hospital," she said.

"Better me than you," wheezed Carlo Magno.

The door opened a third time, and there he was: Don Francisco Maldonado, his black suit neatly pressed but his face puffy from sleep, and his thinning hair hurriedly plastered to his head with too much gel and water. He was flanked by two hulking enforcers, each of them heavily rebuilt with menacing bionics. All three of them froze in unison when Francisco saw Carlo Magno.

"I told you not to come here."

"And I told you I don't care," said Carlo Magno.

"Finally," said Sergio. "Let's get rid of the whole family once and for all."

Hendel put her hand on the sidearm holstered at her hip, completely unintimidated by the massive Maldonado thugs. "Like hell you are."

"I don't mean kill them," said Sergio, and turned to Carlo Magno in a fury. "I mean run them out of town! Get them out of our sight for good!"

"You be quiet," said Don Francisco, hissing each word through clenched teeth. "I give the orders, not you."

"Then give this one," said Sergio. "We've tolerated them long enough."

Whatever the feud was about, Marisa realized, Sergio knew it as keenly as both of the patriarchs. And it infuriated him.

Don Francisco looked at Carlo Magno. "Maybe it's time."

"You promised," said Carlo Magno. "Protection for me and my family."

"Why!" shouted Sergio. "Just because you—"

"I told you to be quiet!" Don Francisco's voice was a mountain of sound, shaking Marisa's ears like a tangible force. "There are some things we don't talk about!"

"She's not worth protecting," Sergio spat.

Marisa was done dealing with their nonsense. "Just get over yourselves," she said. "Screaming at each other like children. You're mad at Sergio for talking? Talking is the only way any of this is ever getting solved."

"Mari," her father warned.

She ignored him.

"You're mad at Omar for releasing the police files?" she continued, stepping toward Don Francisco. "He thought he was helping find his own mother. How was he supposed to know you two pendejos"—she pointed at the don and her father—"were the ones who helped her run away in the first place?" She looked at Omar. "That's what we found in the files, by the way: our fathers lied to the hospital about the body in the accident. She didn't die fifteen years ago."

Don Francisco stared back at her, his face a careful mask of cold, seething fury. "This is the part," he said softly, "where you back up three steps and apologize."

Marisa planted herself directly in front of him, her hands on her hips. "You don't know me very well."

"Marisa, back up," said her father.

"You've heard what he says," she shouted, "and you've heard what he thinks of you—don't you dare start taking his side in this!"

"You don't even know what this is," said Francisco.

"So tell me."

"Leave it alone, Mari," said Carlo Magno.

"Somebody just say something!" she shouted. "Anything!" She felt her frustration boiling inside of her like a cauldron full of superheated magma, threatening to explode out the top and melt through the sides. She shouted again, and realized that she was crying. "You're not the only ones in this! You're not the only ones who get to know! You lost your wife? I lost my arm, and years of my life, and any trust I ever had in my father!" She clasped her hands together, flesh and metal in a viselike grip. "Just tell me where Zenaida is. Just tell me why I was in the car. Just tell me *what happened.*"

And then she was there, popping into existence without a sign or a sound or a rustle of air. She stood behind the bionic enforcers, dressed differently than before and staring at Marisa over Don Francisco's shoulder.

Zenaida.

Marisa took a step back.

"Oh, now you back up?" asked Don Francisco. He saw the direction of her eyes and looked over his own shoulder but didn't seem to see anything.

"Are you okay?" asked Sahara.

Zenaida walked forward, passing through the enforcers and Don Francisco like they weren't even there. She never took her eyes off Marisa.

Her face was cold and cruel and triumphant.

She walked straight toward Marisa, raised a gun, and fired.

FIFTEEN

Marisa screamed, covering her face and flinching away from the attack.

Nothing happened. She opened her eyes, and Zenaida was gone.

"Did you see her again?" asked Sahara.

"Who?" asked Carlo Magno. He was on his feet, shuffling toward her, but Marisa hadn't seen him stand.

"Zenaida," said Omar, looking at Marisa. It wasn't a question but a statement. "She attacked you."

"You saw her?" asked Marisa, but Omar shook his head.

"Not here," he said, and glanced at his father—just for a second, never making eye contact—and then looked away. "But I've seen it before."

"We're leaving," said Don Francisco. He spun his finger in the air, right at shoulder level, gathering his people with a single gesture. One of the enforcers stepped toward the door, triggering the sensor, and held it open with a heavy metal arm. Sergio followed without a moment of argument. Francisco looked at Hendel, and Marisa tried to decipher the look on his face: authority, yes, and resolution, but also . . . fear?

Did he know what Marisa had seen?

Was Zenaida haunting him, too?

"Seal those files," he told Hendel. "You can wait for Chief Grace if you want, but she'll call and tell you the same within the next ten minutes." He turned and walked out, and his enforcers followed.

Omar followed last of all, his head hung low.

"Mari," said Carlo Magno. He tried to put a hand on her shoulder, but she brushed it off and stepped away.

"Don't talk to me," she said.

"Marisa," he said again, though this time his voice had sharpened from consolation to impatience. "We're leaving too. I've called a cab—"

"I'm not going with you," she said, and walked toward the door. The last thing she wanted to hear right now was more excuses, or more hollow platitudes of love or family or letting go of the past or whatever other idiocy he was going to repeat. "And don't follow me."

"Marisa!"

The door opened for her, and she walked out into the predawn haze.

Four thirty in the morning. The city was already shifting from black to dark purple, the ambient light growing faintly stronger as the world slowly came awake. She took a deep breath, closing her eyes and tilting her head up toward the sky.

"Hey," said Omar. Marisa looked to the side and saw him leaning in the shadow of a palm tree.

"I thought you left," she said.

"I left the building," he explained. "But I can't be with my father right now." He jerked his head toward the door behind her. "Sounds like you said the same to yours."

"I don't know if I can ever see him again," she said. "He just makes me so . . . I don't know. Mad, angry, furious, frustrated, confused . . ."

"Betrayed," offered Omar.

"Exactly," said Marisa. She glanced over her shoulder, seeing Carlo Magno inside the police station, talking to Detective Hendel. "Let's get out of here before he comes out."

"I have my car," said Omar, but Marisa shook her head.

"I just want to walk around for a while."

Omar nodded, and fell in step beside her.

Los Angeles was never really asleep, but this time of day was its quietest. Nightclubs and bars and such were finally closed or closing, and nothing else had opened yet except maybe a bakery here and there, or a twenty-four-hour diner selling coffee and artificial eggs. The street with the police station had none of these, and no traffic aside from the omnipresent passage of nulis overhead, shipping goods and documents and everything else in the world, back and forth in an endless dance. Marisa stuffed her hands in her pockets, feeling the different sensations from one hand to another. Even advanced cybernetics couldn't feel things exactly the same way flesh did. It had become a part of her life, familiar and even comforting at times, but now it only made her feel broken.

She walked without purpose, willing to go wherever her feet pointed her. After the third turn she realized that Omar was leading her subtly. "Where are we going?"

"On a different route than an autocab will take your father," said Omar. "Even if he's not following you, I assume you don't want him to accidentally spot you with a Maldonado."

"Ugh," said Marisa, simultaneously grateful for his foresight, angry that it was necessary, and embarrassed that he would accept so calmly his role as a villain. "Thank you," she said. "I'm sorry that . . ." She didn't know how to finish the sentence. Sorry that their families couldn't figure this out? Sorry that they kept giving each other so many reasons not to? There was a time she wouldn't have been caught dead with Omar in any capacity, let alone just the two of them, walking in the dark and sharing . . .

Sharing what? Silence? Emotional weight?

"My mother tried to shoot you," said Omar.

Marisa nodded. She hadn't said it out loud, and yet he knew, which could only mean: "I assume she's shot at you, too?"

"A couple of times," said Omar. "It's one thing to have your mother run away from you, but to have her pull a gun . . ."

She put a hand on his arm. "I'm sorry."

"It's not your fault."

"I know. But I . . . can't stand to see you like this."

He stopped, and turned toward her. His eyes were as dark as onyx, and she was suddenly struck by the way he looked at her—intense and probing, like he was looking at her and into her and through her all at once. She swallowed, and realized her hand was still on his arm. She left it there.

"My sister saw her, too," said Omar, his voice soft but strong. "I only know because I heard her talking in her sleep. I'm amazed anyone can sleep in that house anymore, but . . . I was up the other night, sitting in the library, which is just down the hall from her room, and she started talking to her: 'Mama, please come back. Don't run away from me. I don't want to hurt you.' She's seeing the same things that you are, and that I am, and for all I know our whole family is, but my family never talks to each other. We can't. We can't open up, and we can't trust anyone, and as big of a wreck as I am right now, I think I'm doing better than any of the others because I have . . ." He shrugged. "You. To talk to. And they don't have anyone, not even each other." He turned away suddenly, and took a step away to continue down the sidewalk, but she tightened her grip on his arm, no longer touching it but holding it. She felt his arm move under his sleeve, and his muscle tense under his skin.

"Thank you for trusting me," she said. "And thank you for being someone I can talk to, too."

He turned back, and looked at her again with those dark eyes. She stepped closer.

"Do you ever wish," she said, "that we could just forget who we are? Forget what we've done, and where we come from, and our families and our fathers and everything else and just . . ." She watched his mouth, tinted blue in the morning light. "Just be?"

"Be what?" It was more of a breath than a sentence.

"I guess that depends," said Marisa, and looked up from his

mouth to his eyes. "What do you want to be?"

He stared back at her, not speaking, until finally he whispered, "I want to be here."

Marisa swallowed again. "So do I."

His arm was warm under her real fingers, and she wanted to know what he felt like on her metal ones. She reached up and touched his other arm, feeling the texture of his shirt, and the strength in his bicep, and—very slowly—the warmth of his body coming out through the fabric. The rest of her body felt suddenly cold, and she shivered. He stepped toward her, putting his hands on her waist.

She looked at his mouth again, and parted her lips. She had never wanted to kiss someone so badly in her life.

"Marisa," he whispered, and leaned toward her—

—and froze abruptly, his hands tightening on her, stiff and tense.

"She's here," he said.

The spell was broken. She swallowed, trying to focus. "Zenaida?" she asked.

Omar nodded. "Right behind you. Staring at me, and holding a gun."

"The same vision as before?"

"Yeah." He loosened his grip and turned her slowly. "Do you see her?"

"No."

They were standing on a sidewalk in front of what looked like a mechanic's shop, or maybe an impound lot—a high chain-link fence topped with razor wire surrounded a lot full of autocars, packed too tightly to be a dealership. He pointed toward one of the cars, a red one with sleek, predatory angles. "She's standing in that one," he said. "Her shoulders just come out of the top of it, and I can see her body through the windows." He tensed again. "Now she's coming toward me, right through the fence like water through a sieve."

"Describe her," said Marisa quickly. Could they learn something from the details? "She's dressed differently than in the other vision, right? Not a dress, but some kind of—"

"A vest," he said. "And canvas pants, and . . . it almost looks like tactical gear. She's raising the gun now—she's about to fire it—"

"What kind is it?"

"I don't know—"

"Snap a photo!" she shouted.

He blinked and flinched, and then let out a breath as his body relaxed. "She's gone."

"Did you get a photo?"

"I think so.

"Why didn't I think to get a photo before?" she asked. "Or even video?" She turned away from the lot and grabbed his arm again. "Check the photo—does she show up in it?"

He blinked, then blinked again, then shook his head. "No. Damn it."

"So you can see her but your djinni can't," she said. "How is that possible? It's supposed to be tied directly to your sensory feeds."

"Ghosts don't have to follow the rules," said Omar.

"Holograms do," said Marisa. "So she's not that. I bet she still follows some rules, though; we just don't know what they are." She paced a few steps away. "Something changed: she's wearing different clothes, and she has a gun. She's attacking instead of running away—that has to mean something."

"It doesn't make sense!"

"Just describe her," she said, trying to calm him. "Don't worry about figuring everything out, just tell me what you remember."

"She had . . . like, tac gear, like I said." He shook his head, still staring at the spot where she'd been, as if trying to re-create her with his mind. "Not armor or camo, just black and brown clothes, and the vest had pockets all over it. Like a soldier would use to keep their ammo in."

"Did she have ammo?"

"No." He sucked in a breath. "And I don't think the gun takes normal ammo anyway. It didn't have a barrel."

"Like . . . it was just a grip?" She made a motion with her hand, pulling on an imaginary trigger. "The one I saw was a legit gun."

"It was a gun," said Omar, "with a grip and a barrel and everything, but it didn't have the hole in the barrel. There was nowhere for bullets to come out."

Marisa looked at the same spot by the fence, though of course she couldn't see anything but chain link and cars. She could almost see the gun in her memory. "You're right," she said, closing her eyes. "I couldn't put my finger on it, but I don't remember a hole in the barrel either. And it wasn't a taser or a stun gun or anything, it was—" Her eyes went wide. "Santa vaca."

"What was it?"

"I know where I've seen that kind of a gun," she said, and looked him square in the face. "We use them in Overworld sometimes, when the other team has a lot of nulis. It's a directed EMP."

"She used a nuli gun?"

"Definitely."

"That doesn't make sense," said Omar. He blinked, and after a moment his eyes went wide. "Holy crap." He sent her a link, and she blinked on it immediately, finding an image search with a picture of a thick gray handgun.

"That's it," she said. "That's the gun I saw."

"Me too," said Omar. "It's called an Arvo 350. 'Directed EMP, guaranteed to drop invasive or antagonistic nulis at close range.'" He looked at Marisa. "My mom shot us with a nuli gun."

A slow, wide smile started spreading across Marisa's face. "Did she? Or did she shoot a *nuli* with a nuli gun?"

Omar frowned. "What do you mean?"

"I mean what if this is a recording?" asked Marisa. "A VR recording, but instead of seeing it as a hologram we're seeing through augmented reality. What if Zenaida was being chased by a nuli, like the kind my brother modified for his science project— a seeker nuli designed to follow a specific signal or person or whatever. They even have seekers that can track DNA now; that's how they protect endangered animals. So it found her, and it took video of her running away, and then it found her again and took video of her shutting it down with an Arvo."

"Then why are *we* seeing them?" asked Omar.

"Because we . . ." She struggled to put it all together. "Because it's malware. We got the videos through a virus—" She nodded, the pieces falling into place. "It's got to be your house computer. That's the common factor between everyone who's seen the ghost visions—they've all connected to that computer."

"If this is true," said Omar, "we can find out pretty quick. I'll run a virus scan on my djinni."

"You won't find anything," said Marisa. "I did a scan yesterday, for normal maintenance, and didn't find a thing. This will take a manual search. And it might take a while, so I want to sit down." She looked up and down the street, and then grabbed his hand and pulled him toward a yellow neon light. "Follow me." It was a pancake house, open early or maybe all night long. It tagged them as they got closer, sending a pop-up coupon for cheap coffee; Marisa's djinni automatically trashed it, but she saw Omar blink several times, trying to throw it away manually. Pop-ups were hard to get rid of. Marisa pushed open the door, hearing the jingle of a small bell, and walked immediately to a booth without waiting to be seated. "Cover for me," she muttered, and focused all of her attention on her djinni.

A waitress came over, and Marisa was dimly aware of Omar's conversation with her, but she wasn't listening closely enough to follow it. She started blinking through the layers of her djinni's operating system, looking for the virus. Where would it be hiding? She'd always been so proud of her antiviral package, most of which she'd handcrafted, but if malware was still getting through, she'd have to amp it up a little. Or a lot.

Maybe if she could figure out how it got in, she'd know where it was hiding. She'd connected to the Maldonado house computer directly, through a cable plugged into her headjack. Was that it?

But what were the odds that Omar and Franca ever used a cable? Unless you were doing VR—or trying to bypass some layers of security, like Marisa had been—a wireless connection was all you ever needed.

"Omar, do you ever use a cable at home?"

"Sorry about her," said Omar, "she's working on something."

Marisa looked up, refocusing on the real world to find the waitress—young, plump, and very attractive—leaning against the booth and flirting shamelessly with Omar. Marisa flashed her a glare, then turned to him. "Cable connection to Sofia. Yes? No?"

"No?"

"Thanks."

She refocused on her file tree, running her eyes over the list of folders. It wasn't the cable, then. Did she have any other leads? Of course—the photo. Omar had tried to take a photo of the VR ghost, but the vision hadn't shown up in the image. That meant the video was being added to the brain's perception after the signal had already passed through the optic nerve. It would be easier to build a program that simply projected the image onto your eyes and let your brain perceive it that way, but that kind of program wouldn't be able to simulate a dream the way this one had. And if it was going to overlay a new image directly on top of your perception, there was only one place in the operating system it could be. Marisa entered her private passcode to access the nitty-gritty djinni functions—the hardcore stuff that made the whole thing work, like neural interface and data management. She found the folder for visual processing, blinked it open, and started looking for anything that wasn't supposed to be there.

It took another half hour, cross-referencing the folder's contents against a help forum description from the Ganika Support site, but she found them.

"Three videos," she said out loud.

"Three?"

She refocused on the real world to find the waitress gone, and the table in front of her filled with plates of slowly cooling egg substitute. Omar had mostly finished his.

She nodded. "Three. The one where she runs, the one where she shoots, and . . . a third one I haven't seen yet. Have you?"

"No," said Omar, and his eyes turned inward to his djinni. "Tell me where to look."

She walked him through the file path to find it—he had a Ganika as well, so it was in the same place—and when he had them isolated, he looked her in the eye. "Ready?"

"Ready." She nodded. They blinked in unison, and Marisa grabbed his hand tightly when Zenaida appeared in the aisle next to them.

"I am not yours," said Zenaida. "I used to be, though that was more from my own weakness than from any success or skill on your part. You can't have me, and you can never have me, and you're going to stop looking. Or next time I'll do a lot worse than plant some malware in your brain." She stared into Marisa's eyes for a moment longer, her jaw set and her eyes fierce, and then she disappeared.

"Whoa," said Omar.

"Yeah," said Marisa. "Your mom's kind of scary when she wants to be."

"But this means she's alive," said Omar. "She's not a ghost, and she's not chopped up in an alley somewhere—she's alive, and capable enough that she caught the nuli hunting her and struck back by making these videos." He swallowed, and Marisa almost thought she saw a tear in the corner of his eye. "These are revenge," he whispered. "They were frightening because they were made to be."

She was already holding his hand in one of hers, and now reached out with her other, trying to comfort him. "I'm sure it's not you she's talking to."

"Of course not," said Omar. "It's my father."

SIXTEEN

"Who else could it be?" asked Omar.

"ZooMorrow?" offered Marisa, though even as she said it she knew it wasn't true. It was certainly possible that ZooMorrow thought they "owned" Zenaida—they owned her DNA, after all—but if she was trying to send a message to ZooMorrow, she wouldn't have planted her videos in the Maldonado house computer.

"It's my father," said Omar. He sounded tired, and angry. "He's obsessed with her, and always has been, and now we know that she didn't die in the car accident, but used it to disappear— maybe to get away from ZooMorrow, because they were trying to kill her, but probably from my father as well. And he's never given her up. And since he knows she's still alive he's apparently been trying to find her, hounding her constantly for the last fifteen years, until . . . he sent a nuli to find her? Apparently?"

"He sent a DNA nuli," said Marisa. "That's how this whole thing started. He bought a hunter nuli that targets a specific DNA code, and then stole Zenaida's DNA from ZooMorrow so it would know who to hunt—we knew somebody stole it, but we couldn't figure out who. Now we know."

"I hate him," said Omar.

Marisa watched his face, surprised by the sudden intensity in his voice. "For . . . looking for his wife?"

"For what he did to make her run," said Omar. "For pursuing her even though he knew she wanted out. I know my father: he doesn't like losing, and he doesn't do things halfway. If he's hunting for her now, he's been hunting her for fifteen years. He's been hounding her every step, trying to get her back, and she hasn't had a day's rest!" He gritted his teeth, staring at the table. "She didn't love him. Maybe ever. I don't know much about their relationship, but living in that house, in that family, it's not hard to see at least that much. Whatever other reasons she had, she was also running to get away from him. And he's kept her running for fifteen years, and that . . . that makes me very angry."

Marisa wrinkled her brow, worried he was going to snap. "Don't do anything . . . dangerous."

"No," he said, "but we need to do something." He struggled for words, and then gave up. "I don't know. I was going to warn my siblings, but warn them about what? That our father's the kind of guy who hires merc hackers and seeker nulis to hunt down family members? It's not exactly a surprise."

"We can tell them they're not being haunted by their dead

mother," said Marisa. "Start with Jacinto." He was surely the most alone in this; he'd need all the help they could give him.

Omar sighed and closed his eyes, then opened them again and blinked to start a call. He pulled a handheld mini-tablet from his pocket and patched the audio to its speaker, so Marisa could listen in.

Marisa remembered the time, and looked at her clock app while the phone was ringing: 5:27 a.m., and still before sunrise. "Is he even awake?"

Omar shrugged. "I hope not. I'd rather leave a message anyway."

A ring and a half later the call clicked open. Jacinto didn't say anything.

"Cinto?" asked Omar. "Dónde estás?"

Jacinto's voice was barely audible. "I'm here."

"Did I wake you?"

"I don't sleep much."

Omar nodded. "Yeah, that's kind of what I was calling about." He looked at Marisa, and she squeezed his hand. "Have you . . . had dreams or anything about . . . Mom?"

Jacinto was silent for long enough that Marisa started to wonder if he'd ended the call. Just as she opened her mouth to say something, though, Jacinto responded.

"You're talking about the ghost."

"Yeah," said Omar, looking at Marisa again. "I think we've all seen her."

"You shouldn't worry," said Jacinto softly. "It's not really a ghost."

Omar's eyebrow went up. "You know?"

"Ghosts aren't real," said Jacinto. "It's VR."

"I just now figured that out," said Omar. "How long have you known?"

"I ran a deep diagnostic on Sofia's mainframe after the hacker attacked us the other night," said Jacinto. "I found the three videos then, and the malware program that installs them."

"And you didn't think to tell anybody about it?" asked Omar. "I haven't slept in days because of those things."

"You never asked."

"Jacinto," said Omar, and then closed his eyes, gritting his teeth in what Marisa could only assume was frustration. "Listen. You did a good thing, all right? But now I need you to follow it up. Did you delete it?"

"Of course."

"Good; now send a message to Franca and Father and tell them how to delete it as well. I'll talk to Sergio." Sergio had his own family and his own home; he might not know anything about the visions, and Omar would be better at broaching the subject than someone like Jacinto. "And the next time something like this happens, talk to me, okay?"

"I could say the same to you," said Jacinto, "but that would require talking, so I won't." He hung up, and the line went dead.

"He's so weird," said Omar.

"I hope he's okay," said Marisa. She tapped her fingers on the table, wondering what the next step should be, and then looked up quickly at Omar. "You told him to delete the videos—you don't want to study them?"

"I deleted mine already," said Omar. "I don't want anything to do with them. What we need to do now is go through the financial records and see what I can find there—if my father hired a hacker to get this DNA, he must have paid them somehow, and if I can find the record of that payment I might be able to find the nuli data as well. That could lead us straight to my mother."

"That's going to take forever."

"What other options do we have?"

A woman had sat down at the next booth, directly behind Marisa's head, and was talking loudly to the waitress. Marisa tuned her out and leaned forward to whisper to Omar, but he held up a finger.

"Wait," Omar whispered. He looked wary, and Marisa went tense.

"Wait for what?" she whispered back.

"Shh," he said, and pointed behind her. Marisa stopped talking and listened to the woman's voice.

"And you have no idea, the stress working in a police station," said the woman. Marisa recognized the voice instantly as Detective Hendel. "There are cases—horrible, horrible stuff, you wouldn't believe—but there's so much red tape and sometimes I just can't, you know?"

"I hear you, honey," said the waitress. "You wouldn't believe the backroom politics in *this* place."

Marisa stared at Omar's face, and sent him a text: **Does she know we're here?**

He answered the same way. **She's got to, right?**

"Like right now," said Hendel. "I have a new lead, but the case is already closed and my boss won't let me follow it up. There's a perp we just brought in for a crime—a bioprinter—but in his testimony, he gave us a lead on one of his accomplices. The hacker who sold him the biodata. But they won't let me follow it up. I'm sure you run into this kind of stuff all the time."

"You have no idea," said the waitress. "In a couple of hours this place will be buzzing with the breakfast crowd, and Pita can't stay on top of her tables, but she won't let me help because then we have to split tips, and she doesn't want to give it up. And I keep telling her, and I keep telling the manager, but no. So much red tape."

"That is exactly what I'm talking about," said Hendel. "Anyway, thanks for the coffee. Here's your tip—don't give any to Pita."

"Thank you, ma'am," said the waitress. Detective Hendel stood and walked out, and the waitress walked her to the door.

"She *had* to know we were here," said Marisa. "That had to be a message for us, right?"

Omar nodded. "It sounded like it. She got a lead on our case, and she wants us to follow it up because she can't, but . . . she didn't give us anything else."

Marisa turned to look at the booth. "Maybe she left us something." She glanced across the restaurant, but the waitress had gone back into the kitchen. They were alone. She stood up quickly, moving into Hendel's booth, but all she found was an empty coffee mug and a discarded napkin. "Maybe there's a thumb drive," she muttered. She ran her hands over the seat, and lifted the mug and napkin to look underneath, and was about to drop to her hands and knees to look under the table when Omar stopped her with a hand on her arm.

"She's trying to pass a secret message," he said. "She won't go digital—just old school." He reached for the napkin and flipped it over.

It had two strings of numbers, hastily scrawled with a pen.

"That's a web address," said Marisa. "The second one's an ID signature."

"Let's get out of here," said Omar quickly, stuffing the napkin in his pocket. He looked up, and shouted across the empty dining room: "Thanks for the eggs, and good luck with those finals!" He blinked, transferring credit. "Money's in the till; keep the change." He took Marisa's arm and hustled her toward the door.

"Finals?" she asked.

"You're great with computers," said Omar, "but you need to pay more attention to people."

Hendel was already gone by the time they got outside. "What's the hurry?" asked Marisa.

Omar scanned the street. "For as many illegal things as you do, you suck at thinking like a criminal." He pulled her toward the nearest corner—away, she realized, from the direction of the police station. "If Hendel's sneaking around like this, she's probably being watched. She was careful to never contact us directly, and we don't want to leave any evidence that she contacted us indirectly, so we're getting gone now before anyone has time to snoop around."

"She's probably also terrified," said Marisa. "Two hours ago she couldn't wait to get us as far from this case as possible. Now she's pulling us in, which means something big has happened and she's down to her last resort." She felt helpless and determined at the same time. "We're all she's got."

SEVENTEEN

Sahara and Anja met them in another diner, already bustling with activity. The city was waking up.

"I want to register my official displeasure at your choice of breakfast companions," said Anja, staring at Omar with venom practically dripping from her eyes. She had dated Omar for a while until he'd screwed her over, and this was only the second time she'd consented to see him since. She looked ready to tear his throat out.

"Noted and seconded," said Sahara. Cameron and Camilla hovered over the booth, filming everything, but she'd turned off their microphones—she was streaming a local band over the feed instead.

Marisa was crammed into one side of a booth with both girls, because she had sat first, and neither of the others would sit by Omar.

"I know we have history," said Omar. "I'm willing to put that aside for now if you are."

"How gracious of you," said Sahara.

"Girls," said Marisa, "just listen, okay? This is important. If we find the hacker, we'll have a clear line from the bioprinter to Don Francisco. We'll have evidence that he hacked a megacorp—Detective Hendel can't touch him but ZooMorrow could string him up by his toes if they wanted—"

Sahara's eyes were still locked on Omar. "And you're cool with this? Getting your father arrested?"

"After what he's done to my mother?" said Omar. "Give him hell."

"All right then," said Sahara.

"I thought we already knew who the hacker was," said Anja. "Andy Song said he got the data from Scary Ramira Bennett."

"He said he got the data from a woman, and that she was scary," said Marisa. "We *assumed* it was Ramira Bennett."

"Exactly," said Omar. "The good news is, we don't need to wonder who she is—we can just go find her." He pulled the napkin from his pocket and spread it flat on the table. "There's all the info Andy Song had on her—a web address, and an ID tag."

"The ID's almost guaranteed to be fake," said Anja, scrutinizing the numbers. "No hacker worth her hard drive is going to give a contact a real ID."

"The web address might be useful, though," said Sahara. "Run it through the right software and we could find a physical location. Or at least an approximate one."

Omar frowned. "The hacker wouldn't hide her location?"

"Of course she would," said Marisa, "but this web address includes a time stamp." She pointed at a section of numbers in the middle of the string. "If we can get into the service provider's archive, we can follow the fake trail she used to hide herself."

"But how can you get into the ISP's archive?" asked Omar. "Just . . . hack it?"

"You're so dumb," said Anja. "Just . . . so, so dumb."

"A hack like that would take weeks," said Sahara, "but we don't have to go to all that trouble. See this?" She pointed at a different section of the number string. "The ISP is Johara, and we have an inside woman."

"How can you read these numbers?" asked Omar. "They're just . . . gibberish."

"I am literally running out of ways to describe how dumb you are," said Anja.

"I'm calling Jaya," said Sahara. "And this conversation is moving to text, because it's about to get super illegal, and I don't want anyone listening in."

Marisa waited just a moment before the message icon appeared in her vision. She blinked on it, and entered an encrypted chat with all four of them. Jaya hadn't accepted her invite yet.

"Maybe she's still asleep," said Omar out loud.

SHE LIVES IN MUMBAI YOU WALKING LAMPPOST, sent Anja. **And use the damn chat, that's what it's for.**

Sorry, sent Omar. **Híjole.**

Jaya's icon lit up as she joined the group. **Hey, girls—oh wow. And Omar. Did you guys know Omar's in the chat group?**

Hi, Jaya, he sent.

Yes, we know, sent Marisa. **Let's skip all the insults and explanations and just trust that there's a good reason, okay?**

No insults? asked Jaya. **But I've got a good one.**

Gimme, sent Anja.

Later, sent Sahara. **Jaya, I'm going to send you a web address with a Johara marker in it. I need you to find it in the archives and give us the tightest geographical estimate you can.**

I'm not at work, sent Jaya. **It's, like, eight in the evening here—I'm day shift.**

Can you connect remotely? asked Marisa.

If I call in a favor, sent Jaya. **How worth it is this?**

This is the physical location of the hacker who stole Zenaida's DNA from ZooMorrow, sent Sahara. **At this point there's very little that's worth more.**

Wow, sent Jaya. **Yeah, okay. Let's do this. Give me a second while I call my supervisor.**

Omar looked up at the nulis, watching them while they waited. Sahara had glued a little top hat to Cameron and a bow to Camilla, so they could tell at a glance which was which. He spoke out loud. "You're sure they're not recording us?"

Anja repeated the words in a low-pitched, bucktoothed voice. "You're sure they're not recording us?"

"That's super mature," said Omar.

"That's super mature," said Anja.

Hey, Anja, sent Jaya. **Do you know your dad's corporate phone number?** Anja's father worked for Abendroth GMBH, one of the biggest nuli companies in the world.

Yes? sent Anja. **But . . . why do you need it?**

I'm trying to run a remote search in our server traffic

archive, sent Jaya. **I need an excuse or they're not going to let me in.**

Anja made a face. **If this gets back to him with my name attached to it, there's going to be hell to pay in Anja Land tonight. And I don't even know what kind of currency they use in hell, so it had better not.**

You said this was important, sent Jaya. **Is it or not?**

Fine, sent Anja, followed by a string of numbers. **That's his secretary's line.**

Got it, sent Jaya. **One sec.**

"She's really pulling some strings," said Sahara out loud, and looked at Omar. "You'd better be one hundred and fifty-nine percent sure that you're with us on this."

Omar nodded. "I am."

"I don't want you backing out at the last minute," Sahara pressed. "We are not playing here."

"I told you I'm in," said Omar, and then paused a moment, staring at Sahara for several seconds before shaking his head and looking away. "Look, I know that I haven't exactly earned any trust with you—"

"You have in fact earned the opposite," said Anja.

"But I'm serious," said Omar. "I'm in this to the end. I won't let my father keep doing this."

"You never defended me like this," said Anja. "Where was all this rage when he hurt me?"

"That was different—"

"I could have died," said Anja.

"You were a fling," said Omar. "And you were never more serious about it than I was, so don't look offended. This is my mother."

"A mother you barely knew," said Anja.

"Do not mess with a man's mother," said Omar, and his voice was more serious than Marisa had ever heard it.

Jaya sent another message: **Here's the data.**

That's perfect, sent Marisa. **Thanks, we owe you.**

You owe me nothing, sent Jaya. **Cherry Dogs forever.**

Cherry Dogs forever, sent Sahara, and blinked on the file. She studied it a moment. "It's here in LA, in Eagle Rock."

"What kind of a hacker lives in Eagle Rock?" asked Anja.

"I like Eagle Rock," said Marisa. "They've got that one place, with the pig."

"Oh yeah," said Omar, "the pig place." Marisa looked at him, and he looked back for almost three seconds before laughing. "What exactly do you do with these pigs at this place?"

Marisa laughed with him. "You don't know the pig place?"

"Flirt later," said Sahara. "And call us an autocab to Eagle Rock."

"Not yet," said Marisa, forcing herself to get serious again. "We need a plan."

"We go to this address and start breaking fingers," said Anja. "Done."

"We still don't know whose to break," said Omar.

Marisa nodded. "Look at the satellite view of this address: it's a single apartment building, the size of a city block. It'll have hundreds of rooms, and maybe thousands of people. We need to know which one is our hacker."

"What's your plan?" asked Sahara.

"I think we need a honeypot," said Marisa.

"Smart," said Sahara.

Omar raised his eyebrow. "You want to . . . seduce the landlord?"

"A honeypot's not a person," said Marisa, "it's a tablet. It's a computer that can receive traffic, but doesn't go anywhere or contain anything valuable. Just a dead end, basically."

"No one has any good reason to be there," Anja continued, "so anyone who goes there is, by nature, snooping around where they don't belong. It might not be *our* hacker, but it'll be *a* hacker."

"All we need is some spyware preinstalled," said Marisa, "and we can trace the signal back to the source."

"How can you be sure our hacker will even be snooping around in anything?" asked Omar. "She's busy breaking into ZooMorrow; she's not going to bother with some random tablet on the sidewalk."

"We're talking about a thousand people in that apartment building," said Sahara. "Probably a couple thousand. Those places are notorious for people hacking literally everything they come across—we call it coraling."

"Cor*ral*ling," said Omar, emphasizing the second syllable.

"Not corral," said Anja. "Coral, like a coral reef: the hacker sits there and passively collects data from their thousands of neighbors. They're not breaking into anything, just keeping an eye out for whatever . . . drifts by, unprotected. ID codes, GPS trails, financial info if they're lucky. Nothing she catches will be as big of a score as ZooMorrow would be, but you can still get a lot of good stuff, and you can write programs to do it for you, so it's basically free money every time it turns something up."

"And best of all," said Marisa, "the programs doing the searching are too dumb to recognize an obvious honeypot, so our trap will work perfectly."

"What if more than one hacker is 'coraling' this apartment?" asked Omar.

"Then we get to make some hard decisions," said Sahara. "But first: Where are we going to get a honeypot?"

"I've got systems at home I could sacrifice," said Marisa, "but I don't think I could get in and out without my parents finding me—and they are super not happy with me right now."

"Use mine," said Omar, and pulled out his small hand tablet. "I never really use it for anything anyway."

"Too obvious," said Sahara. "We're looking for a hacker hired by your father—if her software finds a Maldonado tablet in her neighborhood, she'll freak out and disappear."

Omar frowned. "But I thought—"

"Their crawler program won't recognize a honeypot," said Marisa, "but it will recognize ID. We don't want to take the chance."

"I think he should buy a new one," said Anja. She looked at him with her eyes wide, as if challenging him to say no. "You can afford it."

"He doesn't have to buy a new one," said Marisa.

"No," said Omar, "I'll buy it. I said I'm in, and I'm in."

"We need the most expensive one—" Anja started, but Sahara cut her off.

"A cheap and dirty tablet will do just fine," she said. "Call the autocab, and we'll hit a kiosk on the way."

* * *

They bought a MoGan Mini at a vending machine by the freeway, and spent the ride to Eagle Rock filling it with spyware and fake data—nothing that would pass a detailed examination, but enough to fool the coral rig software. Marisa found it hard to concentrate on the ride there, with her thigh pressed up against Omar's on the bench, but what could she do? It was a small cab; there wasn't anywhere else to sit.

And she still really wanted that kiss.

Is there something you want to tell me? Sahara sent her.

Thanks for coming, Marisa sent back.

I mean about Omar, sent Sahara. **You're practically sitting in his lap.**

Marisa glanced down and saw that there was almost ten inches of room between her and the door. She glanced at Sahara, who looked at her dryly, and then she scooted away from Omar with a sheepish smirk. She looked at Anja, but she was focused on programming the honeypot and didn't seem to have noticed.

This time yesterday you'd have spit on him, sent Sahara. **This time last week you would have stabbed him in the heart. What's going on?**

He's different than he was, sent Marisa. **I think it's losing his mom. Again. It's uncovered a different side of him.**

The other side is still there, sent Sahara. **That's how sides work.**

He's helping us, sent Marisa. **He's changed.**

Just don't get hurt, sent Sahara.

Marisa nodded. **I won't.**

Anja told the cab to let them out a few blocks away from the apartment, and Sahara held the honeypot as they got out. "Spoof your IDs now, so she can't follow us later."

Marisa and Anja nodded, blinking to mask their djinni's identity markers, but Omar frowned.

"You say that like it's no big deal, spoofing your ID."

"You are *so dumb*," groaned Anja.

Marisa pulled a headjack cable from her back pocket. "Turn around," she said. "It's faster to just do it for you."

"Ooh!" said Anja, crowding forward. "Let me!"

"Like hell," said Omar.

"Don't worry," said Marisa with a grin. She plugged the cable into his headjack and requested permission to alter his settings. "I'll make sure the new ID I give him is awesome."

"I shudder to think," said Omar, but blinked and granted her access. She made up a fake name, tweaked a bunch of settings, and unplugged the cable.

"Done."

Omar looked at her warily. "So who am I?"

Marisa grinned. "You'll find that out when a confused hacker shouts it at you."

"Let's go," said Sahara, and they walked the last few blocks toward the apartment, listening for the alert of a foreign network connecting to the honeypot.

"Eagle Rock's really gone to seed, hasn't it?" asked Omar.

"I like it," said Marisa.

"You keep saying that," Anja told her, looking around at the run-down buildings. "Are you using those words wrong, or am I?"

"Eagle Rock is great," said Marisa, though she had to admit

that the streets had a lot more trash in them than the last time she'd been there. But then, so did Mirador's. So did most of LA's. Sometimes it felt like the whole city was falling apart.

"Nothing on the honeypot," whispered Sahara. They looked up at the apartment—just one of several that stretched like giant concrete mountains into the sky. "If the coral rig's on a higher floor, we might have to go up to reach it."

"Then let's go up," said Omar. The building looked like it used to have a good lock on it, but these days the door was simply propped open with a cinder block. A scattering of people sat on the front steps, and ignored them as they went inside. Omar hit the up button on the elevator, and when it opened they waited for a pair of old ladies to get out before they stepped in. Omar ran his finger over the buttons. "Thirty floors. We'll go to fifteen and just . . . walk the halls?"

"If we're not in range of a coral rig there, there isn't one," said Marisa. She pushed the button, and the elevator rumbled.

"What are we expecting when we get there?" asked Omar. "Fat lady behind a wall of soda cans? Pasty, feeble girl permanently tethered to her computer system? I don't know a lot of hackers."

"You know three," said Anja, "and we're all super-hot teenage girls."

"Point granted," said Omar, "but what are the odds it's another super-hot teenage girl?"

"Maybe it's a super-hot green-skinned monster woman," said Anja.

"We already ruled her out," said Marisa.

"Maybe she has a clone," said Anja. "It wouldn't be the weirdest thing about her."

Sahara, as always, took control of the situation. "Hackers are only strong in the digital world; in the physical one we should be able to intimidate whoever this is."

"Well," said Omar. "Since our whole plan is apparently just 'be scarier than the scary hacker,' you'll be glad to hear I've got a gun if we need it."

"I'm not *remotely* glad to hear that," said Anja.

"I am," said Sahara. "Just don't do anything stupid." She glared at Anja. "Either of you."

The elevator stopped on the fifteenth floor, and they stepped into the hall. Only some of the lights worked, leaving the corridor in a kind of a half-light gloom. Marisa was glad of it, honestly; it made it that much harder to see how gross the walls and floors almost certainly were. They stayed close together as they walked, avoiding eye contact with the handful of silent people they passed in the darkness. They'd already rounded the first corner when the tablet dinged softly.

"Got one," said Sahara. She held the device up to her face. "Whoever it is, they're poking around in the file system. Standard keywords: financial, banking, etc., etc." She bit her lip, and then grinned. "Backtrack finished: her network ID is listed as 21737. Is that a room number?"

"The one next to us is 15682," said Marisa, reading the door next to her. "Looks like we've got her. Twenty-first floor."

Anja led the way back to the elevators, though this time they had to wait much longer for one to arrive. When a car came, it had a pair of white guys in it; Marisa and her friends stepped in silently, pushed the button for 21, and stood awkwardly while the car rumbled up. Anja farted right as the elevator reached their floor, and blamed it loudly on Omar.

"That's disgusting!" she shouted. "Oh—you smell like a zombie movie died in your intestines."

Omar smirked but said nothing, and they heard the guys in the elevator laughing as the doors closed.

"Follow me," said Sahara.

"Do we have a plan?" asked Marisa. "The honeypot found her, but it isn't going to get us in the door."

"We got in Andy Song's door pretty easily," said Anja.

"Song was a moron," said Marisa. "And he was, let's remember, scared to death of whoever we're about to drop in on."

"There it is," said Sahara, pointing ahead. "Two doors down. I'm going to send Camilla to check it out first." She blinked, and the nuli with the cute red bow flew ahead and turned a slow circle in the hall. "Camera over the door—just a little one, probably narrow field and wireless."

"I should stay out of its sight, then," said Omar. "If she knows me, like you said, we don't want her to know I'm coming."

"We don't want to freak her out with numbers, either," said Sahara. "If all three of us stand there, she might get nervous."

"Hang on," said Marisa. She jogged back down the hall toward the elevators, took the lid off the garbage can, and sifted through it gingerly with her metal hand. She found a paper bag and pulled it out—a fast food sack from something called Casa Rancherita. She filled it with other bits of balled-up junk, to make it look full, and jogged back to the rest of the group. "Food delivery," she said. "Maybe it'll set her at ease."

"Only if she ordered food," said Sahara.

"Don't say it's for her," said Omar, "say it's for a neighbor who isn't home."

"Sounds good," said Marisa, and looked at the logo on the bag. "I guess this giant sombrero means I'm the one to do it."

"That's racist," said Anja, and grabbed the bag. "Don't call me a hero, but I think the world is ready for a white girl delivering Mexican food."

"Let Mari do it," said Sahara, and handed the bag back to Marisa. "Anja, you walk past the door and double back. The rest of us will wait just out of view on either side, ready to jump in if something goes bad."

"So I'm just the face-puncher *again*?" said Anja, feigning offense. "Stop stereotyping white girls."

"Go," said Sahara, and Anja grinned before walking down the hall. She went about one door past 21737, stopped, and crept back silently, staying out of the camera's view. Sahara and Omar crept up into a similar position on the near side, and then Marisa took a deep breath and walked up the door. She held the bag up, logo visible, and knocked loudly.

Who would answer the door? Andy Song had been terrified of this hacker, but was that because she was scary, or because he was just easily scared? What if it was Ramira Bennett, or someone like her? They'd barely escaped with their lives the last time they encountered her. Could they handle another round? Marisa remembered the pinging sound as the tranq dart had hit her metal arm, and turned herself slightly to present that side to the door. Maybe it would provide the split second she needed to avoid getting knocked out again?

If, of course, the hacker was dangerous. But how dangerous could the hacker really be?

The door flew open, and Marisa yelped as she saw the barrel of an assault rifle less than a foot from her face, pointed straight at her. She stared back at, practically cross-eyed, and started to raise the bag.

"Delivery from—"

"Marisa Carneseca Sanchez," said the hacker.

Marisa realized two things almost simultaneously: first, the hacker knew her name, despite the spoofed ID.

Second, and even more shocking, was that Marisa knew who the hacker was. That voice had taunted her too many times. Marisa looked away from the gun and into the blue-haired Latina's face.

"Renata?"

"Thanks for the bag of garbage," said Renata. "I think I'm going to kill you now."

EIGHTEEN

"Wait," said Marisa. Seeing Renata again was . . . well, it was insane. Renata was a mercenary; she'd worked with them on a data heist to take down a telecom company, and then halfway through betrayed them for a payout from the telecom. "What are you doing here? *You're* the hacker?"

"I'm *a* hacker," said Renata. "But I didn't really expect that to be the reason you want to kill me."

"I'm not here to kill you," said Marisa. "I'm trailing a free-lancer. I had no idea it was you."

"No te creo," said Renata. Her left hand was cybernetic, just like Marisa's arm, though the model was older and less sleek. She adjusted her grip on the rifle. "What's with Machote and his gun, then?"

Marisa tried to look innocent. "Who?"

"Come on," said Renata, "I've got cameras all up and down

the hall—you only found the obvious one that everyone finds. I watched you fish that food sack out of the trash, for crying out loud!" She pointed subtly with the rifle: "You've got some galán out there with a gun, though he doesn't look like muscle. And I'm pretty sure his name isn't Rosarita Chiquitita de la Santa Biblioteca."

"What?" asked Omar, still out of view.

"Is that the fake ID you gave him?" asked Anja. "I love you."

"Hi, Anja," said Renata. "And Sahara."

In Marisa's peripheral vision, she caught a glimpse of Sahara rolling her eyes. "Frakkin' Renata," she grumbled.

"I swear we didn't know it was you," said Marisa. "Would we have showed up here with just one dinky little pistol?"

"Hey," said Omar.

Renata still wasn't convinced. "You still brought a gun, though."

"For intimidation purposes only," said Marisa. "We thought we were going to find some snot-nosed little kiddie coder or something."

"Information?" asked Renata.

"That's all," said Marisa. "You did a job for someone, and we want to ask you about it."

"How'd you find me?"

"Honeypot," said Marisa. "Your coral rig pinged it, and we followed the signal back."

"Nice," said Renata, and her suspicious glare slowly turned into a smile. "Time to change that setup, then." She turned the rifle, pointing it at something in a side room out of view, and fired one shot. "Setup changed." Suddenly she smiled brightly. "Come on in!" She stepped to the side and beckoned Marisa with her metal hand.

Nobody moved.

"Look, I'm a mercenary," said Renata. "We can't hold grudges or we'd never get any repeat business. Come in, come in."

Marisa still didn't move, and her friends stayed safely out of sight as well. Along the hall she heard doors starting to open; some of her neighbors had heard the gunshot.

"They're not going to call the cops," said Renata, gesturing toward the other tenants. "Most of them are Krokheads anyway; they don't want the cops here. But they might mug you for cash, because: most of them are Krokheads, as mentioned."

"Fine," said Sahara, finally stepping into view. "Let's go in." Her nulis followed her through the door, and she smiled sweetly at Renata. "We're live, by the way, so don't try anything unless you want ten thousand witnesses."

Renata glanced at the nulis and nodded. "Audio?"

"Just a playlist."

"Good."

Marisa followed Sahara into the one-room apartment, finding it to be nearly empty: a futon, a mini fridge, and several computers and monitors of varying size. One of them, a small black tablet, had a brand-new hole through the center of the screen; behind it was a hole in the wall, through which she could see all the way into the neighboring apartment.

"Don't worry," said Renata, "nobody's home."

Omar came in next. He smiled at Renata—not his

full-on-charm smile, but a modest one that still managed to look rakishly handsome. "Hi," he said, extending his hand. "I'm Rosarita Chiquitita. You're Renata?"

"Most of the time," said Renata, shaking his hand with a smile. "Damn, Mari, this one's a catch."

"Careful which hand you shake," Marisa told him, nodding toward Renata's prosthetic. "One of them explodes."

Renata grinned at Omar, showing her teeth. "It's called a hand grenade."

Omar kept his cool, but allowed himself a small chuckle. "So. How do you know each other, exactly?"

"Renata helped us break into a megacorp," said Anja, stepping in behind him. "Remember KT Sigan? But then she turned on us halfway through the job."

"Oh, we had fun, though," said Renata, and closed the door behind them. "And you still won, in the end, so: respect." She held up her fist, and Anja bumped it with her own on her way to the futon. Renata turned to look at them, the rifle still held somewhat carelessly in her right hand. "You girls heard from Alain?"

"Not recently," said Marisa, with a guilty glance at Omar. She looked away just as quickly. Alain was kind of sort of a prospective maybe boyfriend, maybe, but he was also an anticorporate freedom fighter, and was rarely ever around. Omar was right here.

"Let's talk business," said Sahara. "You were hired by Francisco Maldonado to steal a DNA template from ZooMorrow."

"Maybe I was," said Renata. "What about it?"

"He's my father," said Omar. "Your testimony could put him in jail."

"If it's my silence you're looking to buy . . ."

"You're misinterpreting the situation," said Anja. "We *want* to put him jail."

"The DNA he asked you to steal was my mother's," said Omar. "She faked her death to get away from him, and he's been hunting her ever since. If you can show solid proof that he hired you for that specific purpose—"

"No way," said Renata. "First, because there's no way to give that testimony without also incriminating myself. I'm no criminal mastermind, but I'm pretty sure that's a no-no."

"They could grant you immunity to get to the bigger catch," said Marisa, but Renata shook her head.

"Second," she said, "Maldonado didn't hire me to hack Zoo-Morrow, he hired me to find his wife. ZooMorrow was just my Plan A."

"Oh, come on," said Sahara, looking up at the ceiling. "We were so close!"

"No one's going to arrest him for stalking," said Omar. "Not ZooMorrow or the LAPD."

"Stalking's still a crime," said Marisa.

"You can stop asking," said Renata. "If I started turning on my clients I'd never get any business."

"Are you kidding?" asked Marisa. "You turned on *us*."

"I turned on *Alain*," said Renata, "and only because he was a lone dude, and KT Sigan was paying enough to keep me as a pet. Of course, then you destroyed their US business, so here I am coraling an old apartment block like some kind of moron. So: not eager to start burning more bridges."

"No one would prosecute my father for stalking anyway," said Omar. "He's too powerful. Direct infringement on megacorp property, yes, but stalking some random woman we can't even prove is alive? Nobody's going to care."

"He's right," said Sahara. "Remember that stalker I had from the vidcast? Ganika's rent-a-cops took my testimony and then never did a thing."

"Whatever happened to that guy?" asked Anja.

Sahara gave her an innocent smile. "Nobody knows."

"Feel my arm," said Anja, holding it toward Sahara. "I've got goose bumps *on my goose bumps.*"

"We're not going to just mysteriously 'disappear' my father," said Omar. "Even if I wanted to, he has more bodyguards than most people have friends."

"No," said Marisa. "If we can't stop Don Francisco directly, we have to do it indirectly—we find Zenaida and help her ourselves."

"Two problems with that plan," said Sahara. "First, there's no way Francisco only hired one merc to hunt down his wife. There could be tons of them out there, and we're days behind them. Second, and I want to stress this: one of those mercs is standing in this room, listening to all of our plans, holding an assault rifle."

"Okay, hang on there," said Renata, waving with her free hand. "Seriously, this is perfect: we're both looking for Zenaida, so let's work together! I've already done a ton of legwork, and you've apparently done a ton of your own. We'll share leads, pool our resources, and get this done before anybody beats us to it."

"We have opposite goals, though," said Marisa. "We're trying to protect her—you're trying to take her back to the man she ran away from."

"Po-tay-to, pa-tah-to," said Renata, dismissing the idea with a wave. "That doesn't stop us from finding her, it just . . . complicates the endgame a little bit."

"What exactly did the Don hire you to do?" asked Sahara.

"Gather verifiable data on exactly where and how to find her," said Renata. "As long as Omar's daddy can confirm that my data is real, I get paid."

"We can work with that," said Anja. "Don Francisco pays her to help us find Zenaida, and then we help Zenaida escape before he can grab her or whatever."

Omar looked at Renata. "And we have your word that you won't double-cross us? Try to capture my mother and work out a new fee with my father?"

Renata put a hand on Omar's shoulder. "You sweet summer child."

"If you want her to do something you pay her," said Marisa.

"Fine," said Omar. "We'll work that out later, but for now we're on a deadline. Show us what you've got."

Marisa sent Sahara a private message: **She's going to turn on us. She always does.**

So we know it'll happen, said Sahara, **and we can plan for it.**

That never works.

Trust me.

"Zenaida de Maldonado is a hard woman to find," said Renata, moving across the room toward the computers. She kept the rifle

281

in her hand, and when she sat down cross-legged she placed it in her lap and leaned over it to type on the touch screen. "I know she's back in LA, and I know she's on the west side. I think she might be by one of the docks, but that doesn't really narrow it down. This city has a disgusting number of docks."

"You sent a nuli to find her," said Marisa.

"I sent four," said Renata. "That's how I was able to narrow down her location. I used the ZooMorrow DNA template to give some seeker nulis the scent, and after trolling around for a while they all gravitated toward the coastline. When I lost the first one I figured it had to be drone hunters looking for a free meal, but by the time I lost the fourth it was obvious she was taking them out herself."

"She shot them with an EMP gun," said Omar. "And she used at least one of them to film a video of herself."

Renata looked at him, surprised. "You're kidding."

"Three videos," said Marisa. "Then she broke into the Maldonado house computer and planted them as malware. The whole family thought they were seeing a ghost."

Renata burst into peals of laughter. "Oh, that's amazing! Like, VR videos? In augmented reality?" Marisa nodded, and Renata laughed again. "Ándale, those *would* look like ghosts, wouldn't they? Especially if you already thought she was dead. I'm definitely going to have to use that sometime."

"That's cruel," said Omar.

"Don't blame me," said Renata, typing on her screen again. "It's your mom's idea."

"Where did the nulis disappear?" asked Anja, looking at the screen.

Renata called up the data, and four points appeared on the map. "Kind of all over, honestly. Mostly coastal, like I said, but they go all the way from Santa Monica to Tijuana. And this third one was pretty far inland."

"That's Athens," said Sahara, peering at the map. "That's where Foxtrot is—the club where we spied on the chop shop."

"You spied on a chop shop?" asked Renata. "I really missed you girls."

"It's been in the news," said Marisa. "You've been looking for Zenaida for how long, and you didn't notice when her hand showed up at the police station?"

"Either time?" asked Anja.

"Of course I noticed," said Renata, "but it was obviously just a bioprinter—"

"Because you sold the DNA," said Sahara.

Renata shrugged. "I went to all the trouble to steal it—I may as well make a few extra bucks on the side, right?"

"You have no idea how much trouble you've caused," said Marisa. "This isn't just a couple of bucks, this is people's lives."

"But now you know your mom is alive," said Renata, and looked at Omar. "In a way, I've performed a valuable service."

"You can't just—" Marisa started, but Renata cut her off, spinning around to face them.

"Have you analyzed the videos yet?"

"We've watched them," said Marisa, "and we've looked at the clothing and stuff, but there's not a lot in the way of clues. She's edited out the background too."

"I'm not talking about the image," said Renata, "I'm talking about the files themselves. There's a ton of metadata stored in a video file—even if she cut out some of the assets, there might still be good info buried inside it. Time stamps. Video artifacts. GPS data if we're really lucky."

"That's smart," said Marisa, nodding. "We can do that."

"The third video wasn't taken on the street," said Omar, "it was staged, and she's talking directly to the camera. That might have been filmed wherever she's living."

"Exactly," said Renata. "Dig through that video data and we find the woman."

"Go back a bit," said Sahara. "You said you knew that the severed left hand came from a bioprinter. 'A' bioprinter, not 'the.'"

Renata shrugged. "Your point?"

"You sold it to more than one, didn't you?"

"Argh. Which one borked it?" asked Renata. "Andy Song? Tell me it was Andy Song."

"How many people did you sell the DNA to?" asked Marisa. She could tell what Sahara was thinking, and she didn't like it at all. "Someone is killing to keep that DNA secret—how many people have it?"

"Espérate," said Renata, suddenly serious. "Someone's killing for it?"

"You said you heard about the police report," said Omar.

"It was a gangland turf war," said Renata. "Now they're actually fighting over the DNA itself?"

"Not the gangs," said Sahara. "ZooMorrow. You didn't analyze the DNA you stole from them, did you? You just put it into the drone and started looking for buyers."

"Pretty much," said Renata.

"It had unreleased ZooMorrow gene-tech," said Sahara. "They sent a corporate assassin to recover it."

"Dos diablos dañandose," said Renata, cursing. She looked at her row of computers and screens, and swung the rifle toward their hard drives.

"Whoa!" said Sahara, and she and Marisa and Omar scrambled back away from the computers, expecting her to perform another violent reprogramming. Anja was still reclining on the futon, unconcerned.

"Disconnecting them should be enough," said Anja. "Though I admit it's not as fun."

"Whatever you do," said Sahara, "we need the access data first. Can you still get into ZooMorrow?"

"Why would I want to get back in?" asked Renata. "They already want to kill me from the first time."

"Because we need to protect Zenaida," said Sahara, and looked at Marisa. "Nothing we do to save her is going to matter if they just send another assassin to hunt her down again. We have to delete Zenaida's DNA template and everything else about her from ZooMorrow's database."

"Yeah," said Renata, watching them carefully. "I can get you in. For a price."

"Omar?" said Anja.

Omar grumbled. "Yeah, fine. Whatever my father offered you in the first place, I'll give you that much again for the access data."

"Sold!" said Renata. She sat down in front of one of the computers, looked at a few things, and then shrugged and disconnected it from the others. She handed it to Sahara. "This is everything. Don't let them catch you with it, or they'll think you're the one who hacked 'em." She grinned. "And if you found me, ZooMorrow's not far behind. Let me kill the rest of this stuff and we can go . . . wherever we're going next?"

"Somewhere we can analyze the video files," said Omar.

"Eventually, yeah," said Sahara, "but we have to warn some people, too. Anyone who bought that DNA template could be in danger."

"Do you have a list?" asked Marisa.

"A merc who keeps bad books doesn't get paid," said Renata, and picked up a tablet. "I've got all the names, but here's a little Mercenary 101: we don't just warn them about the assassin; we offer to sell them protection from it. Right? It's like getting paid twice!"

"I can't believe you," said Marisa. "You stole data without any thought to how dangerous it was, or how much the people you stole it from would want to protect it. Then you sold it to a bunch of innocent people, practically painting a target on their heads—"

"They were buying black-market DNA from a nameless internet hacker," said Renata. "They're not exactly innocent."

"They don't deserve to die!" said Marisa. "And you don't even care about protecting them!"

"I can't care about everyone just because they're about to die," said Renata.

"But these ones are your fault," Marisa insisted.

"Just give me the tablet," said Sahara. "Do whatever you need to do to these computers and let's get out of here; we can continue this discussion when we're not sitting on ground zero of an imminent ZooMorrow burn operation."

"Fine," said Renata. She handed Sahara the tablet and slung the rifle over her shoulder before crouching down in front of the largest of the computers.

"Who's on it?" asked Marisa, looking over Sahara's shoulder. "Anyone we know?"

"Let me see," said Sahara, opening the list as she talked. "Just three: Andy Song, a djinni clinic—they probably just use it for blood transfusions—and a hospital—oh." She looked at Marisa, eyes wide with shock. "Oh."

"What?" asked Marisa.

Sahara recovered from her shock quickly, her jaw hardening into crisis mode. "Polo Urias Hospital. Didn't they do your dad?"

Marisa couldn't speak; Polo Urias had replaced her father's liver. She walked to Sahara's side and grabbed the tablet, looking at it. That was the same place. She had the phone number saved in her djinni, in case there were any complications from the surgery; she blinked on it now, and a receptionist answered on the second ring.

"Hello?"

"I need to speak with Dr. Barnes," said Marisa.

"Dr. Barnes isn't in right no—"

"Your office bought black-market DNA from a hacker," said Marisa. "Don't argue with me, I'm standing with the hacker who sold it to you."

"Polo Urias Hospital maintains the highest standards of—"

"Don't argue," Marisa repeated. "I'm not trying to get you arrested, I'm trying to save people's lives. That DNA is dangerous, and everyone who has it could be at risk. Now tell me: Did you use that DNA to bioprint the liver you implanted in my father? His name is Carlo Magno Carneseca, look it up."

The line was quiet for a while, though the receptionist didn't hang up. After a moment she came back. "That DNA's been used to grow five organs, and the only one we've implanted was in Mr. Carneseca—"

Marisa ended the call. "I have to get home," she said, and ran for the door. "The Mantissassin's going to come after my dad."

NINETEEN

Marisa called Detective Hendel as she sprinted to the elevator.

"This is Hendel."

"This is Marisa," she said, mashing the elevator button repeatedly with her thumb. "We talked to the hacker. She didn't just sell Zenaida's DNA to Andy Song—she sold it to the hospital where my father had his liver replaced. The assassin's going to come for him." The elevator doors opened, and she got on, mashing the first-floor button as hard as she could. Sahara slipped in after her, but didn't interrupt her phone call.

"Calm down," said Hendel. "We need to get a sense of how many people took transplants with the black-market DNA—"

"My father has proprietary ZooMorrow technology in his body!" Marisa shouted. "They've killed for less than that in the past twelve hours alone. Isn't there anything you can do to protect him?"

"Of course," said Hendel, "but try to stay calm. You just found out about this, but that doesn't mean ZooMorrow knows it."

"ZooMorrow has alerts set up in whatever central database you use for DNA testing," said Marisa. She was too nervous to stand still, and paced the floor of the tiny elevator as it slowly rumbled down. "They knew when you tested the hand, and they'll know when any of the hospitals that bought the DNA test the patients who have it. My father practically collapsed in the police station this morning, and the medical nuli's standard protocol in a case like that is to run a blood test and look for infections. If any of that blood tests positive for Zenaida's DNA, it'll raise every flag ZooMorrow has, and Ramira Bennett won't be far behind."

"She's not a murderer," said Hendel.

"She's a retrieval agent," shouted Marisa. "She's going to forcibly repossess his liver. What do you call that if not murder?"

Sahara put a hand on Marisa's arm, trying to calm her. The touch made Marisa feel suddenly vulnerable, and she pulled away. "On top of everything else, my father knows Zenaida. He knows the truth about what really happened, and maybe even where she's hiding now. Bennett will interrogate him, and she will kill him." She closed the call, wishing she had one of the old-style phones, like her abuela used to use, that had a big plastic handset you could slam down on the holder. Hands-free technology was awesome and all, but sometimes you really just wanted to slam something.

"I've already called a cab," said Sahara. "Anja and Omar are staying with Renata."

"Good," said Marisa, staring at the door. "And thank you for coming with me."

"Wouldn't miss it."

The door opened, and Marisa sprinted outside to the cab. She sat nervously in the seat, bouncing her legs, and then finally bit her lip and called her father.

"Marisa," said Carlo Magno. She couldn't tell from his voice if he was angry, or tired, or the worst parental emotion of all: disappointed.

"Don't be mad," said Marisa.

"It is way too late for that."

"Someone is coming to kill you," she blurted out.

"What?"

"I'm on my way now, but you have to hide, you have to send the other kids somewhere—"

"What have you gotten into this time?" he demanded. "Is it Chuy?"

"It's not me or Chuy," she said, "it's you! It's the hospital! The new liver they gave you is made from Zenaida de Maldonado's DNA, and someone is—"

"Lupe!" shouted Carlo Magno. "Clear the restaurant! Send Pati to a friend's house!"

"Wait," said Marisa. "What do you know about Zenaida's DNA?"

"I know that this nearly killed us last time," he said. "Stay away. Let me deal with this—"

"Are you kidding me?" she shouted. "You know about the assassins and the DNA and everything? Is this really how it happened fifteen years ago—was she really trying to escape from ZooMorrow? She stole their genhancements?"

"I don't have time to talk right now," said Carlo Magno. "Go home, get your sisters, and get out of here. Take them to Anja's house if you can—"

"Sandro can take them!" she said. "Let me help you!"

"You can help us by staying away!" he barked. "I haven't spent fifteen years keeping you out of the line of fire just so you can jump back in the middle of it now."

"You said you're in San Juanito," said Marisa. "I'm almost there."

"Don't you dare," he growled.

Marisa shook her head. "It's like you said before, Papi: it's way too late for that."

The cab pulled to a stop, and she jumped out as soon as the doors unlocked. The restaurant was shut down; the computer that usually recognized her immediately didn't so much as say hello. She tried the door but found it locked. She blinked, accessed the San Juanito central computer—it wasn't advertising, but it was on—and overrode the controls, causing the door to open with a click. Her parents would kill her when they found out she knew how to do that, but she had bigger concerns right now. Sahara followed her in, and Marisa locked the door behind them with a blink.

"Papi?" she called. "Mami?"

Carlo Magno answered with a low rumble from the back corner. "Marisa . . ."

"Get over here," said Guadalupe, and stepped into view. "No one's come yet. Maybe no one will."

Sahara stayed by the window, watching the street outside, and Marisa walked back to the corner to see her father sitting at table eight, his breathing labored. Triste Chango the medical nuli sat close to him, reading his vitals and murmuring softly. A black handgun sat on the table in front of him.

"You own a gun?" asked Marisa.

"Of course I own a gun," said Carlo Magno. "I live in Mirador."

"We could call the Maldonados," said Marisa. "We pay them protection money, this is what it's for—"

"And what would we tell them?" asked Guadalupe, sitting down next to her husband. "That all the old debts are finally coming due? They're as much a part of this as we are."

"Don Francisco controls everything," said Carlo Magno, and sighed. "But he can't control this."

Marisa sat down across from them. "It's time for you to tell me what's going on. If it helps me protect you—"

"You're my daughter," he snapped. "You're seventeen years old. I'm supposed to be protecting *you*—"

"Stay calm," said Guadalupe. "Both of you."

Carlo Magno sighed. "The past is past," he said. "We can't change it, we can only move on."

"But we can learn from it," said Marisa.

"I've fought for so long so that this wouldn't have to be a part of your life—"

"Look at me," she said, and slammed her metal hand down on the table. She did it harder than she meant to, but they only watched her, waiting for her to finish. She nodded; this, at least, was progress. "This is my arm," she said. "This is my reality. It's been a part of my life for fifteen years."

Guadalupe started to speak, but stopped herself.

"We never wanted this for you," said Carlo Magno. "And you're right: you've had to deal with this in a way we never have. And we've tried, you know we've tried. That's a Jeon Generation prosthetic, Mari. We didn't have the money for it, but we found a way to give you an arm better than the one you lost. We've done everything we could—"

"Except tell me the truth about it."

"The truth is not yours to demand!" he snapped. He looked like he was in pain, but Triste Chango didn't say anything. Whatever he was suffering, Marisa realized, it was more emotional than physical. She tried to speak, but she didn't know what to say.

"You've always been your own person," Carlo Magno continued. "Always self-confident, always self-assured. And always self-motivated, though sometimes it drives me crazy trying to keep up with you."

"I'm only doing what I think is right," said Marisa.

"We know," said Guadalupe. "And we're very proud of you. But when you know things, you meddle with them—"

"Meddle?" asked Marisa. "Someone's trying to kill Papi! Trying to save his life isn't meddling!"

Carlo Magno shouted: "You have no idea the trouble you've caused!"

"I'm not the one who caused it!" she shouted back. "Don Francisco abused Zenaida before I was even born; you and he made a deal when I could barely walk; Zenaida's DNA made its way into your body before I knew anything about any of it. The only part you can blame me for is figuring it out in time to warn you. Now we can do something about it! We can save you, and we can save Zenaida—"

"Zenaida cut off your arm!" Carlo Magno roared.

Marisa's words disappeared from her throat.

Guadalupe closed her eyes.

Carlo Magno stared at Marisa, his face red with fury. "Is that what you want to hear? Is that the truth you're so desperate to discover? Zenaida de Maldonado cut off your arm, Mari! Not in the car, and not by accident. She hacked it off with a shovel!"

Marisa's mouth moved, but no sound came out. She realized she was shaking her head, and somehow that motion helped her find her voice again, though at first there was only one word she could say. "No." She shook her head and repeated it, over and over like a mantra. "No. No. No, no, that's not true. I was in the car, and it hit another car and it pinned my arm between them. That's what you've always told me. I lost my arm in the car accident—"

"You *were* in the car," said Guadalupe. "But you lost your arm a few minutes before that, in Zenaida's garden."

"Why would she . . . cut it off?" Marisa spluttered. "Why was I even there? None of this makes sense!"

"You wanted to know the truth," said Carlo Magno. "This is the truth. You lost your arm even before that garden—you lost your arm before you were born."

"You were born with a limb reduction defect in your left arm," said Guadalupe. "Your upper arm was almost nonexistent, and your lower arm was barely half the length it was supposed to be. You had two fingers and no thumb. And even if we'd had the money to do something about it, at your age there wasn't much anyone could do. They don't make cybernetics for infants. So we figured we'd just wait until you were old enough for a prosthetic, and hope we could afford one once you were. Even then, though, prosthetics were not what they are today. . . ."

Marisa had been five when she'd gotten her first bionic arm—an old SuperYu, the first of many she'd had in her life. It was barely more than a stick and a claw, the best her parents could afford, but it was a trainer arm; it had helped her to form the synaptic connections in her brain, molding the neurons while they were still developing, giving her the baseline she needed to control her later arms, including the current one, as naturally as she did. Before that first bionic, she'd had nothing. Just a stump, an inch or two below the shoulder. She'd lived with it for three years.

Or, she supposed, for all five. Who could remember anything that young?

"This still doesn't make sense," said Marisa. "Why would she cut it off? And why in her garden? And why was I in her garden to begin with?"

"After your first year," said Guadalupe, and then stopped. She was crying, though Marisa couldn't tell if it was the story as a whole that made her do it, or this new specific part of it.

Carlo Magno continued for her. "Zenaida was a scientist with ZooMorrow," he said. "She helped them develop new genhancements, and occasionally . . . stole them. For her own use."

Marisa nodded. "We guessed that much. She used them on some of the enforcers."

"And on herself," said Carlo Magno. "And . . ." He paused for a moment. "After your first birthday, Zenaida . . . came to speak with us. She'd helped ZooMorrow develop an experimental new genhancement that could regrow lost limbs, based on some recombinant animal DNA."

Marisa only nodded.

"We didn't know she was stealing it," said Guadalupe. "We never would have agreed if we had. But she worked there, and she had developed it herself, and we thought it was some kind of . . . trial, I don't know."

"I think maybe we knew it was illegal," said Carlo Magno, "but we said yes, because you were our baby. You deserved a full life, and two good arms, and that's what she offered."

"But why me?" asked Marisa. "How did she even know about my arm?"

Her parents only stared at her. After a moment Guadalupe said, "She . . . saw you at church."

"Your arm grew well," said Carlo Magno, before Marisa's mother had even finished speaking. "Better than we expected. Flawlessly. After eight months your arm was a normal size, and by your second birthday you had all five fingers. It was more than we could have hoped for. She tested you every now and then, making sure it was working, and we thought our problems were over, and then . . ."

"Then ZooMorrow found out," Guadalupe continued. "We didn't know until later, of course."

"Putting the pieces together," said Carlo Magno, "we think the news came while you were in their estate, being tested. Zoo-Morrow agents attacked the genhanced enforcers, and Zenaida knew it was over. The technology in their cells—and in yours—was private property, and top secret, and if another gengineering company got hold of you it could destroy ZooMorrow's plans, maybe their entire business. They had to protect themselves, and they did that by killing anyone who had the leaked tech. Zenaida knew her only hope was to run, and find someplace where they couldn't trace her . . . but then there was you."

"You were just a child," said Guadalupe bitterly.

"She couldn't just take you," said Carlo Magno, "and she couldn't leave you to die, so she—"

"She cut off the genhanced arm," said Marisa. "It was the only part of me that had ZooMorrow tech, so without it I was safe. They had no claim on me, or any reason to even know that I'd been genhanced."

"You were a child!" shouted Guadalupe. "She didn't even sedate you!"

"She didn't have time," said Carlo Magno.

"She used a shovel on my baby!"

"It was sharp," said Carlo Magno. "The cut was clean, and she bandaged you quickly, and she got you in the car and she drove to our house. Or . . . she tried to."

"ZooMorrow hacked the car," Marisa guessed. "They tried to stop her, or turn her around, so she put it into manual mode. And then she crashed." Marisa frowned. "Omar was unharmed—the miracle baby. But Jacinto was crippled, and almost killed. Was that . . ." She couldn't say it.

"As far as I know, that was just the car accident," said Carlo Magno. "She was taking the boys with her into hiding—Franca was out with a friend; Zenaida was probably planning to pick her up on her way out of town."

"And then she got in a crash," said Marisa, "and Zenaida was hurt but wasn't killed. You—" She stopped and looked at her father again. "You helped her fake her death."

"You should have let her die," Guadalupe whispered.

"I probably should have," said Carlo Magno. "Especially now, when her damn liver, of all things, has come back to haunt me."

"She saved my life," said Marisa.

"She's a monster," said her mother.

"She nearly killed you," said Carlo Magno. "The crash was only a few blocks away—I was one of the first on the scene, and I found her on the road, thrown from the car, bleeding to death. It was . . . She told me she was running, and the couple in the other car was already dead. Faking her death was the only way for her to get away from ZooMorrow, so I pulled the dead woman from her car, and when the ambulance arrived I told them a lie about who she was." He was crying now. "You were right there in the car, crying and terrified, and I rode with Zenaida to the hospital instead—not with her, of course, but with the dead woman, holding her hand and calling her Zenaida. I even—" He stopped, and composed himself. "When Francisco and Sergio arrived at the hospital, I explained Zenaida's plan, and the reasons behind it. They went along with it, and confirmed my statement that the dead woman was Zenaida. Meanwhile the real Zenaida was taken to another hospital, and was treated under a false name. By the time Francisco found out which one, she'd already disappeared."

"So Don Francisco promised to protect us because you helped his wife escape from ZooMorrow," said Marisa. "But he hates us because you helped her escape *from him*."

"Yes," said Guadalupe.

Marisa nodded, stunned by the flood of confessions. It made sense, and she'd guessed most of it already, but the real grit behind it—the really painful truths about herself, and her arm, and the sacrifice Zenaida had made to save her . . .

"She saved my life," said Marisa. "Maybe in the moment, if you'd known what she'd done to my arm, you would have been angry, but it's fifteen years later. I'm fine now—you can forgive her."

"I can't," said Carlo Magno. "And I never will."

"It's not like she killed me—"

"When you have your own children you'll understand," said Carlo Magno. "She could have brought you to us, she could have taken you to a hospital, she could have—"

"Any of those choices would have endangered the whole family," said Marisa. "The hospital would have made an official report connecting me to the ZooMorrow DNA. I'd never be safe again for the rest of my life."

"Maybe not," said Carlo Magno, "but at least we could have tried! We could have taken you somewhere—maybe back to Mexico. We could have gone into hiding with her!"

"Never with *her*," spat Guadalupe.

"Why did you even help her after what she did?" asked Marisa.

"If it happened again," said Carlo Magno, "I don't know if I would."

In that moment the lights went out, and the whole restaurant powered down. The computer went offline, the fans stopped spinning, and even the background hum of the giant refrigerator fell silent.

"Someone's coming," called Sahara from the front window. "Not from the front, though—they've cut the power, and looks like they're jamming wireless signals. Where's your solar processor?"

"The solar trees run through a unit in the back," said Marisa, grabbing her father's gun from the table and standing up to face the kitchen. That's where she'd come from; the shortest path from the solar unit to here. She blinked, found her djinni was cut off from the network, and swore. She aimed at the door, ready for an attack, and spoke over her shoulder. "Well, Papi, it's happening again. Let's see what you do this time."

TWENTY

"Give me the gun," said Carlo Magno. He struggled to stand, but Marisa only stepped farther out of his reach.

"Sit down," she said, "you can barely breathe, let alone fight."

"Not again," said Sahara, but her voice was slurring before she even finished the words, and by the time Marisa turned to look at her she was already slumping to the ground, rendered unconscious by a tranq dart. Ramira Bennett strode past her, gun raised, green skin bright against her dark black bodysuit. She'd come in through some other way, a window maybe, silent as a ghost. She fired another dart, past Marisa's ear and into Guadalupe behind her. Marisa turned toward her mother with a shout, too late to warn her, then turned back to Ramira and fired the gun. The assassin dodged it easily, barely moving, and then she was right in Marisa's face, her hands on the weapon, her horrifying mantis eyes mere inches from Marisa's own. She grabbed Marisa's right arm with one hand and her left wrist with another, and twisted in a sudden pattern that sent Marisa and her gun flying in different directions. Marisa hit the wall with a gasp, struggling to regain her senses; her metal arm couldn't feel pain, exactly, but it still had sensation, and she could tell that if it had been a normal human limb, the attack would have broken her wrist.

"Lupe!" shouted Carlo Magno.

"I need information from both of you," said Bennett. Her hands and feet were bare, like before. "Give it to me and she'll live."

"It's a tranquilizer," said Marisa. "A ZooMorrow biotoxin."

"You are in possession of ZooMorrow's proprietary technology," Bennett told Carlo Magno. "Under federal statute 7o.3482, that technology will now be returned to ZooMorrow's custody."

"You can't have it," said Carlo Magno.

"Your demands are irrelevant," said Bennett. "Give me the information I need and your family will be safe. I'm cutting out your liver either way."

"Come and get it," said Carlo Magno, and pulled a long, sharp butcher's knife from under the table.

Bennett smirked. "Are you threatening me?"

"I bet I could do a lot of damage with this thing before you took it away from me."

"I could tranquilize you."

"Then you wouldn't get the information," said Marisa, her anger starting to overrule her logic. "Do you want to interrogate us or attack us? Make up your mind."

Bennett looked at her, then back at Carlo Magno. "Tell me where Zenaida is."

He shrugged. "I have no idea."

"She's dead," said Marisa. "She died fifteen years ago."

"The evidence says otherwise," said Bennett. "She is in possession of stolen ZooMorrow technology, and as such she is a fugitive from the law."

Carlo Magno held the knife in front of him. "I'd give her to you in a second if I could, but I don't know where she is. I haven't talked to her in fifteen years."

"You, then," said Bennett, turning back to Marisa. "You've been looking for her; I've seen you. You were in the shantytown building last night."

"Mari . . . ," growled her father.

"I was at Bao's house," she told him, and then looked back at Bennett. "I've been looking, but I haven't found anything."

"Your mother is dying," said Bennett. "Tranquilizers aren't the only biotoxins I have in my arsenal."

Marisa looked at Guadalupe, unconscious in her chair, and thought about the acid they'd found at Omar's house the night Bennett had raided it. It had eaten through brick and metal like they were nothing—what would that do to a human body? And what other toxins did Bennett have in her arsenal?

"It's a slow-acting poison," said Bennett. "She'll be fine for the next half hour, but after that her heart will begin to shut down, and there will be very little that I or anyone else can do to stop it."

Marisa felt her chest constrict. "But you have an antidote?"

"That depends," said Bennett.

"I don't know where Zenaida is," Marisa insisted. "I know she's near the coast."

"This entire city is near the coast."

Marisa tried to remember what Renata had said about her drone data. "She's near a wharf or a dock or something—that's all I know."

"A minute ago you swore you didn't even know that," said Bennett. "See how much you can remember with a little motivation?"

"That's everything!" shouted Marisa.

"Then I suppose I'm done here," said Bennett, and turned on Carlo Magno. "It's time. Do you want to do this the easy way?"

"You can let me live," said Carlo Magno. He was pleading now. "This medical nuli can keep me alive until an ambulance gets here—"

"I am not a surgeon," said Bennett. "This procedure is going to be very imprecise."

"It's attached with a plastic valve," Carlo Magno said. "All you have to do is find it and unplug it. Just be careful, and you can take the liver without killing me."

"I do not have time to be careful with thieves," said Bennett.

"I'm not a thief," shouted Carlo Magno. "The hospital gave it to me—I had no idea it was ZooMorrow DNA."

"The hospital has been dealt with," said Bennett. "As has the bioprinter. After I deal with you and Zenaida, there will only be one loose end."

"Who?" said Marisa.

"Guillermo Alcalá received a transfusion of Zenaida de Maldonado's blood," said Bennett. She pulled Memo's djinni from a pouch on her waist. "A freelance surgeon purchased it from a djinni clinic and used it during the surgery when he removed this djinni. Since the djinni was in your possession, I assume you know where the owner is?"

Carlo Magno looked at Marisa. "What is she talking about?"

"I know where he is," said Marisa, nodding. "Leave my father alive and I'll tell you how to find him."

"I'm not here to barter," said Bennett. "They have both stolen proprietary ZooMorrow property, and megacorp rights outweigh those of humans. Federal statute 4b.1: 'The ability of a corporation to pursue the mandate of its shareholders shall not be infringed, by force or by law or by the intervention of private citizens.'"

"This is madness," Carlo Magno growled.

"This is the world," said Bennett simply. "Console yourself with the knowledge that you will not be in it for long." She walked toward him, pulling a knife from a sheath on her belt, and Marisa knew that her gambit had failed. She called out the last remaining chip she had to bargain with.

"I have videos!" she shouted. Bennett paused, the knife held high, and Marisa spoke as quickly as she could. "Zenaida planted videos in the Maldonado house computer, one of which she filmed herself, maybe in her own home or apartment. We can analyze them for data that might tell us where she is." She looked at her father. "Just let him live."

Bennett thought for a moment, her face unreadable behind those wide mantis eyes. Finally she spoke: "So that's what those are," she said, and turned back to Carlo Magno. "I was infected with those videos when I infiltrated the Maldonado house computer. I'll analyze them when I finish here."

"No!" shouted Marisa. She jumped in front of her father. "I won't let you hurt him!"

"I will hurt you both if I have to," said Bennett.

"Marisa," said Carlo Magno.

She kept her eyes on Bennett. "I'm not leaving you, Papi."

"The nuli can keep me alive," he said, and there was something new in his voice this time. Resignation? Yes, she thought. But something else as well; something that reminded her, in that moment, of herself.

A grim, fierce, unstoppable determination.

"Papi, what are you doing?"

She didn't dare to take her eyes off of Bennett, but when the corporate assassin frowned and tilted her head, staring past Marisa at whatever Carlo Magno was doing, her curiosity grew. And when she heard the tape from his bandages ripping open, she couldn't stop herself any longer. She turned her head, just enough to catch her father in her peripheral vision.

He had pulled up his shirt, exposing his brown belly and fat white bandages, and as he tore the bandages away she saw the wide, grisly scar of his surgery, the skin puckered around the stitches, the wound still only partially healed. He should have been in a hospital, under the care of a doctor, but they couldn't afford anything more than a slapdash surgery and Triste Chango. The scabs had stuck to the bandage, and new blood was seeping out now that he'd ripped it free. It mingled with the old, and he held the knife in a trembling hand.

"Papi," she whispered, "what are you doing?"

"The funny thing is," he said, "I think now I finally understand

Zenny and her shovel. It's terrible, but sometimes terrible is the best you can do."

And then she knew what he was planning.

"Papi, no!" She lunged for him, but he was too quick. He sliced open the wound, parting stitches and scabs and flesh while a blossom of blood spilled into his lap.

TWENTY-ONE

Marisa screamed, and her father roared—a long, loud, gravelly shout designed to drown his own pain in anger. She tried to take the knife from him, but he gripped it tight and clenched his teeth and sliced through more of the stitches, and she didn't dare to wrestle it away from him. The liver is up high, just at the bottom of the ribs, almost directly next to the heart. If they started fighting for the knife, who knew how much damage she might do?

Triste Chango sprang into action. "Emergency!" he shouted. "Your vital signs are crashing. An ambulance has been summoned. I am administering pain medication now." It was already by his side, practically touching his leg, and now it reached out with a small retractable arm and sprayed him with the hypodermic, pumping a massive dose of narcotic painkillers into his system. Carlo Magno's hand started trembling almost instantly.

"Stop him from the sealing the wound," he said, dropping

the knife and hissing with his teeth clamped tightly shut. "I only have about thirty seconds before those narcs make me too stoned to work."

"Papi, stop," cried Marisa, tears streaming down her face. "You're killing yourself."

"Better me than you," he said, and then gasped in pain. He growled again, fighting to regain control, and then shoved his hand into the open wound. "And better I do it than her."

Triste Chango reached out with another tube, trying to insert it into the wound. Marisa moved to let it get closer, but Bennett pulled the nuli away.

"Let it help him!" Marisa shouted, but Bennett said nothing. Marisa turned back to her father. "You can't rip out your own liver!"

"No manches," he said, his hand still shoved inside. She stepped toward him, and he gasped and pulled his hand out of his chest.

It was clutching his liver.

"I'm really good with a knife," he said. He forced a smile, though his eyes were already closing.

Marisa screamed. Bennett stared, letting go of the nuli, which surged forward again with its tube extended. It placed the end in Carlo Magno's wound and fired a burst of white foam pellets; they expanded, soaking up the blood and filling the wound, stopping the bleeding almost instantly.

"Papi," Marisa sobbed.

"I'll be fine," said Carlo Magno. His eyes were still closed, and his speech was starting to slur. "This is what Triste Chango is for."

Marisa stared at him in shock, then grabbed the liver in her hands and whirled around, standing to face Bennett. The plastic

310

connection valve dangled from it, dripping gobbets of blood on the floor. "This is what you wanted, right? Take it! Take it and get out of here!"

Bennett's face was still unreadable, with those faceted, inhuman eyes. She looked at Marisa for a moment, then sheathed her knife, pulled a thin square of plastic from a pouch on her belt, and shook it. It unfolded into a plastic bag. She held it out, and after a moment of shocked disbelief, Marisa reached forward and slid the bloody liver into it.

"Now go," said Marisa.

Bennett sealed the bag and attached it to a strap on her side. She looked at Carlo Magno again, staring for a couple of seconds, then turned and walked away.

Marisa screamed again. "What about the antidote!"

"That was a bluff," said Bennett. "She doesn't need one." And then she disappeared around a corner into a different part of the dining room. Marisa rushed after her, but by the time she reached the same corner, the restaurant was empty. However Bennett had entered the building, she'd gone out the same way.

"Marisa," mumbled Carlo Magno, and she raced back to his side.

"Papi! Are you in pain? Can I get you something?"

"No pain, mija. Just high as a kite." He smiled broadly, half asleep and covered with blood and sealant foam. "At least," he said slowly, "I had a knife instead of a shovel."

"Don't worry, Papi," said Marisa. "She's gone. It's over and you lived, and the ambulance is on its way, and we'll get you to the hospital and get you a new liver."

"Good, good," he said, and then smiled again. "Make sure it's not from a wanted criminal this time."

She smiled with him, laughing through the tears, praying that he would survive until the ambulance arrived to help him. Triste Chango was still closely attentive, taking readings and giving him more drugs—antibiotics, she assumed, and stimulants. Marisa held her father's hand, talking to him softly, trying to keep him awake. He murmured strange things, only barely coherent from the drugs, and then he blinked, and Marisa leaned closer.

"What are you doing?" she asked.

"I . . . know you," he said. His eyes were still closed, though he was struggling to open them. "And I know we can't afford a new liver. You're going to follow that woman and try to get my other one back, and I'm not letting you."

"No, Papi," said Marisa, "I'm staying with you."

"The doctors won't let you," he said. "I'll go into surgery, and you'll be alone, and you'll start getting ideas." He blinked again. "I'm stopping you."

"What are you doing?" she asked again. "You're stoned out of your mind, Papi, don't do anything you can't undo; you're not thinking straight—"

"I'm using my parental controls," he said. "Those videos are your only lead."

"Papi, stop."

He blinked again. "Now you can't follow them."

Triste Chango sounded another alarm, a loud klaxon that stunned Marisa and jerked her father awake. "Please do not go to sleep, Mr. Carneseca. You must remain conscious."

Marisa shook her head, trying to clear the ringing from her ears, and then blinked to check her djinni. What had he done? It still worked, and when she tried to get online—

"A la verga," she muttered, and ran for the door. Bennett had blocked the local wireless signals, and she had no idea if Triste Chango's call for an ambulance had actually gone out. She tried the door but it wouldn't open; the locks were digitally controlled, and with all the power shut down they couldn't unlock. She tried a window instead, and forced it open with a grunt.

"Help!" she shouted, trying to climb through to the street beyond. "My father's been stabbed! Call an ambulance!" She made it through and fell to the ground with a grunt; she twisted, and managed to land on her bionic arm, which saved her from a nasty scrape on the cement but knocked the wind out of her instead. She clambered to her feet, finding a few people staring at her; she recognized most of them as regulars in the neighborhood, and shouted again. "My father's been stabbed, and our djinnis aren't working. Call an ambulance now!"

Several of the people shouted back assurances, and more still ran to help her. They called for paramedics and helped force the door open, and soon the restaurant was filled with friends and neighbors tending closely to Marisa's parents and to Sahara. Marisa found the solar unit in the kitchen and turned it back on, restoring power to the building, but whatever Bennett had done to the wireless signals was still in place. One of the old señoras in the neighborhood pulled Marisa to a chair and made her sit down, holding her hand and trying to calm her. Marisa nodded, recovering from yet another adrenaline rush, praying one more time that her father would be safe. She took a deep breath, holding the woman's hand, and then remembered her djinni.

What had her father done? She hunted through her system, trying to see what he had changed, and then she remembered that he'd mentioned the videos. Her heart froze, and she looked in the folder where she'd put them.

And started crying again.

"Whoa," said Anja, "whoa, it's okay. It's okay."

Marisa looked up to see Anja and Omar and Renata walking through the crowd. Marisa stood up, and Anja ran to her, wrapping her in a tight hug.

"It's okay," Anja said again. "Everything's going to be okay. We're here to help now."

Marisa looked at Omar. "Do you still have those videos? Of Zenaida?"

"No," he said, shaking his head. "Why?"

"Does Jacinto?"

"He got rid of them," said Omar. "In his djinni and everywhere else. What's going on?"

"They were our only way to find Zenaida," said Marisa. "And my dad deleted them."

The ambulance took Carlo Magno back to Polo Urias Hospital. Guadalupe was already starting to wake up, and went with them to help take care of him and sign the various papers and forms they needed. When Marisa explained to her what happened, she broke down in tears—getting stabbed was one thing, but losing the liver was something they couldn't feasibly recover from.

They'd already spent all their savings buying him the first liver. There was no way they could afford another. They couldn't even afford the hospital stay.

"Take care of the other children," Guadalupe told Marisa. "Don't—" She stopped, took a breath, and recovered. "Don't tell them how bad it is. We might still find a way to save him."

And then the paramedics pulled Guadalupe outside, and she got into the ambulance and drove away. Marisa looked around at the devastation in the restaurant—the overturned tables, the massive puddle of blood—and sank down into a chair. What could she possibly do now?

"We can get him another liver," said Anja.

"We can't afford one," said Marisa.

Anja shrugged. "I can."

"Your father will never agree to it."

Anja thought for a moment, then sighed and shook her head. "No, he won't."

"Neither will mine," said Omar. "Though I suppose that goes without saying."

"I still don't know the exact terms of their truce," Marisa said, closing her eyes, "but yeah. Papi said this is the one thing he wouldn't save him from."

"We need to get that liver back," said Sahara. She was awake again, too, and propped up in one of the booths while she waited for her equilibrium to return. "You already own it, and it'll still be good for a few hours."

"Organs don't last that long outside of the body," said Omar. "And Bennett didn't put it on ice."

"She did it one better," said Sahara. "That black sack Mari described sounds like a stasis bag. Assuming she sealed it right, it'll last until tomorrow at least."

Marisa felt her heart swell with hope, but she let the air out almost immediately. "No," she said. "Bennett has it, and we've never been able to find her. There's no chance we can get the liver back at all, let alone tonight."

"We can find Zenaida," said Renata. She'd been hanging in the back, avoiding the conversation out of respect or discomfort, but now she joined it eagerly. "Find her and this Bennett chick will find you, guaranteed. Then you can trade for the liver."

"Maybe," said Marisa, "but my father deleted the videos. That was our last lead." She stood up and paced away, too agitated to sit any longer. "Is it just the danger, like he said? Or is there something he's still trying to hide from me?"

"You might be able to recover the videos from your djinni's memory," said Sahara. She was sitting up straighter now. "Deleting a file doesn't mean that it's gone, it means that it's no longer cataloged or protected. That section of the hard drive can be freely written over, but until it is, the file you deleted is still in there."

"Probably not an option," said Anja. "Djinnis have very little local storage, and Marisa's is almost certainly full of install files for Overworld and other games. Anything else, especially big stuff like VR video, will be stored remotely on a cloud server somewhere."

"You can still find that, though, right?" asked Omar. "I've seen you girls hack into virtually anything—this can't be that hard."

"Yes it can," said Anja. "How many times do we have to tell you this? Hackers aren't magic, missgeburt; it takes time and massive amounts of prep and research. Hacking KT Sigan took seven of us days, and that was with weird windfalls to help get us access. Hacking into a Ganika cloud server would be just as complicated, without the back doors, and by that time they'll surely have been written over with someone else's cloud storage."

"So it's hopeless," said Marisa. "My father's going to die."

"It's not hopeless," said Sahara. She sat up fully, swaying slightly before centering herself and staring at Marisa with fierce intensity. "We can do this."

"What's 'this'?" asked Marisa. "What can we do?"

"Something," said Sahara. "Anything. Ramira Bennett is out there somewhere, and she has your father's liver, and we can find it and bring it back. Maybe there's something on Lemnisca.te that can help us get into Ganika's cloud servers, I don't know. Let me check." She blinked, frowned, blinked again, then refocused her eyes on Marisa. "Why doesn't my djinni work?"

"Bennett killed our satellite access," said Marisa. "Local connections work, but we can't get onto the internet."

"Sounds like a Faraday cage," said Sahara.

"Sounds like a Suppression Bubble," said Renata. "Did the power go down at the same time?"

"Yeah," said Marisa, "she killed the solar unit. I got it started up again, though."

"Sure," said Renata, standing up, "but did you unplug the Bubble? Show me where it is."

Marisa stood, curious, and led her into the kitchen. Anja and Omar followed, but Sahara stayed where she was, still too unsteady to walk. Apparently being tranqed twice in twelve hours really messed with your head. Marisa found the solar unit by the back door—a private power plant that collected energy from the solar trees and panels on the roof and distributed them throughout the building. It was about three feet tall, two feet wide, and one foot deep, attached to the wall about two feet up. Renata smirked and crouched down, feeling under the unit with her hand.

"There's always a big outlet right under the unit, but they're hidden so no one ever uses them. Yep, here it is."

"Pull it out," said Omar.

"And kill us all?" asked Renata. She lay on her back and put her head under the unit. "We used to use these all the time when we hit a target—pretty standard stuff. I'm surprised you girls don't know about them."

"We're not terrorists," said Marisa, "so that might have something to do with it."

"You wound me," said Renata. She reached up with her hands and started fiddling with whatever device she was studying. "We prefer the term 'freedom fighter.' Though to be fair, we did set traps on our Suppression Bubbles. Your green repo agent apparently does not. Plug your ears in case I'm wrong."

"What? No!" Marisa barely had time to react before Renata unplugged the device, pulled it out, and looked up at their shocked faces.

Renata looked confused. "What?"

"You could have leveled the entire block!" shouted Omar.

"Cool," said Anja, reaching for the device. "Gimme."

"What'd I miss?" asked Sahara from the kitchen doorway. She

was leaning against the doorframe, her eyes out of focus. "Everybody shouted."

"She almost killed us!" said Omar.

"Meet Renata," said Marisa. "You get used to it."

"It's called a Suppression Bubble," said Renata, handing the device to Anja. "You plug it in and it shorts out the solar unit, giving itself a burst of power that it uses to set up an EM field in a big sphere around itself. Signals can bounce around inside of it, but they can't go through it, and turning the power back on just keeps the thing going. If you're trying to take someone out quietly, or even just rough someone up a little, these things are amazing."

"My djinni's already reconnecting," said Sahara. "Give me a minute, I'm going to sit down and check Lemnisca.te for Ganika hacks."

"Mine's reconnecting too," said Marisa. Text alerts and missed calls were already popping up in her vision—apparently Anja and Omar had both tried to call her while they were en route, which was right in the middle of Bennett's interrogation. She had some texts from her siblings, asking what was going on, and one from Chuy, who'd apparently heard about the attack.

Then another message caught her eye, and she had to sit down in shock.

"Girls," she said quietly. "I got an email from Grendel."

"Like, a Lemnisca.te message?" asked Anja.

"No," said Marisa. "A direct email."

Anja and Sahara looked at her with wide, fearful eyes.

"Who's Grendel?" asked Omar.

"There's no way it's from his real ID," said Sahara. "He'd never give you that kind of info about himself."

"Spoofed ID," said Marisa, scanning the email for viruses. "The account was created twenty minutes ago. Five bucks says it was deleted five minutes later."

"Answer the man's question," said Renata. "Who's Grendel?"

"We're competent, mid-level hackers—" said Sahara.

"Speak for yourself," Anja interjected.

"Grendel is the real deal," Sahara continued. "Some shadowy monster from the darknet. Mari ran into him back during the Bluescreen fiasco, and he's been popping up ever since."

"He's contacted her a couple of times," said Anja. "Mostly he helps us with whatever mess we've gotten ourselves into, but there's always some kind of angle in it for him. Even when it looks like we're helping someone else, he benefits."

"And he knows about the accident," said Marisa. "I was trying to find him because he knew the truth about what happened to me in that car. Which means that on top of everything else, he's connected to this somehow."

"Maybe he's Severov," said Sahara. "Or that other name we heard, who works for Severov—Teofilo? Something like that?"

"He could be someone inside of ZooMorrow," said Omar.

Anja nodded. "Like the original assassin who tried to kill Zenaida."

"How about we stop talking and read the damn email," said Renata. "Does that seem like a good way to maybe answer some of these questions?"

Marisa swallowed. "Virus scan came up clean. It's safe to open."

Sahara nodded. "Do it."

Marisa took a breath, looked at her friends, and opened the email.

I can't save her. You can.

It had four attachments.

"Santa vaca," Marisa breathed.

Omar put a hand on her arm. "What is it?"

"All three videos," said Marisa, "and another video that seems to be patched together from their background data."

"Scheiss," said Anja.

"I take it all back," said Sahara. "You are one hundred percent being haunted."

"How did he know?" Marisa demanded. She blinked to open the first video and saw that it had already been broken down and analyzed, just like Renata proposed. "Did he hear us? Was he listening? And how did he know I needed them—is he still listening now?"

"My camera nulis have been with us all day," said Sahara. "Even with the mics turned off, he surely has programs that could figure out what we were saying."

"Then how did he get the videos?" asked Renata. "Even if he knew about them, he couldn't just find them and decrypt them in an hour."

"Yes he could," said Marisa. It all made so much sense now. "Grendel can find anything, and know anything, but he can't save Zenaida. He said it himself. So who cares this much about Zenaida de Maldonado, and had access to the videos, and is a frakking wizard with computers . . . but can't do anything in the real world?"

"Holy crap," said Omar. "It's Jacinto."

Another email appeared in Marisa's vision, from another fake address, with a simple subject line:

You're wasting time.

"Right," said Marisa. "We'll deal with this later. However Grendel got this data, and whoever he really is, we have it now, and we can use it to find Zenaida and save my dad." She looked at Omar's face, and saw empathy there for the first time ever.

"Okay then," said Sahara. She nodded, thinking, the gears of a strategist already turning in her head. She pointed to one of the wall screens; normally they cycled ads for daily restaurant specials, but now they were newly rebooted from the power failure, and played a screensaver slideshow of Mexican landscape photos. "Play the video."

Marisa smiled, tight-lipped, and squeezed her friend's hand. "Thank you. Thanks to all of you."

"Cherry Dogs forever," said Anja. "Plus . . ." She waved at Omar and Renata. ". . . assorted others."

Marisa blinked, connecting to the San Juanito computer network, and synced the nearest wall screen to her video player. She loaded the fourth video from Grendel, the one marked "reconstructed data," and played it.

The screen was black, followed almost immediately by a short paragraph of small white words: **The files from Zenaida de Maldonado were full 3D video, filmed on an Arora Huntress 559 guardian nuli. She scrubbed out all visual data other than herself when she created the malware. Approximately 62 percent of that data was recoverable.**

After a moment those words faded, and the first video appeared: Zenaida, terrified, looking over her shoulder and running away. She was on a street somewhere—black patches where the data was corrupted left holes in the picture, but it was on some innate level recognizably Los Angeles. Rolling hills, with crumbling brick houses. Marisa had seen streets like it in old San Diego, but she wasn't completely certain that this was there. The video ended, cutting to black, and moments later the second video appeared: Zenaida, her jaw firm, her eyes alive with hatred, advancing toward the camera and firing.

"Demonios," muttered Renata. "I paid a lot for that nuli."

The street in this video was different, though similar, and Zenaida was wearing the same clothes so it was probably the same day. The end of the same long chase, Marisa supposed.

The screen cut to black, and then the third video appeared. Zenaida was dressed in a black shirt and pants and an olive-green military vest, her hair tied back, all business. She sat in a small room, the walls some kind of corrugated orange metal; behind her was a small cot, a backpack, and a low table covered with equipment.

"Engineering tools?" asked Anja.

"Medical," said Renata. "That's a field kit for a combat medic."

"Is she in a war zone?" asked Omar.

"I am not yours," said Zenaida. "I used to be, though that was more from my own weakness than from any success or skill on your part." The background, like in the other reconstructed videos, was patchy and full of black holes, but even then it was easy to tell that the room she was in was small and cramped. The nuli was up high, almost at head level, and Marisa thought it must be sitting on top of something—or more likely, she realized, hanging from a hook on the wall. "You can't have me," Zenaida continued, "and you can never have me, and you're going to stop looking. Or next time I'll do a lot worse than plant some malware in your brain." The video froze and rewound slightly, and some more words appeared in the corner:

Audio enhanced to amplify background noise.

The video started playing again, and weird bass clicks and rumbles covered Zenaida's voice while she spoke: "—a lot worse than plant some—" On the word *some*, as clear as day, a horn sounded, deep and distant. It boomed again on the word *brain*, and then a third time while Zenaida simply stared at the camera.

And that was it.

"Well, that was a waste of time," said Renata. "That didn't tell us anything."

"It told us she's in a shipping container," said Sahara. "Did you see what those walls were made of, and how long and narrow the room was?"

"She must be . . . living there," said Omar.

"I've heard about this," said Marisa. "It's a shantytown by the coast—La Huerta. An old dock that was abandoned when the company that owned it went under. Most of the shipping containers were still there, so people just . . . moved in." She looked at Renata. "So you were right—she's near the docks."

"But where?" asked Renata. "We don't have time to turn over an entire shantytown."

"I can borrow my brother's nuli," said Marisa. "We can give it Zenaida's DNA template and let it go to work."

"I still have the data," said Renata. "All we have to do is plug it in."

Marisa sent Sahara a private message: **She's going to betray us. You know she is.**

I told you, Sahara sent back, **I have a plan. Two wrongs are going to make a right.**

Two wrongs? sent Marisa.

Sahara smiled and sent another message: **Who do we know who hates Don Francisco more than anything in the world?**

Before Marisa could think of an answer, a small bell chimed in the corner—someone had opened the front door. The group fell silent, and Omar and Renata pulled their guns out. Marisa crept to the kitchen door, listening to the footsteps in the other room. One person? She couldn't tell. Whoever it was wasn't trying to hide; she could hear a voice muttering softly, and then suddenly it swore loudly in Chinese.

"Mari!" said the voice. "Where are you?"

"Bao!" She opened the door and saw him standing white-faced, staring at the blood.

"What happened?" he asked

"The Mantissassin came back," she said. "She has my dad's liver, and we're going to go get it back, but first we have to find Zenaida in an abandoned dockyard."

Bao looked at her, and at the other friends filing out of the kitchen, and did a double take. "What the hell? It's Traitor Hot Girl!"

"Her name's Renata," said Marisa, pulling away from him. "She's helping us again. I forgot to mention that part."

"I can see why," said Bao. "It was weird enough already before the Great Betrayer showed up."

"Hey, Bao," said Renata, and Marisa glanced over to see that the girl had somehow pulled her neckline lower. "How you been?"

Bao looked at her, then back at Marisa. "None of this makes any sense."

Memo's djinni was still on the bloody table, where Bennett had dropped it; Marisa picked it up and put it in her pocket. "I know," she said, and grinned. "Are you in?"

"For you?" Bao shrugged. "Always."

TWENTY-TWO

Anja called an autocab, and Bao described the container village as they rode through the city.

"It's a shantytown," he said, "like the building I live in except it's an entire city. The Rodolfo Guzman Huerta Dockyard was built to be the biggest in LA, and missed the rise of nuli labor by about a year—it was obsolete almost immediately. The company couldn't even afford to pull out the goods that were already there, so they just abandoned it, and looters showed up. It became a criminal market, and by the time they sold off everything in the containers it was already pretty established, so they stayed. La Huerta is still a market, plus now it's a neighborhood, and a maze, and everyone there is a criminal and it's super dangerous."

Sahara raised her eyebrow. "This is usually the part where you tell us it's *too* dangerous, and we shouldn't go."

"You're not dragging my sisters into it this time," said Bao. "Knock yourselves out."

"Good," said Sahara. Her nulis clung to the roof above her, watching everything. "Here's my plan—"

"Just don't literally knock yourselves out," said Bao. "They will straight up steal everything you own."

"Thanks," said Sahara. "Now—"

"Including your kidneys," said Bao, interrupting again. "You'll wake up naked and burglarized in a tub full of ice, possibly also missing an eye."

"Naked and robbed," said Renata. "Burglary is when you break into a building, not a human body, and the police are *very* specific about the difference." She looked around at their surprised faces. "What?"

"Can I say my plan now?" asked Sahara.

"Can I give some more advice first?" asked Bao.

"Why not?" said Sahara, falling back into her seat and folding her arms.

"Get your djinnis locked down," said Bao. "Like, crazy locked down. La Huerta is riddled with coral rigs and spyware and every nasty thing you can imagine. They'll strip your ID and your credit numbers and everything else they can find."

"Come on," said Anja smugly, "who do you think you're talking to? We've got firewalls on our firewalls here."

"Is that really a thing?" asked Omar. "Can you double up a firewall—"

"Heiliges Schwein!" shouted Anja, and looked at Marisa with wide eyes. "Do we *have* to bring the four-year-old?"

"I can spoof him again," said Marisa, and pulled out her head-jack cable. "Turn around."

Omar did so, reluctantly. "This is getting kind of emasculating."

"Maybe try not being a useless idiot," said Anja. "Just a thought."

The autocab stopped at Marisa's house, and she looked up from Omar's djinni settings. "Crap, I forgot." She held up the cable. "Sahara, can you finish this?"

"Fine," Sahara groaned. "Be quick."

Marisa nodded and jumped out of the cab. Olaya, the house computer, recognized her immediately, and unlocked the door as she ran toward it.

"Welcome home, Marisa," said Olaya. "Your calendar has three items today—"

"Cancel them all," said Marisa, running for the stairs. She stopped suddenly. "Where're the rest of the kids?"

"Pati is at Isa's house," said Olaya. "Sandro and Gabriela are in their bedrooms."

"Thanks," said Marisa, and continued up the stairs, taking them two at a time. She ran past Gabi's door and knocked on Sandro's.

"Gabi?"

"Mari," said Marisa. "Can I come in?"

"Sure," said Sandro. She opened the door to find him working at his desk, tinkering with his seeker nuli. "So what's going on with the restaurant?" he asked without looking up. "Olaya told me it was closed?"

"Dad was attacked," said Marisa. Sandro set down his tools and stood up immediately.

"Bad?"

"Yeah." She licked her lips, trying to think of what to say. "He's in the hospital. Mom's with him. They told me not to tell you, but . . . it was pretty bad."

"He's alive?"

"For now," said Marisa. "He . . ." She stopped. "Do you want short or long?"

"Long," he said, but blinked, and after a moment he shook his head. "Olaya says Sahara and Anja are outside, plus two IDs it doesn't recognize. You're going somewhere."

"I promise I'll give you the long version later," said Marisa. "Here's the short one, and I know it doesn't make sense, but if you've ever trusted me on anything, trust me on this: Omar Maldonado's mom is alive, and an assassin is chasing her, but first that assassin stopped by the restaurant to steal Papi's liver."

"What?"

"I know it doesn't make sense—"

"Why does an assassin need Dad's liver?"

"That's part of the long version," said Marisa. "For now, just . . . She has the liver, in a stasis bag, and we need to find Omar's mom so we can head off the assassin and get the liver back. So I need your seeker nuli."

"You'd also need her DNA template," said Sandro.

"Got it," said Marisa, and pointed toward the street with her thumb. "One of the unidentified IDs in the cab."

Sandro stared at her, and she braced herself for one of his

lectures on reckless endangerment, but instead he simply sat down, screwed a panel back onto the nuli, then stood up again and handed it to her. "Here." He blinked, and a message popped up in Marisa's djinni. "That's the access code," said Sandro. "It should give you total control."

"I'm going to be straight with you," said Marisa, "the nuli might not make it through this."

"As long as Dad does," said Sandro, and shook the nuli a bit. "Take it."

"Thanks. You'll talk to the girls?"

"Just come back alive," said Sandro. "I love you."

Marisa felt her eyes grow hot. "I love you too." A tear rolled down her face. "Lechuga."

"Now you ruined it," said Sandro, and pointed to the door with a smile. "Go."

"Thanks," said Marisa, and ran back down the stairs.

"Good-bye, Marisa," said Olaya. "Make good choices."

Marisa almost tripped in surprise. She looked up at the nearest speaker in the wall, the source of Olaya's voice. "Did my parents tell you to say that?"

Olaya said nothing, and Marisa paused for only a moment before running outside, closing the door behind her, and jumping into the cab.

"Got the nuli."

"And my djinni's all set," said Omar.

"I uploaded Renata's laptop for Fang and Jaya," said Sahara. "She'll break into ZooMorrow and cover Zenaida's tracks."

"Now," said Renata, "all we need are my guns."

Sahara shot her a look from the side of her eye. "I'm disturbed by how plural that word was."

"I'm not," said Bao. "As long as she's on our side, I want her to have every gun she can carry."

"You're my favorite," said Renata, blowing him a kiss.

"How can we be sure she *stays* on our side?" asked Anja.

"Just make sure you stay on Bao's side," said Renata. "I'm his till I find someone cuter."

"Then I guess we know what Bao's job is," said Marisa, and gave him a helpless smirk. "Stay cute."

La Huerta, when they arrived, felt to Marisa as if it was almost as large as Mirador: giant, rusting cranes stretched over dark green canals; old derelict ships hiding small, illicit new ones; and endless rows of shipping containers, each the size of an autohauler truck: twelve meters long, and two and a half meters both wide and tall. Some were rusting, some were toppled, and some were stacked seven or even ten levels high. The makeshift streets between them were filled with people of every variety, and none of them looked friendly.

"This looks terrifying," said Marisa.

"Good," said Bao. "That means you're appraising it correctly."

Even the cab was nervous: "It may be difficult to find another taxi quickly in this area," it said. "Would you like me to stay nearby?"

"Nein," said Anja, and thumped it on the roof. "Hit the road, buddy."

Renata surveyed the container village, blowing a puff of hair out of her eyes. "If it tried to hang around, we'd find it up on blocks with its tires stripped."

"Now I'm wishing we all had guns," said Sahara.

"I've got a gun," said Omar, "but I'm starting to think there's no way I have enough bullets."

"How many you packing?" asked Renata. She was armed with a long rifle, tipped with a thick black suppressor, and at least one handgun that Marisa could see; she also wore a rubberized backpack, which might have been carrying several more, though Marisa didn't know for sure what was in it. For all she knew it was full of replacement explosive hands.

"Eight in the gun," said Omar. "Spare mag with eight more."

"Well then," said Renata. She propped her rifle against her shoulder. "Try to only piss off sixteen people at the most."

"And don't miss," said Sahara.

Anja raised her eyebrow at Renata's armory. "You're just going to walk around like that?"

"Trust me," said Bao. "She'll fit right in."

"The DNA template is loaded in the nuli," said Marisa. "Ready to launch."

"Wait," said Sahara, putting her hand on Marisa's. "We gotta name it."

"Never launch a nuli without a name," said Anja.

"Guess that's what I was doing wrong," said Renata.

"I want to name it Pancho," said Omar.

Marisa looked at him, then back at Sahara. "That's the short version of Francisco."

"My father's been looking for my mother for fifteen years," he said, and then grinned. "When we finally find her, I want it to be a fat little bastard with a nickname he hates."

"I love it," said Anja, but then immediately scowled. "Still hate you, though. Don't get any ideas."

Marisa blinked, powering up Pancho's wings, and then heaved it up into the air. It was small, about the size of a toaster; it hovered over them for a minute, calibrating its DNA sensor, and then approached Omar for a few seconds before apparently deciding that, while similar, his DNA wasn't Zenaida's. He circled around them slowly, then flew up higher and zoomed off into La Huerta.

"Do we hang out?" asked Marisa. "Or . . . follow it?"

"Let's at least move in toward the market," said Bao. "If you're carrying a wallet, throw it away now and save yourself the trouble of being pickpocketed."

He walked toward the wide gate in the dockyard's chain-link fence, and the rest of the group followed him warily.

The entrance to La Huerta was thronged with kiosks and food carts, just like any high-traffic border point, though these merchants weren't selling kitschy souvenirs. A man shouted at them in a thick Pakistani accent, hawking his street-rip IDs; beside him, a white man with long, shaggy hair called out a repeating, almost singsong ad for his premium stock of aftermarket memory chips: "Everything they never thought you'd find! Two chips for a dollar! Everything they never thought you'd find! Two chips for a dollar!" Marisa saw a little boy selling Yerba Buena, a marijuana hybrid laced with mint; on the other side of the road an old woman sat curled up in the imperfect corner of two shipping containers, a few dozen cybernetics spread out before her on a multicolored shawl. Her spread had eyes, ears, drug ports, djinnis, and even a foot. Anything an illicit shopper might want—all the overpriced, questionably legal, don't-ask-where-it-comes-from merchandise that an otherwise upstanding citizen might try to buy—were laid out on tables or hanging from wires or lining the jackets of shady vendors in darkened alleys.

"Anyone want some black-market goods?" asked Sahara. "I think we found the mother lode."

Bao shook his head. "These are all black-market bads, trust me."

"How long have you been saving that one?" asked Omar.

"We don't really have the kind of relationship where you get to mock me," said Bao. "That said: most of the ride over here. And totally worth it."

"Don't buy anything in the entrance," said Renata. "I've seen this kind of place before, in Mexico City—all the good deals are inside."

"Don't buy anything at all," said Marisa. "Half of these places probably have undercover runners to follow you home: they sell you a tablet, they mug you and steal it back, and then sell it to the next sucker."

"Probably," said Anja, "but that really just makes me want to buy something and see what happens."

"Don't," said Omar.

"Okay, now I'm definitely buying something," said Anja. "That place sells Huckleberries, hang on—"

"No," said Sahara, grabbing Anja's arm as she started to move out of the group. "We stick together."

Marisa got an alert from Pancho: he'd found a concentration

of people, probably a marketplace or an apartment, and checked it out before moving on. "Nothing to report," she said out loud.

"Ten o'clock," said Bao. "Ferrat. Ooh, two of them."

Marisa looked to her left and saw them—two black rats, each about the size of a small house cat, gnawing hungrily on the corner of a shipping container. A group of small children shouted at them, waving sticks, and the Ferrats scurried away with the children in hot pursuit.

"They eat metal?" asked Omar.

"Courtesy of ZooMorrow," said Sahara. "We looked them up a few days ago: gengineered chimeras designed to eat scrap metal and break it down. People harvest their excrement for manufacturing."

"Most of them are controlled," said Bao, "but it's hard to keep something that eats metal locked up. A lot of these places have wild ones running around."

"What happens when they start running through the city?" asked Marisa. "That's a doomsday scenario if I've ever heard one."

"They'll probably all die trying to chew on power cables," said Renata.

"Or a railroad track," said Marisa. "And take a whole commuter train with them."

"If they're dangerous, someone will pay to have them killed," said Renata, and made an imaginary check mark in the air with her finger. "Note to self."

Pancho sent another alert: **population concentration number two scanned and cleared.** She blinked into its app, where Sandro had prepared a map to track its movements. It was going quickly, but La Huerta was almost impossibly large.

How long did they have?

They walked deeper into the village, passing out of the initial tourist zone and into a more residential-looking area: here the shipping containers had been emptied and inhabited, and the enterprising squatters who lived in them had added little touches to make them more livable: windows cut into the sides, or ladders and stairs welded onto the outer walls. The shipping containers were stacked neatly, like blocks, in an almost artful arrangement of different colors and corporate logos.

"Oye!" yelled a man, and Marisa ignored him like all the other eager vendors, but the next word took her by surprise: "Bao-chan!"

"Friend of yours?" asked Sahara.

"I skim credit cards for a living," said Bao. "Gotta fence those IDs somewhere." He walked to the side of the road, where an old Japanese man with a long, curved mustache leaned against the corrugated wall of a container. "Salaam, Mugen."

"Salaam, Bao-chan," said the man. "Here with friends today?"

"Just visiting," said Bao. "Nothing to sell you right now, I'm afraid."

"Just visiting," said Mugen slowly, giving a long, meaningful look to Renata's rifle. "Buying or selling?"

"Just keeping ourselves safe," said Sahara.

"That's a sniper rifle," said Mugen. "Most visitors to La Huerta are more concerned with close-quarters threats."

"While we're here," said Bao, pulling out his phone, "have you seen this woman anywhere?" He called up a picture of Zenaida, which Marisa had screenshotted from the video and passed around to everyone.

"I don't think so," said Mugen, "but I'll be sure to tell you if I do."

"Thanks," said Bao, and tapped the screen a few times. "How about this one?" He showed another picture, and Mugen whistled.

"Suteki!" he said. "I *wish* I'd seen that one."

Marisa leaned over to see the screen and saw a picture of Bennett. "You have a picture of Bennett?"

"I snapped it in the high-rise the other night," he said, "right before I distracted her for you." The photo was taken with a night-vision filter, but showed Ramira Bennett in profile and captured her unearthly beauty almost perfectly.

"What's wrong with her eye?" asked Mugen.

"You'll know it when you see it," said Bao.

"Instantly," said Anja. "She's bright green."

"We're going to head in to Incheon, okay?" said Bao. "Let me know if either of those women show up."

"Of course, Bao-chan," said Mugen, and proffered the tiniest hint of a bow. Bao returned a much deeper bow of his own, and they continued down the road.

"Incheon is another marketplace," said Bao. "The one locals actually shop in. I've got a contact there who might know something."

Pancho searched and cleared another area while they walked, and three more while Bao asked around with his local contacts. The rest of them sat under a plastic awning, eating cold congee and avocado ice cream. The afternoon heat was oppressive every-where, but here in the labyrinth of hard metal shipping containers it was focused and reflected and magnified. Every now and then a breeze blew by, bringing a salty, welcome chill from the ocean, but these were few and far between, and gone too quickly.

Hard-eyed locals watched them from every side, each sporting a veritable catalog of weapons and physical upgrades—rail gun pistols, cybernetic attachments, and even some bizarre genhancements that Marisa knew couldn't possibly be legal. One woman walked by, grizzled and dangerous, with a circular saw in the place of a hand and a rusting respirator replacing her mouth and nose. Her skin puckered at the edges, where some back-alley surgeon had bolted the bionic to her face. Marisa wondered what injury or illness had necessitated the change, and then, the more she thought about it, wondered how the woman managed to eat. The woman's strangeness was almost immediately superseded by a tall, lanky man in a loose-fitting shirt, whose eyes were mounted on the ends of gently waving stalks, extending four or five inches out of their sockets. Whether the eyestalks were cybernetic or gengineered, she couldn't say.

Another alert came in from Pancho, and Marisa blinked on it idly, wondering which jury-rigged apartment building had been searched and cleared this time, but what she saw made her stand up in shock.

"Pancho's dead," she said.

"That might be nuli hunters," said Anja.

"I lost four nulis thinking it was hunters," said Renata, and checked the magazine in her rifle. She slapped it back into place. "It's Zenaida."

"Good news," said Bao, returning from one of the vendors. "The mushroom guy thinks he knows Zenaida—says she buys from him sometimes. If he's right, she lives over in—"

"A container tower two streets that way," said Marisa, pointing in the direction of the nearest canal.

"Yeah," said Bao. "How did you know?"

"We just lost Pancho."

"That's definitely Zenaida," said Sahara. "Let's go."

Anja dropped her congee cup in a recycling basket and stood up. "Did the merchant recognize Bennett?"

"No," said Bao, "but unless she's a local mushroom customer, that's not saying much."

"I'm starting to think that she might blend in a little too well around here," said Marisa. "We'll be lucky if anyone remembers her at all."

"Mugen noticed her face before her eyes," said Omar. He stood up to follow them to the container tower. "Abnormalities become pretty normal after a while, but a beautiful woman will always stand out."

"I know," said Renata. "It's my curse."

"Let's go," said Sahara again, and they followed her through the marketplace, weaving between tables and stalls and standing vendors wearing high racks of trinkets on their shoulders. At the edge of the Incheon, Marisa took over, leading them along the path Pancho had taken through the streets—narrow, junk-filled canyons between tall blocks of shipping containers. They reached one of the tallest stacks, where an old white man in cargo shorts and a white mesh T-shirt sat in a weathered folding chair under a fraying beach umbrella.

"Excuse me," said Bao. "Can I ask you a question?"

"You mean not counting that one?" asked the man.

"Oh wow," said Bao, "that's even better than my 'black-market bads' joke. How about you just tell me how many questions I can ask, and we'll skip all this negotiating?"

"Just ask your damn question," said the man.

Bao produced his phone and showed him the picture of Bennett. "Have you seen this woman?"

He studied it for a moment before shaking his head. "No. Should I have?"

Bao swiped the screen, and showed him Zenaida. "How about this one?"

"What do I look like, a dating service? Get out of here."

"Can you tell me where I can find the landlord?" asked Bao.

"He's not a dating service either," said the man.

"Listen," said Omar, stepping forward and taking Bao's phone. "You see this second photo? That's my mother. She's in trouble, and First Photo is trying to kill her. Now, if you're done making stupid jokes, tell us where she is."

The man stared at them a moment longer, examining Omar's features and the photo. "Yeah, I suppose you could be Zenaida's kid. What's your story, then? She's lived here long enough, and you've never bothered with her before."

"We thought she was dead," said Omar. "How long has she been around?"

"Four years, maybe?" The man leaned to the side and spat something dark and juicy on the ground. "I've only been landlord for three, so I don't know for sure."

Omar looked shocked.

"Which room does she live in?" asked Sahara. "Or . . . how does it work here?"

"She has a room," said the man, nodding, "but I don't know which." He leaned forward, and grunted with the effort of standing up. "We'll have to check the files." He didn't blink, and Marisa raised her eyebrow.

"Physical files?" she asked.

"They're a lot harder to hack," he said, turning toward a door cut into the side of a container. He walked with a painful waddle, as if his legs or his back didn't work right. "Nobody who lives in La Huerta is eager to be found."

"Are you sure you haven't seen the other woman anywhere?" asked Anja.

The landlord pushed open the metal door and led them into the shipping container; it was practically an oven in the heat. "Don't touch that outer wall," he said, pointing to the one they'd just come through. "This isn't one of those fancy insulated cans." The inside of the container was filled with furniture, not in a livable arrangement but as some kind of storage room—chairs and tables and beds and hammocks, carefully stacked from floor to ceiling. Marisa figured he probably sold them to tenants. Another hole was cut into each one of the narrow walls of the room, connecting it to the neighboring containers, and the landlord pointed toward the left one dismissively. "That's my private room, so stay out. The files are over here." He sidled between the stacks of furniture, working his way to the back corner. He reached something, crouched down to fiddle with it, and suddenly stopped short. "What the . . . ?"

"What is it?" Sahara followed him through the narrow pathway and looked over his shoulder. "Hot damn," she muttered, and then turned to shout to the rest of them. "His file cabinet is padlocked shut, but the padlock's been eaten through by some kind of acid. It's gotta be Ramira's biotoxin."

"She's here," said Anja, looking at the doors. "Or she was."

"Hang on," said the landlord, his earlier lazy attitude completely gone. "Let me see what they took." He pulled open the drawers, one by one, running his fingers over the files. "I have these listed in numerical order, one for each can in the building. If I can find which can whoever broke in here was looking for . . ."

He trailed off, muttering to himself as he searched. Marisa looked at Omar, who was standing by the wall with wide eyes, staring at nothing.

"You okay?" she asked.

"Huh? Yeah, I'm fine." He looked at her a moment, then spoke again, almost to himself. "Four years, he said. This place is barely an hour from my house, and she lived here for four years, and she never tried to see me, contact me, nothing. . . ." He shook his head. "Maybe we shouldn't be here at all. We haven't known anything about her for fifteen years, but she's known everything about us, and never once visited us or tried to tell us she was okay or even just check in and see how we were doing. Not once."

"She might have tried," said Marisa. "We don't know."

"As capable as she's proven herself to be?" said Omar. "If she'd wanted to contact me, she could've done it anytime."

"Here it is," said the landlord. "Or isn't: the files for can 47 are missing."

"That's got to be Zenaida," said Sahara. "Where's 47?"

The landlord handed her a piece of orange paper, a crude copy of a copy. "Here's a map. Just don't go anywhere you're not supposed to—like I said before, people who live here don't want to be found."

"Let's do this," said Sahara.

"Yes!" Renata slung the sniper rifle over her shoulder and pulled out a pistol, racking the action to chamber a round. "Let's earn some money."

Sahara looked at the map and blinked, taking a photo and forwarding the image to each of them. Omar pulled out his pistol as well, and Sahara's camera nulis swirled overhead, taser prongs extended and ready. Anja and Marisa were armed with the same one-shot tasers they'd had the other night, and Bao produced a similar weapon from under his shirt.

"Renata, take the lead," said Sahara, "followed by Marisa, me, and Omar in the back. Bao and Anja, stay in the street and watch for anyone trying to slip out behind us."

Marisa locked the image of the map in the corner of her vision and followed Renata through the door on the right of the storage room. Sahara and Omar came close behind. The door led to another container, where a sheet of scrap metal had been welded to the walls, cutting the narrow can in half; one side was a tiny room, where two small children peeked out of the crack in the door and watched them go by. The other side was a steep staircase—a rusted ladder bolted to the walls and floor at a forty-five-degree angle, forming a dangerous walkway through a hole in the ceiling. They climbed the rungs, finding themselves in another half can, and went through a ragged, doorless hole that turned into a narrow hallway. They followed this trail deeper into the stack of containers, twisting through a maze of breaks and cuts and modifications, pausing at each crossroads to try to figure out which branch the map wanted them to take. The entire system was a warren: sometimes it led them down, other times up, other times even outside, where the trail continued on a series of catwalks high above the ground.

"This can't be the most direct route," said Sahara. "He's trying to waste our time so she can escape."

"He didn't create this map just to mess with us," said Renata.

Marisa sent a message to Anja: **Anything out there?**

Plenty, sent Anja, **but no Zenaida.**

Keep us posted, sent Marisa, and followed Renata through another twist and up another ladder. Several turns later they were on the roof, seven containers high, with a smaller sort of penthouse block rising several containers higher in front of them.

"Should be that one," said Renata, pointing with her gun at the second container in the elevated row. It had a metal door, currently closed, though the padlock on the door hung loose and open.

"No way she's inside," said Sahara. "Anyone who wanted could come by and lock her in."

"She wouldn't have just walked away with the door unlocked," said Marisa. "This isn't that kind of neighborhood."

"Cheekbones, check it out," said Renata. Omar cast her a sidelong glance, probably more annoyed at the nickname than the order, but he said nothing and held up his gun, approaching slowly. Marisa followed a few steps behind, taser ready, wondering what they would find inside: Zenaida, lying dead? Ramira Bennett, lying in wait?

Or something even worse?

TWENTY-THREE

Omar opened the door with the tip of his foot, gun raised. Inside the container was the room they'd seen in the video, down to the last detail—including the salvaged seeker nuli she'd recorded with, hanging on the back wall. The only difference was a hole, at least half a meter wide, the edges still sizzling from an acid burn. The center showed clear sky and loading cranes in the distance. Marisa ran inside, looking out the jagged hole at the wasteland of La Huerta beyond.

Across the street, only one building over, Ramira Bennett was scuttling up the side of another stack of shipping containers, her bare fingers and toes clinging to the metal as if gravity meant nothing. She looked over her shoulder, fixed Marisa with those inhuman eyes, and then turned back to her path and raced up the side of the containers. Marisa's gaze tracked up, finding the roof of the makeshift building.

There she was. Zenaida de Maldonado, dressed in combat fatigues, sprinting away at top speed.

"There!" Marisa shouted. "She's on the next building."

"Out of the way," said Renata, and shoved Marisa to the side. She dropped her pistol, pulled her long rifle from her shoulder, and lined up a shot—not at Zenaida, but at Bennett. She pressed her eye tightly to the scope, her right hand on the trigger and her left arm propped up with her elbow on her knee, her left hand cradling the rifle. She slowed her breathing, drawing a close bead on her target. "Plug your ears."

"Careful!" shouted Marisa. "She's got my dad's liver."

Renata pulled the trigger gently, but just as she fired, Bennett dropped, letting go of the wall and then grabbing it again several feet lower. She had dodged the bullet perfectly; the projectile slammed into the side of the container, punching through like it wasn't even there. The suppressor on the rifle dampened the sound, but not completely; instead of a deafening boom, it was merely a loud bang, like someone had whacked the inside of the metal container with a hammer. Zenaida looked back but gave no sign that she recognized them and kept running. Renata swore and resteadied her gun, ready to fire again, but Bennett scuttled to the side, rounding the corner of the container and disappearing out of view.

"Lost her," said Sahara.

"Not . . . yet . . . ," said Renata. She was still tracking the rifle smoothly, aiming at where Bennett probably would have been if the containers hadn't been in the way. She fired again, shooting straight through the corner of the container, and as the bang died away they heard a cry. Marisa's jaw dropped, and a second later Bennett reached the top of the stack, bleeding from her upper left arm and scowling at Renata.

"That's right, bitch!" shouted Renata, cupping her hand around her mouth. "These are AP rounds!"

"The stasis bag is on her waist," said Marisa. "Make sure you're aiming high."

"She's getting away," said Sahara, but Bennett was already ducking behind one of the containers on the opposite roof. Sahara pointed out the hole and down, to a narrow catwalk connecting this stack to the next one. "Follow me."

Marisa balked, terrified of the height, but Omar was already throwing a blanket over the jagged edge of the hole and climbing out onto the ledge.

"I'm going up," said Renata. "I can give better sniper support from a few cans up."

"Hurry," said Sahara, and followed Omar out. He'd shoved his pistol into his waistband, and was climbing down the ledge to the catwalk. Marisa looked at the next building over, fixing a spot in her mind and then blinking on it, setting a marker through her GPS. She sent the link to Anja and then opened a call to the entire group.

"We found them," she said, climbing out after Sahara. They were on top of containers stacked seven cans high, and Marisa did the math as she tried not to look down: that put them eighteen meters above the ground, with nothing but an I-beam catwalk between them and the ground. Omar was already working his way across the gap, with Sahara close behind. Marisa kept her eyes up, refusing to look down, and hoped that the person who'd welded the catwalk to the containers had been good at their job. "Go to my marker, and watch the tops of the walls."

"Got it," said Anja. "What were those gunshots we heard?"

"That was Renata," said Marisa. She took a deep breath, let go of the wall, and started across the catwalk.

"Shooting at who?" asked Bao.

"You wound me," said Renata. "Obviously I shot at the bad guy."

"I never doubted that," said Bao. "I just want to make sure we define 'bad guys' the same way."

"Everyone shut up," said Sahara, two-thirds of the way across the catwalk. "I'm trying to not plummet to my death."

Marisa swallowed her fear and focused on walking, one foot after the other, keeping her eyes on the narrow catwalk. Omar had already reached the other side, and moments later Sahara did the same. They stood at the edge, arms outstretched for Marisa, and when she was finally close enough they grabbed her hands and hauled her to safety.

"We're on the next building," said Sahara. "Renata, can you see Bennett?"

"I'm not at the top yet," Renata answered. "Flying isn't one of my superpowers."

"We can't see anything from down here," said Anja.

Marisa blinked onto the internet, looking for a map site and then zeroing in on her current position, zoomed in to show the building they were standing on. She pinned it to the corner of her vision, in the same space the apartment map had been in. It gave her a better sense of the terrain as she raced off after Omar and Sahara, pelting across the rooftop. Most of it was open and clear, but here and there another container rose up one or two levels above the others.

A sudden gunshot rang out, and the three of them dropped to the ground, scrambling for cover.

"Is that you?" asked Bao.

"Bennett," said Omar, crouching in the lee of a container. "She's got us pinned down."

"Then she's pinned Zenaida, too," said Sahara. "If she were still chasing her, she wouldn't have time to ambush us like this."

"There's a doorway in the roof over there," said Marisa, looking at her map and pointing to the left. "It's the only way in, so unless Zenaida just jumped off the ledge, that's where she is."

"Bennett's shots came from the right," said Omar. "We're in between them."

"Great," said Sahara.

"We've reached the street below your marker," said Anja. "Doesn't look like anyone's jumped off your roof. Zenaida's probably in the hole."

Marisa studied her map. "There's another stack of I beams on the far side of this can," she said. "More catwalks they never installed, I guess? We can crawl behind them in cover and get to the doorway that way."

"How old's your satellite photo?" asked Sahara.

"Couple of months," said Marisa, checking the date. "Should be good." She ran to the edge of the container, peeked around the edge, and saw the beams. "Still there. I'm going to risk it." She ran, and gunshots rang out from both sides. Marisa threw herself to the floor behind the steel beams, breathing rapidly. "Santa vaca."

"We're definitely between them," said Omar.

"I'm trapped here," said Marisa, crawling on her chest toward the far end of the I beams. The doorway she'd seen on the satellite photo was there—just a hole in the roof, with Zenaida and who knew what else inside of it. "There's a good ten-foot gap between me and the doorway. I can't make it without getting shot."

"Renata?" asked Sahara.

"I had a complication," snarled the mercenary. "Give me a minute."

Marisa shot a look back at Sahara, who shook her head suspiciously. *What is Renata doing?*

"I'll cover you," said Omar. "Three, two, one: go."

Marisa heard more shots behind her, and hoped it was enough for Bennett to take cover. She jumped to her feet, sprinted across the last ten feet, and leaped into the hole. It had a wooden staircase inside of it, about two feet below the level of the roof, and Marisa tumbled down it in a series of painful whacks.

"Freeze!" said a woman.

Marisa held up her hands, too disoriented to know where the voice was coming from. "Don't shoot. I'm looking for a friend."

"There's no one else here," said the woman, and Marisa's eyes finally found her: standing in the far corner, one hand trying to unlock a door, the other holding a fat black pistol pointed square at Marisa. Instead of a normal magazine it had an ammo drum, like an old-style tommy gun, and Marisa shuddered to think how many bullets it could fire, and how fast.

"It's you," said Marisa.

Zenaida kept her gun trained on Marisa but said nothing as she continued fiddling anxiously with the lock.

"You're Zenaida de Maldonado," said Marisa, and the woman stopped moving. She turned her head slowly, keeping the gun up.

"How do you know that name?"

"Because I know you," said Marisa. She struggled to stand, keeping her hands up so the woman wouldn't shoot. "And you know me, too." She paused, thinking, and then used her human finger to point at her prosthetic arm. "I'm Marisa Carneseca."

The woman stared at her, and then lowered the pistol. "Dios mio."

"It's really you," said Marisa.

Zenaida stared at her a moment longer, then shook her head and looked back at the door lock. "I don't know how you found me but you need to turn around and forget you ever did—"

"Omar's outside," said Marisa, and Zenaida froze again. Marisa risked stepping closer, and Zenaida didn't stop her. "We've been trying to find you ever since ZooMorrow sent that assassin—that's how we knew you were alive, because they were still hunting you."

"Then you should have stayed away," Zenaida insisted. She crossed toward Marisa now, waving her gun and frowning. "Did your father ever tell you how you lost that arm?"

Marisa grimaced, backing up and placing a hand on her prosthetic. "Yes."

"Then you should know better than to get yourself back into this mess. Move." She pushed Marisa aside and climbed the first few stairs. She crouched down, just below the hole in the roof, and readied her gun. "I'm not going to let my boy die on this roof, so call your friends." She popped up suddenly, holding the gun with both hands, and strafed the roof with bullets once again, pinning Bennett behind the container she was using for cover.

"Run!" shouted Marisa, scrambling up after Zenaida and waving to Omar and Sahara. They saw her, and Sahara started sprinting toward the hole. Omar paused, frozen by the sight of his mother, but Marisa yelled at him again, gesturing wildly, and he ran. Marisa jumped down out of the way, and Omar and Sahara leaped down after her, both landing better than Marisa had. The camera nulis zoomed in with them. Zenaida ducked down after them, and she and Omar stood staring at each other.

". . . Mom?"

Zenaida looked at him, and Marisa couldn't read her face. After an agonizing silence, she looked back up at the hole in the ceiling, raising her gun in case Bennett came charging into view.

"You have any bullets left?" asked Zenaida.

"Spare mag," said Omar. He ejected the empty one and slapped a new one into place.

"Watch the hole," said Zenaida, and went back to the door. She pointed her ammo drum pistol at the lock, pulled the trigger, and filled the room with a deafening cacophony of shots and sparks and ricochets. The lock and door tore open like paper, and she kicked the debris out of the way. "Go!"

"Not without you," said Omar.

"You think I'm staying in this death trap?" growled Zenaida. "Go!"

Marisa went first, and was surprised to find the container beyond filled with electrical equipment. Most of it was storage, but some was active . . . and some had been riddled with bullets.

"Damn," said Zenaida, shoving past her to look at the equipment. "Sorry, Rodney." She looked over her shoulder at Omar. "You still watching our backs?"

"Of course."

"Good," said Zenaida, and started digging through a cardboard box full of cables and motherboards. "This belongs to a local named Rodney Burls; he uses it to look for aliens. Somewhere in here he's got an encrypted radio—a handheld shortwave, like they used to use in the Coastal Defense Force. Though I guess that was before your time."

"Um, the only major invasion of United States soil," said Sahara. "They kind of teach it in schools."

"Here it is," said Zenaida. She pulled out a round white tube, maybe a foot long, and pressed a button on the side. A light started beeping red, and she nodded. "Time to run."

"What are you doing?" asked Marisa. "Who are you trying to contact?"

Zenaida shook her head. "The less you know, the safer you'll be when they interrogate you."

"Oh, not you too," said Marisa. "Why don't adults ever tell us anything?"

"You can't leave!" said Omar. "Not again."

"Watch the back door!" she shouted. She walked to the other door in the container and opened a heavy latch. "Let's go. But I can't lock any of these doors behind us, so watch our backs!"

Suddenly the entire container rang like a bell, and Marisa felt a rush of air. She looked up in shock and saw a bullet hole in the ceiling; a finger of sunlight shone through, the beam pointing to another bullet hole that had just opened in the wall. The bullet had passed mere inches from Marisa's face.

"Is Bennett shooting through the roof?" asked Omar.

"That was me," said Renata. "It's called covering fire."

"You almost shot me in the face!" screamed Marisa.

"But I didn't," said Renata, "and now Bennett's too scared to get near that hole you went into. She ran off the other way."

"We'll watch for her," said Anja from the street.

"Who are you talking to?" asked Zenaida.

"We've got friends outside," said Sahara.

"Loosely defined," added Marisa.

"Suffice it to say that our backs are being watched," said Omar, lowering his gun and turning toward Zenaida. "Now, you . . ." He seemed as if he was going to ask her a question, but he either couldn't find the words or he couldn't bring himself to say them. "You're here."

Zenaida didn't meet his eyes. "If she's circling around, you're safer if you stay here." She paused, looking at Omar, then put a hand on his shoulder. "I'm sorry this couldn't be . . . you know. I'm sorry. Say hi to your siblings for me." Then she turned and ran out the door, and Marisa shot a pained glance at Omar before chasing after her.

Sahara followed, and sent Marisa a message: **I'm not sure what I was expecting.**

A paranoid survivalist? Marisa sent back. **I feel like we**

should have seen that coming.

Paranoid and kind of a blowhole, sent Sahara.

The door led into another container hallway, so narrow Marisa had to turn sideways to walk through it. She looked back, making sure Omar was coming with them, and then hurried to catch up to Zenaida, following the twists and turns and hoping they led somewhere useful.

"How many exits does this container block have?" Sahara called out.

"You're safer if you don't follow me" was Zenaida's only answer.

"We're not leaving you!" shouted Marisa. She jumped down another staircase to find Zenaida paused at a junction in the tunnels, and stormed up to her with a frown. "I think we deserve some answers."

"Probably," said Zenaida. "This isn't exactly the time, though."

"Are you planning to stick around for a better one?" demanded Marisa. "We've torn this city apart trying to find you; not just for the last week but for the last fifteen years." She saw Sahara and Omar drawing close to them, and laid into Zenaida with a fury. "This is your son!"

"We don't have time," said Zenaida, and turned back to the junction. She chose the left tunnel, and walked down it with her gun raised. "I'm sorry you found me," she called over her shoulder. Marisa and the others hurried after her. "It would have been easier for all of us if you hadn't."

"We're not very good at 'easy,'" said Marisa.

Zenaida stopped at an open door, looking out onto another

catwalk. She turned back toward Omar. "I'm a terrible mother, and the last fifteen years have probably only made that worse; I'm not apologizing, I'm just letting you know. You look like you've become a decent young man, which I can only assume is in spite of your father's influence. I'm glad of it. I . . ." She trailed off, and then stopped. "I don't know what you're expecting from me. I don't need your help, and I don't have anything to give you except my absence: I'm a wanted fugitive, and the farther you stay away from me the safer we'll all be. If you . . . care about me at all, stay here, and keep these two with you." She didn't wait for a response; she raised her gun and ran out the door.

"Wait!" shouted Marisa, and jumped to follow her, but the street outside was already ringing with gunfire, and she fell back inside; Bennett was shooting at the catwalk from somewhere, the bullets pinging off the metal as Zenaida ran. Zenaida fired back, her heavy machine pistol pumping out bullets at a ridiculous rate, sweeping them across the wall of shipping containers in a loud, sparking wave.

"She's right above us!" shouted Anja.

"Got you," said Renata, a gleeful whisper in Marisa's ears, followed by the loud double explosion of her sniper rifle: the first when she fired it, and the second when the huge, armor-piercing round slammed into something heavy and metal outside of Marisa's view. Bennett stopped firing, and Marisa jumped up and peeked out the door. The street below was full of shocked locals, staring up at the firefight above them, and Marisa felt a wave of dizziness as she looked down.

Bao and Anja waved at them, and then pointed urgently to the far side of the next building. "There's a crane over there!" shouted Bao. "She's trying to reach the docks!"

Marisa gathered her wits, keeping her eyes up and focusing on her balance. Zenaida ran into another door on the far side of the catwalk, and Marisa ran to follow her.

"Right behind you," said Sahara.

Bennett popped up in front of them, one floor up and about five meters to the side; before she could shoot, Marisa heard a burst of gunfire from behind her as Omar unloaded the second magazine of his pistol. The bullets pinged off the metal edges of Bennett's window, and Bennett dropped back out of view. Marisa kept running, and all three of them reached the end of the catwalk, tumbling into the narrow hallway before Bennett could pop back up again.

"I'm going to shoot below her window," said Renata, and Marisa covered her ears as the noise of the impact rang through the container stack. A moment later Renata clucked her tongue. "No way to tell if I hit her."

"Stop shooting," screamed Sahara, "we're in here!"

"Bao and I are running to the other side," said Anja. "Try to get to the roof!"

"This way," said Marisa, and ran to the wall of the container, where some enterprising resident had cut a set of handholds into the corrugated metal wall. She climbed up into a dimly lit hallway and drew her taser. Was Bennett in this container, or the next one over? Sahara joined her, and then Omar, and they followed the hallway as it wound through the stack, past makeshift doors and piles of garbage and the shocked faces of locals. Marisa could hear footsteps in the hallway ahead, but didn't know if they were Zenaida's, or someone else's, or simply their own footsteps echoing back to them.

"I'm looking at a satellite image of the whole area," said Anja on the group call. "One of the crane arms next door to your container stack collapsed at some point, and it's leaning against the top. It looks like you can cross from your roof to the crane, and from there to the edge of the water—I bet you anything that's where Zenaida's going."

"Roger," said Sahara, and pointed to another metal ladder. "This way."

They climbed up, saw a shaft of daylight, and followed it to another ladder that led to the roof of the makeshift building. They reached the top of the containers just in time to see Zenaida picking her way across the gantry of a fallen crane, and Marisa ran toward her with a shout.

"Wait!"

Zenaida looked at her, but didn't stop or slow down.

"I can see you," said Renata on the phone. "I've got a clear view of the whole rooftop. No Bennett."

Marisa reached the edge of the fallen crane, where it leaned heavily against a pair of crumpled shipping containers. She'd been expected something smaller, but this wasn't a construction crane—it was a loading crane, the kind that reached out over the massive ships and picked up the containers. It was thick and heavy, and she was amazed the stack of containers hadn't collapsed under its weight. The locals had bolted and welded the two structures together as well as they could, trying to make it as secure as possible, but Marisa still felt her heart leap into her throat as she stepped to the edge and put a hand on the gantry. It stretched far ahead, past another crane and out to the water—not the ocean, but a wide canal where a derelict container ship was rusting at the dock. A series of cargo nets formed a kind of tether, connecting the crane to the ship in what looked like a well-traveled ladder.

"She's trying to reach the ocean," said Omar, planting his feet next to Marisa's. Zenaida was picking her way across the gantry, where the locals had long ago created handholds and guide ropes. "That radio she turned on—she must have signaled someone offshore."

"Renata," said Sahara. "Can you cover us?"

"Any bright green head that pops up is getting shot in nano-seconds," said Renata.

Marisa looked back; the container stack they'd started in, now two blocks away, was the tallest in the area and, perched on the top of it, Renata would have a commanding view of La Huerta.

"All right, then," said Sahara. "Let's do this."

Sahara went first, probing the gantry with one foot and then, when she was confident it wasn't going to collapse beneath her, putting her full weight on it. She found a handhold, and then another, working her way out toward Zenaida; Omar followed, with Marisa taking up the rear. Wind whipped past her on every side, and she gripped the handholds with white-knuckle terror.

Step by step. Inch by inch.

"There's Bennett," said Bao.

"I can't see her," said Renata.

"She's under the gantry," said Anja. "Crawling along the bottom of the crane like a spider."

"I don't have a shot," said Renata. "She can cross the whole gantry like that."

"Don't shoot through the crane!" shouted Sahara. "This thing could collapse any second as it is."

"Call Fang and Jaya," said Marisa. "They were researching ways to stop Bennett—it's now or never, so let's pray they've got something."

"Zenaida's reached the second crane," said Sahara. "We have to hurry."

Marisa was halfway across, with nothing but a broken metal ruin to stop her from a five-story plummet to the concrete below.

"We've got a perfect view but no weapons," said Bao.

"Give me your nulis," said Anja. "I can hit her with their tasers."

"Transferring control," said Sahara. There was a pause, and Marisa held her breath as she reached for another handhold. "Done. Knock her off this thing."

"Yessss," said Anja. Marisa watched as Cameron and Camilla froze in midair, hovering in place, and then dove down on either side of the crane as Anja steered them toward her quarry. Marisa didn't dare to blink into the camera feed and watch their progress; the crane curved up as it crossed the gap, and she was now nearly six stories up. Maybe seven. She reached the ends of the handholds, and tentatively gripped the rope instead. It was connected to the crane by metal bars every few meters, like a railing, but it wiggled and jerked in her hand, moved by the wind and by Omar and Sahara clinging tightly to it ahead of her. She took a step, barely able to breathe for the fear of it.

"Scheiss!" yelled Anja. "She dropped them both!"

"She killed my nulis?" said Sahara.

"It was unreal," said Bao. "Bennett let go with both hands, stood *upside down* on the bottom of the crane, and shot one with her gun. The other was behind her and she literally punched it out of the air."

"It was kind of awesome," said Anja. "But now you're all going to die so it's hard to really enjoy it."

"Do something else, then!" shouted Omar.

"We can try to run around to the far side of the canal," said Bao, "but it'll take us too long to get there. The crane's the fastest way."

"She's coming back," said Sahara. "I reached the second crane, and Zenaida's coming back toward me."

Marisa kept walking, holding tight to the guide rope, and reached the second crane just as Zenaida did. They were perched on the top of a small platform, so high in the air Marisa didn't dare to guess at the measurement.

Zenaida scowled. "Damn it, I told you to run. Move." She pulled out her pistol, and Sahara and Marisa shuffled to the side.

"Can you get a good shot from here?" asked Sahara.

"We'll see." Zenaida dropped to her knee, then all the way to her chest, trying to see the underside of the crane. She closed one eye, gripped the pistol in both hands, and fired a long burst. Bennett swung up and out of the way, dodging the gunshots and landing on the side of the crane.

"There she is," said Renata, and they heard the sound of her sniper rifle echoing through the air. Bennett jerked to the side, barely keeping her gecko grip on the crane; she dropped back down underneath it, one arm hanging loose, and scuttled across from one side of the crane to the other while Zenaida fired another long burst. The gun clicked, the giant ammo drum finally running dry, and Zenaida cursed under her breath. Renata fired again, but Bennett hadn't gone far enough out, and the shot missed.

Bennett hung below the gantry, staring at them, her right arm and both of her feet clinging to the metal like a spider. Her left arm dangled uselessly, dripping blood.

"Hurts, doesn't it?" called Marisa. She raised her taser and spoke more softly. "Is this our last weapon?"

"Yup," said Sahara.

Marisa steeled her nerves. "Awesome."

Ramira Bennett pulled her dart gun from her waist, aimed, and fired twice. Both Zenaida and Omar started slumping to the floor, hit by her sedatives, and Marisa and Sahara hurried to grab them before they rolled off the sides of the narrow platform. Bennett moved forward, but Marisa raised her taser again, aiming at her with one hand while steadying Omar with her other.

"You don't have the range," said Bennett.

"So come closer," said Marisa.

Bennett smirked, raised her pistol again, and fired. It clicked on an empty chamber, and it was Marisa's turn to smirk. "All those gengineered upgrades, and you can't count your rounds?"

Bennett said nothing, watching her, then put the pistol away. She was standing on the bottom of the crane with only her gengineered gecko toes to support her. She winced, adjusting her broken arm, and started unzipping her black stealth bodysuit.

"Oh, come on," said Bao. "Is she doing what I think she's doing?"

"It's not as hot as you think," said Marisa.

"It is *kind of* hot," said Sahara.

"Don't forget," said Anja. "Her body is a weapon; if she's stripping, it's because she has another trick up her sleeve. No pun intended."

Bennett zipped her bodysuit to the waist, then disconnected her belt. The top half of the bodysuit came loose, like a shirt, and she shrugged it off with another grimace of pain, pulling it over her broken arm and then discarding it. It fluttered to the ground, drifting on the wind, and Bennett stood upside down in nothing but black pants and a tight black sports bra. Her bright green skin glowed in the sun, and she spread her good arm to the side, exposing a thin membrane between her arm and her torso. The membrane shone almost yellow in the sun, with small red blood vessels tracing pathways like the veins of a leaf.

"What is she doing?" asked Marisa.

"She's eating," said Fang, her voice jumping into the shared call. "She uses photosynthesis for energy—it's one of the few things I was able to find out about her. That's why she's green. If she's uncovering skin, she's probably trying to maximize her surface area."

"She's trying to accelerate her healing," said Sahara.

"Jaya and I managed to find an old archive," said Fang. "They upgraded to better server hardware and only wiped about half the data from their old one. If she's the same model of gene-tech we found the plans for, she has chlorophyll in her skin, gecko-style microhairs in her fingers and toes, and poison sacs in her neck. And of course the eyes, which you already know about."

"So how do we stop her?" asked Sahara.

"I wish we knew," said Jaya. "We haven't found any weaknesses yet."

"I still have a taser," said Marisa. "All it takes is one shot."

"She's way harder to hit than you think," said Anja. "Trust me. She's even dodged most of Renata's shots, and she can't even see those coming."

"Fire that gun and miss," said Sahara, "and we lose every advantage we have."

"And you'll definitely miss," said Anja.

"I'm not giving up!" Marisa shouted. She waved the taser in Bennett's direction. "Stop waiting around and bring it, lady! You scared? I'll give you two million volts, right in that pretty green face—" Marisa stopped suddenly. Gengineering. Bennett *did* have a weakness, and Marisa had just figured it out. "Hey, Sahara," she asked, keeping the taser trained on Bennett, "will my dad's liver survive the fall from here?"

Bennett narrowed her eyes, wary and alert.

"In a stasis bag?" asked Sahara. "Probably. Unless she has a bomb in her pocket she forgot to tell us about, the bag will protect it from anything."

"I will not fall," said Bennett. "I am a highly trained operative—"

"Blah blah blah," said Marisa. "You're a ZooMorrow MyPet

with a pretty face and some gecko toes. And who knows how gecko toes work?"

"They use Van der Waals forces," said Fang, her voice playing through the speaker on Omar's tablet. "Very tiny interactions between the microhairs on her body and the electrons in whatever she's touching. The more surface area the better, because it creates a stronger electrical field, but unless you can reduce the surface area she's clinging to—"

"Short version," said Marisa. "Your weakness is science." She adjusted her aim, pointing the taser at the crane gantry itself, and fired. The prongs hit the metal with a weak fizzle—two million volts spread across an entire loading crane was barely noticeable—but it was enough. The charge in the taser restructured the electrical field around Bennett's feet, and her gecko toes couldn't hold on anymore. She dropped like a stone.

"Yes!" screamed Sahara.

Marisa leaned over. The green woman plummeted, then spread her arms, extending her inner membrane to its full width; it caught the air, slowing her fall, and she swooped to the ground with a cry of pain and triumph. She looked up at Marisa, cradling her broken arm and screaming in fury—

—and then Bao and Anja both shot her with their tasers from behind, and she fell to the ground in an unconscious heap.

TWENTY-FOUR

Sahara held Omar steady, perched high on the top of the crane, and looked at the unconscious boy with a smirk. "I'm just glad it wasn't me this time," she said. "Those tranqs really mess with your head."

"Anja, can you check the stasis bag?" asked Marisa. She held Zenaida tightly, making sure nobody else fell. "Make sure Papi's liver's okay." She waited through an agonizing silence until Anja finally answered.

"Liver's good. Stasis bag's indicators are green all around."

"Gracias a dios," said Marisa, and closed her eyes in silent prayer. She sent her mother a message, letting her know she had the liver back. It would still cost them a fortune to have it reimplanted—they'd probably lose the restaurant—but they could save her papi. "How are we going to get down?" she asked.

"We have to wait for them to wake up," said Sahara. "These tranqs wear off in about thirty minutes."

Marisa couldn't think of any better ideas, so she kept her arms on Zenaida and waited.

Down on the ground, Anja and Bao tied up Bennett as tightly as they could, and then laid her flat on the edge of the dock and hung her head over the side, puncturing each of the biotoxin sacs on her neck and draining them into the water.

"Renata, you out there?" asked Marisa. "You're being pretty quiet."

Renata didn't answer.

"That's no good," said Anja.

"And here comes the long-awaited betrayal," said Sahara. "Activating Cygnus Protocol . . . now."

"What's Cygnus Protocol?" asked Bao. "It sounds exciting."

"It's just a text message," said Sahara. "The exciting part comes later."

"She's waking up," said Marisa, watching Zenaida begin to stir. She was recovering far ahead of schedule, and Marisa wondered if one of her genhancements was some kind of metabolic boost. The woman opened her eyes, and Marisa smiled. "Qué onda?"

"What's going on?" asked Zenaida. She blinked, still trying to clear her head. "Where's the ZooMorrow agent? Where—oh, damn it, she shot me." She tried to sit up. "We've got to move."

"Definitely don't move," said Marisa. "The agent's tied up, and you're still too groggy to walk down off this thing, so give it a minute."

Zenaida's eyes went wide. "How'd you tie her up?"

"Zip ties," said Marisa.

Zenaida closed her eyes. "That's obviously not what I meant."

"Marisa bent the laws of physics to her will," said Sahara. "She hacked a genhancement."

"You can't hack a gen . . ." Zenaida trailed off, and shook her head. "Obviously you can. I've underestimated you since you got here, and it's time I started taking you seriously."

"Thanks," said Marisa. "Most people never get there."

"I still have to go, though," said Zenaida, and finally managed to sit up. She tapped the white radio rod in her pocket. "This is a signal beacon for an offshore flotilla—an independent commune in international waters. I'll be safe there."

"You can't just leave again," said Marisa.

"You want me to stay here?" asked Zenaida. "After all this?" She shook her head. "With ZooMorrow and Francisco and who knows how many other people all looking for me, I think it's time to clear out again. Maybe I'll go back to Lagos—though if anyone asks, you didn't hear me say that."

"ZooMorrow's not looking for you anymore," said Sahara. She picked up Omar's tablet and turned it to face Zenaida. Fang and Jaya were on it, in a split-screen video call.

"Hello, Zenaida!" said Jaya, waving enthusiastically. "So good to finally meet you!"

"Nǐ hǎo," said Fang.

"What's this?" asked Zenaida. "Who are you?"

Jaya grinned. "This whole mess started when someone broke into ZooMorrow's database and stole your DNA template. Fang and I broke back in and deleted every record of you that they had. There's no DNA, there's no employment history, there's no sign that you ever worked on or took or used their technology. They'll be lucky if they can *spell* 'Zenaida' after this, let alone find you in their archive."

Zenaida looked shocked. "I don't understand."

"As far as ZooMorrow's concerned," said Sahara, "you don't exist. People will still remember you, obviously, including Admiral Greenboobs down there, but they no longer have any legal claim on you or your DNA. And once she wakes up and syncs with the server again, she won't even have a copy of your DNA left to help look for you."

"If they come after you again, it will be murder," said Marisa, "not trade law. And murder, as I've recently learned, is one of the only crimes left where the police force has full jurisdiction."

"You're safe now!" squealed Jaya. "Isn't that wonderful!"

"That's . . . great," said Zenaida. "Truly, it is. And I thank you. But there's still Francisco—he's been hunting me since the day I left, and I can't go back to that. You know what he's like, I assume."

"Well enough," said Marisa.

"Maybe you just need to talk to him," said Sahara. "Tell him how you really feel, and that you don't love him anymore."

"It's never been about love," said Zenaida, "just control. He hasn't given up in all these years, and he's not going to now."

Omar shifted but didn't wake. Zenaida looked at him, pursing her lips, and Marisa couldn't fathom what thoughts might be running through her head.

"He missed you, you know," said Marisa. "He's all tough and macho and tries to act like everything rolls off of him—and most things do—but not you. He's missed you every day you've been gone."

"I missed him, too," said Zenaida softly.

"He wants you back," said Marisa.

Zenaida stared at him a moment longer, then shook her head. "No he doesn't."

"But look at everything he's done for you—"

"He didn't do it for me," said Zenaida. "He doesn't love me—he doesn't *know* me." She looked at Marisa, her eyes as deep and sad as dark black pools. "He's his father's son, not mine. Not anymore."

"You don't know him either," said Marisa.

"Of course I do," said Zenaida, and she smiled, but it wasn't any less sorrowful than the loss in her eyes. "Why do you think I live in La Huerta? I've been watching him and the other children for years. And I love them, but . . . I know what they're like."

"So come back," Marisa insisted. "Show them another way to be."

"They're adults now," said Zenaida, shaking her head. "The time to raise them is long past—and don't assume that I would have been any better at it than Francisco was. I worked too much, and when I wasn't at work I was almost never home, because Francisco was there. It was more important to me—I can see this now, looking back—to avoid my husband than to be there for my children. Sergio's the only one who remembers me, and what does he think of me?"

"He . . ." Sahara began, but trailed off. They all remembered what he had said in the police station.

"Exactly," said Zenaida. "And can you blame him? I abandoned them. What kind of a mother does that?"

"You tried to take them with you," said Marisa.

"But I didn't," said Zenaida. "And who can say if they'd be better or worse? Francisco is a monster, but he raised the kind of son who risked his life for a stranger. That's worth something."

"You're not a stranger," said Marisa. She clung to the idea stubbornly, refusing to concede the point. "You're his mother."

Zenaida sighed, not in frustration but in sadness. She studied Marisa's face, and after a moment she spoke again. "You have wonderful parents, Marisa. Not everyone does—most of us are just old children, chasing after dreams and running from our nightmares. We're weak and we're flawed and we're . . . Well. We're imperfect. And the fact that you don't see that is the finest testament I can imagine to how good your parents really are."

Marisa felt a tear in the corner of her eye, and wiped it away. "It doesn't always seem that way from my side."

"It never does," said Zenaida. "But Carlo Magno told you about me, right? That cost him more than you realize."

"He still won't tell me everything," said Marisa. "Even after he told me about the arm, and how you cut it off, there was *still* one more secret he didn't want me to know." She wiped away another tear. "But you know it, don't you?"

Zenaida only stared at her, watching her, and after a long, solemn moment she nodded. "I do. But that's your father's story to tell, and he'll tell you in his own time."

Marisa looked down at her hands, one flesh and one metal. She didn't know what else to say.

"Run," Omar croaked. The three women looked at him, startled. He tried to open his eyes. "Bennett's almost here," he said, his voice dry and hoarse from the sedative. "We have to run."

"It's okay," said Zenaida, and reached toward him, tentatively, stopping just before touching his face. Her fingers hovered there, uncertain, and then she put her hand gently on his cheek. "Shh," she whispered. "It's okay. Everything's going to be okay."

Omar shifted, slowly waking up, and after a moment he opened his eyes. He saw her hand, and her face, and added it together. He looked at her for a moment, then pulled away.

Zenaida's fingers curled slowly as he left them, holding loosely to nothing. Omar watched a moment longer before speaking. "You're not safe here."

"It's over," said Marisa. "Bennett's tied up, and ZooMorrow's been neutralized."

Omar frowned. "Neutralized how?"

"Hi, Omar!" said Jaya from the phone.

Fang stuck out her tongue, and sank low in her seat.

"Her records are erased," said Marisa. "They can't look for her anymore, physically or legally."

"Maybe ZooMorrow," said Omar, "but not my father."

"No," said Zenaida.

"Speak of the devil," said Sahara, and nodded toward the dockyard below.

A low, black car was gliding slowly toward the base of the crane. Two more followed it.

"Hey, guys," said Renata, jumping back into the voice call. "I hope you don't mind that I called Don Francisco, right? I mean, he is my original employer, and I'd hate to get a reputation as a traitor."

"Scheiss," said Anja.

"Time to hide," said Bao.

"Don't worry," said Sahara, and pointed down the dock in the other direction. "Cygnus Protocol swoops in to save the day."

Marisa looked, and saw another trio of cars coming toward them, almost identical to the first: black paint, black windows, and the menacing bulk of some very expensive armor upgrades.

"Yeah, we're definitely hiding," said Bao, and Marisa looked down to see him and Anja dragging Bennett's body into a small control shack at the base of the crane. "I know a mobster showdown when I see one."

"What did you perras do?" demanded Renata.

"Who did you . . . ?" asked Marisa. She looked at Sahara, questioning, and then she figured it out.

"Who hates Don Francisco even more than we do?" asked Sahara, and grinned. "Lavrenti Severov."

"A la verga," Renata muttered. "If you screwed me out of my payday—"

The first motorcade stopped, and Sergio stepped out of the lead car. Two armed men joined him, each holding an assault rifle, their eyes hidden by jet-black optic implants. The second group stopped several meters away, another trio of men ready to face the first—dressed the same, armed the same, and ready for the same trouble.

"This is the coolest thing I've ever seen," said Anja.

"They're children," said Zenaida dismissively. "Always trying to prove they're the biggest boys on the playground."

Sergio started talking, and Marisa tried to listen, but they were too far away to hear. "Anja," she whispered, "what are they saying?"

"They're introducing themselves," said Anja. "The Russian mobsters seem like they were expecting the Mexican ones, but it's all a big surprise to Sergio."

Zenaida turned to Sahara. "You called them here—what's your plan? Just let them kill each other?"

"That's my brother down there," said Omar. He looked at Zenaida. "That's your son."

"I sincerely hope that nobody kills anybody," said Sahara. "And I don't think they will—Severov has had people in LA for years, and if all they wanted to do was murder some Maldonados, they could have done it anytime."

Zenaida scoffed. "That doesn't mean they won't take advantage of the opportunity now that you've dropped it in their laps."

"I offered Severov something better," said Sahara. "He doesn't want to kill Don Francisco—he wants to hurt him. And what would hurt Don Francisco more than anything else in the world?"

"The same thing that's been hurting him for the last fifteen years," said Marisa. "Knowing that his wife is alive and well and somewhere he can never reach her." She looked at Sahara in shock. "You're giving Severov Zenaida?"

"Never," said Zenaida.

"He promised to keep you safe," said Sahara. "Killing you just gives Don Francisco a reason to come after him. Keeping you alive and safe and far away will eat Don Francisco alive."

"I'm not a bargaining chip," said Zenaida, and looked down

at the arguing mobsters. "And I'm not someone's tool of revenge." She looked back at Sahara, and her eyes were fierce. "You girls have a lot to learn, but learn this now: if I go with Severov, the thing that bothers Francisco won't be losing me, it will be losing me *to another man*. I'm just a prize to him."

"We know that," said Sahara, "that's why—"

"You don't know," said Zenaida. "Or if you do, then you don't understand, because this whole plan of yours is using me in exactly the same way. I am not leverage, for him or for you or for anyone else."

Sahara stared at her, then sighed. "You're right," she said. "I'm sorry."

"What else can you do?" asked Marisa. "You can't just stay up here forever."

"I can leave the way I'd always planned to," said Zenaida, and held up the radio beacon. "See this yellow indicator? They've answered my call, and they're on their way. They probably think I'm Rodney, because this is his beacon, but they'll take me. Everyone needs a doctor."

"Is that what you've been doing in La Huerta?" asked Omar. "Hiding out here, and working as a medic?"

Zenaida nodded. "My training's in biology, but for most of these people that's close enough."

Marisa felt her heart lift, thinking of her father. "Do you do surgery?"

"No," said Zenaida, and Marisa's heart sank again.

"So that's it?" asked Omar. "You're just leaving?"

"Can you honestly say your life would be better if I stayed?"

asked Zenaida. She stood up, and Omar struggled to stand with her. Sahara helped him up, and he gripped the platform's narrow railings for support.

"I . . . don't even know you," said Omar.

"It's probably better that way," said Zenaida. "Whoever I turn out to be, I can promise you that I'm not who you think I am. Or who you think I ought to be."

Omar studied her for a moment, then nodded. "Well. You have my ID. If you can't stay, maybe we can at least stay in touch."

Zenaida paused before answering. "I'd like that." Her radio beacon started beeping, and she looked toward the derelict ship on the far end of the crane arm. "My ride's here. Tell . . ." She stopped, and bit her lip, and looked back at Omar. "Tell Pancha I miss her. Tell her that she's beautiful, and that beauty doesn't matter half as much as she thinks it does. Tell Sergio that I'm sorry, and tell Cinto that . . . that he's a better person than he realizes."

"And my father?" asked Omar.

"Tell him everything we said here," said Zenaida. "He'll ask, so you might as well. But I have no special message for him—or no, I do. Tell him that I don't live in his world anymore. If he still insists on searching for me, it's because he lives in mine." She smiled faintly at the thought, and then put her hand on Omar's arm. "For you, I'll just say this: don't become him. There's a good man in you, if you can find him."

Omar watched her for a moment, then nodded. "Okay." Marisa couldn't tell what he was feeling as he said it.

"And you," said Zenaida, and turned toward Marisa. She put her hand on Marisa's arm—the metal one. "Don't become me."

"That's . . . not what I was expecting you to say," said Marisa.

"I don't know you," said Zenaida. "I think you're a good person, because there's no other reason to be up here on this crane trying to save the woman who cut off your arm with a shovel." She patted the arm, then let her hand drop. "So be yourself, because it's obviously working well for you, but don't forget to be the kind of self that other people need."

Marisa stared back at her, not certain how to take that. Finally she just looked at Omar, then back at Zenaida, and said the only thing she could think of. "Okay."

"Say good-bye to your friends for me," said Zenaida, and turned and climbed out onto the arm of the crane. Marisa glanced down at the mobsters, still arguing, and wrote a message on her djinni: **She left. She didn't choose either of you.** She found their IDs, bounced the signal through a handful of different satellites, and sent the text to both of them. She looked back at Zenaida, almost halfway to the ship, and then sat down and watched her as she finished her climb, clambered down the cargo nets, and disappeared.

"They're leaving," said Anja. Marisa looked down from the crane to see both groups of mobsters getting in their cars and driving away.

"I promised them Zenaida," said Renata. "If you pinche migas cost me my money—"

"You did everything he hired you to do," said Omar. "Maybe for the first time in your life. I'll make sure you get paid in full."

"I . . . okay," said Renata. "Sold. What else can I do for you?"

"Send me an account where I can send your money," said Omar. "And then never bother us again."

"How much to not bother you again?"

"I'm not paying you to leave."

"Too bad," said Renata. "It won't be my fault if we run into each other again sometime."

"Bennett's awake," said Bao.

"Say hi from me," said Marisa.

Bao paused, and Marisa heard muffled speaking from his end of the phone; it was a handheld, so it picked up a lot of ambient noise. After a moment he spoke again. "She says you're a stinky doo doo head. I had to clean that up a little."

"Put her on," said Sahara. They heard the muffled talking again, and then Bennett spoke. Bao must have been holding the phone to her ear.

"What do you want?" asked Bennett.

"Nothing," said Sahara. "You're free to go. Nothing you did was illegal, as stupid as that is, so we're not going to turn you over to the cops or leave you here or anything else. Your current objective, as I assume you've noticed, doesn't exist anymore, so you're done here, and we're done with you. Anja and Bao will untie you, and no one's going to hurt you, and we assume you're enough of a professional to not hurt any of us."

"You shot me," said Bennett. "My arm is broken."

"That was Renata," said Marisa. "And I told her not to."

"Thanks a lot," said Renata.

Sahara smiled. "Do you need a ride to the hospital?"

Bennett groaned. "I'll be fine. Cut me out of here and help me get my jacket back."

"Done," said Anja. "Hold still. Here's your jacket, and—oh. New hologram."

Marisa looked down and saw Bennett walk out of the shack at the base of the crane. She was cradling her arm, and her skin wasn't green anymore—it was bronze. Marisa frowned. "She activated her holomask?"

"You could say that," said Bao.

"What face is she wearing?" asked Marisa.

"Yours," said Anja.

Ramira Bennett turned and saluted the top of the crane, and Marisa saw her own face looking up at her. She waved back, stunned. Then Bennett walked away, disappearing into the streets of La Huerta.

"You don't see that every day," said Sahara.

"Actually I do," said Marisa. "That's what makes it so weird."

Sahara moved to the side of the platform, putting a hand on the ladder that led down the side of the crane. "Let's get out of here. I've got a date tonight, and it's going to take hours to clean up from this . . . running gunfight through a black-market shantytown? Is that really what we just did?"

"I love us so much," said Anja.

"Hot date," said Marisa. She stood up, stretching her legs after the half hour of crouching on the platform. "Who with?"

"A girl from Omar's party," said Sahara. "Yuni."

"Yuni's awesome," said Marisa.

And then she looked at Omar. Did she still want that kiss?

She tried to parse her own feelings. She still wished she had kissed him, but she didn't really want to kiss him now. The moment had passed, and the confusion had returned; it was something about the way Zenaida had talked about him, she thought. There was a good man in there somewhere, if Omar could find him.

I'll wait, Marisa told herself, *and kiss that good man if he ever shows up.*

"Well," said Sahara, starting down the ladder. "First things first: let's go get your dad his liver back."

"Absolutely," said Marisa. She paused, and smiled. "And you know what? I think I've figured out how to pay for it."

"How?" asked Jaya.

"Thanks to you and Fang," said Marisa. "You purged Zenaida from ZooMorrow's records, which means that she's free now— and so is everybody else who has her DNA."

"We know that already," said Fang. "That's why we can give this liver back to your dad."

"Yeah," said Marisa, and pulled Memo's djinni from her pocket, "but it's also why a certain gangster is no longer being targeted for assassination. I figure Memo owes me a favor."

TWENTY-FIVE

On the lowest level of a forgotten parking garage, Carlo Magno Carneseca lay in a hospital bed, surrounded by makeshift walls of thin plastic sheets, to keep the area clean. An electrical choir of machines beeped softly around him, lights blinking and IV drips cycling quietly in the darkness. The residents had left for the evening, gone up to higher levels, and the stark concrete room had the feeling of a sepulcher, solemn and alone.

Marisa sat by the bed, and held her father's hand.

Sometime in the night he stirred, slowly waking up from the anesthetic of his surgery. Marisa watched him as he woke.

"Nnnnn," he groaned.

"Do you need something?"

"Nnnnnnnn," he said again. His eyes fluttered. "Dnnnnn. Dónnnde 'stoy?"

"Estás vivo," said Marisa. "You just came out of surgery. We put your liver back in."

"Murrrrisa," he slurred, his eyes still closed. "I went. To a lot of trouble. To take that out."

Marisa smiled. "Sorry, Papi. You've got to piss me off a whole lot more than you already do if you don't want me to save your life."

"I shudder to think," said Carlo Magno. He paused, breathing slowly. "Where's your mother?"

"At home with Sandro and the girls."

"Good," he said. "Hospitals are depressing." He finally managed to open one eye, squinting even in the dim light of the recovery room; he focused on the plastic wall, and then his eye roamed around the room, looking at each piece of overused medical equipment in turn. "This isn't a hospital."

"Not officially."

He blinked, and then frowned. "My djinni doesn't work."

"We had to turn it off," said Marisa. "Mine too. They wouldn't let us in otherwise."

"Where are we?"

"Do you want the long version or the short?"

"I want the version that doesn't involve me having surgery in a crack house somewhere."

"How about a gang lair?"

He shifted suddenly, trying to sit up, and grunted in pain so strong he collapsed back onto the bed. "Eitale, qué fea."

"Don't move," said Marisa.

"Why are we in a gang lair?"

"Because the gang lord owed me a favor," said Marisa. "Stay still and I'll tell you about it."

"Did you kill anybody?"

"No."

"Did you sleep with anybody?"

"Papi!"

"There's only so many ways a gang lord can owe you a favor!"

"It's Memo, Papi, it's Memo and Chuy. We're with La Sesenta."

Carlo Magno sighed, keeping his eyes closed and trying not to move. "Mija . . ."

"You were dying, Papi."

"I saved my own life, thank you."

"Sort of," said Marisa. "You mostly just postponed death. And you don't want to hear this, but the only way to save you was to get your liver back, and the only way to do that was to track down the agent who took it."

"I'm hallucinating," said Carlo Magno, raising one finger in the air. "That's the only explanation. I'm still drugged, and I'm imagining this."

"We got your liver back, and we purged Zenaida's records from ZooMorrow's database," said Marisa. "Which means she and you and Memo are all no longer targets. And after we saved his life, he was kind enough to offer us the use of his surgeon."

"Gangs don't have surgeons."

"He's kind of a . . . black-market freelancer," said Marisa, and winced at the next admission: "From the Foundation."

Carlo Magno moved again. "That's—ow!—a terrorist group!"

"Technically, yes—"

"Mari, how do you . . . how many times . . ." He couldn't find the words he wanted, and sighed again instead, shaking his head in defeat. "What am I going to do with you?"

"I was hoping you'd thank me," she said with a grin, "but we can work up to that."

Carlo Magno grumbled in exasperation, which turned into a groan, which soon turned into a high-pitched laugh. He laughed until his belly shook, pulling on the stitches, and then he winced again and went back to a groan. "Ay, mija. I'm so sorry. You saved my life, and I'm being an ass."

"Cool, are we allowed to say ass now?"

"No," he said. "I'm on hospital drugs, I can say whatever I want." He paused. "I wish I could blame not trusting you on the drugs, too, but we both know that's not true."

Marisa didn't answer, only sat and watched him.

"I love you, mija. And I thank you from the bottom of my heart. Which is currently next to a liver instead of a giant bloody hole, so, thank you."

"Don't forget my friends," said Marisa. "And Chuy, believe it or not. He helped a lot."

Carlo Magno stared at the dark ceiling, his lips in a thin line, and after a moment he nodded. "I'm sure he did." He held Marisa's hand tightly, thinking silently in the darkness. After another long moment, he spoke again. "You saw her?"

"The ZooMorrow agent? Yeah."

"No," said Carl Magno. "Zenny."

"Yeah," said Marisa. She watched his face carefully, trying to read it. "You called her that before. That seems a little more familiar than 'local mob geneticist who randomly decided to help my daughter.'"

"Tell me something," said Carlo Magno. "Am I going to live?"

Marisa frowned. "Yeah—that's what I've been saying this whole time."

"But I mean really," said Carlo Magno. "No one's going to kill me, the transplant's not going to fail, I'm not going to catch some . . . evil doctor cave infection and die in this hole?"

"I promise," said Marisa. She pursed her lips, considering him for a moment. "Why are we talking like this all of a sudden?"

"I have to know that I'm living, because I want what I say next to matter. This is not a deathbed confession. This is a father talking to his daughter, telling her a truth that she's deserved to know for a long time, and . . . I've just never been ready to tell you before."

Marisa waited, holding her breath.

"Zenaida wasn't just a random mobster who decided to help a handicapped girl," said Carlo Magno. "She didn't know you, but she . . . she knew me. We . . ." He stopped, pausing to think or breathe or steel himself, and in that pause Marisa knew exactly what he was going to say, suddenly and with perfect clarity, because it was the only thing he *could* say, the only thing that answered all the riddles and dotted all the *i*'s, and her heart screamed for him to stop—for her to never have to know the secret he was about to reveal, but it was too late, and she had worked too hard, and now the time had come and he said it, and it was real: "We had an affair."

And there it was. Truth, like an immovable monolith, called

into being by her own stubbornness. Her father had had an affair. He hadn't wanted to tell her the truth, because the truth was that he had been unfaithful to Guadalupe—to Marisa's mother—and that awful reality sank into the middle of Marisa's mind like a black hole, warping her entire life around itself. An affair.

"No you didn't."

"I did."

"You wouldn't!"

His voice was calm. "I did. It was—"

"Does Mami know?" she asked.

Carlo Magno nodded. "Of course she does. Revealing it was the only way to make it work."

Marisa closed her eyes, imagining her father in the arms of another woman, betraying the bonds that formed their family. She started to cry, and her tears turned hot and her sadness turned to rage. "How could you?"

"Do you really want to know?"

"No!" she screamed. "Yes! I don't— How could you?"

"It was wrong," he said, "and it was shameful. It is the greatest mistake I have ever made."

"Mami had a baby," said Marisa. "A crippled, one-armed baby, and she was at home taking care of me and you were out screwing that—"

"No," said Carlo Magno, "it was before you were born."

"Don't lie to me," she snapped. "You said it was why Zenaida helped with my arm."

"That was later," said Carl Magno.

"And that makes it okay?"

"Of course not!" he shouted, and then grimaced and put a hand to his bandages. "Mari, look. Nothing I'm about to say is 'okay.' None of it is good, or excusable, or right. But it is true, and you wanted the truth. Do you still want it, now that you know what it is?"

Marisa felt like she was tearing in half: part of her wanted the truth, and part of her wanted to run away and never see him again. Another part of her, small but furious, wanted to tear out his tubes and his stitches and leave him to die.

"What's the point?" she asked. "Why should I listen to any of it?"

"To understand," said Carlo Magno.

Marisa stared at him for a long, slow pause, and then nodded. "Okay. Tell me why."

"Because I was stupid," said Carlo Magno. He looked up at the ceiling. "It was just after Chuy was born—so yes, I was leaving your mother with a brand-new baby. We were young and in love, but we were also ambitious, and we'd started too much new life at once. Maybe not too much for others, I suppose, but too much for me. I had a new wife and a new child and a brand-new restaurant, and that's what really did it—I worked the night shift and Lupe worked the day, and we never saw each other awake for more than five minutes at a time, and those five minutes were so frantic or preoccupied or . . . whatever. They were never happy. We were stressed, and we were unprepared for it, and we were apart so much that I guess I just . . . forgot. I lost track of what was really important, and what I need to be doing, and why I'd married your mother in the first place. And that's not an excuse, because Lupe was going through exactly the same stuff and she never faltered for a second. I was the villain here, and I'm not trying to gloss over that. Just to help you understand."

He paused, like he was expecting her to say something, but she had no words to say. He watched her, waiting, and after a silence started talking again.

"Zenny—Zenaida—felt just as alone: she hated her husband, and she hated going home, and we saw each other at church and at the restaurant and all around the neighborhood, and eventually, we just . . . made bad decisions. It didn't last long—just a few months—and then Lupe got pregnant with you and I ended it immediately. I knew that I couldn't be the father I needed to be—that I wanted to be—unless I reevaluated and rededicated and re . . . built my entire life. And it was you who made me realize that, Mari, or the thought of you, at least. That sounds cheesy but it's true. I broke it off, and it was over, and I thought no one would ever know, and then when Zenaida came back almost a year and a half later with this horrible plan to regrow your arm we said yes, because why not? I still wasn't great at thinking through the consequences. Zenaida thought it would be safe, so we all went along with it." He paused again, though this time he wasn't waiting for her—he was deep in his own thoughts, considering his past from every angle. The one event, the one decision, that would come to define everything.

"I heard the car accident before I saw it," he said. "I don't know if you've ever heard one, because they're so rare these days, but they're horrible: the tires squeal, and when you grew up with this like I did that puts you on alert already, asking yourself if this will be a wreck or just a bad driver slamming on the brakes. Is it just a squeal? Or will there be a crash? And then I heard it—two giant metal autocars slamming into each other, breaking and crushing and tearing and clanging. And I ran, and there was Zenaida, half dead on the street in a shower of broken glass. I heard . . . crying, in the car, and I found Omar in the back seat wailing away, and you next to him, strapped into a car seat, your arm in a bandage. Jacinto looked dead already. I wanted to save you first, but I didn't know if I could move you without causing any more damage, so I went back to Zenaida, and she told me the story, and she begged for my help. They were coming to kill her, and the only way to escape was to convince them she was dead. Switching the bodies was easy, but then what? How could I convince the paramedics that I had any authority or familiarity with Zenaida's identity? A bystander wasn't enough—it had to be a close relative or a neighbor or a friend. I tried to spin a hundred other stories to explain it, but inevitably the truth came out. I was her lover, and I knew her beyond a doubt, and they accepted my testimony and entered it into the hospital records. When Don Francisco showed up he saw through it immediately, but he accepted the ruse as the only way to save her life. He just never accepted me."

"And thus the feud," said Marisa.

"And thus the feud," he agreed.

"But . . . how did Mami forgive you?" asked Marisa.

"Lupe is a better person than I am," said Carlo Magno simply. "It took a lot of time, and a lot of work, but she forgave me, and we stayed together, and we had three more children and a thriving business and a life we're both proud of. It's a life of mistakes, to be sure, but isn't that what they talk about in church every week? That a person can change and be better?"

"I . . ." Marisa stopped, struggling to find a grip on her own feelings. "I don't know."

"I know you don't," said Carlo Magno. "Sometimes I don't either. And I understand that this is a lot, and that it changes everything, and I never wanted you to know because I knew that it would hurt you. That I might lose you forever. And I'll understand if you feel like you can't . . . be my daughter anymore. But it's like you keep saying: you're practically an adult now. So maybe if you don't want me as a father, I hope you might at least want me as a friend."

Marisa nodded, staring at the floor. How could she answer him? What could she say?

"You know," she said at last, "Zenaida told me something on top of that crane."

"On top of a crane?"

"Never mind that part," said Marisa quickly. "She told me something, and I wasn't sure if it was true or not, but now I think it is."

His voice was quiet. "What was it?"

"That I didn't realize how good you were."

Carlo Magno scoffed. "And now telling you my greatest shame is what finally convinces you?"

"Maybe," said Marisa, nodding. She looked up. "Because anyone can make a mistake, but you're the kind of person who spends your whole life trying to make up for it. I just watched a very long parade of people do exactly the opposite of that." She took his hand, and smiled, and used her metal fingers to wipe another tear from her cheek. "I'm going to tell you something now that my father once told me. Are you ready for it?"

"Hit me."

"The past is in the past," she said. "It can't hurt you unless you let it. So we're not going to let it."

Carlo Magno smiled. "I like that plan."

"I like it too," she said, and put her other hand on his. "Here's to the future."

ACKNOWLEDGMENTS

This book could not have been written without the unflagging support of my editor, Jordan Brown; my agent, Sara Crowe; and the many, many people who work with them. I also give huge thanks to my assistants, Kenna Blaylock and Allison Hill, and to my amazing business manager and wife, Dawn Wells. These are the people who make my books possible; I'm just the guy who writes them, usually in my pajamas.

On this particular book I want to give an extra shout-out to my daughters. I didn't really set out to write a series about a father-daughter relationship, but that's what it turned into, and most of the credit goes to them for being amazing and for making me want to tell their story. And don't worry: we don't fight NEARLY as much as Marisa and Carlo Magno. :)